Other historical fiction books
by
Paul W. Feenstra

Published by Mellester Press

Boundary

Moana Rangitira Series
The Breath of God
For Want of a Shilling

Gunpowder Green

Into the Shade

Falls Ende short story eBooks
    1. The Oath
    2. Courser
    3. The King

Falls Ende full length novels.
Falls Ende – Primus (eBooks 1,2 & 3)
Falls Ende – Secundus
Falls Ende – Tertium
Falls Ende – Quartus
Falls Ende – Quintus
Falls Ende – Sextus
Falls Ende – Outlaw

Leonard Hardy's
A Sinister Consequence
A Questionable Virtue

A Gentleman at Heart

Boundary

Historical Fiction

Published in 2018 by Mellester Press

Copyright © 2018 Paul W. Feenstra
The right of Paul W. Feenstra to be identified as author
of the Work has been asserted by him in accordance
with the New Zealand copyright act 1994.

This book is copyright. Except for the purpose of fair
review, no part may be stored or transmitted in any form
or by any means, electronic or mechanical, including
recording or storage in any information retrieval system,
without permission in writing from the publishers. No
reproduction may be made, whether by photocopying or
by any other means, unless a licence has been obtained
from the publisher or its agent.

Published in New Zealand
A catalogue record of this book is available from the
National Library of New Zealand.
Kei te pātengi raraunga o Te Puna Mātauranga o Aotearoa
te whakarārangi o tēnei pukapuka

Cover design by Chris Largent
Edited by Mea

www.PaulWFeenstra.net

ISBN 978-0-473-43621-6 Softcover
ISBN 978-0-473-43623-0 Hardcover
ISBN 978-0-473-43622-3 ePub
ISBN 978-0-473-43624-7 Kindle
ISBN 978-0-473-43625-4 iBook

Published by
Mellester Press

BOUNDARY

by

PAUL W. FEENSTRA

Published by
Mellester Press

ACKNOWLEDGEMENTS

It is doubtful that I could have completed this novel without the generous help and assistance of a wide range of people and organisations, many of whom endured my persistent questions and enquiries. While I have sought to honour their expertise and advice and to maintain a high level of accuracy, any errors or omissions are entirely my own.

My heartfelt thanks to the New Zealand Institute of Surveyors; Robin Slaughter; the National Poisons Centre / Te Pokapū Mātauranga Tāoke; Dr Carolyn Fowler (CA, CMA), Victoria University of Wellington; Narlene Ann Nganeko Ioane (Ngaarauru, Ngāti Ruanui, Pākakōhe, Muaupoko); the dedicated staff at the Pātea and Waverley Libraries; Archives New Zealand; and the Alexander Turnbull Library, National Library of New Zealand.

In particular, I wish to thank and Chris Largent for his creative brilliance.

FOREWARD

While Boundary is a work of fiction, it is largely based on real historical events and, with some exceptions, uses the names of people who lived and held prominent positions during the period in which the story is set. Colonisation is an often misunderstood and dark passage in New Zealand's early history, and for many, its consequences remain deeply felt today. This novel does not seek to exploit that suffering for mere entertainment. Rather, my hope is that *Boundary* encourages readers to ask questions and seek informed answers.

No disrespect is intended towards the descendants of those whose names appear in this book. For the most part, the personalities, behaviours, and private lives of the characters are products of my imagination. Any resemblance beyond names and historical presence is unintentional. The use of fictitious names may not have served this story's best interests, possibly weakening sequences that relied heavily on historical accuracy.

Paul W. Feenstra.

BOUNDARY

by

PAUL W. FEENSTRA

For Wilma and Allan.

Without you both, this novel would never have been possible.

Excerpt from chapter I, from the book –
'Information Relative to New Zealand:
Compiled for the use of Colonists'

There is, probably, no part of the world which presents a more eligible field for the exertion of British enterprise, or a more promising career of usefulness to those who labour in the cause of human improvement, than the islands of New Zealand. The relative position of those islands, their soil, climate, rivers, harbours, and valuable natural productions, – all invite Englishmen to settle there. And it is obvious that great benefits may be conferred upon the natives, by the introduction among them of the habits and arts of an orderly and civilised British community.

–   John Ward Esq,
Secretary to the New Zealand Company
1839

New Zealand
Russell
Auckland
North Island
Kapiti
Te Awaiti
Britannia
Wairau Valley
Wellington
South Island

PROLOGUE

John Lambton cleared his throat — a call for quiet and a signal that he was ready to begin. Faces turned expectantly toward the New Zealand Company's Governor as he waited for the scattered pockets of conversation to subside.

The Board of Directors was fully assembled that evening, along with several company principals, including John Ward, the Company Secretary, and the inevitable clerk, poised to record the minutes. Outside in the hall waited Ngaiti, a young male Māori in the employ of Edward Wakefield, should his knowledge of New Zealand be required.

The room fell still, the silence broken only by the snoring of William Hutt, MP, who had predictably nodded off. John Buckle leaned across and gently jostled Hutt's shoulder. Hutt awoke with a start.

"If it pleases the Speaker—"

Laughter rippled through the room. Those present were well acquainted with Hutt's habit of taking unscheduled naps during Company meetings.

At one side of the room, Colonel William Wakefield was recounting an anecdote to Sir William Molesworth, his laughter drawing a sharp look from his elder brother Edward, who stood at the front, visibly impatient for proceedings to commence. When the room finally settled, Joseph Somes, the Deputy Governor, nodded to Lambton to proceed.

"I have received a letter from the Colonial Secretary, Lord John Russell—"

"That pompous ass!" came a shout from John Abel Smith in the far corner.

Lambton ignored the interruption. He paused deliberately, letting the weight of his words gather.

"The Colonial Office has withdrawn its support for the New Zealand Company's efforts to colonise New Zealand. Parliament has refused to pass the bill."

The room erupted. Chairs scraped; voices collided. Eilker Boulcott jolted upright and spilt brandy across the trousers of Arthur Willis, who remained blissfully unaware amid the uproar. Across the room, Edward and William Wakefield exchanged a brief, knowing glance.

"We've come too far to stop now!" Molesworth protested.

"Gentlemen, please!" Somes called above the din.

Order returned gradually. Arthur Willis at last noticed his damp trousers as a cloth was pressed into his hand.

"Sir William is correct," Lambton said, meeting Molesworth's eye. "We have come too far to stop now."

"How much capital have we raised through land sales?" asked Francis Baring.

Lambton turned to Edward Gibbon Wakefield.

Wakefield stepped forward, surveying the assembled men. "At one pound per acre, land has been sold to the value of one hundred thousand pounds."

A murmur swept the room, this time edged with optimism. A few men applauded.

"Why has the Colonial Office reneged?" someone demanded.

"Lord Russell has received representations from the Church Missionary Society and the Wesleyan Methodists," Lambton replied. "They are hostile to our proposal."

"Those missionaries would do well to confine themselves to salvation and scripture," Molesworth snapped, "and leave commerce to businessmen."

"Hear, hear!"

Somes raised both hands. "Gentlemen. We have much to discuss."

"Despite Parliament's decision," Lambton continued, "we still have an opportunity to honour our obligations to the colonists. Edward Wakefield will outline our strategy."

Wakefield waited until silence returned. "Our objective is to acquire extensive tracts of wasteland suitable for immediate habitation. This land will form the foundation of a planned settlement — a modern city, designed by our surveyors and draughtsmen."

He crossed to a large map mounted on a trestle: orderly streets, public buildings, harbour, gardens and green belt meticulously laid out — familiar territory from earlier discussions.

"For such a settlement," he calmly said, tapping the map, "we require flat land, a viable harbour, and a vendor prepared to sell at the lowest possible price."

Lambton rose. "You refer to this land as '*wasteland*'?"

"Correct," Wakefield replied. "Land that is neither settled nor cultivated."

"And if the land is inhabited?" Lambton asked, resuming his seat.

"Then under the principles of Systematic Colonisation," Wakefield said calmly, "the inhabitants will be relocated."

Lambton nodded.

"We must act quickly," Wakefield continued. "Before Parliament legislates to prevent us from doing so — as I believe it eventually will."

"Hear, hear!" cried an unknown voice.

"I propose we purchase a fast vessel and dispatch an expedition to New Zealand without delay. My brother William, as Principal Agent, should lead it, accompanied by the necessary personnel — surveyor, draughtsman, interpreter, surgeon and accountant. Discretion will be essential. We must avoid alerting the Government to our intentions."

Smoke drifted thickly through the room as the men listened and nodded in support.

"Dammit, Eddie — just find a ship and set sail!" cried Lord Petre.

Wakefield smiled. "I am pleased to say we already have. She is called *Tory*."

From the darkened street outside, their laughter spilt into the London night.

PART ONE

CHAPTER ONE

Te Awaiti Whaling Station, Ships Cove, Marlborough Sounds, New Zealand. Sept 1839

Like funeral pyres, dark columns of oily black smoke rose solemnly from well-fed furnaces on the foreshore of the Te Awaiti whaling station. In vain, the smoke tried to follow the unsettled wind, but the erratic gusts unfairly dispersed the pungent fumes, assaulting the senses of anyone near and far. Adding to the stench and the pall of death, rotting pieces of flesh, bone and oil littered the beach, providing ample opportunity for scavengers to gorge themselves in undisguised ecstasy.

To fuel the hungry flames, and oblivious to the distasteful task of boiling whale blubber, heavily muscled whalers in stained, dirty clothing threw waste off-cuts, or *scrag*, into the furnaces beneath the large iron boilers. With special cutting tools called *spades*, other whalers removed two-foot-square sections of blubber from slaughtered whales that hung nearby, and threw them into boilers, known as *trypots*. The blubber was boiled, allowed to cool, and the separated oil was removed, casked, and shipped to Australia, where it was sold by the tun.

The whalers were hard men. Many were runaways or parolees known as *ticket-of-leave men*; some were sailors who had deserted their ships, and others were simply *currency lads*, men born in the harshness of Australia. Approximately forty European and two hundred Māori adults were living around the Te Awaiti whaling station, and most were gainfully employed in various aspects of whaling. Unsurprisingly, disagreements were common and not limited to men alone. They were settled quickly with knuckles in lively brawls fuelled by cheap, potent rum. The enticements of wealth, lawlessness and women were enough to overcome the unpleasantness and bring these desperate, fearless men across the sea to this newest frontier.

The New Zealand Company-owned barque *Tory* lay at anchor two hundred yards offshore. She had been here for almost two weeks, while the New Zealand Company's principal agent, Colonel William Wakefield, waited anxiously for the whaling season to end so that his newest employee, Richard 'Dickie' Barrett, could join them before *Tory* departed.

"This is hell, and I don't like it, Andrew Stewart! I never, ever wish to set my eyes on such a God-forsaken and miserable place as this for as long as I shall live!" Eleanor looked up into her husband's eyes, her own filled with tears, emphasising her feelings. "This smell, the odour of death, doesn't wash off. I go to sleep tasting it. It's in my clothes, in my hair. It's a constant reminder of how evil this place really is." She buried her face protectively into Andy's chest.

He knew how she felt and understood her discomfort, and, like her, wanted nothing more than to be rid of this foul place. He wrapped his arms around her small frame and held her close.

After a few moments of silence, she pushed herself away and looked up at him. "Andy, we have sailed to the far side of the world to find a better life and raise a family, and this is where we have been brought. Is this what we can expect?"

"Ellie, we'll be leaving here soon. You know this. Colonel Wakefield reassured us all that this was only a temporary layover." He lowered his head to look intently into his lovely wife's face. "He's a good man, Ellie. He'll honour his promises. You'll see. We must continue to trust him – we have little choice." He pulled her towards him, gave her a tender squeeze, and rested his chin gently on her head as he leaned back against the rail at the bow of the *Tory*.

Tory quietly departed Plymouth, England, almost four months ago, and, at Colonel Wakefield's express wishes, hurried to reach New Zealand before the English Parliament passed legislation preventing them from conducting business there. Captain Edward Chaffers had ensured the voyage was trouble-free. They out-sailed other ships they encountered, and even the weather had been kind to them. However, Ellie complained bitterly that the captain's willingness to spread copious amounts of chloride of lime throughout the ship to avoid pestilence was a little excessive. They had arrived in New Zealand without incident and had immediately made landfall at this detestable location, where they had since remained.

A male Māori, comfortable in the clothing of an English gentleman, walked slowly along the deck towards them. Lost in thought, he was oblivious to the young couple at the bow watching him.

"What ails you, Ngaiti?" inquired Andrew as he approached, "Is everyone in despair aboard this fine vessel today?"

Ngaiti looked up in surprise and offered a friendly smile.

Eleanor detached herself and leaned against her husband, linking her arm through his as she greeted the young man. "Don't listen to him, Ngaiti, I believe he is the only person here who enjoys this horrid place."

"Good morning, Miss Eleanor, Andy. And since you ask, yes, I am worried."

"Oh, could we help?" Eleanor inquired with some concern.

"I've been trying to make Colonel Wakefield see reason and have him understand that his plan won't work." Ngaiti paused, leaned on the rail and looked out across Te Awaiti as if searching for something. "He wants to buy land from Māori, but this, er, concept is something that is unknown to us."

"Nonsense," replied Andrew, "Everyone is familiar with the notion of buying and selling."

"That is what the colonel believes, too, but you are both wrong."

"If you go ashore now, you will see Māori selling potatoes to anyone with money."

"Potatoes aren't land, Andy."

"I still don't understand Ngaiti. Why is this a problem?" asked Eleanor.

"What do you think will happen when the New Zealand Company goes to Māori chiefs and he says to them, 'I want to buy this land, how much will you sell it to me for?' Money has no meaning, so the colonel will offer trinkets, weapons and blankets. Those things will interest the chiefs, and of course, they will want them. But as Māori do not believe in land ownership as you Europeans do, they will agree to his terms without fully understanding what will happen next. Māori will still believe they are free to roam the land, travel through it and live wherever and whenever they want, just as they've always done." Ngaiti turned to face Eleanor, the conviction of his belief evident on his face. "I have seen the fences in England. You are forbidden to walk on your neighbour's property without asking him first. Māori will not know of this and when they are refused permission to travel across the land or to use it, there will be trouble."

"Ngaiti, Colonel Wakefield has the support of many learned and educated men, they are politicians, doctors and academics, and I do not believe that these men haven't considered these implications you speak of. My friend, I think you concern yourself needlessly," offered Andrew.

"Thank you, Andy, I wish you were right, but you don't know Māori."

Ellie looked up at Andrew, her face betraying the unease she felt.

"And about time too," Ngaiti said, as he observed a small rowboat that was making its way towards *Tory*, carrying a single passenger.

"Who is that?" Ellie asked.

"That is Dickie Barrett, the gentleman we've been waiting for," replied Ngaiti.

The small rowboat pulled alongside, and within moments a small, round man clambered aboard the *Tory*, where he was met by Colonel Wakefield. The two men disappeared below deck into the colonel's cabin.

"With luck, now that the whaling season is over, we shall be leaving here, as soon as the colonel has decided where we are going," laughed Ngaiti.

"Not soon enough," quipped Andrew.

"What do you mean, they've sold one million acres?" shouted Colonel Wakefield, as he began pacing in his small cabin, the low ceiling height forcing him to bow his head.

"Jackson and Guard, sir, two whalers, purchased one million acres from local Māori," replied Dickie Barrett amiably.

"And what prompted them to purchase this land?"

"I believe they knew that was your intention, why you are here in New Zealand; they wanted to beat you to it."

Wakefield continued pacing, ignoring Dickie, who sat quietly watching.

"The land around here is too hilly for our needs; those whalers can have it. I don't want it." Turning to face Dickie, Wakefield continued, "We can't dilly-dally here any longer, Barrett. Where do you suggest we should go? I want a suitable harbour and flat land, lots of it?"

"I agree, sir, and if I may, let's head to Port Nicholson, where there is a large area of flat land on the north side of a large, protected harbour."

"Show me."

Wakefield pulled a chart from his writing desk, and Dickie Barrett stabbed a grimy finger at the area he had spoken of. Wakefield studied the area carefully.

"Yes, yes, this will do nicely, Barrett. I suggest you get your family aboard as soon as is conveniently possible."

"They will be aboard by tomorrow afternoon, sir. If the weather holds, we can leave on the morning tide, the following day."

Wakefield nodded in assent, "Are you acquainted with the Māori chief of that area?"

"Yes, sir, there are many chiefs, but I do know a senior chief; we have met on a number of occasions. I'm sure you will find him agreeable to any reasonable offer you make," said Barrett with confidence.

Wakefield raised his eyebrows at the turn of good news. "Does he speak any English?"

"No, sir, perhaps a word or two, that is all."

"And how well do you speak the language Dickie?"

He shrugged. "I get by reasonably well sir."

Wakefield looked closely at Barrett, weighing his options.

"Perhaps you should be my interpreter."

"I thought you had an interpreter, that young Māori bloke?" said Barrett.

"Ngaiti? Yes, he's becoming something of a nuisance. His goals and those of the New Zealand Company seem to be at odds. He's opposed to the New Zealand Company purchasing land from Māori. He claims our plan is flawed and will cause trouble." Wakefield laughed, and Dickie Barrett joined in.

"I don't think we can have that, sir. Perhaps if you no longer require his services, I could assume his responsibilities?"

"Yes, I think that may be best. I will be sorry to see him go; he's been a good lad to my brother over the past two years." Wakefield returned to studying the chart. "I will make an announcement at dinner this evening to inform everybody of our destination, and I will speak with him."

As usual, the dawn of a new day brought no change to the bleakness of the whaling station and its morbid activities. Furnaces continued to spew oily black smoke, and the stench of rotting flesh and the pungent, vicious smell of boiling blubber were attracting nature's more opportunistic foragers.

Gaily painted whaling chase-boats, many of them owned by Dickie Barrett, departed the station in search of one last whale, their bright colours in sharp contrast to the dangerous and grisly task they performed.

Andrew and Eleanor were at their customary position on the foredeck of the *Tory* when Ngaiti ambled up.

"We missed you last night, Ngaiti. We had a rather rigorous debate," said Andrew.

"What was the topic?"

"In the married state, which constitutes the greater evil, love without money, or money without love?"

"And you supported which side?" asked Ngaiti with a grin.

"Money without love."

Eleanor directed her elbow firmly into Andrews's ribs.

"Ellie wouldn't let me choose that point of view," Andrew laughed. "So we debated whether the greater evil was money without love, and we lost. Captain Chaffers' team put up a good fight." Andrew rubbed his side. "But where were you, Ngaiti? We looked everywhere for you, and could have won with your help."

Ngaiti looked around to ensure they were alone. "I went ashore to see my cousin, Honi."

"How thoughtful of you, Ngaiti," said Eleanor, "saying goodbye before we depart tomorrow morning?"

"No, Miss, I spoke with my cousin over the land purchases."

"And did your cousin make you see sense, that your concerns are for nought?" asked Andrew.

"No, my cousin sees it as I do. We were trying to decide what to do to warn Māori."

"Ngaiti! If Colonel Wakefield hears of this, there will be trouble. You risk your employment," warned Andrew.

Ngaiti looked out towards a small cluster of boats tied to a rickety pier. He frowned. "It is too late for that, Andrew."

Andrew's mouth opened in surprise.

"Ngaiti, what is going on?" asked Eleanor, expressing concern.

He paused for a few heartbeats, then turned to face her. "I am no longer employed by Colonel Wakefield; my services to the Company have been terminated," he responded sadly. "Once we reach Port Nicholson, I must leave the ship."

"Oh no." Eleanor looked concerned. "Who will perform your duties for the colonel?" she asked.

"The man you saw yesterday, Dickie Barrett, he is now the interpreter for Colonel Wakefield.

"He seems a happy and agreeable chap," offered Andrew.

"Yes, that is what he wants everyone to see, but he is a hard and unpleasant man, as are most whalers. Do you believe an honest man could survive and do business in this place, amongst this?" Ngaiti again turned and leaned over the rail, waving his arm to take in the beach and the squalor.

Andrew and Eleanor turned and grimaced as they looked outward.

A longboat with a mast slowly made its way from the pier, heading out of the bay. Four men rowed, while another sat at the stern at the tiller.

Ngaiti smiled and pointed. "Look, there goes my cousin now."

The three friends watched in silence as the longboat cleared the bay and the young men aboard quickly raised a tattered canvas sail. Immediately, the boat heeled over and gathered speed as they headed towards the Cook Strait, the body of water separating New Zealand's southern and northern islands. The winds were favourable, and the sea was calm.

"Where are they going?" asked Eleanor.

Ngaiti looked nervously around and again spoke quietly, "They are going to Port Nicholson to visit a Māori chief called Te Wharepouri. I have instructed my cousin, Honi, to tell the chief of Wakefield's plan to purchase land around Port Nicholson. Hopefully, Honi can help the chief understand the English concept of land ownership and what it will mean to them. With luck, Te Wharepouri and other chiefs can give thought to what they will do, hopefully avoiding any misunderstandings."

"Ngaiti, you are stepping into dangerous waters," warned Andrew. "If the colonel finds out what you have done, there will be problems for you."

"Andy is right, Ngaiti. You must be careful."

"Yes, I know this, but I am doing what is right for my people ... and your people too."

"Our people?" asked Andrew.

"What will happen if colonists and settlers don't receive what they expect?

"What they've always done, complain bitterly! The British Empire has survived on its resolve, superior strategy and a fine cup of tea," Andrew laughed, with the others joining in.

"Isn't it dangerous to travel all that way in a small boat?" asked Eleanor.

"Yes, it is, but Honi and his brothers are experts on the ocean, they know the weather will not cause problems for them today."

"I still think you are over-reacting to this, Ngaiti," said Andrew quietly.

Three years earlier, at Te Awaiti, Ngaiti was tricked by the captain of a French whaler into sailing with them as a crew member, on the promise that he would meet French royalty. During the long voyage to Europe, Ngaiti began to learn French. By the time they arrived at Portsmouth, Ngaiti almost spoke the language fluently. Edward Wakefield, researching New Zealand, approached the newly arrived whaler and sought information from the captain about the route taken, the weather, and any challenges faced on the journey. Speaking English with some fluency, Ngaiti acted as interpreter for the two men.

Impressed by the young man's intelligence, quick learning, and pleasing disposition, Wakefield offered Ngaiti employment. Eminently impressed by the young man's hard work and honesty, Edward Wakefield ensured Ngaiti was taught to speak the Queen's English correctly, to read and write, and, more importantly, introduced him to the finer points of English culture and society. Ngaiti became a gentleman. It was only natural that, when the time came, he would assist Edward's brother, Colonel William Wakefield, in his quest for the New Zealand Company in New Zealand. Now twenty-five years old, he was offered free passage in exchange for his language and cultural expertise. An astute and strategic thinker, Ngaiti also provided pleasant company and had endeared himself to both Mr and Mrs Stewart, quickly becoming good friends.

Ngaiti turned to face both Andrew and Eleanor, taking a big breath. "Andrew, your family is of Scottish ancestry, isn't it?"

Andrew nodded.

"You have clans. These clans fight amongst each other. They form bonds through marriage, and relationships between clans change when one clan offends another. Some clans even have a long-standing hatred for each other. The power of alliances determines who lives safely on their land and on their neighbours' land. Am I correct?"

"Yes, you are correct." Andrew nodded.

"I ask you this. What would happen if you gave one clan leader weapons that no one else had? How would the other clans behave, and what would happen?"

"The clan leader would celebrate his good fortune with a wee dram, then they'd fight," said Andrew with a laugh. His wit earned him another elbow in the side. Eleanor was not amused.

"It would likely cause jealousy, envy, and probably create many disagreements," replied Andrew in a more serious tone.

"Then this is the only way I can describe the similarities between Māori and *pakeha[1] to you*. Do you now see the danger of what Colonel Wakefield will do when he upsets the balance?"

"Yes, I concede your point, Ngaiti, but the Europeans will live alongside Māori, and if the balance is upset, as you believe," Andrew raised

---

[1] *Pakeha - Māori word for Europeans*

an eyebrow at Ngaiti, who leaned on the rail, "then we have laws to protect us all."

"Whose laws?"

"Ours, of course," laughed Andrew.

"Do Māori have laws, Ngaiti?" Eleanor asked.

"Yes, we do."

"Then what will become of them, Andy? Will we have to abide by both Māori laws and our laws?" she asked.

"I can't say, but the Company has told us they are introducing a modern civilisation to a primitive culture, so I expect Māori will learn to appreciate that the laws of a modern society are fair and just for everyone."

Ngaiti turned from the rail. "Do you believe that Māori should ignore and forget their laws?"

"Our laws are probably better, but I've not really thought about it. What do you think?" Andrew asked.

"If Māori invaded England and, as conquerors, we said, 'We have come in peace and will live together in harmony, and you will now obey Māori laws', how would you feel?" Ngaiti gave no time for a response. "I think there will be conflict, Andy. Colonel Wakefield and the Company need to be aware of this before they go too far."

"But we are not invading, Ngaiti."

Ngaiti raised his eyebrows. "Then you come to Aotearoa[2], as guests?"

Andrew paused, mulling over what he said.

"I understand Ngaiti," said Eleanor sympathetically. "And you do too, Andy. You are just being stubborn and hate to admit you are wrong."

"Colonisation is just another word for invasion," said Ngaiti with contempt.

---

[2] *Aotearoa - Māori word for New Zealand*

CHAPTER TWO

Port Nicholson - Te Whanganui a Tara

The moderate south-westerly winds were kind to Honi as he and his brothers sailed across the Cook Strait, the body of water separating New Zealand's two main islands. As they approached the southern point of the northern island and headed towards the entrance to Port Nicholson, known to Māori as Te Whanganui-ā-Tara, the wind shifted and the swell rose, slowing their progress. Unable to resist the temptation, some of the brothers cast lines over the side and caught a reasonable quantity of fish, certainly enough to offer as a gift on their unexpected arrival. It was late in the day when five tired and cold sailors entered Port Nicholson and, still under sail, made their way to the sheltered western shore of the large bay.

Warmly greeted at Kaiwharawhara and their gift of fish well received, Honi and his brothers were seated by a fire, enjoying its warmth, when Chief Te Wharepouri arrived and sat beside them.

Typically dressed in European clothing, he wore his hair long and loose, not tied in the customary knot. A traditional Māori facial tattoo, called a *moko*, covered his entire face. To some, it was intimidating; to others, the *moko* told a story. His hands were large and calloused, familiar with work and the highly skilled craft of canoe-building. Scars crisscrossed his lower, muscular arms, mementos of past battles and victories, reminders of the fallen. Saying nothing, he turned to look at Honi and studied the young man before him. Te Wharepouri's gaze was intense and inquisitive, perfectly matching an intelligent, handsome face. The silence wasn't uncomfortable; it wasn't awkward - the unspoken words were reassuring, strengthening the family bond.

Te Wharepouri knew Honi's visit was important. Travel across the Cook Strait was always dangerous, especially in a small boat. These men before him had shown bravery, maturity and patience. They hadn't babbled like gossiping women when they arrived. They had brought fish as *koha*[3], which pleased the women, and then waited patiently for him without complaint. Te Wharepouri nodded. Despite their youth, he respected the young men before him.

"The *koha* will put food in our bellies tonight, thank you."

Honi nodded, holding Te Wharepouri's piercing gaze.

"You bring news of your father, Honi?"

"He is well, and healthy. He asks after you, sir."

"I hope you are looking after your mother?" Te Wharepouri looked to Honi's brothers for a response.

Shifting nervously, they nodded, murmuring that they did.

"And how is your life at Te Awaiti with the *pakeha*?"

Honi looked at the chief's face, "It is not a good place, it is a place of death."

Te Wharepouri understood. These were good young men, reminding him of when he was young and their age.

The brothers began to relax as Te Wharepouri intended.

"Why have you come to see me, Honi?"

Honi began to tell Te Wharepouri exactly what Ngaiti told him. He recited word for word all his concerns and passed on the intentions of Wakefield and the New Zealand Company; he left nothing out.

"And Barrett will now be the interpreter for Wakefield?"

"Yes, Ngaiti will no longer work for Wakefield and Barrett will speak for him."

Te Wharepouri poked the embers of the fire with a stick, deep in thought. After coming to a decision, he called for a warrior and asked him to go to his cousin, Te Puni, and request that Te Puni come to

---

[3] *Koha - Gift*

Kaiwharawhara as soon as possible. The warrior acknowledged the instruction and immediately ran off.

"It is time to eat, we will talk later, for now I must think," said Te Wharepouri, dismissing the young men.

Barrett was no stranger to Te Wharepouri. Several years earlier, Barrett had taken Te Wharepouri to Sydney, New South Wales, aboard the schooner *Tohora* to purchase muskets and powder. Chief Te Wharepouri had even urged Barrett and his friend Jacky Love to set up a trading base some distance north of Port Nicholson in the Taranaki area. This proved very useful, as the information he received far outweighed the unpleasantness he encountered in Barrett's company.

Te Wharepouri knew that Dickie Barrett was involved in many things; trading, whaling, and now he was working with the New Zealand Company. He followed the *pakeha* money like a dog chasing a bitch in heat. He'd also heard stories of cruelty, lies and deceit. Yes, Barrett was clever and outwardly friendly and agreeable, but when no one was near, he was very different – he couldn't be trusted. *He is a man without honour*, thought Te Wharepouri.

Now Barrett was bringing more *Pakeha*; their arrival was not unexpected. As Ngaiti correctly noted, this would create problems for Māori. *When Te Puni arrives, we will discuss our actions*, he thought. With a heavy sigh, he rose from the fire and went to join the others to eat.

Chief Te Puni arrived, and after formally greeting elders and family members, the two chiefs retired to a hut to discuss Wakefield's imminent arrival and his desire to acquire land. A September evening chill lingered in the air, and a small fire was built in a pit in the earthen floor to keep the two men comfortably warm.

Calling for Honi, Te Wharepouri and Te Puni sat cross-legged before the fire as Honi recounted everything he'd been told by Ngaiti. Unusually, no one else was present.

"It's simple cousin," said the older Te Puni, once Honi departed, "refuse to allow them our lands!"

"Is it that simple?" Te Wharepouri turned to look at Te Puni. "Wakefield will go to another chief, then another; finally, someone will accept the gifts he offers. Then what will happen? A weak chief will have these gifts. And what will Wakefield offer?" The chief looked back into the flames. "Amongst other things, he will tempt them with muskets and powder. Yes, we can be certain of that. Then we must protect our lands and ourselves from a chief who has weapons he should not have. …No, sadly, cousin, it isn't that simple."

Te Puni nodded. The flames cast orange, flickering shadows across their faces as they stared into the fire, seeking answers.

"Did you know that the missionary Henry Williams came here and wanted this land?" asked Te Wharepouri after a few moments of silence.

Te Puni shook his head.

"Yes, he came here a short time ago, when you were in the Wairarapa. He brought men from Australia with him and warned me about this man Wakefield. I understood what Williams wanted to do. He is a good, peaceful man, but what he proposed would not prevent war. They wanted this land but would not live here."

"You are happy with your decision to turn away the missionary?" asked Te Puni.

"No, I did not want to turn him away at all, but I don't think I had any choice," said Te Wharepouri in frustration.

Te Puni nodded.

They both stared at the dancing flames.

"What is our greatest fear? Te Wharepouri asked after another lengthy pause.

"We all fear being attacked while we sleep on our mats, at that moment where we are feeling safe and with the warmth of a woman beside us," Te Puni stated.

Te Wharepouri raised an eyebrow with a hint of a smile.

"I fear for my people," Te Puni added in a more serious tone.

"If we allow *pakeha* to build their homes on this land, we are less likely to be attacked by our enemies. These *pakeha* all have muskets and soldiers. They will protect each other and us if they truly come here to live in peace."

"Do you really believe that?" asked Te Puni.

"I want to believe it, cousin. When they come, and they will, we can live without fear of being killed or taken as slaves by other Māori."

"You have forgotten a very important thing."

In question, Te Wharepouri turned his head to look at his cousin.

"Te Rauparaha!" said Te Puni.

"He is no longer a young warrior; he has no fire in his blood anymore," said Te Wharepouri dismissively. He'd not forgotten what Te Rauparaha had done to him.

Te Rauparaha was a very senior and powerful chief who lived a good day's run from Port Nicholson and controlled most of the lands in the region. A few years earlier, Te Wharepouri was fighting a northern iwi and sought the help of Te Rauparaha. When asked, Te Rauparaha declined to come to the aid of Te Wharepouri, yet in spite of their chief's wishes, half of his people had thankfully come to help him and aid in his victory.

"You do know why Te Rauparaha did not support you?" Te Puni said with a grin.

"Because of a woman?" Te Wharepouri looked at Te Puni, who began to laugh.

"You've met her, you know what Te Rauparaha must have endured - you should be offering him pity, not anger."

Te Wharepouri laughed, then spoke with gravity. "We must consult with Te Rauparaha and receive his blessing before we accept *pakeha* gifts in exchange for allowing them to use our land."

"Ngaiti said Wakefield will be here tomorrow, so we have no time to talk with Te Rauparaha," Te Puni offered.

The two men sat silently, thinking about the problem.

Finally, Te Wharepouri spoke. "We will allow Wakefield to use our lands, and we will accept the gifts he will offer."

"But cousin, you can't do that without Te Rauparaha's approval," said Te Puni with concern.

"Wakefield doesn't know that," Te Wharepouri said with a sly smile. "We should send a message to Te Rauparaha to tell him exactly what Ngaiti told us. Perhaps we should send Honi. He can also tell him that we will accept Wakefield's gifts."

Te Puni looked at Te Wharepouri with some hope.

"I believe Wakefield will seek to speak to Te Rauparaha very soon. And when he does, Te Rauparaha should say to Wakefield, 'I know nothing of what Te Wharepouri has done; I was not consulted, and so I do not recognise any arrangement you have made with Te Wharepouri.' Do you see, cousin? That means Wakefield has to offer Te Rauparaha gifts in exchange for the use of our land. This will cost Wakefield much." Te Wharepouri laughed.

"But why is this a good thing?" asked Te Puni.

"Because, cousin, those gifts of muskets and powder will go to us and to Te Rauparaha, not to those chiefs who would take our homes and enslave us. It means the *pakeha* will live amongst us and we will be safer."

"You will be seen as a fool by Wakefield and some Māori. They will see you as nothing more than greedy, in love with power and the trinkets they offer."

"Let them think that. I care about the safety of everyone, not just Māori. This plan offers peace, even if I am seen as a fool."

With a devious smile Te Puni said, "And we are making it very difficult for the *pakeha*."

The next morning, Honi and his brothers, accompanied by some guides to ensure they didn't lose their way, were sent overland to see Te Rauparaha. Te Puni and Te Wharepouri went to the *waka*[4] to prepare and await Wakefield's arrival.

---

[4] *Waka - Canoe*

CHAPTER THREE

Port Nicholson, Sept 20th 1839

With a flourish, the pencil danced across the paper, almost as if it had a mind of its own. Deft strokes left dark lines, while gentle, precise sweeps created lighter shades and textures, highlighting the artist's skill. The increasing wind caught the paper's edge and attempted to free the unfinished drawing. Unperturbed and with infinite patience, the artist held the page in place with his palm and continued to transform random marks into a recognisable image that represented the panorama before him. Charles Heaphy, the young draughtsman employed by the New Zealand Company, sat on a chair amidships as the *Tory* made her way into Port Nicholson for the first time. He continued to sketch, oblivious to the wind and changing scenery, but honest to the image captured in his mind that his pencil created.

Beside Heaphy sat another young man and friend, eighteen-year-old Edward Jerningham Wakefield, the nephew of expedition leader Colonel William Wakefield. He also applied his skill with pen to paper. Not to sketch and create visual impressions; Jerningham, as he preferred to be called, created sentences and literary accounts of the sights he witnessed. He scratched his journal entries with pious dedication, interpreting life's experiences and familial loyalties through the lens of youthful naivety.

Closer to the bow, Eleanor Stewart stood at the rail, enjoying a respite from the unpleasantness of the whaling station. Her buoyant mood was reflected by all aboard, the excitement and nervousness about the unknown in sharp contrast to the idleness and boredom they had felt at Te Awaiti. She looked behind her and checked on her husband. Predictably, he sat reading the magazine of the *Society of the Diffusion of Useful Knowledge,* which he was never without. She smiled, comforted by his presence. Married only a few months before they departed from England, the couple had yet to enjoy the normal life of a husband and wife deeply in love.

Both Andrew and Eleanor were indentured to the New Zealand Company, he as an accountant and she as a housekeeper and cook for Colonel Wakefield. Their passage and accommodation, along with a modest salary, were provided.

She continued to watch her husband, oblivious to her loving gaze. He was special, she knew, in more ways than one. Andy possessed a gift for numbers. He could instantly arrive at a result that would require the most complex calculations. Numbers were a game to him, and he could instantly recall a page of numbers, discern a pattern, a discrepancy, or add, multiply, or subtract – it mattered not. He was never wrong and, with some smugness, enjoyed being challenged on his summations. No profession was better suited to Andrew Stewart, and he practised it with passion. Possessing a rather quick and dry wit that often led him to apologise, he was tender, loving, and genuine – they were also best friends. It didn't matter to her that Andrew carried a little excess weight and was not the physical specimen other women sought in their men. Eleanor knew she was beautiful and that other men coveted and desired her; she could have had any man. Instead, she fell in love with her childhood friend; for her, Andy was perfect. She turned her reflections outward, leaving Andy to his magazine, and enjoyed the changing sights and dynamic scenery of coastal New Zealand.

Tory tossed aside the increased swell effortlessly as she entered the channel. The change in motion drew attention to their arrival, and all heads turned to look outwards at the unfolding splendour. Pencils were returned to their cases, and books and papers were stowed out of reach of sea spray and damp. Through the ocean's haze and the smudge of distant green, the unidentified landscape dissolved to reveal lush vegetation, wooded hills, and the clarity of sharp rocks that ringed a brutal and savage coastline. Maintaining protective vigilance, a mountainous range of hills surrounded Port Nicholson but allowed an expansive, wide, flat valley that narrowed as it disappeared northwards. The sun's intensity heightened colours; the blues deep and mysterious, the greens vivid and calming, and the white clouds so bold - an exclamation point. It wasn't tropical, it wasn't temperate; it was distinctly unique. For the colonists and immigrants, it was familiar and would offer comfort, hope and a future. According to Colonel William Wakefield, this would be home.

Eleanor felt Andrew's presence. They stood shoulder to shoulder at the rail, each enjoying the closeness. Without a word, he placed his hand on hers, and together they shared the wonder before them.

"Māori call this place *Te Whanganui-ā-Tara*, it means the great harbour of Tara," volunteered Ngaiti who came on deck to join them.

"And who is Tara?" questioned Andrew.

"Legend has it that Tara was the son of a Polynesian who came to New Zealand many hundreds of years ago. It is said that Tara discovered this place," he answered.

"Then it is good to see that Māori is no different from Europeans in that way."

"Why is that?" asked Ngaiti, puzzled.

"The penchant for naming places after themselves."

Eleanor shook her head.

Further aft on the quarterdeck stood Colonel Wakefield and Dickie Barrett. Dickie pointed out various landmarks and features as they came into view and passed. Wakefield nodded appreciatively and asked a few questions, which Barrett answered with informed confidence.

As the *Tory* moved further into the channel, the swell decreased. On Barrett's advice, Captain Chaffers slowed the ship and ordered some of the sails lowered. Barrett pointed out a dangerous reef on the port side to the captain and indicated a safe course for the *Tory* to follow. Captain Chaffers instructed the navigator to record the reef on their charts, keeping them updated with Barrett's expert local knowledge. Wakefield had the captain's telescope and was studying the entrance to the large bay that lay directly ahead.

"That island is called Matiu," said Barrett, "and there is a smaller island to the right called Makaro."

Colonel Wakefield swung the telescope to study the two islands. "I can see the larger island is of considerable strategic importance; the smaller is nothing more than a large rock."

"Māori have lived on Matiu Island from time to time, and yes, they recognised its importance," said Barrett.

Wakefield grunted and continued his appraisal of the bay.

"The mast look-out reports seeing two Māori war canoes heading in our direction, Colonel," said Captain Chaffers, indicating from where they would appear.

Immediately, all heads turned anxiously to the West, the canoes too distant to be seen.

"Are we in any danger?" asked Wakefield to Barrett.

"No sir, I doubt it. It's most likely they have come to talk, but you never know. If I could use the telescope?"

Barrett studied the distant canoes, he knew there was nothing to fear from them, it wasn't a war party, but it wouldn't hurt to let others feel a little anxious and cement their dependence on him.

"Captain, ensure that we have adequate protection. may I suggest running out our guns and having muskets at the ready in the event we are threatened?" offered the colonel.

"Very well sir, I concur," replied Captain Chaffers with a hint of nervousness.

Within moments, activity below deck saw the portside gunports opened and muskets were brought on deck. As it offered an ideal vantage point, some muskets were brought into the rigging where the lookouts were located.

On hearing the lookout's warning of approaching canoes, Ngaiti leaned in closer to Andrew and Eleanor, "I suspect chief Te Wharepouri is in one of the *waka*, although I have no idea who is in the other."

"Should Eleanor go to her cabin for safety?" asked Andy with a concerned look.

"I'm not going below to my cabin, Andrew Stewart!"

"I think she is safe here; they aren't coming to cause us harm," suggested Ngaiti.

"There!" Eleanor nodded her head emphatically as she crossed her arms in defiance – she wouldn't go below.

The two war canoes, *waka taua,* were drawing closer, but still too far away to make out faces. In synchrony, the thirty paddlers in each *waka* drove their hoes into the water with short, aggressive, and powerful strokes, propelling the craft quickly.

Captain Chaffers ordered all passengers back and to stand in a group on the quarterdeck, not out of fear or threat of danger, but out of respect and to be welcoming, he reassured. Jerningham Wakefield positioned himself to document the arrival, and Charles Heaphy, using the navigator's chart table, began to sketch the two canoes as they approached. Colonel Wakefield disappeared to his cabin to suitably attire himself for the occasion.

The large, ornate, black-painted prow, *tauihu,* of each canoe rose proudly, dismissing the large waves with ease in an explosion of spray as the ornately carved *waka* drew closer. At the rear, a warrior controlled the *waka* with a large steering oar. At times, he crouched for balance, applying his weight to keep the heavy craft on course; occasionally, he stood straight and proud. Even from a distance, Ngaiti could see the man grinning, enjoying every moment. The short, powerful strokes of the warriors, dictated by the chant of a caller, kicked up copious amounts of water as the *hoe* plunged repeatedly into the ocean. With ample freeboard, seawater still managed to find a way inside, and a couple of dedicated men bailed furiously, emptying the accumulated seawater from the bottom of each canoe.

It was obvious to everyone on board the *Tory* that the approaching *waka* were putting on an impressive display of speed, handling and physical endurance; it was clearly a demonstration for the benefit of the onlookers. As they drew closer, Ngaiti identified features and immediately pointed out Chief Te Wharepouri to Andrew and Eleanor. He couldn't see who the chief was in the other *waka* but thought it might be the older Chief Te Puni.

Colonel Wakefield returned on deck, looking resplendent in his finest livery. He requested to Captain Chaffers that the *Tory* heave-to and that a ladder be made ready to lower on his command, but, in caution, held back until he knew the intentions of the natives bearing down on them. The entire crew and passengers gathered, watching the *waka* with attentive fascination and some anxiety, which Barrett did little to allay.

Ngaiti was also nervous. He had no way of knowing whether Honi had spoken to Chief Te Wharepouri, and if he had, what Te Wharepouri's response would be. He hoped that Te Wharepouri would not say anything to Colonel Wakefield about being forewarned. There was little he could do but wait.

"Do they carry weapons on board those canoes?" asked Eleanor.

"Yes, it is common for warriors to be armed while on a *waka*, but I do not know whether they are armed now," replied Ngaiti.

"Even if they were hostile, there is little they could do against the cannons aboard this ship," said Andrew proudly, feeling secure.

"And how accurate are those cannons against swiftly moving *waka*? They could be within the cannons' line of fire in seconds, and you'd have sixty Māori clambering over the sides of this ship in moments," Ngaiti responded with a grin.

Eleanor looked nervously at Andrew, who wisely chose to remain silent.

"You are safe, Miss Ellie. If they were going to attack, we would have known by now," reassured Ngaiti with a laugh.

So that they could be formally introduced, Colonel Wakefield had all officers and senior passengers assemble at the front of the group. Ngaiti, Andrew and Eleanor were deemed less important and stood further back. Finally deciding that they were in no apparent danger, the colonel instructed the ladder to be lowered, an invitation to come aboard. However, the two *waka* did not approach; instead, they paused at some distance from the ship.

"Why won't they come?" queried the colonel to Dickie Barrett.

"I don't know sir," replied Barrett, equally puzzled.

"Tell them it's safe, we will not hurt them."

"They cannot hear us sir, they are beyond hailing distance."

"Then we shall wait," informed Colonel Wakefield.

Doctor John Dorset, the official colonial surgeon, suggested they go below to escape the sun and wind until their presence was required on deck. Wakefield put an end to that request with a sharp retort.

"Perhaps we should lower a ship's boat and go to them," offered Wakefield to Barrett.

"Yes, we could do that, sir. It may help."

"Colonel Wakefield, sir?" Ngaiti spoke.

"Yes, what is it, Ngaiti?" Wakefield replied, without taking his gaze from the *waka*.

"If you ran the guns in and lowered the gun ports, then the *Tory* may appear less threatening."

Wakefield turned to face Ngaiti, then slowly to Barrett. "Yes, a splendid idea. Captain?"

"Aye, aye, sir," responded Captain Chaffers.

Within moments, orders were barked out, and the crew began securing the guns and lowering the gun ports. Immediately, both *waka* began to move and slowly approached the *Tory*.

When all attention was focused outwards, Dickie Barrett stole a glance at Ngaiti. Gone was the affable whaler cum interpreter; the inimical look was intense and dangerous, and it lasted but a second. Its meaning and intent were made very clear to Ngaiti.

"Now, why didn't I think of that?" said Wakefield as he straightened his jacket and adjusted his cover.

Eleanor had seen Barrett turn to look at Ngaiti; she was surprised by the vehemence Barrett displayed over such a trivial matter. She moved closer to Andrew, who was craning his neck to catch sight of the spectacle.

Colonel William Wakefield looked down at the medals that hung resplendently from his left breast. Noticing an errant medallion slightly askew, he straightened it so it now lay as it should. It was imperative that he and the other employees of the New Zealand Company, assembled on the quarterdeck, project a dignified air and that their appearance and behaviour inspire trust and confidence among the natives they were about to meet.

For the brothers, Edward and William Wakefield, this first encounter with Māori was a significant milestone towards fulfilling their dreams and ambitions. Opportunists to the core, they'd fancied creating an empire founded on Systemic Colonisation and enterprise, which they hoped would eventually mirror the East India Company's success. Buying cheap land, building a community, and watching it expand into a town represented the culmination of that dream.

A shame Edward couldn't be here now, thought the colonel.

He'd always been at his older brother Edward's side, even during the darkest times, when they were both incarcerated for kidnapping. Even when Edward's attempt to colonise South Australia failed, he'd remained supportive. It wasn't Edward's fault that guileless and conniving company officials from the South Australia Colony, which Edward helped found, wrested control from him. He believed in Edward with unflinching loyalty and devotion.

Colonel Wakefield glanced down at his medals and laughed to himself. It was Edward's idea for him to obtain an officer's commission by supporting the Emperor of Brazil in his war against Portugal. Having no military experience, William was, to everyone's surprise, able to join with the commissioned rank of Captain. After fulfilling his obligations to the emperor, he enlisted to fight for Queen Isabella II of Spain. With a total of five years' military service, he emerged with a chest full of medals and holding the rank of colonel. Edward was delighted and immediately recruited William to the New Zealand Company's cause.

CHAPTER FOUR

Port Nicholson.

In deference to age, the older Chief Te Puni climbed aboard the *Tory* first and immediately stepped aside, allowing his younger cousin, Chief Te Wharepouri, to climb the ladder and stand beside him. Once on deck, Te Wharepouri stood relaxed, facing the assembled group. As usual, he wore his longish hair loose and appeared comfortable in a shirt, trousers and a jacket, with an impressive cloak, a *kahu kuri,* draped over his shoulders. This cloak was special and signified his status. Te Puni was dressed similarly, although his *kahu* was less intricate.

Te Wharepouri studied the group gathered before him. He looked slowly from one face to another, taking measure. His neutral expression gave no indication of his mood or thoughts. He also knew that his *moko*, a facial tattoo, would create some unease, especially among *pakeha* women.

He immediately recognised the little portly man, Barrett, standing in front. The only indication that Te Wharepouri was familiar with him was the uncontrolled tightening of his mouth; it was unlikely anyone noticed. At the back, behind the others, he recognised Ngaiti. He exchanged the briefest eye contact, giving an imperceptible nod. Te Wharepouri could not help staring at the young woman standing beside him; the colour of her hair and skin was as unusual to him as his *moko* was to her. He thought she was a vision of pure beauty, and, to his surprise, she did not demurely look away as he expected; instead, she returned his gaze with equal intensity and open, intelligent curiosity. There were older men and younger, some in uniform and others not. He noted two young men, almost boys; each appeared to be writing on paper or drawing. He continued his appraisal and stopped at the person he assumed was the *pakeha* chief, William Wakefield.

When in Sydney, Australia, Te Wharepouri had seen many soldiers and noticed the uniforms they wore. He was puzzled at how a man could fight wearing such clothes. He was even more astonished by the uniforms worn by their chiefs, or officers, as he'd been told they were called. Those uniforms were so tight and restrictive, preventing the physical movement needed to be a good warrior. To the battle-hardened Te Wharepouri, this indicated that the officers were not fighting men. How could they be, he wondered. In front of him now stood such a man. He looked at Wakefield closely and noticed his carefully disguised unease and nervousness.

Wakefield cleared his throat, and Dickie Barrett stepped forward to greet Te Puni with a traditional *hongi*. Te Puni bent down to the shorter Barrett as they briefly pressed noses and foreheads together in the traditional Māori greeting. As Barrett welcomed Te Puni, Te Wharepouri continued his appraisal of Wakefield, studying his uniform and the many adornments he wore. Te Wharepouri was impressed. The fabric looked strong and held colour easily. It was not coarse but was woven finely and looked durable. He must obtain such cloth, but without the useless decorations, he thought.

Barrett then greeted Te Wharepouri with a *hongi,* who returned the gesture by holding out his arm and shaking Barrett's hand in the *pakeha* custom that he'd learned.

Once Te Wharepouri and Te Puni had been formally announced to Wakefield, they were introduced to the group's senior members. Barrett's attempt at translating amounted to little more than a few words and half-sentences. Te Puni, who did not understand the *pakeha* language, struggled with Barrett's interpreting skills and, with the odd whisper in his ear from Te Wharepouri, eventually understood all that was happening.

Chief Te Wharepouri had been around many *pakeha,* including those he met during his two visits to Australia and the whalers and missionaries who now lived scattered throughout this land. He was certainly not fluent, but he had made every effort to learn the language these men spoke and could understand much of what they said. Te Wharepouri enjoyed the fact that no one was aware of this, and he wasn't about to be forthcoming now.

After the introductions, Barrett and Wakefield led the chiefs down to Wakefield's cabin, where Wakefield would make his intention to purchase land known. Young Jerningham, as secretary, was invited to attend and take notes.

"What interesting men," stated Eleanor, once the deck had been restored to order.

"Yes, it was unsettling at first when the younger chief Te Wharepouri was looking at us," replied Andrew.

"He is a great warrior and fought in many battles," said Ngaiti proudly.

"What do you think they are they doing now?" asked Eleanor.

"I presume Colonel Wakefield will be making his intentions understood, and hopefully Te Wharepouri and Te Puni will agree to sell land, I'm sure we will know soon enough," replied Andrew.

Ngaiti was leaning over the rail and shook his head.

In *Te Reo* Māori, the language of his people, Te Puni said with formal dignity, "We are honoured that you have come to visit us, and we welcome you here as our guests. What is the purpose of your visit, and how can we be of help?"

Wakefield turned to Dickie Barrett for the translation.

"He asks, why have you come?"

"We have come here to offer you a wonderful opportunity. We bring many valuable gifts that we can exchange for the purchase of some of your land," said Wakefield, with the confidence of a hawker.

"The *pakeha* want land and bring gifts," Barrett said to the chiefs.

Te Puni and Te Wharepouri conferred briefly.

"How much land do you need, and what do you intend to do with it? Will *pakeha* make this land their home?" asked Te Puni.

Wakefield turned to Barrett expectantly.

"What will *pakeha* do here?" Dickie replied.

Wakefield nodded and pretended to give his reply dutiful consideration. "We intend to build a modern township on suitable land so that the colonists can prosper and live in peace."

To Te Puni Barrett said, "They will live here in peace."

Again, the two chiefs conferred quietly.

Jerningham was writing furiously, trying to keep up with the dialogue. His own impressions were positive, and this was reflected in his accounts. He was impressed with Barrett's translation skills; his responses were direct, succinct and delivered with confidence.

"How many *pakeha* will come here to make this land their home?" asked Te Puni.

To Wakefield Barrett translated, "Will many white men come here?"

"Tell him yes," said Wakefield.

"Yes, many *pakeha* will come," said Dickie Barrett.

Te Wharepouri spoke. "Ask Wakefield again, how many *pakeha* will live here?"

For the briefest of moments, Dickie Barrett's eyes flashed at Te Wharepouri.

"Chief Te Wharepouri asks, how many will come here?" said Barrett.

"Tell the chief, ships will bring many, many people here. People who will fill the streets and build many grand homes and farm the land," said Colonel Wakefield enthusiastically.

"Some ships will bring *pakeha* to walk on the paths and live in their homes," Barrett responded to Te Wharepouri.

Chief Te Wharepouri held Barrett's gaze, his eyes narrowed.

William Wakefield suggested he'd like to see the land and its features first-hand. An agreement was quickly reached, and Te Wharepouri would guide Wakefield the following day for an inspection. Te Puni would not accompany them, as he was needed in his village. A halting, polite discussion continued for a short time, after which the two chiefs quietly returned to their waiting canoes. After the two chiefs departed and were heading back to their village, the *Tory* moved further into the bay and dropped anchor safely in the lee of Matiu Island.

Colonel Wakefield sat alone in his cabin. After a glass or two of wine, he loosened his tunic, rested his feet on his writing desk, and contemplated the day's events. He was eminently pleased, feeling that the preliminary discussions with the two chiefs had gone rather well. Tomorrow, he would be able to see the land for himself and establish the location of the town he wanted to create. If all went according to plan, the first ship, the *Aurora,* would soon arrive, full of colonists eager to settle the land they had paid for, land he had yet to purchase. Wakefield knew he needed to obtain land, and soon. His smile disappeared at the thought of Colonial Secretary Lord Russell's reaction to the news that the New Zealand Company had acquired land and begun colonisation. He would be rather displeased. What steps would the Colonial Office take? He wished his brother Edward were here; he always dispensed sound advice.

CHAPTER FIVE

Pito-one

Ngaiti was on deck, waiting to board the ship's boat that would take him ashore. This was the day he would leave the *Tory* and end his employment with the New Zealand Company. He was saying goodbye to his best friends, Andrew and the tearful Eleanor. Promises were made to keep in contact, to see each other often, and not to become strangers. Colonel Wakefield, Charles Heaphy, Jerningham Wakefield, and Doctor Ernst Dieffenbach, the Company's naturalist, appeared on deck and began descending the ladder to the boat below. Eleanor gave Ngaiti a final sisterly hug and said her emotional goodbyes. After shaking hands with Andrew, Ngaiti hoisted his canvas sack onto his shoulder and, with a wave, climbed over the side.

Andrew and Eleanor watched as the ship's boat made its way towards the northern shore of Port Nicholson.

"Do you think we shall ever see him again, Andy?"

"I'm sure we will, he knows that Colonel Wakefield intends to build a settlement here and that is where we will live, so he can find us easily enough."

"It is beautiful here. I can see us living happily in a cottage near the foreshore, taking evening walks," she said wistfully. "We can get some animals. And I want us to have pigs too. I want to cook lovely pork dinners for you. Once we are settled, can we get pigs, Andy?"

"Of course, Ellie," He was already salivating, "Do you think this climate will support growing apples?"

On reaching the shore, Te Wharepouri warmly greeted Ngaiti, who had been waiting patiently for the boat's arrival. After saying farewell to everyone and politely thanking Colonel Wakefield, Ngaiti immediately walked west, around the bay, towards Te Wharepouri's *pa*[5] at Kaiwharawhara.

True to his word and accompanied by a single *waka* and warriors, Te Wharepouri guided the group on an extensive tour of the wide valley. They began by heading north up the river, then slowly worked their way back down, making frequent stops to explore. They traipsed across the valley from one side to the other, fording small streams and thankfully avoiding any hills. Charles Heaphy drew pictures, and Jerningham Wakefield continued to document the day's activities in his journal. With exuberance, Doctor Dieffenbach studied the fauna and the unusual birds, and at every opportunity, he peppered Te Wharepouri with questions about his observations, while poor Dickie Barrett struggled to translate the complex inquiries to the doctor's satisfaction.

Unaccustomed to physical exertion, Dickie was exhausted, his feet hurt, and he lost his jovial manner, complaining and grumbling as Te Wharepouri led the group along narrow paths, across grassy meadows and through dense woods and swamps. They now waited back at the beach for the doctor, who was some distance away, engrossed in observing the antics of an unusual native bird.

Wakefield ambled along the shelly beach on the exposed northernmost shoreline of Port Nicholson, which Te Wharepouri said was called Pito-one. His head swivelled this way and that as he marvelled at the beauty of the steep wooded hills on either side of the valley. There was much to see – this rich and fertile land held his interest, and he could easily imagine it being inhabited by colonists and becoming a thriving town.

---

[5] *Pa - Village*

In England, The New Zealand Company had employed Samuel Cobham, a draughtsman, to prepare a map and design their first planned settlement. Aligned in a neat, orderly grid, the symmetrical streets and facilities of the new township were intended to remind colonists of England, a perfect model of English society without its faults, as the advertising brochures indicated. Never having visited New Zealand, Cobham assumed the land was flat and that deep harbours were plentiful. It was this settlement that Wakefield was now imagining.

If he closed his eyes, he could see gentlemen strolling casually along neat, tree-lined streets that ran parallel to the beach. He could hear the clip-clop of horses pulling wagons and carts carrying merchandise, competing with the delightful laughter and giggles of playing children. Wakefield turned to the ocean, where the vivid image of ships tied to piers, unloading goods, became clear. He could see it all before him, the hustle of a busy port, so integral to the commercial success of a settlement. He intended to develop this thriving township into the capital city of this frontier land. This was what he and his brother Edward had dreamed of. This would become Britannia and the beginning of Systematic Colonisation.

Not far from Wakefield, Te Wharepouri sat on the beach. He casually drew patterns in the coarse sand with a small stick and studied the *pakeha* soldier. He felt Wakefield was a dreamer, a man with fanciful ideas, and entirely focused on accumulating wealth. As Te Wharepouri knew, *pakeha* wealth was measured by money. Men like this conveniently overlooked the realities of life, fuelled by naivety, their actions driven by greed and the certainty that they could take what they wanted. They were convinced of their dreams and stood heavily on the toes of many to reach those goals. He knew that, with little or no thought for the consequences, they would exploit Māori to the fullest. Te Wharepouri had little faith in the objectives of Colonel William Wakefield and the New Zealand Company he represented.

It was frustrating that he knew so little about *pakeha* ways. Still, from fragments of conversation he'd overheard and understood, it was clear that Wakefield might not be pleasing his own people in England - something he would discuss with Ngaiti later. Despite that, Te Wharepouri still believed that *pakeha* who wished to make this place their home could live peacefully amongst Māori, without fear of exploitation. Having *pakeha* living near the village and trading with Māori would be useful, and the odd farmer from whom Māori could learn new agricultural techniques would be welcome. Perhaps there might be someone to teach the children the *pakeha* way of writing. For now, he had no real option but to appear willing to help Wakefield, though he would not make it easy for him.

Te Wharepouri believed that a man's life was simple; you provided food for your family and ensured their safety. This was done through the support of the *whanau* (family), the *hapu* (clan), and the *iwi* (tribe). Te Wharepouri was under no illusion; he knew his own existence here was precarious at best. Other *iwi* wanted this land; they wanted slaves and had many warriors to accomplish this, more than he had to defend the area. Given the opportunity, those Māori who wanted this land would eventually fight to obtain it. If his people lived in peace with p*akeha*, an attack from other Māori *iwi* was very unlikely, and everyone could sleep safely at night.

Te Wharepouri sighed, turned his attention to the sea, and watched the small waves gently folding onto the shingle beach. He didn't want *pakeha* living here, nor did he want to share his land with them, but he knew he could not prevent them from coming, just as he could not stop an angry ocean.

He laughed. Perhaps he and Wakefield were similar, both dreamers.

Colonel Wakefield made a decision. After signalling Barrett, they approached Te Wharepouri, who stood as they approached.

Wakefield spread his arms and pivoted, "This land, as far as the eye can see, this is what I want to purchase from Māori."

"He wants all this land," said Barrett

Te Wharepouri nodded in response. He had yet to hear from Chief Te Rauparaha and could not technically commit or agree to anything with Wakefield.

"I will give this thought and will discuss this with my people."

"He said he will think about it," translated Dickie.

"We need to decide on this quickly. Ask him when he can give me his answer?"

"When will you know?" asked Barrett to Te Wharepouri.

Giving the matter some thought, Te Wharepouri responded, "Tell him, I will have a decision by tomorrow."

"Tomorrow," Barrett told Wakefield, who smiled in response.

Later that day, after returning home to Kaiwharawhara, Te Wharepouri received a message from Te Rauparaha. The message was typically brief. Te Rauparaha understood what Te Wharepouri and Te Puni intended and agreed to the plan.

Immediately, Te Wharepouri sent word to all the chiefs in the area, instructing them to meet urgently at Kaiwharawhara for a *hui*, a meeting, where they would gather to discuss the proposal. The *hui* was a matter of some concern to Te Wharepouri, as all the chiefs needed to agree, and unanimous agreement was never a certainty.

Māori are a freethinking and independent people. Māori chiefs do not order their people to obey. Instead, through discussion, a chief will make his case and seek support. He cannot order warriors to fight. If the warriors do not believe in the cause, they are under no obligation to follow the commands of their chief. Te Wharepouri could not order the chiefs to obey him and accept his plan; he had to convince them it was the right thing to do, and he needed total support.

CHAPTER SIX

Port Nicholson, Sept 24th, 1839

Colonel Wakefield paced *Tory*'s deck in growing frustration. No one was listening to him; again, he repeated his instructions to the hapless sailors.

"Keep the muskets further back!" he yelled. "I told you, place the larger items to the rear and the smaller items near the front, where they can be easily seen. Spread everything out so it appears there is more!"

Items of all descriptions were arranged on the deck; there were dozens of shirts, pants and nightcaps. Tomahawks, axes, adzes, boxes of soap, wax, lead and shaving brushes were stacked in neat, orderly rows. The New Zealand Company had brought from England cotton, calico, ribbon and handkerchiefs, all quality fabrics, now proudly displayed. Nor had they forgotten the much-sought-after gunpowder, muskets and cartridges. The sailors were arranging scissors, umbrellas and Jew's harps, filling all available deck space.

"Put the blankets over there, man!" fussed Colonel Wakefield, "No, no, behind the pencils!"

"That's 'bout it, sir," said a frustrated sailor carrying a box of combs, the last items to be brought up from the ship's hold.

"Where are the pipes? I know there are pipes somewhere."

"Yes, sir, they're here." With exasperation, the sailor pointed to a small box partially hidden by forty-eight iron pots.

"Are you sure that's it? I thought there was more," questioned the colonel.

"No, sir, that's everything you assigned for the Port Nicholson purchase," replied the sailor, rolling his eyes.

The colonel looked across Port Nicholson, hoping to spot the ship's boat that was to bring six Māori chiefs to the *Tory*. He walked to the bow, dodging neatly arranged items on deck, and looked again across the bay. Still nothing. "Damn it, where are they?"

Captain Chaffers approached and stood beside Wakefield, "I will inform you immediately once the boat has been sighted, Colonel."

He sighed, "Thank you, Captain. I will go to my cabin in the meantime. Can you find Jerningham and send him to me, please?"

"Yes, of course, Colonel."

It had always been the intention that young Jerningham would record the land transactions and draft the deed-of-sale documents on behalf of the New Zealand Company. It mattered not that he wasn't a legal scholar or familiar with the nuances and expertise required to create binding legal documents. He was an intelligent young man, quick to adapt, showing promise with pen and paper, and was the obvious and preferred choice to undertake that responsibility. In preparation, and with youthful confidence, Edward Jerningham Wakefield had briefly reviewed some deeds in England and felt confident he could easily act in the company's best interests.

It was in his uncle's cabin that Jerningham was reminded of his obligations and the expectations placed upon him. The colonel needed reassurance that the deed-of-sale would be executed so as to withstand the scrutiny of any court of law should the company's purchases ever be challenged.

William had confidence in his eighteen-year-old nephew, but he was unimpressed by the callousness and attitude young Jerningham displayed. Perhaps this was just a sign of the times. Young people today showed little respect for responsibility and authority, thought William. Wakefield was about to reiterate this point to Jerningham when a knock at the door informed him that the boat had been sighted and was approaching.

The colonel gave Jerningham a final look, patted him on the shoulder, and the two men headed on deck to wait for their guests.

Symbolising status, the six Māori chiefs were each resplendent in their *kahu kuri* as they were welcomed aboard *Tory*. To Barrett's displeasure, Chief Te Wharepouri had invited Ngaiti to attend. After the formal introductions, Colonel Wakefield immediately began summarising the territory the New Zealand Company would purchase.

Te Wharepouri outlined the boundaries by drawing a map on the deck of the *Tory*. The area he described, approximately 160,000 acres, encompassed land controlled by the six chiefs present here today.

Colonel Wakefield made an impressive show of highlighting the merchandise on display. The chiefs made no secret of the value they placed on these items, and possession would change their lives dramatically. One chief, Nga Pakawa, stood further back, scowling. He was visibly unhappy and spoke in hushed whispers to Te Wharepouri as Barrett finished his irregular translations.

The *hui* held at Kaiwharawhara the previous evening had not gone well. Initially, Te Wharepouri and Te Puni were the only chiefs willing to deal with the New Zealand Company. The others wanted nothing to do with the *pakeha* or their intrusion onto their lands. After much discussion and argument, all but one finally agreed. A lesser chief, Nga Pakawa, was unwilling to consent.

His argument, perhaps the most compelling of all, left the other chiefs chilled when he asked, "What will you say when many, many white men come here and drive you all away to the mountains? How will you feel when you go to the white man's house or ship to beg for shelter and hospitality, and he tells you, with his eyes turned up to heaven and the name of his God on his lips, to be gone, for that your land is paid for?"

Famous for his wisdom and intelligence, Te Puni paused to consider his reply. Turning to face Nga Pakawa, the older chief replied with gravity, "How will you feel watching your women being raped and your children carried away to become slaves by warriors from northern tribes? How will you feel when you ask for help, with the *Pakeha* God in your heart and no weapons to fight with?"

It was an undeniable stark reminder of the constant danger they were all in. As the five chiefs looked at Nga Pakawa, he looked down - his doubts were fuelled by the words and advice he'd received from the missionary Reverend Henry Williams.

Missionaries were active in New Zealand, spreading God's word and selling muskets to Māori for many years. The Christian Mission Society and the Wesleyan Methodists travelled extensively throughout the northern island, achieving some success in converting many Māori to Christianity. The Reverend Henry Williams, whose CMS church was vehemently opposed to the actions of the New Zealand Company, had previously spoken to Nga Pakawa and made his church's views on land purchases and colonisation perfectly clear.

The words of Reverend Williams were familiar to all who attended the *hui,* but to the insecure Nga Pakawa, they unsettled him. It was finally agreed that Nga Pakawa would accompany the other five chiefs to the *Tory,* keep an open mind, and, with hope, that Te Wharepouri would change his opinion so the group would reach consensus. Te Wharepouri had a quiet, encouraging word with Nga Pakawa.

Although not a chief, Minarapa Rangihatuake, a Māori Christian preacher and respected leader from the Te Aro *Pa,* came to see Te Wharepouri. He expressed his concerns and insisted that the Te Aro land not be included in the agreement. As outlined to him, Te Wharepouri agreed. Many in the Te Aro *Pa* had once been slaves and, within the Māori community, were perceived as having a lower social standing. Politically, Te Wharepouri couldn't be seen to openly support them without risking being perceived as weak, but yes, he thought, he would quietly raise this issue with Wakefield and insist that the land around the Te Aro *Pa* not be included.

The array of merchandise, fabric, tools and weapons, carefully laid out on the deck of the *Tory,* was alluring. It was a slow, deliberate seduction, and each chief yearned to own such wonderfully well-made items. Crates full of muskets beckoned, and the finely woven cloths were enticements difficult to ignore. Tools with sharp edges for chopping wood and tending the gardens were useful items that made life easier for the people of Te Wharepouri. This wasn't just about vanity or greed; it was about necessity.

Te Wharepouri cast a casual glance at Nga Pakawa and saw that he, too, was transfixed.

Colonel Wakefield stepped closer, "Is there some apprehension? Are you displeased?"

"Problem?" translated Barrett.

"We wish to discuss this briefly amongst ourselves," replied Te Wharepouri.

"They want to talk, sir," stated Barrett.

"Very well, let's give them some time," said Wakefield, tactfully grabbing Barrett's elbow and leading him away.

Jerningham Wakefield had finished transcribing his notes and had now begun writing the deed of sale. The colonel approached him and looked over his shoulder. "Any questions?"

"No, Uncle, all is well," he replied.

The colonel continued, ensuring that Dickie Barrett was listening, "It is vital to the integrity of this company, and to those fortunate enough to enjoy its association and business activities, that any and all transactions are legal." Colonel William Wakefield turned to look at Barrett and spoke slowly. "And that there be no merit or foundation for a challenge to its covenants." He pointed to the deed.

Jerningham paused, looked up at his uncle and casually nodded.

"Of course, sir, wouldn't expect nuttin' else," said Barrett quickly.

"Very well, carry on," instructed the colonel, who turned his attention back to his guests.

Speaking for the assembled chiefs and to appease Nga Pakawa, Te Wharepouri stepped forward. "We have a concern."

Barrett translated, "He has a question."

Wakefield indicated for Te Wharepouri to continue.

"In time of need, will *pakeha* come to the aid of Māori?" Te Wharepouri looked closely at Colonel Wakefield. "Will your people help us if we come to your homes, or will you turn us away?"

Wakefield, understanding the serious tone of the question, turned to Dickie.

Barrett cleared his throat, allowing time to formulate his reply. "He wants to know, if he needs help, will you lend him a hand?"

Colonel Wakefield nodded and looked at Te Wharepouri, smiling, "Of course I will help."

"Yes," translated Barrett.

Edward Jerningham Wakefield, the eighteen-year-old son of Edward Gibbon Wakefield and nephew of William, had almost completed the deed of sale. William invited the six Māori chiefs to his cabin, where the deed would be explained, and they could share a glass of wine to celebrate while they waited for young Jerningham to finish.

Jerningham sat at his uncle's writing desk and began to read the completed documents aloud. He paused after every few paragraphs, allowing Dickie Barrett time to interpret the legal terminology and translate it into *Te Reo*, the spoken Māori language. Predictably, Barrett's translations were vague and omitted detail. The translation didn't take long. While Te Wharepouri did his best to understand Jerningham's oratory, many words and sentences were unfamiliar. He was also aware that Barrett's translation was inaccurate and incomplete. He guessed it was essentially a loose, general translation that contained very few specifics.

Te Wharepouri had doubts - many of them. If he refused to sign the documents, Wakefield would approach other chiefs who would eagerly sign, giving little or no thought to the significance of their actions. The lure of displayed merchandise was too tempting. It would shift the power balance between Māori chiefs and increase the threat of war between them.

Would *pakeha* honour their word? Te Wharepouri looked at the deed, the marks and scribbles on the paper that meant so much to Europeans yet meant nothing to him. What did Māori care for words on paper? Was not a man judged by his actions, by his honour, his *mana*? No one in the cabin saw Te Wharepouri's brief look of contempt as he turned his head to look at Wakefield. Ngaiti, who stood at his side, also appeared unhappy.

Barrett finished the deed translation, and Wakefield waited anxiously as the six chiefs talked amongst themselves. Finally, to Wakefield's immense relief, Te Wharepouri informed him that they had unanimously agreed to sign the precious *pakeha* paper that was so important.

Colonel William Wakefield was overjoyed. He'd not only completed his first land purchase but also stolen a march on the English Government, and it would cost only three hundred and sixty pounds' worth of purchased merchandise. They all returned to the deck of the *Tory*. Ngaiti stood near Chief Te Wharepouri as everyone gathered to witness the signing of the Port Nicholson agreement.

In contrast to the smile of Colonel Wakefield, the Māori chiefs were not smiling, their expressions grim.

"My heart tells me this is wrong," whispered Ngaiti to Te Wharepouri. "Barrett's translations were inaccurate; it would be wrong to proceed."

The chief nodded in understanding to Ngaiti. After a moment's consideration of Ngaiti's recommendation, he turned away from the group and spoke quietly, for Ngaiti's ears alone. "If we do not sign, others will. I have no choice."

Before departure from the Te Awaiti whaling station, a whaling ship from England delivered a dispatch from Edward to William. The message detailed that, in response to *Tory*'s covert and hurried departure from England, a ship called *Druid* was on its way to New South Wales, carrying Captain William Hobson RN, who had been proclaimed Lieutenant Governor of the British Colony about to be established in New Zealand. Hobson's task was to ensure that Māori title and sovereignty over their lands were indisputable. Hobson would likely inform the New Zealand Company that the British nation was taking possession of New Zealand and that the Company's actions were illegal.

Edward had instructed his brother William to purchase as much land as possible before Hobson arrived to take office and begin passing any laws. They would deal with any repercussions later.

Fiercely loyal to his brother, that was exactly what William intended to do. He must hurry.

CHAPTER SEVEN

Britannia

The Heretaunga, or, as Wakefield renamed it, the Hutt River, flowed with an elegant yet moody grace through the low-lying plains of the fertile valley. Fed by a dynamic range of hills called Tararua, it meandered generally southward and flowed into the north-eastern end of Port Nicholson. It was mostly wide and shallow, and when the sun shone, the water appeared golden, sparkling with an almost majestic serenity. During the frequent winter rain, the Hutt River changed personality, and little could be done to temper its fickle disposition.

Heavy, torrential downpours lasted for days, and the passive river that Wakefield admired so much eventually burst its banks, flooding all the dwellings in the new settlement. Silty brown water flowed freely through tents that had not been washed away, and even through the few hastily constructed permanent structures. At times, disconsolate residents waded knee-deep through mud and water, watching helplessly as valued possessions, transported with loving care across the world, perished. Treasured family heirlooms such as portraits, Bibles, books and clothes floated away like flotsam, while those items lucky enough to be saved were plagued by mould and mildew, becoming indelibly water-stained. Just as quickly, the waters receded, and settlers began cleaning up and repairing the damage.

Exposed to the savage southerly winds borne on the howling gales from vicious southern ocean storms, the winds were numbingly cold. Without compassion, the winds raced up Port Nicholson and struck the fledgling community head-on, delivering a chill that thick layers of clothing could not repel.

On the advice of his surveyors, Wakefield chose this location to begin building the first settlement. Māori called the area Pito-one. Located on the north side of Port Nicholson, it lay at the head of a large, arable valley that gradually narrowed as it disappeared northwards, merging into the distant, rugged, bush-clad hills. Colonel Wakefield's enthusiasm and eagerness to colonise Pito-one and turn it into a model of British society blinded him to the practicalities of creating a functioning, viable township. It had no harbour. The coarse shingle beach was shallow and offered little prospect of creating a thriving port. With grim determination, the newly arrived colonists, now numbering around two hundred, endured the hardships but were not inspired by the vision that this settlement was the much-heralded 'Britannia' the Company touted.

The urgency for Wakefield lay in satisfying the growing number of unhappy, newly arrived colonists who'd still not received title to the good, fertile land they'd bought and paid for. Nevertheless, Company surveyors were busy surveying one-acre plots as quickly as possible. With the addition of a steam-powered sawmill brought from England to process timber, the small settlement grew quickly, although many homes were still made of canvas and were temporary structures at best.

Andrew and Eleanor's temporary home was little more than a tent with a mud floor, draughty and cold. Exposed to the biting southerly winds that raced up the harbour, the canvas walls and roof were ineffective against damp and chill.

Eleanor sat down inside her tent with a heavy sigh and stared at the stained, dirty canvas that protected them only from rain. Unable to keep the bone-chilling wind out, Andrew was constantly tightening the ropes to prevent powerful gusts from ripping the entire structure loose. Tears ran freely down her face as she sat facing the canvas, her shoulders heaving in quiet misery. Now and then, a sob escaped, and she buried her face in her hands, overcome by the adversity of their situation and ashamed of her weakness. Andrew was with Colonel Wakefield, reviewing Company accounts, unaware of her distress.

"Ellie! Ellie, are you there, dear?" came a woman's voice from outside. "Ellie?"

Eleanor quickly wiped her eyes, recognising the voice of her matronly neighbour. "Yes, Mrs Moore, coming!" she said, and opened the tent flap to step outside.

"I have something for you, Ellie," Mrs Moore said with a big smile, handing her a small sack. "It's flour. The new mill is finally operating, and we've been testing the machinery..." Mrs Moore saw Eleanor's tear-streaked face. "Oh, Ellie dearest, what's wrong?"

Mrs Moore stepped forward, opened her arms and enveloped Eleanor in a motherly embrace as Eleanor burst into tears again.

"It's everything... the cold... wet... damp..." Eleanor sobbed. "Everything is dirty..."

Mrs Moore stroked Eleanor's hair and patted her gently on her back. After a minute or two, Eleanor pulled herself away.

"I'm sorry, I need to be stronger," Eleanor said with resolve.

A handkerchief magically appeared from the copious folds of Mrs Moore's skirts and she handed it to Eleanor, who gratefully wiped her eyes.

Two young men, labourers, squelched past. Seeing her crying, they slowed to stare at the two women.

"No one said this would be easy, Ellie," said Mrs Moore, bending forward to look into Eleanor's eyes. She held her by the shoulders.

"We suffer because of the decisions of men who claim they have our best interests at heart, yet have little understanding of what we must endure. And just like little boys, they get upset when we don't pay them attention."

Eleanor returned the look; her bottom lip trembled as she listened.

"And then we must cook and clean for them, in impossible situations."

Eleanor nodded in understanding.

"These very same men who act like children bear great responsibility, too. They work hard and toil to provide for us, often in situations we can't. They worry about our children and us, and sometimes not enough about themselves. More often than not, they don't feel the need to share their burden with us."

The labourers slowly walked past again.

"Look at me, Ellie." Mrs Moore insisted.

"Those men, they're staring…"

"Yes, I know, try to ignore them," Mrs Moore turned and gave them a withering, contemptuous look. "When you feel despair, think of your husband and the duty you have to him. It helps."

"Thank you, Mrs Moore. Sometimes I believe I'm selfish, thinking only of myself and my discomforts, not of others." Eleanor returned the handkerchief.

"Why don't you use the flour and make something nice for your husband, surprise him."

"Thank you, I shall do exactly that," Eleanor replied.

"It appears we are being watched," said Mrs Moore with a smile as she looked over Eleanor's shoulder.

Alarmed, Eleanor turned quickly. "Oh, that's Pork-Chop," she said, relieved. "We just bought her."

With small grunts and covered in mud, the small pig stood in the small rickety enclosure and looked up at them.

"I'll give you some food scraps for her." Mrs Moore offered. "Now I need to return, cheer up, dear."

She leaned forward and gave Eleanor a quick hug, hoisted her skirts and waded with determination through the glutinous mud back to the flourmill.

Eleanor went back to clean her face. She had already decided to bake some bread and a pie for Andrew. She felt better and welcomed her neighbour's timely appearance and the comfort offered.

The firewood was damp, some even sodden. With difficulty, Eleanor lit the fire in the oven Andrew had built for her. It was nothing elaborate, just bricks carefully stacked into three sides, with a steel plate on top. To turn part of it into an oven, Andrew had devised a system to slide another plate down and block the opening to the oven section. It worked well when the wood was dry.

She felt more cheerful after Mrs Moore's visit, and the thought of the surprise she would have for Andrew brought a smile to her face. Eleanor added more wood to the fire to bring her oven up to temperature, and, with the flour given to her, she began to prepare her meal.

She turned to the pigpen – it was empty! Pork-Chop had disappeared. She ran over and looked more closely, seeing that the animal had simply pushed aside the loose mud and crept beneath the lower railing. She knew the little pig must have only just escaped and couldn't be far away. She examined the area but couldn't see her anywhere. She continued to search, carefully peering into the shadows, and then she saw her. There she was, heading towards the river, Pork-Chop's little legs powering through the thick mud.

Quickly covering the food she was preparing, Eleanor gave chase, dodging dangerous puddles of unknown depth as she ran along the deep, muddy track. She lost sight of the animal as she approached the river, then saw it emerge from behind a tent, running along the raised bank beside the. River.

Risking a glance to ensure no one was watching, Eleanor lifted her skirts and quickly bore down on the errant and determined little beast. Only a step or two away, Pork-Chop, realising she was being chased, instinctively tried to evade.

After heavy rains, the swollen Hutt River threatened to overflow its banks yet again. No longer a meandering, golden, sparkling river, it was now an angry, swiftly moving, muddy, brown mass. Felled by mudslides and strong winds, trees and debris floated downstream. Caught in the current, the debris posed a serious threat to boats and people in its path.

As Pork-Chop slowed, she turned to see Eleanor bearing down on her – the game was up. With a frightened squeal, the small pig slipped on wet grass and rolled over, tumbling into the river. Seeing the animal about to slide into the water, Eleanor desperately reached out. She skidded on the same wet grass and fell heavily, sliding down the small embankment into the fast-flowing, very cold Hutt River. With a yell, she landed on top of the struggling pig, briefly submerging it before lifting it safely from the water. She held the frightened animal firmly with one arm and reached out with the other towards the bank and a clump of overhanging grass. The roots weren't strong enough to hold her and pulled free from the wet soil. The river's current slowly dragged her and Pork-Chop away from the safety of the bank.

The two labourers watched in delight as Eleanor pursued the fleeing pig. To their surprise, they saw her hoist her skirts and chase after the animal with athleticism normally reserved for boys, not attractive young women. They were still watching Eleanor run along the low embankment when they saw her arms flail and then disappear from sight.

Realising what had happened, they ran quickly and reached the bank, where they found Eleanor fighting to keep her head above water, her sodden clothes weighing her down. They needed rope or a long stick, neither of which was handy.

Further downstream, they could see a bend in the river where Eleanor would be closer to the shore and easier to reach. Shouting for help, they ran, but few people were about to hear their panicked yells. They could hear Eleanor's cries as they sprinted past. Slipping frequently, they managed to keep from sliding into the river and arrived at the river's bend. Breathing hard, they searched for anything they could use. Every tree they saw had all its low-hanging branches cut, used for firewood or tent frames. There was nothing accessible unless they could reach higher limbs.

"Up there!" shouted Danny, pointing to a dead branch that was a suitable length.

Young Willy stared up helplessly at it.

"Here," Danny bent down, interlacing his hands together beneath the branch. "I'm gonna toss you up, grab the branch, it'll snap if you can reach it."

Willy stepped onto Danny's hands and, with a huge heave, launched himself upwards. Willy's upstretched hands found the branch and he grabbed it, but it didn't snap. He hung by his hands, suspended.

"Jiggle, Willy! C'mon! Hurry!"

Willy began bouncing. With a crack and a resounding snap, Willy and the branch landed on the soft, muddy ground with a painful grunt.

"Hurry!"

Danny grabbed the branch and ran to the bank. He extended the branch, hoping the young lady would grab it. She was almost there, drifting towards him, and he could see her fighting to keep her head above water.

Eleanor was cold, her extremities numb, even though she'd only been in the river a short time. The frigid water drained her of vital energy, and her heavy skirts threatened to pull her under. She was struggling, and her attempts to keep afloat were weakening. She still held Pork-Chop, who was suffering from the frigid water as she was. It was cold – so cold.

"Grab it!" yelled Danny, snapping her back to reality. "Grab it!" he yelled again.

She was drifting down towards the outstretched branch the young man held. She reached out with numb fingers and clutched the proffered branch. Her downstream momentum slowed, and she was pulled towards the bank, but she had no strength to hold on, and the branch slipped through her numb fingers.

Danny quickly threw off his coat and leaped into the water as Eleanor passed. He lunged – snatched at her, seized a fistful of clothing – and pulled and held on, but was now in danger of being carried downstream.

Willy had stood rooted to the spot as he watched his friend leap into the water.

"The branch, get the branch!" spluttered Danny.

Finally understanding what was needed, Willy retrieved the branch Danny had dropped and ran a few steps to catch up with them. He extended it across the water as Danny and Eleanor drifted past. Danny reached out and easily grasped the branch. He held on tightly as Willy pulled them all to safety.

Eleanor lay shivering, her lips blue. Danny put his coat over her, then took Willy's coat and put it over her as well.

"Find some dry wood, we need to light a fire," shivered Danny. "Get some from the tent over there," his teeth chattered.

A fire raged, and Eleanor sat beside it, shivering and savouring its warmth. Her clothes were still wet, but until she could return home, she would remain in them. Pork-Chop was tied to a tree, apparently recovered and, like her, enjoying the fire's heat. Danny had stopped shivering, and his shirt lay steaming on a stick near the flames. Willy had gone in search of more wood.

"Thank you again, so much," Eleanor said. "You saved my life. If you hadn't saved me when you did, I think I would have given up."

"You were lucky, Miss, I tell ya," said Danny. "If we hadn't seen you chasing that pig, I don't think anyone else would 'ave, either."

Eleanor nodded in understanding.

"I just want to go home and get into some dry clothes," she said quietly as she hugged her knees, her skirts beginning to steam.

Willy returned and stoked the fire, the heat beginning to take effect. Pork-Chop began digging around the tree she was tied to.

"I think I'm able to walk home now," said Eleanor.

"Good, we'll take you home safely Miss, you'll be right," offered Danny.

Willy nodded and grinned.

Andrew arrived home to find a small group of people gathered around their tent. Mrs Moore was fussing over Eleanor, and two youngish lads, strangers, were eating bread.

He began to shake as the near-tragic incident was recounted to him, and he realised he could easily have returned home to find he had lost Eleanor. Mrs Moore helped Eleanor change into dry clothes, then brought tea and freshly baked bread for the two lads. Grateful to Danny and Willy, Andrew held back his emotions as Eleanor sat by the fire. She stopped shivering and said she felt better, though she still looked pale.

Rain threatened, and Danny and Willy said farewell. They needed to return to their tents to ensure everything was protected and dry. Mrs Moore returned home to prepare the evening meal for her husband, leaving the couple alone. Andrew and Eleanor sat quietly together in their tent as she cried into his shoulder. He held her tightly and rocked her gently as darkness and rain began to fall again.

In absentia, much of the time purchasing land, Colonel Wakefield was spared the misfortunes of cold prevailing winds, persistent rain and the unpredictable river that brought misery to so many. Engineers and surveyors were convinced they could control the river with levees, but the capricious waterway randomly changed course, rendering their efforts useless. The harsh conditions tested couples. Relationships were strained, people became ill and tempers flared. After the bitter disappointments of

Britannia, and with their patience exhausted, some settlers moved to the south-western corner of Port Nicholson, where flat land was scarce and hills, in abundance, offered shelter and protection. Reluctantly, Wakefield eventually supported the relocation of Britannia and followed the disgruntled settlers. However, confusion reigned over the name. There was the old Britannia in Pito-one, which they'd mostly abandoned, and now there was a new Britannia. Honouring an avid New Zealand Company supporter and friend, the Duke of Wellington, Arthur Wellesley, the Company directors promptly named the new township Wellington. The aspirations of the New Zealand Company to create Britannia, the flawless, beautiful township they had meticulously designed, would not be realised in Pito-one.

Immigrant ships transported prefabricated buildings for easy assembly, and they were quickly erected along the Wellington foreshore and on the surrounding low-lying hills of the growing community. Recognising the futility of trying to make Britannia the model township, Wakefield finally accepted that it was an abject failure and selected a new prime location near a low hill close to the new harbour for his new Wellington home and office.

To the immense relief of many, Wellington offered shelter from the cold southerly winter winds. There was no river threatening to burst its banks, and a deep, protected harbour allowed easier access for ships to offload cargo.

PART TWO

CHAPTER EIGHT

Wellington Township, June 1840

Intense brown eyes stared at him from behind the leafy cover of a thick bush. They watched malevolently as the figure slowly approached. Carefully repositioning itself, it tensed, poised to strike and catch him unawares. Her small eyes narrowed as Andrew squelched through the mud, his voice carrying easily in the early-morning chill.

"Why do animals need to be fed so early in the morning?" he grumbled as he approached the small pen housing the waiting sow. "Especially on a Sunday morning."

Carrying a bucket of food scraps and slops, he stopped a couple of feet from the rickety fence as the sow sprang from behind the bush to attack.

Andrew laughed, "Not this time, Pork-Chop, you'll have to do better than that."

With the bucket raised, he threw its contents into the pen, half of which landed on the head of the disgruntled pig. Pork-Chop immediately began to eat, keeping a wary eye on Andrew, who in turn assessed her.

"Soon, my dear, soon," he said over his shoulder, as he carefully made his way back up the short muddy path to the small, prefabricated cottage he shared with Eleanor.

Andrew and Pork-Chop did not enjoy a harmonious relationship, and when the opportunity arose, she took great delight in giving Andrew a swift head-butt. When she was younger, it was of little concern, but as she grew, so did her strength, and her blows often caught him unawares, leaving him sitting on his backside in the mud. Pork-Chop had a lot of growing to do; she was young but still carried enough weight to inflict damage. It was highly unlikely that the two would ever form a bond and reach an amicable understanding. Pork-Chop was jealous of Andrew and protective of Eleanor. With Eleanor, she was always gentle and affectionate.

It was early on a beautiful Sunday morning, and on Ngaiti's urging, they would attend a service at Wellington's first church, built at the Te Aro *pa*. Eleanor was preparing breakfast as Andrew came in, returning the bucket to its place in the corner.

With much joy and celebration, the couple had only recently relocated to their modest cottage, assigned to them by Colonel Wakefield. It was quickly assembled on the gentle slope of a low hill overlooking Lambton Harbour in Wellington. After the hardships they endured in Britannia, their new home was heaven. Eleanor even had a real stove.

Wellington lay on the southwest side of Port Nicholson. Ringed by hills, it offered adequate shelter from the cold southerly winds and a deep, protected harbour, perfectly suited for shipping and serving the growing community. The New Zealand Company divided Wellington into two areas; hilly Thorndon Flats, where Colonel Wakefield built his single-storey home and office, only a few minutes' walk from where Andrew and Eleanor lived. The New Zealand Company named this neighbourhood Thorndon Flats, after Thorndon Hall in Essex, the residence of the New Zealand Company board member, Lord Petre. However, locals now refer to the area simply as Thorndon. The other area, mostly inhabited and cultivated by Māori, was named Te Aro Flats, which contained sizeable portions of reasonably flat, fertile land and was home to the Te Aro *pa*.

Eleanor was excited, and with her mouth full of bread, she waved a letter she had received from her Aunt Mary, who lived in Van Diemen's Land.

"You're going to get marmalade all over that letter if you don't put it down."

Eleanor mumbled an unintelligible reply that made them both laugh.

The letter explained the difficult economic times and the family's struggles after the loss of two ships they owned. Uncle Charles owned a small shipping company and had met with moderate success. By expanding the business, they began delivering needed goods and merchandise to whaling stations in New Zealand, but two quick accidents saw their business suffer. The letter went on to explain how Charles was considering moving the family to New Zealand and beginning a new life. He felt New Zealand offered a better future for them.

"When will they arrive?" asked Andrew.

"She doesn't say anything, only that this is something they are considering and that they will let us know," said Eleanor, finally able to speak.

Andrew smiled, he knew Uncle Charles and enjoyed his company and humour.

"It will be wonderful to see Uncle Charles again. You must be pleased, Ellie?"

"I am. This is good news." Eleanor put the letter down and realised the time. "Andy, if we are to go to the church service, we must leave soon."

"I'm ready," he replied, helping her clean up from breakfast.

"He says he asked God for land to build a place of worship," Ngaiti translated quietly. "And God provided."

Minarapa Rangihatuake stood at the pulpit of the newly completed Wesleyan Church, built within the extensive Te Aro pa in Wellington. Appointed as a preacher by Wesleyan leaders Rev Hobbs and Rev Bumby, Minarapa now stood facing his congregation, his eyes blazing with spirit, taking in the faces of those seated before him as he finished his sermon. He spoke in *Te Reo*.

"God will always provide, open your hearts and allow him in."

Built from *raupo,* a type of wetland rush, local Māori carefully tied clumps of the stems together and bound them to create strong, well-insulated walls and an elaborate high ceiling. Decorations and Māori paintings adorned the interior walls, and a large wooden cross stood protectively over the mostly Māori congregation, who sat attentively on mats, listening to the sermon.

"And now we have a fine church. A church we can all be proud of."

A murmur of agreement rippled through the ardent flock as they acknowledged the hard work of everyone who had contributed to its construction.

Minarapa nodded and smiled before continuing.

"But more challenges face us, and we can overcome them as we have confronted and surmounted others." Ngaiti continued his interpretation for Andrew and Eleanor. "We will not allow the New Zealand Company to take our lands – just because they covet them!"

Minarapa thumped his fist on the pulpit to emphasise his point, again glancing at the faces around him.

Andrew raised his eyebrows and turned to Eleanor, both surprised by the change in direction and tone of the sermon.

A man's voice shouted out.

"What did he say?" Andrew whispered.

"He said we should kill them when they come," Ngaiti whispered.

Andrew winced.

Minarapa paused at the outburst, shaking his head, looking perturbed. "Christians shouldn't kill; that is not our way." He raised a finger towards the heavens, emphasising his point. "But we can stop them; they will not trespass, and we will prevent their illegal claim on our land!" Again, his excited flock murmured in support.

"And we will forgive them. We *will* forgive them!" said Ngaiti.

"Who is the preacher, is he a chief?" asked Eleanor.

They were standing outside in the sunshine shortly after the service's conclusion.

"The Te Aro *Pa* has no ranking chief to speak of. Minarapa is much loved by the people here, and because most of them are Christians and members of the Wesleyan Methodist church, they turn to him as a leader."

"Why is this land in question?" asked Andrew.

"The people here believe that the area known as Te Aro was never included in the original land transactions agreed at the early stages of the negotiations aboard the *Tory*. Chief Te Wharepouri quietly insists that this was a condition of the agreement and that this land was never included in the original Port Nicholson land purchase. Colonel Wakefield maintains that it was included and believes he has every right to begin surveying and determining allotment boundaries for colonists."

"I've heard the colonel talk with Mr Park, the surveyor, about it. I believe they will begin plotting the area soon, regardless of any Māori opposition. I can see why the Company wants this land; it's almost flat and perfect for colonisation," said Andrew, appraising the area.

"Te Wharepouri made a point of telling the colonel that it was not included in the purchase. I was there and heard him."

Andrew laughed. "Yes, the colonel believes this is nothing more than a ploy to extract more weapons and blankets from him."

"What does Chief Te Wharepouri say about this?" Eleanor asked.

"Te Wharepouri told Wakefield, 'Your heart and mind are divided by the wealth you gather. When they become one, your *mana* will be strong, and you will do what is right.'"

"What is *mana*?" she asked.

"*Mana* for Māori is central to our culture; it defines character, spirituality, the essence of a person, and what he is."

"Ah, yes. I understand …I think," said Eleanor.

Ngaiti continued, "It is a little difficult for Chief Te Wharepouri. Many Māori who live here at Te Aro *Pa* were once slaves, so they are of a lower social standing. Te Wharepouri can't be seen to be too sympathetic or active in their interests."

"Is that why you are here?" she asked.

"Yes, Miss Ellie. With Chief Te Wharepouri's quiet blessing, I am here to help them."

"Help them? In what way?" Andrew chimed in.

"To protect their land."

"From what I've heard, Colonel Wakefield has no qualms about sending surveyors into Te Aro. As far as he is concerned, this tract of land is owned by the New Zealand Company, and Māori have no legal rights to it."

"Look around here, Andy. What do you see?" Eleanor asked.

Andrew shrugged his shoulders.

"These people plant crops and cultivate this land. That is what they do. I can see that if this land, or even large parts of it, are taken, it will ruin them," Eleanor stated.

"Yes, I suppose that if they lose their land, they'll have nothing here. I see it now," conceded Andrew. "From what you've said, that means you anticipate difficulties for them when the surveyors come?"

Ngaiti nodded.

CHAPTER NINE

The confident swagger of men carrying swords and muskets into the Te Aro Flats posed little threat to Māori, who stood at a safe distance and watched. Fanning out, the well-armed men advanced, inviting Māori to challenge them. Content to observe, Minarapa repeatedly instructed his people to avoid confrontation and to allow the *pakeha* to go about their business.

Some *pakeha* carrying weapons toyed with their muskets, hoping that today Māori would resist. As they slowly approached, some began to provoke them by hurling insults and slurs. Many of Minarapa's people didn't understand the *pakeha* language, but reinforced with aggressive sneers, they could grasp the intent and tone behind the taunts. Sensing Minarapa's mounting agitation, many men eagerly awaited the word to respond; they wanted nothing more than to chase the invaders from land that did not belong to them.

Chief Te Wharepouri knew that the situation was volatile and asked Ngaiti to go to Te Aro to observe on his behalf, to watch carefully, and to help Minarapa persuade the Te Aro people to demonstrate calm and restraint in the face of the self-assured white man.

"Do nothing. These men want us to react and fight. It will be a battle we cannot win today," urged Ngaiti to the watching Māori.

"This is our home, our *pa*, these people have no right to come here," replied a warrior in frustration.

"Wait until darkness, then we will act," said Minarapa quietly.

The warrior grunted in growing impatience.

Behind the armed militia came other men carrying chains and scientific equipment. Every now and then, the nervous surveyors and their assistants looked anxiously over their shoulders, half expecting a horde of crazed Māori warriors to charge down upon them.

Assistant surveyors, or 'chainmen', began laying out the specialist one-hundred-link Gunter's Chain to its full sixty-six-foot length, then placing steel arrows into the ground to mark the end of each chain length as they began surveying and marking boundaries.

With an assortment of scientific equipment, surveyors triangulated the necessary parameters using theodolites securely mounted on tripods and began to mark out one-acre, or ten square chain, plots of land. Surveying was a precise science, and surveyors were proud men who took their profession very seriously. They sought to remain faithful to their craft and to measure accurate boundaries, even when threatened with attack. With some urgency, surveyors were told to chart this area expeditiously and to mark out parcels of land that had already been sold. In the interests of time, and under increasing pressure from unhappy colonists, it was of little concern to an insistent Colonel Wakefield if slight errors were made. The colonel assured the pedantic surveyors that any minor surveying mistakes could easily be resolved at a later date. Most surveyors disagreed with that point of view.

On the surveyor's instructions, the assistant would drive a white boundary peg into the ground with a large hammer at a specific location. Drawing perimeter lines from peg to peg would outline the boundary. The details and position of each plot were given a lot number and accurately recorded in the surveyor's field book. The lot number was also carved onto one side of the boundary peg facing the plot that had been surveyed; eventually, each side of the boundary peg would bear a different lot number. Colonists who paid in advance were given possession of their land once the information in the field book had been transferred to the master plan held at the New Zealand Company's Wellington office.

Robert Park, one of many surveyors for the New Zealand Company, stood straight and stretched his back, easing his cramped muscles. He repositioned his hat and placed his hands on his hips, looking out across the land before him. Much of this area had been cultivated and was growing vegetables, mostly potatoes and a variety of other produce that Māori sold to settlers. He wasn't happy to see his men damaging plants by walking through the crops, or seeing the chain ripping through vegetables as it was straightened and pulled tight. He'd repeatedly demanded that the chainmen be respectful and avoid damage. He shook his head in quiet sympathy. Some surveyors didn't care and showed little or no respect for Māori buildings or crops, pretending they didn't exist.

Surveying was a thankless task. No one appreciated the physical effort required to climb steep hills, wade through swamps and fight through dense bush and scrub to survey land. It mattered not to his employers whether it rained, was cold or hot, or whether his body provided nourishment for hungry insects, often leaving painful, raised bumps that became infected in the harsh conditions of the wilderness. Mr Park smiled. He knew that tomorrow he would return here and begin surveying the same land all over again. For the foreseeable future, he would sleep in a real bed, enjoy a hot bath and not spend nights in a tent perched on a windy, wet hilltop.

"How's it goin' then, Mr Park?" came a voice from behind.

Robert Park turned and looked down at the man who greeted him. Saying nothing, Park reached into his vest and drew out a well-worn pipe and tobacco pouch.

"Without the distractions, we could work much quicker, Mr Barrett." He began the slow, therapeutic task of packing tobacco into the bowl.

"I gathered a few lads to keep an eye on you and make sure you aren't in any danger," Barrett said with a smile as he watched Park lightly compress the tobacco in the bowl with his thumb.

"I'm just sorry it's come to this. There's no need for your men to display open hostility, issue threats, or provoke Māori, Mr Barrett," suggested the surveyor disapprovingly.

Barrett remained silent and continued to watch Park complete his routine.

Satisfied with his pipe, Park placed it in his mouth, struck a match and began to suck. As the tobacco smouldered, Park lightly tapped the tobacco a final time for good measure, then looked at Barrett. "I don't want trouble here, in any shape or form. Make certain your men know this."

"Yes, sir, Mr Park. We can't have trouble, can we?" Barrett looked out across the field. In the distance, he could easily see Minarapa, with that meddlesome Ngaiti beside him. Barrett's eyes narrowed. Ngaiti was becoming more of a problem, a ringleader sowing the seeds of discontent. Barrett smiled, pleased with the irony of his joke. "Good day, Mr Park," said Barrett as he trudged away.

"Mr Barrett," Park replied, happy to see the irksome man leave.

The surveyors marked out the required one-acre plots for the day, and it was expected that they would return tomorrow and every day thereafter until the entire area had been surveyed. As dusk fell over Te Aro Flats, assistant surveyors began packing their equipment and withdrawing from the area.

Protecting the delicate optics from damage, Robert Park removed his beloved theodolite from the tripod and thoroughly wiped away dust and moisture. Assured all was well, he carefully wrapped the theodolite in a cloth, placed it in its protective wooden box, and then put it into a leather bag with stout straps, allowing him to wear it on his back. Of all the surveyor's equipment, the theodolite was the most valued and treasured.

Because of the nature of their work, surveyors often found themselves in remote and dangerous places, and unfortunately, accidents happened from time to time, with lives regrettably lost. In such a situation, if a choice was required to save the life of a chainman or to save the theodolite from damage, the surveyor would save his theodolite first - a chainman could easily be replaced. Something surveyors enjoyed reminding chainmen all too frequently.

With the theodolite secured on his back, Robert Park hoisted the tripod onto his shoulder and strode off to the wagon and the waiting chainmen, his thoughts consumed by the prospect of a hot bath and dinner.

Most of the musket-wielding militia had since departed, leaving half a dozen men to stand guard. The call of an evening meal was more pressing than the need to protect insignificant white pegs hammered into the earth. Those men remaining would be rotated throughout the night, guarding the area to ensure the surveyors' work remained untouched.

From the perimeter, a few Māori remained, watching the surveying party load their equipment onto wagons and depart. As the shadows lengthened, quiet descended over Te Aro, a distant barking dog the only indication that something was amiss.

Darkness finally enveloped Te Aro Flats. The watery moonlight provided only enough illumination to make out indistinct shadows moving slowly through rows of neatly laid crops. The occasional voice could be heard as the men exchanged a pleasantry or grumbled about being hungry or bored. They all carried muskets and were instructed to warn away any intruders, shooting only if threatened.

Not far away, dozens of eyes watched the unsuspecting guards. Minarapa and a group of men waited in readiness, patiently looking for patterns in the guards' patrols. Feeling confident, Minarapa finally gave a signal, and two men slid out from concealment and began to crawl along the rows of potatoes towards the surveyors' pegs they had identified earlier in the day. The positions of the pegs were committed to memory. One man carried a bag woven from flax, which held a short, thick log, while the other grasped a *taiaha*, a spear.

With skill and patience, the warriors advanced slowly, slithering across the ground and through rows of cultivated crops. When a guard approached, the warriors remained motionless and cleverly blended into the earth or nearby foliage. They made no sound and gave no indication of their presence.

Two more men left the group and began to crawl in a different direction. Before long, ten groups of men entered the large area the guards were patrolling, each carrying a flax bag, a log and a *taiaha*.

The first group, who had the furthest to travel, eventually crawled to the nearest boundary peg. As rehearsed, one man extracted the log from his bag and laid it flat on the ground, firmly against the peg, while the other pushed the sharp-pointed *taiaha* horizontally into the peg, immediately above the log. Still prone, he slowly levered the *taiaha* down against the log. The peg moved and lifted slightly. He removed the *taiaha*, pressed it firmly into the peg again, and pushed down, levering the peg upwards. The silent process was repeated until the peg could be removed by hand. They then placed the log and the peg into the flax bag. The hole was filled with soil and smoothed over, and they moved on to the next peg some distance away.

Although there was nothing to see, Minarapa and Ngaiti watched and listened closely, hoping there would be no cry of discovery. Throughout the night, all the surveyors' boundary pegs were removed, and the guards patrolling the area were completely unaware of the subterfuge.

Ngaiti stayed until all the men returned, then they all went back to the Te Aro *pa* to burn the surveyors' pegs. Dawn wasn't far away when Ngaiti finally departed Te Aro and began the long hour-and-a-half walk to Kaiwharawhara.

The walk took him down to the harbour, where he followed the well-used track towards Thorndon. A few early risers were out and about, greeting him warmly as he passed by, but his mind was lost in the confusion of what was happening to his country, to his people and his family. He was at a loss as to what he could do. As usual, his thoughts returned to the concept Edward Wakefield created and called 'Systemic Colonisation' and to what it meant. Unlike most other people, Ngaiti had both the Pakeha and Māori perspectives, and no matter how he tried to understand Systemic Colonisation and its philosophical meaning, he couldn't bring himself to support the idea.

Systemic Colonisation was a concept proposed by his old mentor, Edward Wakefield. In theory, quite simple, but in practice, as Ngaiti admitted to himself, much more complex and fraught with problems. A new colony would attract investors and capitalists who would purchase land. A plot of land for an urban dwelling, another for a country estate, and another for farming. As Edward Wakefield believed, this would provide an abundance of jobs for hand-picked migrant labourers – skilled men to work the land and build.

Labourers were promised jobs and sufficient wages so they could save and eventually fulfil their dreams, purchasing property and a home of their own. In practice, the land was frequently unaffordable, and jobs were difficult to find. Some suggested the concept was purely a ruse, a scheme in which labourers were always kept wanting, and the wealthy enjoyed control of the new model society. Ngaiti yawned.

Tired after a long night and lost in the confusion of conflicting emotions, he never saw the two men waiting for him in the darkness of a small warehouse as he walked by, nor did he sense their presence as they quickly approached him from behind. The only indication that something was wrong was the intense pain at the back of his head as one of the ruffians struck him with a vicious blow from an expertly wielded sap. Ngaiti collapsed unconscious on the ground, bleeding profusely from his head.

CHAPTER TEN

Thorndon Flats, Wellington.

As customary, Andrew and Eleanor were enjoying a leisurely breakfast together. He had a busy day ahead and, in preparation for creating the balance sheet, he needed to finish entering all invoices and receipts into the daily journals and then begin recording entries in the accounting register. For Andrew, this was easy; the most difficult part was making his handwriting neat and legible. His office was situated at Wakefield's residence and accessible through a public side entrance. All those seeking business meetings with Colonel Wakefield would pass through an outer office and waiting room, then through Andrew's workplace to reach the colonel's office. As the colonel wasn't in residence today, Andrew felt no compunction about arriving at work early and disturbing him.

"I hope the colonel can sort out the problems with the Government," Andrew said between mouthfuls of porridge.

"Should we be worried, Andy? What will happen if they challenge the legality of the land sales to the Company?"

"All I know is that the colonel made sure every transaction was completed with meticulous care." Andrew picked up his teacup and took a small sip. "I've seen all the documents. The numbers add up, and there's no indication of any improprieties by the Company, so I do not know why the Government is angry."

"Could Jerningham have made errors in his documents and in the deeds he created?" asked Eleanor as she began to clean the small kitchen table where they ate.

"I doubt it. While Jerningham is no trained scholar or lawyer, he's a very accomplished writer, and if he made mistakes in writing those documents, they are probably only minor ones, not worthy of serious attention." Andrew stood, handing his empty cup to Eleanor.

"Then I would be very disappointed in the Wakefields and the Company if they were involved in any deceit," said Eleanor with a frown. "For one, I would not want any association with the Company if they were involved in any illegal activities."

"I wouldn't worry, Ellie, if you are imprisoned, I shall visit you once a month, bring you a pot of tea, a change of clothes, and I will even bring Pork-Chop to visit."

Eleanor flung the tea towel at him, then launched herself into his arms. Andrew held her tightly, enjoying a moment of closeness before he left for work.

"Promise me, Andy, that you will keep an open eye on anything that looks inappropriate or you think is illegal. I don't want us to be caught up in this and be held responsible."

"Of course, Ellie. Don't worry."

"You had better go to work, or I will change my mind and hold you captive," Eleanor said with a twinkle in her eye. She pushed herself back and straightened her clothes.

Andrew left the cottage in contemplation. He knew the English Government had appointed Lieutenant Governor Hobson to oversee its interests in New Zealand, and he wondered what the Company might have done to provoke Hobson's displeasure. He quickened his stride and continued towards the Company's office at Wakefield's home.

Down the path, a short distance along, a small group of people had gathered and were carefully inspecting something by the side of the track. As Andrew approached, he could just make out a man who appeared injured. Not a common occurrence, and with his curiosity piqued, he paused briefly to observe. Two strangers who had come to the injured man's aid were helping him into a sitting position. Andrew saw the face clearly and instantly recognised him.

"Ngaiti!" he yelled, pushing past the onlookers to crouch down beside his friend.

Dazed, with blood trickling down the side of his face, Ngaiti stared at Andrew blankly.

"What happened? Are you badly hurt?" Andrew asked.

Recognition dawning on him, Ngaiti could only reply with a grunt.

Understanding that Ngaiti required medical attention, he asked one of the onlookers for help carrying Ngaiti back to his home, a short distance away. Andrew and the stranger managed to half-carry, half-drag Ngaiti, who was unable to walk, back to the cottage.

On hearing a commotion, Eleanor met them at the door.

Taking charge, she instructed that Ngaiti be brought to the guest bedroom and placed on the bed. She immediately fetched water and began cleaning and caring for the bewildered young man.

The stranger explained that no-one had seen the cause of Ngaiti's injuries and that he'd only just been found lying on the side of the track moments before Andrew arrived. After thanking the man, who quickly departed, Andrew returned to Eleanor.

"What happened, Andy?"

"I don't know. There were no witnesses; no-one saw a thing. Presumably, Ngaiti succumbed to an accident of sorts."

"Andy, fetch the doctor, while I continue to clean the wound."

The doctor inspected the deep gash on Ngaiti's head and sutured the wound, declaring that he was suffering from severe shock to the brain, or, as he described it, *commotio cerebri*, and needed rest to recover. He dispensed laudanum to ease the pain, which left Ngaiti sleepy. The cause of the incident was still unknown, and until the effect of the opiate had worn off, it was unlikely that Ngaiti would be able to communicate coherently.

It was decided that Eleanor would remain with Ngaiti, and Andrew would continue working, returning home during his midday break to see how he was doing.

Andrew sat at his writing desk. The journals lay open in front of him, and a large accounting register beckoned. He had been unable to shake the image of Ngaiti's injury from his mind, the sight of blood streaming down the side of his face disturbing. The doctor explained that head wounds bled profusely and often looked worse than they were.

With a long sigh, he looked at the column of numbers in the register; at least they were predictable, made sense, and provided logical order in an often-chaotic world.

In his small office, Andrew recorded all the expenses and income for the Company's activities in New Zealand. He'd often receive smudged and soiled paperwork; sometimes rainwater ran the ink, leaving the documents all but illegible. Others were torn or stained with mud, or the handwriting was indecipherable. It was a never-ending, thankless task to keep reminding everyone, including the colonel, to obtain legible receipts for all expenses so that the register could be reconciled. Auditors in England would hold Andrew responsible for any discrepancies.

He could recognise numerical patterns easily; when a colonist's ship arrived, the relevant documents would eventually reach Andrews's desk, and he would record the expenses in the daily journals. With so many ships arriving in Wellington carrying colonists, he could accurately predict the expenses submitted by the Company's chartered ships. After a while, he could recognise discrepancies or errors with ease and would immediately bring them to the colonel's attention for clarification. If the colonel was unavailable, as was frequently the case, he would speak directly with the ship's captain or find the responsible person.

Andrew marvelled at how the Company generated huge profits from land sales. Agents for the Company were busy selling land to colonists in England at one pound an acre. In response, the Company needed labourers to work the land, build homes and do the hard graft. After careful vetting, they were now arriving on New Zealand shores by the shipload, ready to begin a new life.

After reviewing some past journal entries, he calculated that the Company had purchased about 20 million acres from Māori for less than

9,000 pounds. An incredible return on a modest investment, he thought. Surprisingly, he also discovered that Barrett was nearly always involved in these purchases.

The relationship between Colonel Wakefield and Richard 'Dickie' Barrett was curious, noted Andrew. Barrett was constantly receiving thanks for his work in creative ways. The Company recently granted him a lease for a large building in Wellington, which he quickly converted into a hotel. Barrett had his finger in many pies. He was a whaler, a trader, and an agent for the New Zealand Company, for which he received an annual salary of one hundred pounds, and he was now also a publican. There wasn't much that happened in Wellington, or within the Company, that Dickie Barrett wasn't involved in. He was indispensable and reaping the rewards. More recently, a few colonists had come to the office to complain about Barrett. In Andrew's eyes, this somewhat tarnished his image as a convivial philanthropic businessman.

Focusing on his work, Andrew returned to his accounting register. In a few hours, he could finish work for the day and return home.

Andrew was relieved to find Ngaiti talking quietly with Eleanor when he arrived home. Much to everyone's relief, he seemed a little better, though pale and still in pain.

"You gave us a frightful scare, Ngaiti. What happened?" asked Andrew.

Ngaiti allowed Eleanor to reposition the pillows and give him some water.

"I was attacked when I was walking back to Kaiwharawhara. Someone was waiting and hit me with something," said Ngaiti.

"Did they take your money?" inquired Andrew.

After a brief pause, Ngaiti replied, "No, I wasn't robbed."

"Then why on earth would anyone attack you? Did you see who it was?"

"I caught a glimpse, and I think I have seen him before." Ngaiti didn't elaborate further, realising he'd said more than he intended to.

Eleanor and Andrew exchanged a look of concern.

"Then who was it?" Andrew pushed the matter.

"I- I'm sleepy," replied Ngaiti groggily.

Understanding that they would get nothing more from him, Eleanor took the glass of water from Ngaiti's hand and indicated that they should let him rest and sleep. They returned to the kitchen.

"What do you think, Andy?"

"He knows more than he is willing to share, that's for certain."

CHAPTER ELEVEN

Staplehurst, Kent, England

Mr Whiting peeked from behind the threadbare curtain, moving it aside carefully to remain unseen as he considered the local residents who had come this evening to hear him speak. The fifty seats were all filled, and the audience waited with growing impatience for the lecture to begin.

George Whiting was an agent for the New Zealand Company. He travelled from town to town throughout Kent, England, delivering lectures on New Zealand. Each lecture varied and was tailored to the Company's immediate needs. Tonight, he would focus on attracting the attention of skilled people, such as mechanics, carpenters, and agricultural workers, who could be persuaded to emigrate.

His deliberate delay in appearing before the townsfolk was part of his well-rehearsed 'act'. He knew the exact moment to appear, and within a short time, his audience would be sympathetic and eating from his hand. He judged the moment carefully and decided - it was time. Taking a few deep breaths, he parted the curtain and rushed onto the slightly raised platform, looking flustered.

"Ladies and Gentlemen," George gasped, appearing out of breath. "Please forgive me for my tardiness. I would have been here earlier, but sadly, I was accosted on the street by a rather discourteous and dishonest vagabond who insisted I provide him with some gratuity." George frowned disapprovingly to reinforce his point. "He was trying to rob me!" His audience, caught in the spell, looked on in sympathy as George spread his arms wide to emphasise the gravity of the offence. "Yes, Ladies and Gentlemen, the audacity of the man who dares to impose on me and then demand that I hand over a shilling!" Mr Whiting paused and looked openly at the faces of those who sat before him. He shook his head and spoke slowly. "He demanded that I hand over a shilling!" Mr Whiting repeated, with practised gestures and oral theatrics.

With impeccable timing, a voice in the crowd yelled out, "Wha' did ya do?"

In response, George held up a finger. "I explained to the would-be robber that I was a hard-working man of poor means, unable to provide adequately for my family, and that a future of financial independence and comfort was very unlikely." George surveyed the room, soliciting compassion, and spoke dramatically. "That I would starve myself if need be, so that I may see my children adequately clothed and fed." Heads nodded in support and understanding, an all-too-familiar circumstance for those in attendance. George never felt the need to add that he didn't have children, nor was he married.

The unknown voice again asked the question on everyone's mind, "Did ya give him a shilling?"

Appearing troubled, Mr Whiting scanned the faces of the residents seated in the small hall, heightening the drama and tension. He casually reached into his vest pocket. "No!" he exclaimed. "He gave me sixpence!"

He extracted a coin and tossed it into the air.

The fifty curious residents of Staplehurst who attended this evening's lecture broke down into fits of uncontrolled laughter.

George had them exactly where he wanted them. Now, the real performance would begin.

Once the audience had settled down, George Whiting revisited the argument of being poor with no future.

"Such a place exists, Ladies and Gentlemen. The Directors of The New Zealand Company have begun to colonise our newest frontier." George spoke with confidence as he paced across the raised platform, which may have been a theatrical stage. His performance was worthy of accolades.

"They have carefully selected colonists of character and reputation and granted them land and opportunity in New Zealand. The failings of our culture will remain here. They have begun to create the perfect English society!"

All attendees at tonight's performance received a handbill upon entering the hall. It was an advertisement from the New Zealand Company offering free passage to New Zealand and a guarantee of work for selected applicants upon their arrival.

"These gentlemen colonists have need of your skilled talents." George paused to drive his point home.

"The Directors have already begun to create Britannia, a township designed to emulate the finest qualities of English civilisation. Wide boulevards, parks and public amenities are set within undulating plains suitable for the cultivation of grapevines, olives and wheat. A natural green town belt surrounds Britannia, where no buildings or structures will ever be permitted; these designated areas are for your enjoyment and leisure. Ladies and Gentlemen, the New Zealand Company is offering suitable applicants the opportunity to emigrate to New Zealand and to afford them a future that is presently unattainable. If you are aged between fifteen and thirty years, and you possess the necessary skills, are healthy and of sound character and mind, then I urge you to consider this fine offer," appealed Mr Whiting with passion.

George fielded questions and answered each with confidence. He'd given this talk so many times that it was unlikely anyone would ask a question he couldn't answer. At the end of the evening, George Whiting received fifteen more applicants and slipped a coin into the hand of the audience plant before returning to his lodgings.

Over the next three days, Mr Whiting would interview each applicant to assess suitability, then refer the applications to the New Zealand Company Directors for final selection and approval. As Mr George Whiting was one of the Company's more productive agents, he would pack his bag, depart for the next town or village, and begin the process all over again.

CHAPTER TWELVE

Thorndon Flats, Wellington

The morning ritual was the same. Andrew made his way down the muddy path towards the pigpen at the bottom of the garden. The birds were waiting, and a chorus of chirps and tweets greeted him as he approached the pen. The birds always helped themselves to the food Pork-Chop missed. As usual, the sow was waiting behind the bush, and Andrew could see her glistening, moist snout poking through the branches as she lay in wait for him, her eyes fixed on him.

With a loud series of grunts and snorts, Pork-Chop flew out of the bush towards Andrew, scattering the few birds who had already landed in the pen in anticipation of the morning feast. She slipped, one leg sinking into the mud, her shoulder taking the brunt of the fall as she slid a foot or two towards the fence where Andrew stood watching.

"Easy, Pork-Chop. Don't bruise the meat. Take care of yourself," he said with a big grin as he up-ended the bucket into the pen. Foiled again, Pork-Chop turned her attention to the food scattered before her, one eye still watching Andrew.

Colonel Wakefield had two guests with him in his office when Andrew arrived at work, and Andrew found him in a rather disagreeable mood. The colonel was livid at the lack of progress in surveying Te Aro and at the delays caused by repeatedly re-surveying the same land. For three consecutive nights, the boundary pegs mysteriously disappeared, despite the assurances given to him by Barrett.

Wakefield voiced his displeasure with Barrett and now demanded an explanation from the Company's 'Surveyor General', Captain William Mein Smith. Captain Smith, who was surveying the land for the Botanical Gardens that Wakefield wanted so much, offered little in the way of a solution that hadn't already been tried. Frustrated, Wakefield made it clear to all that surveyors were a troublesome breed of men and that surveying was a simple job anyone could do. This didn't endear him to the 'measuring men' fraternity, with whom Wakefield had recently become unpopular.

It was decided that the New Zealand Company would open its coffers and, with one hundred pounds, create an elementary law-enforcement infrastructure, hiring two men and bestowing on one, the title of 'Policeman' and on the other the honour of 'Magistrate'. Under Wakefield's control, this would now make New Zealand Company law enforceable. All immigrants, both colonists and settlers, signed a contract stating that they must abide by all laws created by the New Zealand Company.

If they could apprehend the vandals, an example could be made to deter others from committing any further seditious acts.

On further reflection, Wakefield also decided to offer a bribe, whereby, if Te Aro Māori received a gift of twenty blankets, perhaps they could be persuaded to stop the peg-pulling.

Having overheard the entire exchange, Andrew decided it was best to keep his head down and immerse himself in the small stack of receipts, invoices and bills awaiting his attention. After Dickie Barrett and Captain Smith had departed, Colonel Wakefield remained quietly in his office, writing to his brother Edward in England.

The morning hours passed by quickly and, before long, it was time for Andrew to return home during his mid-day break.

Ngaiti was asleep and had volunteered no further information to Eleanor.

"There is something going on, and he isn't telling. Do you think he's in trouble?"

"After work, I will insist that he tell us, Ellie. That's all we can do. Beyond that, it really isn't our affair."

"Yes, but as his friends, we have a duty to help him."

"And we are doing just that," said Andrew, giving his wife a hug and a kiss.

Andrew returned to work a few minutes early. As he entered, he could hear raised voices seeping through the walls of the colonel's office. Not every word was audible, but he easily recognised Barrett's voice. The gist of the conversation became clear. Barrett was again reassuring, confirming to the colonel that one of the peg-pulling perpetrators in Te Aro had been dealt with, which explained why no pegs had been removed the previous evening and why Robert Park should have no further problems surveying the land a final time.

The delays in allocating the pre-sold properties in Te Aro to the waiting colonists were adding to the pressure Wakefield already felt. As principal agent, he was responsible for all land purchases in New Zealand; he suffered at the pleasure of England's Colonial Office's constant haranguing, and, adding to the growing burden, the hostile voice of Lieutenant Governor Hobson. As a result, Colonel William Wakefield was growing more frustrated day by day. Not helping matters was his brother Edward, who was becoming less responsive to letters sent to him.

Andrew couldn't help but listen with fascination. After a moment, Wakefield's door opened, and Barrett strode out. Surprised to see Andrew at his desk, Barrett paused, offering a polite smile.

"Good afternoon, Mr Stewart. I hope you and the missus are well."

"Yes, thank you for asking, Mr Barrett," replied Andrew with equal politeness.

"As long as you're both happy and healthy, that's the important thing, isn't it?" said Dickie, smiling as he left the room.

Andrew was growing to dislike Dickie Barrett. Although Barrett had offered no particular reason, there was a shallowness and insincerity about the man that irked him.

The colonel didn't want to be disturbed and spent the rest of the afternoon in his office, preparing for the inevitable showdown with Lieutenant Governor Hobson.

Ngaiti was feeling better and more talkative, though he was still unwilling to discuss the assault. He told Andrew and Eleanor he would return to his home in Kaiwharawhara later that evening. However, Eleanor insisted he remain their guest for another night. Ngaiti wasn't silly and didn't protest. Andrew was about to raise the subject of Ngaiti's mysterious injury again when a knock at the door surprised them both. They didn't receive many callers. A brief look of concern flashed across Ngaiti's face.

Eleanor rose and went to answer the door, leaving Andrew and Ngaiti alone.

"My friend," began Andrew. "I know you are keeping something from us about what happened to you yesterday, and we are very concerned for you. Tell me what happened?"

Eleanor opened the door and recoiled in surprise. Before her stood the imposing figure of Chief Te Wharepouri and another man, also Māori. Te Wharepouri stood facing Eleanor, saying nothing.

Recovering quickly, she smiled nervously. "Good evening," she said slowly, holding up her hand in front of the chief to wait while she called for Andrew.

Andrew came quickly and was equally surprised to see Chief Te Wharepouri standing outside the door to their small cottage.

"Good evening, sir, uh, how can we help you?" Andrew inquired nervously.

The chief stood and looked at them both, a small smile playing across his face.

"Hello," said the chief, the first English word anyone in New Zealand had heard from him. The second word was in the Māori language and very understandable. "Ngaiti?"

Eleanor, taking the initiative, returned the smile and invited both men to enter her home. The chief said a word or two to his companion, who then remained outside. Te Wharepouri slowly entered the cottage and looked around the room with curiosity. He saw Eleanor's ornaments, paintings of their homes in England, and family portraits. He pointed to the painting of an older couple and looked at Eleanor questioningly.

"My mother and father," she replied slowly.

Te Wharepouri nodded in understanding.

The small cottage was warm, cosy and inviting. A kitchen table dominated the main living area, with two armchairs strategically placed in the corner facing low bookshelves along the far wall. There were two other rooms, the main bedroom and a storage room that Eleanor insisted be called the guest room. Andrew considered it more of a storage room, as Ngaiti had been their only guest since they moved in, and they weren't expecting anyone any time soon.

Andrew went to fetch Ngaiti, who gingerly walked from the bedroom. Chief Wharepouri's expression failed to hide his concern as Ngaiti approached and sat at the kitchen table. Eleanor indicated that Te Wharepouri should do the same, offering him a chair.

Ngaiti spoke briefly to Te Wharepouri and then translated.

"Chief Te Wharepouri thanks you both for welcoming him to your home," said Ngaiti. "He asks that you forgive him for his unannounced visit. He'd heard that I was injured and that you had come to my aid. He came to see whether I needed any further help."

Eleanor and Andrew both looked at the chief and smiled.

"You are very welcome, sir," replied Andrew, wondering how the chief knew where Ngaiti was.

Te Wharepouri nodded his head in acknowledgement.

Eleanor went to make tea for her guests as Te Wharepouri and Ngaiti spoke. Periodically, Ngaiti would translate something for Andrew and then continue. At one point, Te Wharepouri became visibly angry, prompting Eleanor to look at Andrew with apprehension. Eventually, Te Wharepouri stopped talking, looked at Eleanor, and waited for Ngaiti to speak.

"Te Wharepouri apologises for his anger. He is not angry with you or me; he is angry about what happened to me and what is happening around us. He has also asked me to tell you about my injury."

After Eleanor gave her guests, including the grateful man outside the door, a cup of tea, she joined the three men at the table. As Ngaiti began to talk, Chief Te Wharepouri watched Andrew and Eleanor closely. He recognised her as the captivating woman on the *Tory* the day he had first come aboard. At the time, he had dismissed Andrew as unimportant, but now he assessed him differently. Te Wharepouri had survived many battles and attempts on his life. He attributed his survival not so much to his fighting ability as a warrior as to being a good judge of character. While he was undeniably strong, skilful and brave, he prided himself on being astute and observant. He could accurately assess people; determine their motives, intentions and *mana*. This was why he had risen in power as a chief and survived.

Ngaiti had often spoken of this young *pakeha* man and woman. He trusted and liked them, calling them his friends. As he observed the couple, Te Wharepouri silently agreed with Ngaiti. Their *mana* was good; it was strong.

Ngaiti began, "I was at Te Aro, helping Minarapa. Do you remember that I told you the New Zealand Company does not have a claim on the land they are now trying to survey in Te Aro?"

"I know there have been problems. Colonel Wakefield and Dickie Barrett were shouting about it earlier today. They mentioned the surveyor Robert Park," replied Andrew. "But other than that, I know only what you've told me."

"Yes, I told you that Te Aro was never included in the original land deal and that was made very clear to Wakefield through Barrett on the *Tory*."

"I've never heard Wakefield speak of that," replied Andrew.

Ngaiti looked to Te Wharepouri, who indicated for him to continue.

"After the land was surveyed, all the boundary pegs were pulled out that evening and again over the next two evenings," said Ngaiti.

"Oh my God," said Eleanor, her hands covering her mouth.

"Ngaiti, were you involved in this?" asked Andrew.

"No, I didn't pull the pegs, but I was there and was seen by Barrett during the day. It was his men who were guarding the surveyed land."

Te Wharepouri spoke quickly to Ngaiti, who then continued.

"I was walking from Te Aro back to Kaiwharawhara to report to Chief Te Wharepouri when I was attacked," Ngaiti said. He looked to Te Wharepouri for support to continue. "We know it was Barrett who ordered his men to attack me. Recently, we have seen men watching us closely, *pakeha* men. These men have followed us from a distance, trying to remain hidden."

Andrew interrupted Ngaiti with a question. "These men, have they been following you only, or Chief Te Wharepouri as well?"

"They have followed Chief Te Wharepouri and me when he leaves the village. We also know those men are watching to see who visits the village," replied Ngaiti.

"Then these men have seen you come here?" asked Eleanor, looking at the Chief.

Ngaiti spoke to the Chief and translated his response.

"No-one has seen Chief Te Wharepouri come here tonight. The men outside are watching to make sure we are safe."

"Safe?" Andrew raised his voice. "Safe from what, Ngaiti? Tell us. What is going on here?"

"We think the person who attacked me was one of the men who have been following us. I saw him briefly when he struck me and recognised him from the whaling station in Te Awaiti. He is a whaler and a friend of Barrett."

"But why would he attack you unless you have done something wrong? You were there when the surveyor's pegs were pulled," Andrew responded.

Again, Ngaiti turned to the Chief and spoke briefly to him.

"Te Wharepouri has asked me to talk to you about this," said Ngaiti, shifting into a more comfortable position.

Andrew and Eleanor sat quietly, occasionally exchanging a glance as Ngaiti began. Te Wharepouri drank his tea and observed. The man who had been outside the door was gone, his empty teacup on the step. He slipped into the shadows and watched the cottage carefully from a distance.

"Many settlers and colonists are unhappy. They feel the New Zealand Company was not truthful about the land they purchased. They were told they would be buying flat land and that a modern planned township was being built. Instead, they live on steep hills. Flat land is scarce, and Wellington looks nothing like a planned township. The jobs that were promised don't exist. They are worried because they feel insecure." Ngaiti looked at both Andrew and Eleanor, who listened carefully.

"The New Zealand Company, as you know, has sold flat land in the township they do not own, and they need it quickly to give to the colonists who arrive by ship almost every day. That land is in Te Aro, but Wakefield does not have a claim to it, and he believes he does. This uh… dispute is causing difficulties for the Company and Wakefield. The English Government disagrees with the New Zealand Company over these land deals, and the colonists who have purchased or been given land believe their land could be taken from them. You are aware of this, Andrew?"

"Yes, I have heard. Colonel Wakefield has dismissed these complaints as mere nuisances," replied Andrew. "He said there is no basis for the claims you mention."

"It's not a nuisance. Look at what has already happened. The English made New Zealand part of New South Wales. They appointed Hobson as Lieutenant Governor, and he will proclaim that all land purchased from Māori will be considered illegal," stated Ngaiti carefully and deliberately.

Andrew was speechless, "Preposterous!" He finally exclaimed. "That can't happen, because…"

"Because that could affect the New Zealand Company's plans," interjected Ngaiti. "But there is more. The English government believes that Māori were unfairly taken advantage of, that the Company did not disclose all details or all the terms of the sale of land-"

"Ngaiti, that's untrue. I am aware that Colonel Wakefield was very particular about ensuring everything was legal in case the land sales were ever challenged."

"Yes, but perhaps the problem does not directly lie with Colonel Wakefield in that regard."

"What do you mean?" Andrew asked, becoming more confused.

"How did Wakefield communicate the terms of the sale?"

"Jerningham prepares the deeds, and then Richard Barrett explains them to Māori," Andrew answered.

"We know that the deeds are not correctly written, and we also know that Barrett has not translated accurately, far from it," informed Ngaiti.

Andrew had no reason to doubt this assertion. After giving the matter some thought, he asked, "Ngaiti, this is all very well, but what does it have to do with your being attacked?"

"Chief Te Wharepouri has had many men visit him, mostly *pakeha*. They seek information to determine what action the English Government will take against the New Zealand Company. I have been translating for these men, and I have also witnessed many of Barrett's translations aboard the *Tory*. What do you think will happen if the Company can no longer do business? What will happen when it becomes public that Barrett translated incorrectly? Seeing me in Te Aro during the surveying incident was enough to incur Barrett's anger. I believe Barrett sent my attacker. It was a warning for me to stay away. Barrett has much to lose."

"Why are you telling us all this, Ngaiti? What is the purpose?" asked Eleanor.

Te Wharepouri spoke quickly to Ngaiti, who then continued. "We believe Barrett is achieving great status and wealth amongst *pakeha* and has benefited enormously from the land sales, but he has not been honest with either Māori or *pakeha*. He is misleading everyone, including Wakefield. Chief Te Wharepouri believes Barrett will continue to protect his position with Wakefield and line his pockets. He thinks Barrett's greed and power will cause many problems for all of us."

Andrew silently agreed with Te Wharepouri. His own observations supported what he'd been told. He indicated for Ngaiti to continue.

"Chief Te Wharepouri asks that you share with him any information you come across about Barrett, especially if you suspect it's immoral or illegal. This information will be given to Lieutenant Governor Hobson."

Andrew looked at Eleanor and could see the worry on her face. This was putting them both in a delicate situation. He looked at Ngaiti, then turned to face Chief Te Wharepouri. "I understand why you have come to me, and I agree with what you have said about Barrett. I cannot jeopardise my position or the trust placed in me by Colonel Wakefield and the New Zealand Company." Andrew looked directly at Te Wharepouri, holding his gaze. "I am sorry. Regardless of how much I agree with you, my responsibility is to my wife and our future. If Colonel Wakefield were to hear of this, we could lose everything." Andrew waved both arms, encompassing their home and possessions. "We live here because of our work. This cottage belongs to the Company."

No one spoke; the room remained quiet as everyone digested what Andrew had said. Eleanor placed her hand on Andrew's arm, a gesture of support and love. Ngaiti's expression showed his disappointment, and Te Wharepouri continued to look at Andrew. A tightening of his mouth and a nod indicated that he understood.

Chief Te Wharepouri spoke to Ngaiti; the tone of his words was calm and soft.

Ngaiti turned to Andrew and translated. "He asks me to tell you that he respects your decision. He believes your motive is honourable and sincere. If the positions were reversed, he would have responded the same way. Chief Te Wharepouri apologises to you both for placing you in this difficult situation and hopes this will not harm our friendship. He welcomes you both to visit us at Kaiwharawhara at any time you choose and hopes to see you soon."

Te Wharepouri stood and extended his hand to Andrew, then, astonishing everyone, turned to Eleanor and offered her his hand.

After saying farewell, Ngaiti, with Te Wharepouri at his side, slowly walked into the evening, protected by six men who emerged like ghosts from the darkness.

CHAPTER THIRTEEN

Sydney, New South Wales.

Captain William Hobson, the newly appointed Lieutenant Governor of New Zealand, swatted at the fly that continued to pester him. Convinced it had singled him out and that its sole purpose in life was to torment and antagonise - he'd had enough. Hobson finally dealt with the troublesome insect using Thomas Peacock's *'The Misfortunes of Elphin'*. The fly was caught unawares between the book and the unforgiving desk as the ornately bound, heavy volume, a gift from Aunt Harriet, slammed into it, quickly extinguishing its futile life. Captain Hobson unceremoniously named the fly 'William' after Colonel William Wakefield, flicked the misshapen object off his desk, and picked up the letter he'd just received to read it again.

Against the policy of the English Government, the New Zealand Company continued to purchase land from the natives in a manner that called into question the integrity of its principals. It continued to take advantage of indigenous people unfamiliar with the tenets of English law, business, and the cultural norms of a modern permissive society. Adding to his woes, this newly arrived letter provided further information that could fuel civil unrest, possibly even violence. Not to mention the disgusting and unfashionable philosophy of some of the New Zealand Company's proponents. Hobson glanced down at the paragraph that offended him.

Hobson discarded the letter with distaste, wishing he could deal with the New Zealand Company as efficiently as he had with that irksome fly.

'Manifest Destiny', good God! He laughed at the irony. Indigenous people existed at the whim of their superior and aristocratic masters. Heaven forbid; the practice of slavery was banned. Hobson was furious.

Determined to put an end to the Company's uncontrolled activities, Hobson began pacing the confines of his office. His conscience and the directives placed on him left little option but to act swiftly. He would transfer his office to New Zealand and immediately begin enforcing the laws protecting Māori sovereignty as detailed in the 'Declaration of Independence'. The troublesome Wakefield would have no choice but to desist immediately from acquiring land directly from Māori.

Hobson stopped pacing and looked out of the window. Let the politicians in England deal with the backslapping, self-congratulatory Directors of the New Zealand Company, many of whom had no qualms about boasting of the wealth they'd accumulated. Allow the Directors to confront the unfortunate colonists who had invested money in illegally obtained land. Hobson felt no pity; they'd been fairly apprised.

Mounting pressure against the Company was coming from every quarter; from the displeased colonists who had believed they were purchasing flat premium land in planned townships, the missionaries who felt Māori were being exploited and treated unfairly, and the Government, which insisted that the right of sovereignty be observed. Who would be next to enter the fray? Hobson decided that he would again write to Colonel Wakefield, enlightening the man as to the significance of his actions and instructing him to terminate the Company's pursuits.

Another fly buzzed past his ear. Captain William Hobson saw no reason to delay his departure from Sydney. He found New Zealand's temperate climate far more agreeable, and fewer flies.

CHAPTER FOURTEEN

Wakefield Residence and New Zealand Company Office, Thorndon Flats

"Samuel Revans believes it's a good idea, sir," said Barrett to Colonel Wakefield as they both walked past Andrew towards the colonel's office.

"Yes, and that is what Edward has been telling me. It could, however, have far-reaching implications if we fail," protested Wakefield. "But then again, if we succeed, it means the Crown no longer stands in the way of private enterprise, does it?"

As the two men entered Wakefield's office, leaving the door partly ajar, Andrew turned his head to listen.

"I could make the hotel available for a public forum, let the settlers and colonists speak, and you'll see the support will be there," encouraged Barrett.

Colonel Wakefield was silent as he mulled over the idea. Revans had already published the first edition of the Company's newspaper, the *New Zealand Gazette,* in England. He could print another edition here locally, which could be used to spread the word and solicit further support.

He leaned forward across his desk towards Barrett. "You'd better be right about your assumptions." He wagged a finger at the sycophantic Barrett. "Make sure you let Revans know. He's one of the biggest proponents - he'll bring people to your meeting."

"It's a splendid idea, sir. Well done," Barrett replied.

"Yes, perhaps we should wait and see first." Wakefield leaned back in his chair. "When Hobson hears of this, he'll be beside himself."

"I wouldn't worry too much about Hobson, sir," said Barrett. "Or his cronies, for that matter." Barrett sat smugly.

"We are moving against the Crown, Dickie. Of course, I'm worried."

Andrew sat up. What were they scheming? It sounded treasonous at best. Hearing footsteps, Andrew put his head down and pretended to be immersed in the ledger before him.

"Good day, Mr Stewart," said Barrett, leaving the office.

"Pardon me?"

"I said good day," Barrett repeated.

"Oh, yes, good afternoon, Mr Barrett. I do apologise. I was concentrating."

"Let's hope it was on your work and not on other matters," said Barrett over his shoulder as he left the office.

Confused, Andrew rubbed his hands through his hair.

The hours passed by slowly and Andrew couldn't wait to return home to discuss with Ellie what he'd overheard.

When it was finally time, he almost flew out the door and arrived home, breathless.

"Should we tell Ngaiti?" asked Eleanor.

Andrew walked towards his armchair, removed the magazine that lay on the seat, and sat down. "What happens if Wakefield finds out?" he replied, crossing his legs.

"Do we not have an obligation to say something? As you say, it does sound treasonous."

"I don't know whether it is treasonous, and I don't know what they are planning," Andrew replied.

Eleanor rose from the table, walked to Andrew, and sat on his lap. "We must do what is right, Andy."

"Yes, that's what worries me."

"Neither of us has work tomorrow. Perhaps we could take a picnic near Kaiwharawhara, and we may encounter Ngaiti. It can do no harm to inform him, and he can decide what to do." Eleanor suggested.

"Yes, we could do that, but we shouldn't be seen in Ngaiti's village. According to Ngaiti, Barrett has his men there watching. If we are just in the general area, that should work nicely," Andrew replied. "And, uh… what food were you thinking of taking on our picnic?"

The mile-and-a-half walk from Thorndon to Kaiwharawhara was a pleasant stroll along a well-used track that ran parallel to the coast. The sun shone brightly, and a gentle north-westerly breeze kept the temperature moderate. The couple waved politely to a few people they met walking in the opposite direction, and a wagon or two passed them by. They walked happily together, enjoying the chance to be outside and exploring. It didn't take them long before they could see a few small huts ringed by a wooden palisade in the distance, presumably the village of Chief Te Wharepouri, which Andrew had pointed out to Eleanor.

They veered off the path and headed towards the ocean, looking for a suitable spot where they could enjoy a picnic lunch. Andrew hoped someone would see them and send word to Ngaiti or Te Wharepouri that they were nearby.

As Eleanor began to prepare the food, Andrew looked around. From where they sat, he could see the track and anyone walking along it quite easily. Not far away, he could see the village, but the figures were too small to identify. A few ships lay at anchor in Lambton Harbour, and he could even see a few pleasure boats sailing to and fro. This was a beautiful area. The hills that surrounded the harbour were like stately sentinels, watching over them and keeping them safe. It was peaceful and serene. Small waves lapped the shore, gently rolling rounded pebbles backwards and forwards with a mellow rattle.

Andrew watched Ellie as she fussed over the food and smiled. He was content and hungry.

They talked about their future, the adventure of being in this unusual country, and, like any young couple, made plans and promises to each other. The afternoon passed quickly, and soon it was time to leave. As they packed away their few utensils, Andrew saw a figure approaching.

"Ngaiti," Andrew said to Eleanor, pointing.

"How wonderful to see you!" called Andrew as Ngaiti approached.

Ngaiti was frowning but broke into a smile as he shook Andrew's hand. Eleanor enveloped him with a hug.

"You look better than when we last saw you," said Eleanor, looking at his head.

Ngaiti laughed. "Yes, I feel better, thank you, Miss Ellie. It is good to see you both. I hope you enjoyed your picnic here?"

"This is a beautiful area," said Andrew, indicating for Ngaiti to sit with them.

Ngaiti's smile disappeared as he sat. Andrew and Eleanor exchanged glances.

Ngaiti paused, "You have been followed here."

Andrew immediately stood, looked around, and saw no one. The track was clear.

"We didn't see anyone. Are you sure we were followed, and why would they follow us?" asked Andrew.

Ngaiti's expression conveyed his thoughts. "I don't know Andrew, but you are safe now. We chased them away some time ago and kept watch to make sure you were not disturbed or harmed."

"What!" exclaimed Andrew, who again stood to look around. Where moments earlier he had seen no one, there were now about six Māori, some with spears, others carrying muskets. "Where did they come from?"

Eleanor moved closer to Andrew, unconsciously seeking protection.

"When you first walked here from Thorndon, two men followed. They were whalers and kept far enough away that you couldn't see them; then they hid nearby, watching while you ate. We saw them, chased them away, and kept watch over you from a distance. The whalers did not see me, and they certainly do not know I am talking to you now. They have gone."

"Oh, Andy, what is happening?" Eleanor asked, her agitation mounting.

"Did you come here for a picnic, or was there another purpose?" Ngaiti looked enquiringly at them.

Again, Andrew and Eleanor looked at each other.

"Go on, Andy, tell him," she urged.

Andrew recounted the conversation he'd overheard between Barrett and Wakefield, then asked Ngaiti whether he understood what they had been referring to.

Ngaiti remained silent as he digested the information.

"Well?" asked Andrew after a minute.

"Thank you for sharing this information. I think I understand what they were talking about," Ngaiti eventually replied.

"Is it important?" Eleanor asked.

"Yes, let me tell you. Samuel Revans, the man you spoke of, was the editor of a newspaper printed in England. The newspaper was financed by the New Zealand Company and published as a single edition. It was intended to advertise and support the Company's activities in New Zealand for English people interested in coming here. Revans now lives in Wellington, and from what you overheard, I expect he will begin publishing another edition, as Wakefield suggested. However, he is known for being a republican."

"Oh no!" declared Andrew. "I think I know where you are going with this, Ngaiti."

"Chief Te Wharepouri has heard rumours that, if New Zealand becomes a republic, the Company can continue to do business and ignore all the restrictions imposed on them by the Imperial Government. They would no longer be required to listen to Hobson or the Colonial Office in England, and New Zealanders would no longer accept Queen Victoria's sovereign rule. If that happened, the New Zealand Company could make its own laws to suit itself, and no one could do a thing about it. We have heard that the proposed name for this republic is New Victoria."

Andrew laughed. "These people want to create a republic, yet they honour the Queen's name. How absurd!"

"How does Chief Te Wharepouri come by all this information, Ngaiti? He doesn't even speak English," said Eleanor.

"He knows a lot more than you think." Ngaiti paused, choosing his words carefully. "Do you think for one moment that Te Wharepouri would allow *pakeha* to come here to our country, invade it, and subject our people to the rule of English law without making every attempt to understand what is happening?" Ngaiti's voice rose with passion. "He has people come to him with information; he pays attention and is very astute. He cares for Māori, and although you may find this difficult to understand, he also cares for *pakeha*."

"Yes, I can believe that," Eleanor said.

"Chief Te Wharepouri knows everything that is going on in Wellington and the surrounding areas. In this case, he will probably inform Lieutenant Governor Hobson, who now resides in New Zealand, about the news you have shared with me."

Andrew looked down, deep in thought.

"Chief Te Wharepouri is a good man, Andrew."

Andrew nodded in agreement.

"Many *pakeha*, including young Jerningham Wakefield, have written unfavourably about Te Wharepouri. They say he is a greedy Māori chief who is happy to sell his land for trinkets, blankets and muskets. They say these things because they do not understand him or his motives. I also believe they fear him, not because he will go to war and fight, but because of his mind and intelligence. Do you understand this?"

"Yes, I am beginning to understand," said Andrew.

"Remember, I have attended many of the New Zealand Company Directors' meetings. I have heard all that these men have to say, and I have heard them speak of riches, wealth and prosperity. I was with the Wakefields for over two years in England. Never once did I hear them speak of humanity or the effect their actions have on indigenous people. Tell me, Andrew, who is the greedy one?"

"Ngaiti, you have spoken well, perhaps more than at any other time. I feel I understand what is happening here. I am not proud of what the Company is doing, and it doesn't reflect how I feel or how I was brought up to think. Andy and I are not like the Wakefields; we just want a happy future together, with opportunities that were not available to us in England. Isn't that right, Andy?"

"Ellie is correct, Ngaiti, but our future currently hinges on the New Zealand Company and the agreement we have with them. Until we can find an alternative, we must continue to work for them."

"But can you continue to help the people of New Zealand?" asked Ngaiti.

"As long as we aren't in danger, and I'm worried about that now." Andrew reached for Eleanor's hand.

"Please tell Chief Te Wharepouri that we will do all we can," said Eleanor.

Ngaiti smiled and nodded in response.

"Why were those men following us?" asked Andrew.

"Who do you know that associates with whalers? Certainly, Wakefield isn't seen in their company," offered Ngaiti.

"Barrett!" the three said simultaneously.

"One day, when the opportunity presents itself, I will tell you all about Edward Gibbon Wakefield and his brother William. You will not like what you hear from me," said Ngaiti earnestly.

CHAPTER FIFTEEN

Wellington Township.

The building now known as Barrett's Hotel was originally brought to New Zealand on an immigrant ship as a prefabricated two-storey structure. Located at the northern end of Lambton Harbour, it was separated from the beach by a narrow boardwalk and a well-used track known as Lambton Quay. It quickly became the focal point and meeting place for activities and social events for Wellington's residents. With Dickie's subtle encouragement, it was only natural that the hotel would be the venue for the meeting of the 'Wellington Settlers Constitutional Association'.

It wasn't offensive to those who attended the meeting that the pungent odours wafting from the foreshore, scant yards away, were from raw sewage that drained into Lambton Harbour. Braced with enough alcoholic beverages the hotel provided, any unpleasantness experienced by the attendees would seem inconsequential, as they themselves contributed in volume to the outflow that poured into the harbour.

Inside, the hotel was still quite unfinished. Rumour had it that Dickie's purse was as tight as his waistline, though occasional improvements occurred. However, these updates were linked to questionable deals and transactions that cast doubt on the principals' moral integrity.

Dickie sat at the back of the room, surreptitiously surrounded by his associates, many of whom were ex-whalers, hard men conscripted and lured to Wellington to perform a variety of tasks for the enterprising and ambitious man. As always, in the presence of the public and respectable gentlemen, Dickie was unobtrusive, agreeable and jolly, a persona he went to great lengths to maintain.

With a pleasant smile, Dickie warmly greeted those who approached him and watched the attendees carefully. He paid particular attention to who spoke to whom, any open animosity, and, of course, the development of acquaintanceships.

The meeting had progressed from preliminary introductions and a statement of purpose when Samuel Revans took the floor as the guest speaker. His views were widely known within the community, and many had heard his arguments for republicanism. He again embraced the opportunity to expound his views to inform and educate.

"We are all god-fearing men, and we have infinite compassion and empathy for those indigenous peoples who exist on this wonderful land," said Revans, staring intently at the audience, his eyes shining with the certainty of his beliefs. "Let me quote to you a most persuasive passage about Māori from a book that many of you have read, titled '*Information Relative to New Zealand: Compiled for the use of Colonists*', authored by the esteemed Secretary for the New Zealand Company, Mr John Ward." Revans reached down and retrieved the book from the table before him, waving it with a flourish at the attentive members. Positioning himself so he could clearly see the small text in the poor light, he began to read with dramatic vigour.

"The spirit of revenge is implacable in their breasts; the law of retaliation is their only rule for the reconcilement of differences, and their hatred of their enemies is deep and deadly. Many of them are covetous of accumulating property and thieve with little scruple. The licentiousness of the women is subjected to no restraint until after their marriage."

Revans paused to take a drink and continued with his recital.

"Polygamy prevails, and it is usual for the head wife to commit suicide after her husband's death. They have a propensity for ridicule and insult; and, in short, with the physical powers and passions of men, they have at present the intellect of children and, in moral principle, are often little above the level of the brute creation."

Again, Revans paused to add credence to the assertions he read aloud.

"Such are the unhappy characteristics of a thoroughly savage nation."
He slammed the book shut and flung it onto the table.

"This is why, my friends," Revans spread his arms wide, rotating to take in the room, "we must divide New Zealand and allow native Māori to live amongst themselves in the lands beyond that which is known as Cape Kidnappers. South of that boundary, we will create a self-governing province, and it shall be named New Victoria!"

"I want you to take me home, Andy, right now," whispered Eleanor.

Andrew's mouth dropped open in disbelief as he listened to Revans speak. He was astounded that people actually believed and agreed with the man. They sat near the hotel entrance and had heard enough. Andrew helped Ellie with her cloak, and the couple quietly left the hotel and began to walk up the gentle hill towards their home.

Barrett had seen the couple leave and gave a slight nod to a man standing casually near the doorway. The man nonchalantly left the premises and followed the couple at a discreet distance.

"Now I understand what Colonel Wakefield was talking to Barrett about," said Andrew, visibly upset and angry.

"And Wakefield supports that, - that, twaddle?" exclaimed Eleanor with disgust.

With his arm protectively around her shoulder, the couple walked in the darkness.

"You weren't at the meeting for very long," said Ngaiti as he stepped from the shadows near their cottage.

"I'm outraged, Ngaiti!" Eleanor said, detaching herself from Andrew and walking down the path, leaving Andrew and Ngaiti surprised. "It's made me feel rather ill," she added, disappearing indoors.

From behind a nearby tree, hidden in the tangle of branches, stood Barrett's man, watching.

Andrew and Eleanor decided to attend the meeting at Barrett's hotel and, as arranged, then recount to Ngaiti the subject and context of what had been discussed. The three sat at the kitchen table, assessing what Revans had been so eager to share.

"That man, the author of that book-" began Eleanor.

"The New Zealand Company Secretary?" asked Andrew.

"His name is John Ward," answered Ngaiti.

"Yes, him. He must have had a torrid experience when he came to New Zealand, to write such terrible things…"

"He has never been to New Zealand, Miss Ellie," interjected Ngaiti quietly.

"That makes it worse, and it sickens me, and now I really do feel ill," said Eleanor.

"You know of this book?" asked Andrew.

"Yes, I have read it, he even writes of me in it," Ngaiti laughed, "but he offered me a discourtesy by misspelling my name."

Eleanor looked at Ngaiti, "Why did you not tell us of this book and the philosophy of the Company Ngaiti?"

"There is much I could tell you about the Wakefields that would surprise and shock you, Miss Eleanor. But why did I not tell you?" He returned and met her gaze with equal intensity. "I tried."

Eleanor claimed it was something she had drunk at Barrett's hotel that disagreed with her, and she retired early to bed. Andrew believed that what Ellie had heard this evening was the cause of her distress, and that in the morning she'd be her normal self. He wasn't overly worried.

Ngaiti returned to Kaiwharawhara, where he informed Chief Te Wharepouri of the meeting's details. If he deemed it necessary, the chief would ensure the information was passed on to Lieutenant Governor Hobson with urgency.

After an unpleasant night, the morning brought no improvement for Eleanor, and Andrew insisted on fetching the doctor, leaving the house early to find him. The doctor was unavailable, attending a difficult birth for a local woman. Andrew returned home disappointed, and Ellie ordered him to go to work; she would remain in bed and rest.

Worried about Eleanor, Andrew was distracted and unable to focus on his beloved numbers. Noticing something was amiss, Colonel Wakefield spoke to Andrew and, on learning of Eleanor's condition, immediately suggested that he ask his own physician, Doctor Isaac Featherston, to consult with her. Andrew readily agreed, and the colonel quickly sent for him.

Dr Isaac Featherston was a long-time friend of William Wakefield. On Wakefield's persistent urging, Featherston finally succumbed to his pleas and, with his new bride, immigrated to New Zealand, arriving only a few weeks earlier. A supporter of the New Zealand Company, Featherston readily accepted the challenges of establishing himself in a new colony. An advocate of many causes, he fully intended to immerse himself in politics and make his mark on New Zealand and its people. He'd looked forward to settling in the new township of Wellington, touted by the New Zealand Company as being without paupers and free from the ills of British society. On arrival, he was disheartened to discover it was not so, as were many others when they first set foot on New Zealand shores.

Featherston was outspoken, possessed a lively wit, and, on rare occasions, demonstrated a rather disagreeable short temper. Some suggested it was nothing more than the effects of a night of insobriety that prompted the infrequent flare-ups.

Dr Featherston finally arrived at Wakefield's office, and after introductions by the colonel, Andrew and the doctor made their way to see Eleanor. They soon discovered a common bond when Isaac learned that Andrew was also an avid reader of the magazine '*Society for the Diffusion of Useful Knowledge*'. Isaac informed Andrew that he had only reached 'FU' and began to recite exactly what a 'Fulgurite' was. The two were laughing like old friends as they entered the cottage.

Andrew remained in the kitchen while Eleanor was being examined.

Dr Featherston listened patiently as Eleanor described what she had eaten and drunk the night before, and was quite surprised to learn that the couple were interested in the extreme activities of the 'Wellington Settlers Constitutional Association'. *No wonder the poor woman is feeling less than perky,* he thought. After a careful examination, he concluded that her symptoms were consistent with food poisoning and advised her to drink plenty of water to stay hydrated and to rest. He left a small bottle containing pieces of ginger root, which she should take twice daily.

Dr Featherston returned to the kitchen, explained his diagnosis to Andrew, and reassured him that there was no need for concern, adding that Eleanor would return to her normal self in a day or two.

Still puzzled by the revelation that they had attended the meeting at Barrett's hotel the previous evening, the doctor asked Andrew why they had gone. It seemed so out of character, he added.

Caught unawares, Andrew struggled to answer. "We were interested in learning more about a concept unfamiliar to us," Andrew finally suggested. "But we were rather displeased with what we heard and left early," he quickly added.

Dr Featherston made no further mention of it, then left carrying an armful of magazines, promising to return the following evening to check on the patient.

CHAPTER SIXTEEN

Thorndon

Lieutenant Best screamed at his soldiers, his voice cutting through the ambient noise and normal activity of the Thorndon docks. In response to his curt command, the soldiers of the 80th Regiment eventually lined up and snapped loosely to attention. Best strode down the first line of soldiers, sneering at the disgraceful turnout. Some men had become seasick and spent nearly the entire journey retching over the side as *Integrity* sailed from Auckland to Wellington. They had only recently arrived and disembarked; it was no excuse for slovenly behaviour, thought Best. He was unimpressed and made a mental note of the offending characters. Once they returned to Auckland, he would devote some much-needed time to the regiment's discipline. A subtle cough from behind reminded him of the reason they had assembled.

With a crisp about-face, Lieutenant Best marched towards the New Zealand Colonial Secretary and informed him all were present and accounted for.

"Thank you, Lieutenant," said the secretary, who also held the commissioned rank of captain in her Majesty's Royal Navy.

A crowd began to gather, curious about the reason for the military presence.

"What's goin' on then?" yelled a voice from the crowd.

Another voice yelled, "Wot's it all about, General?" prompting laughter.

The secretary waited until more inquisitive people had gathered, then, with as much *gravitas* as he could muster, he walked forward, stopped in front of the soldiers, and turned crisply to face the crowd.

Adding drama to the occasion, he held a document before him to read. His audience quietened, curious about the nature of the event. He cleared his throat and spoke loudly and clearly.

"In the name of Her Majesty Victoria, Queen of the United Kingdom of Great Britain and Ireland. By William Hobson, Esquire, a Captain in the Royal Navy, Lieutenant-Governor of New Zealand..." shouted the Colonial Secretary.

The crowd grew and listened as they learned that Queen Victoria now ruled the northern island of New Zealand as sovereign, under a treaty signed by Māori chiefs.

After reading the proclamation, he folded the document and returned it to the pocket of his uniform. Without loitering to field questions, the Colonial Secretary clasped his hands behind his back and headed up the hill to the residence and office of Colonel Wakefield and the New Zealand Company.

Lieutenant Best ordered his soldiers to about-face and begin marching after the colonial secretary.

The announcement came as no surprise, but the Secretary's quick departure prompted speculation; the small crowd was abuzz.

Against the vocal protests of Wakefield's newly hired private secretary, an officer of Her Majesty's Royal Navy strode into the office with an air of absolute authority. Flanked by two soldiers, he paused briefly to assess the obstacles and immediately plotted a course for Wakefield's door. Andrew, caught reading a newspaper with a sweet pastry mid-bite and firmly held between his teeth, looked at the three imposing men with a start and promptly removed it.

"Wakefield?" asked one of the soldiers, wishing to confirm their destination.

To Andrew, it sounded more like an order than a request.

He waved his pastry, pointing to the colonel's closed door. With his mouth agape and crumbs liberally scattered over his coat, he just watched.

He remembered to close his mouth just as the new arrivals burst into Colonel Wakefield's office.

"What is the meaning of this intrusion? How dare you enter this office unannounced!" cried Wakefield, who sprang to his feet.

The naval officer paused, looking around the room with clear contempt.

"Explain yourself, sir!" Wakefield appealed again. "You have no right—"

"Colonel William Wakefield? My name is Captain Willoughby Shortland," the naval officer announced, cutting Wakefield off. "By the powers and authority granted to me by the Imperial Colonial Secretary and Lieutenant-Governor of New Zealand, Captain William Hobson, I have been appointed New Zealand's Colonial Secretary and Police Magistrate." Shortland turned to the waiting soldiers and casually waved an arm, indicating they should wait outside the office.

"I suggest you take a seat, Colonel."

"You can't intrude in here and order…"

"Sit, Colonel!"

Red-faced with anger, Wakefield sat slowly.

"We have a number of items to discuss," said Captain Shortland, seating himself uninvited. "Beginning with a proclamation."

Shortland again removed the document from his tunic, emphasising its importance by unfolding it dramatically and holding it close to his face.

"In the name of Her Majesty Victoria, Queen of the United Kingdom of Great Britain and Ireland. By William Hobson…" Shortland intoned.

Andrew was reeling, and although he was trying desperately to listen, his attention was also on the two soldiers who stood protectively near the door.

"…do hereby proclaim and declare to all men that from and after the date of the above-mentioned Treaty, the full sovereignty of the Northern Island of New Zealand vests in Her Majesty Queen Victoria, her heirs and successors - forever." Shortland concluded. "Do you fully understand this proclamation?"

Wakefield nodded.

"Do you understand, Colonel Wakefield?" insisted Shortland, raising his voice.

"Yes, yes, I do understand, Captain," spat Wakefield, finally responding, his mind reeling.

Under the scrutiny of both soldiers, Andrew slowly stood and positioned himself to hear more clearly and catch a glimpse through the open door into Wakefield's office.

"Excellent, then we are making progress, aren't we? This proclamation has already been made public," Shortland stated arrogantly, waving the document in the air before neatly folding it and returning it to his pocket. "However, there are other matters to bring to your attention. Namely, I have been instructed to inform you that Lieutenant Governor Hobson intends to commence land hearings to determine the legality of the means by which the New Zealand Company obtained title to the lands around Port Nicholson from local Māori."

"Then I have nothing to fear," said Wakefield confidently, recovering from the initial shock. "All land purchases were entirely legal, a matter I personally supervised, and I stake my reputation on it."

Captain Shortland laughed. "Come now, Colonel, you and your brother have both been incarcerated and are convicted felons. Three years, was it? How do you expect your word to be taken seriously?"

Wakefield, incensed, stood at once, his chair clattering against the wall. The two soldiers at the door quickly entered, ready to subdue the enraged man.

"Have I offended your honour, sir?" chided Shortland, who remained seated. "We both know it's true, so your precious little probity remains intact." Shortland levelled a withering look at Wakefield. "Sit down, man, I'm not through yet," he said dismissively.

The soldiers stood menacingly, waiting for Colonel Wakefield to sit.

The colonel remained standing, facing Captain Shortland, breathing hard and trying to control his anger. After a moment he repositioned his chair and sat.

"What is it you want?" Wakefield asked after the soldiers returned to their position and they were alone.

Shortland returned Wakefield's hateful stare, then removed a speck of dust from the sleeve of his finely tailored uniform. Assured his livery was once again impeccable, he faced Wakefield. "I want you to stop the Company's activities."

Colonel Wakefield was trying to gather his thoughts, but his anger clouded his judgment. He decided an offensive rebuttal might yield a more satisfactory result.

"May I inform you, Captain, that the New Zealand Company is governed by extremely influential and respected gentlemen. Your self-serving, abrasive demeanour will not serve you in good stead when I make my report. Your actions will be noted."

"Yes, you may be correct, sir. That is why I am only the messenger. If you wish to protest, as is your right, His Excellency, Governor Sir George Gipps, will make himself available to hear your argument." Captain Shortland stood as if to leave. "However, make your case soundly, or your fall from grace and the reach of your powerful associates will not prevent you and your brother from facing the full consequences of your actions. Good day, sir." Captain Shortland walked to the door and stopped.

"Oh yes, I nearly forgot. Please forgive me, Colonel. Lieutenant-Governor Hobson has some doubts about your faith and commitment to the Crown. He requests the pleasure of your company to reaffirm your loyalty and devotion to Queen Victoria. I'm sure you will enjoy a pleasant journey to the Bay of Islands to swear your allegiance." Shortland waited for Wakefield's response, the smirk on his face indicating the pleasure he felt at wielding power over Colonel William Wakefield.

Wakefield contemplated his response.

"Tell Hobson I accept his invitation. Now get out!" yelled Wakefield.

"Then I can also tell Lieutenant-Governor Hobson that you've disbanded your cosy little republican association? May I remind you, as Police Magistrate, that I'm empowered to enforce the Law, Colonel? Treason is punishable."

"Of course," stated Wakefield, he knew he was beaten.

With the soldiers following in his wake, Captain Willoughby Shortland navigated to the outer office door and quickly left the building.

CHAPTER SEVENTEEN

Bay of Islands, Northern Island, New Zealand.

James Busby raised his glass and toasted Lieutenant-Governor William Hobson upon hearing that Hobson was to become New Zealand's first Governor and Commander-in-Chief. The two men sat outside in the warm afternoon sun and shared a bottle of Busby's finest claret.

Accepting the toast, Hobson leaned forward and raised his glass, taking a healthy sip and savouring the taste. He placed the glass gently on the table, leaned back in his chair, rested both hands behind his head, and stretched.

"I think we did an outstanding job, James."

After a lengthy pause, Busby replied with a sigh, "Time will tell."

"You don't appear very confident."

Again, Busby held the silence for a moment. "I'm not convinced that Māori understand the treaty's true nature and why we had to create it."

"When signing the Treaty, they appeared to understand the content of the document," replied Hobson.

"No, that's not what I mean, although in all honesty, I sincerely doubt they do understand it," said Busby.

He knew Busby held a lot more experience than he did in Māori affairs and so Hobson listened carefully.

James Busby leaned forward on his chair, "Five years ago I was forced to create the 'Declaration of the Independence of New Zealand'. Why?"

"Because of that rogue Frenchman Baron de Thierry."

"Yes, exactly, because if I hadn't acted as I did, we would have a rooster embroidered on our hats and be drinking French wine instead of the fine nectar we enjoy today."

"And your point?" smiled Hobson, "Other than to brag about your wine."

"Be patient. I'll get to that in a moment. This 'Treaty of Waitangi' – why was it created? No, don't answer with your uninformed drivel," laughed Busby. He leaned across and stabbed his finger at Hobson's chest. "Other than the obvious, you had to find a way to prevent the New Zealand Company from fulfilling its vision of Systemic Colonisation. Now the Company cannot act with impunity and is answerable to the Imperial Government." Busby removed his finger and continued. "If allowed to proceed unchecked, the Company would have destroyed Māori culture, taken all the land and alienated them."

Hobson raised his eyebrows at Busby's assertion.

"Don't look at me like that," Busby grinned. "I'm sincere when I say they would have eventually taken *all* the land and annexed Māori, forcing them to eke out a pitiful existence in the far north or the extreme south, on land the Company didn't want."

"It's all gloom with you Scots," teased Hobson.

"We're realists," replied Busby, his face showing mock indignation. "But as a supposed Officer in the service of Her Majesty's Royal Navy, you'd understand the concept of not reacting to your enemy's strategy. Or were you too busy with wine, women and song?" jibed Busby, taking a sip from his glass.

"I protest at that uncalled-for allegation," stated Hobson.

"It's probably not far from the truth," laughed James.

Hobson joined him.

"Look, we had to create a treaty to protect Māori from European decimation. The damned French would have behaved no differently from the New Zealand Company, and don't attempt to tell me otherwise. Our response then was reactionary. The result of those treaties is that New Zealand is now a place where Māori must adjust to European influence. We couldn't prevent Europeans from coming, just as Māori couldn't. We did the next best thing," stated Busby with conviction.

"And what could have been the alternative?" Hobson asked. He leaned forward to listen.

"Now, my friend, that is the real issue. We could have created a place where Europeans had to adjust to Māori. And I'm sorry I didn't have the vision five years ago to see it."

"Māori came to New Zealand for exactly the same reason Europeans came to live here, for a better life and a promise of a future. So what's the difference?" asked Hobson.

"They arrived here first."

"And this is why you believe the new treaty I created, the 'Treaty of Waitangi', may cause problems?" Hobson asked.

"How could you possibly convey to Māori the concept of regressive imperialism I just described, and in a way they could truly understand? I don't believe Māori even have a word in their vocabulary for 'Sovereignty' or 'Rule'. When Reverend Henry Williams translated the document into Māori, he had to be creative, devising words to describe European concepts that were unfamiliar to them. From a Māori perspective, interpreting one aspect of the treaty suggests that we created it simply because the glorious British Empire wanted total exclusivity to exploit Māori and take their land. I know that you didn't create it for that purpose." Busby paused to look at Hobson intently. "But that doesn't mean others within the Imperial Government, either now or in the future, won't see it that way. Māori will question your motives, if not today, then tomorrow. I ask you, soon-to-be Governor, how will New Zealand respond to that?" Busby folded his arms and sat back in his chair with a smirk.

"I will have to give that some thought," replied Hobson.

"Don't take too long," warned Busby, leaning forward again. "Look at those colonists who have already purchased land from the New Zealand Company; from their viewpoint, they feel very threatened. They will fight you tooth and nail because they want security and the realisation of the dreams Wakefield and the New Zealand Company fed them. You, my friend, have come between them and those dreams. Be prepared; in the days ahead, your boat will encounter some turbulent waters."

"You have successfully ruined a perfectly splendid afternoon, James."

James Busby laughed and refilled both glasses.

"What of Wakefield, have you trodden on his ambitions yet?

"I sent Shortland down to pay him a little visit." Hobson winced.

"You should have just sent for him, William."

"Perhaps, but I wanted that disagreeable man Shortland away from me for a while. And I expect Wakefield will be visiting me soon. Apparently, he'll be reaffirming his loyalties to the Crown."

"Ah, wonderful, you took my advice," said Busby with a laugh.

"Yes, and also from that chief down there, what's his name? … Ah yes, Te Wharepouri. He's been instrumental in keeping me apprised of Wakefield and his nonsense, which is why we've been able to act so quickly."

"The rogue chief, the one they call greedy and so enamoured with European gifts and weapons?" laughed Busby.

"If only they really knew."

"You seem concerned," stated Busby.

"I fear that if his involvement were made public, he'd be in grave danger."

"Don't let it happen, William."

"Your glass needs refilling," stated Hobson.

The late-afternoon sun cast long shadows across the small community of Russell in the Bay of Islands. The two men, who had quickly become friends, enjoyed their spirited camaraderie, the wine and the spectacular view.

CHAPTER EIGHTEEN

Thorndon, Wellington.

Anyone walking past the small cottage nestled on the gentle slope of Thorndon could see the Union Jack draped between the white lacy curtain and one of the two windows facing the track. It had been Eleanor's idea, a signal for Ngaiti to come and visit. She positioned the flag carefully, and to any passerby it appeared casual, almost insignificant. She and Andrew decided to signal Ngaiti soon after Andrew arrived home, much earlier than normal, after Colonel Wakefield had ordered Andrew and other staff to leave the building following Captain Willoughby Shortland's departure.

The flag had been visible for over twenty-four hours, and as yet there'd been no indication that Ngaiti was aware of the signal. Andrew and Eleanor finished their evening meal and settled into their chairs to talk and read for a while before bed when a knock at the door interrupted their chat.

As hoped, it was Ngaiti and he immediately expressed curiosity at the signal and the reason they needed to see him.

Seated at the kitchen table, Andrew explained what he had witnessed and overheard during Captain Shortland's visit. Ngaiti shook his head in amazement.

"Perhaps we will finally solve some of these problems," stated Ngaiti, with a big smile.

"Ngaiti, Colonel Wakefield is very assured that the land hearings will not rule against him, he said as much to Shortland," Andrew said.

"I believe the issue is not so much with the accounting for the land purchases, but with the communication through the deed of sale and the translations," replied Ngaiti.

"Then that would mean you could play an important part in the hearings, as you overheard many of the translations Barrett made," said Andrew. "You'd be a witness."

"Yes, I expect so."

"Considering you have already been attacked once, you should be even more careful. If the only witness to the translations were to meet with an unfortunate accident..." Eleanor suggested.

"I don't think Barrett will do any more than threaten me. He cannot risk implicating himself," Ngaiti responded.

"And what of the allegation made by the captain that both the colonel and Edward Wakefield are convicted felons?" Eleanor asked. "Surely he wasn't serious in suggesting that?"

"Miss Eleanor, let me assure you that, according to what Andrew told me, Shortland is correct. They both spent three years in prison for kidnapping an heiress."

"Kidnapping!" Andrew laughed.

"Oh, my goodness!" exclaimed Eleanor, "That's astounding."

"Yes, it is," replied Ngaiti.

Their discussion was interrupted by the sound of raised voices coming from outside.

Andrew and Ngaiti ran to the door, flinging it open to find two Māori holding Dr Isaac Featherston.

"Doctor!" exclaimed Andrew in surprise.

"This is quite a welcome, Andrew. Who are these men?"

Ngaiti spoke briefly to the Māori who had released the doctor, then disappeared into the night.

"We are very sorry, doctor, please forgive us. It wasn't their intention to cause you any harm," Eleanor said, inviting Featherston inside.

"Then who were they intending to harm?" asked the doctor, regaining composure.

Ngaiti and Andrew exchanged looks.

"Doctor Featherston, may I introduce our friend Ngaiti?"

"I believe we have met in England," said the doctor, holding out his hand.

After the introductions, Eleanor made tea, and everyone was seated around the table. Andrew hoped no one else would come to visit, as they had no more kitchen chairs.

"What brings you by, Isaac?" asked Andrew, hoping to lighten the tense atmosphere.

"I was passing by and wanted to leave you some magazines we agreed to swap. I saw a light on and thought it was appropriate and still early enough to call in. But I must say, your welcome was less than friendly." Featherston opened his bag and extracted a handful of magazines, which he handed to Andrew.

"The two men outside are there to protect me, sir. I do apologise if they frightened you. They had no way of knowing who you were," offered Ngaiti.

"What, or who, is it you need protection from?" asked Featherston, looking from face to face with some concern.

The table remained quiet, as the other three exchanged uncertain looks.

As neither Andrew nor Ngaiti was willing to explain, Eleanor began to inform the doctor about Ngaiti's recent attack and injury, and the suspected reason for it. Ngaiti supplied details.

Doctor Featherston nodded as he began to understand. "I must say I am surprised by what has happened. I have met Barrett on numerous occasions since arriving and have found him quite disagreeable, so what you've told me reinforces my opinion of the man. However, the New Zealand Company and the Wakefields do appear to be in a spot of bother. They pulled the wool over my eyes when they lured my wife, Bethia, and me here to New Zealand, and between the four of us, I am quite unhappy about it. I believe William was less than forthcoming."

Andrew was surprised by Isaac's feelings towards William Wakefield; he had assumed they were close friends.

Not wishing to intrude any longer, Ngaiti excused himself and said he would pass on the good news. With a promise to be vigilant, he wished everyone good night and left.

"An intelligent young man, speaks well," Featherston said after Ngaiti had left. "He was highly thought of in England by Edward Wakefield's friends and associates."

"Yes, we are very fond of him," said Eleanor.

"And very worried about him, truth be known," volunteered Andrew.

CHAPTER NINETEEN

Lambton Quay, Wellington.

New buildings, warehouses and wharves sprouted in a mishmash of shapes and sizes along the full length of Lambton Quay, while hillsides, mostly cleared of bush, were yielding healthy crops to feed hungry colonists and settlers. Recently arrived ships anchored in the protective lee of Lambton Harbour were disgorging merchandise or loading supplies in preparation for departure.

Colonel Wakefield acknowledged that the settlement of Wellington was still little more than a large village, but as the days and weeks passed, the growth was noticeable. A muddy path became a track and then a road. With elements of design and aesthetics, a shack morphed from a temporary patchwork of miscellaneous planks and sidings into a solid, permanent structure. Merchants were advertising and selling not only essentials but also luxury and extravagant items to ladies and gentlemen of means. Wellington was far removed from the ordered, planned community named Britannia that the Company advertised in England, but as long as the ships continued to arrive with colonists, he didn't give a damn.

"Wellington will grow into a spectacular city one day, eh Dickie?"

Barrett quickened his pace to catch up with Wakefield. "Yes, sir, I think she's coming along nicely. You've done a splendid job, sir, and should be congratulated."

"Not everyone shares that view," Wakefield said, continuing to walk along Lambton Quay, which ran parallel to the foreshore. "I care not for their unjust opinions, and as time passes, they will see me for who I am and appreciate all I have done," he added confidently.

"You're in a chipper mood this morning, sir." He knew enough about Wakefield's personality to recognise that something had happened, good news, Barrett guessed.

"We all have reason to feel grand, Dickie. News from England offers hope for our future and the continued realisation of our plans."

Barrett had to increase his pace again. "And what would that news be sir?"

Wakefield continued to walk, ignoring Barrett's question.

"Sir?"

Wakefield stopped and waited for Barrett. "Rather than deem all purchases void, the Colonial Secretary, Lord Russell, has agreed to honour our land purchases."

"That is good news, sir. Will all the purchases made by the Company be honoured?"

"Not entirely, Dickie. Joseph Somes, the Company's Deputy Governor, has considerable influence with the Secretary and has persuaded him to see reason." Wakefield continued at a brisk pace.

"Yes, influence does help considerably, doesn't it, Colonel?" Barrett offered, struggling to keep pace.

"However, we just have to prove that the purchases we made, specifically around the Port Nicholson agreement, are legitimate, and I don't believe that should be a problem for us at all."

"Prove to whom?" asked Barrett suspiciously.

Wakefield laughed. "Dickie, you will never understand the intricacies of politics."

"Yes, sir," said Barrett, his face remaining impassive.

"The Governor has appointed two men to investigate our land purchases. They are up north in Russell, snuggling up to Hobson and that loathsome man, Shortland. However, there appears to be a disagreement between the Governor and the Imperial Colonial Secretary. Lord Russell has decided to send his own man here from England to govern and investigate the land hearings. He believes his man will appear more impartial."

"So, the argument is about who has the final word, either the governor's men or Lord Russell's man?" stated Barrett.

"Yes, correct Dickie. As I think the colonial secretary has seniority over the governor, then I will, in all likelihood, make my case to Lord Russell's appointee. The word is, Hobson will not back down, and so we may well have three commissioners."

"Do we know who Lord Russell will send here?" asked Barrett, feeling a stir of worry.

"I've been told that the lawyer William Spain is the likely candidate."

"Is that a good thing, sir?"

"Yes, perhaps I understand he is honest. But I do need time, Dickie. I'm not sure when he will leave England, and I need to present my case at the land court hearings with adequate preparation. Not to mention all the communiqués between the Board of Directors and me. Questions I need answered take approximately six months to receive a response."

"Oh, that is far too long, I agree, sir."

"I have it on good authority that a change in the English political landscape may view the Company's actions here in New Zealand more favourably. A change in Parliament may not happen for a while, so any delay by Spain in arriving here will certainly work to our benefit. If Spain departs England within six months, we will certainly be disadvantaged. There is much to organise and prepare if we are to win. Additionally, I will not be informed of specifics until Spain is familiar with those frivolous complaints lodged against us, so I need to account for every possibility."

"I understand, sir. Uh, have you requested a delay?"

"Lord Russell fears that delaying the hearings will provoke Māori into hostilities. So, the short answer is no. But don't fret, dear boy, I know I took every possible step to ensure the land purchases were entirely legal."

"Legal, sir?"

"Yes, of course, what do you mean?" Wakefield asked.

"Well, sir, when you say legal, do you mean under the laws of England?"

"Good grief, man, what other laws could there possibly be?"

They walked on in silence for a few minutes.

Barrett was extremely concerned. He knew that his ability as a translator would be called into question and could ultimately affect the healthy relationship and economic benefits he'd been enjoying with the New Zealand Company. He surmised that if the hearings were governed by provincials, rather than by an appointee from England, he'd have a greater opportunity to influence the outcome and, of course, hopefully come through the hearings with his reputation unscathed.

It was easy for Barrett. He saw things as either black or white. He quickly decided he didn't want this slick English lawyer, Spain, to come to New Zealand. Perhaps there was a way…

"Delays are commonplace, sir. You know how these things go. The weather, someone's ill health, or ship repairs. I'm sure Spain's visit could be delayed."

Wakefield turned around and began to walk back from where they had started.

He knew what Barrett was suggesting and that it was a very dangerous course of action. However, in the unlikely event that the hearings went against him, the Company could lose everything. Stacking the deck in his favour only improved his chances. He had to win!

"And you feel confident that Spain's voyage to New Zealand will be delayed, Dickie?" Wakefield slowed his pace, much to Barrett's relief.

"Oh yes, sir, without any doubt," Barrett said as he caught up with Wakefield. "As you are well aware, Colonel, delays are, uh, costly."

Wakefield said nothing, and Dickie dropped back a step.

Turning his head, Wakefield asked, "What do you think such a delay would cost?"

When it came to money, Barrett was always ready. "A delay of such magnitude would cost one hundred pounds, sir."

Barrett did not see Wakefield wince.

They arrived outside Barrett's Hotel, and Colonel Wakefield said, "Come and see me tomorrow morning, Dickie." He lengthened his stride and walked off.

While Colonel Wakefield wanted Spain's New Zealand arrival delayed, Barrett didn't want him to come at all.

The following morning, Barrett turned up at Wakefield's office and was handed the required one hundred pounds.

"This is a lot of money, Barrett," Wakefield informed.

"Of course, sir."

"I need to account for this and will need a receipt from you."

Barrett looked aghast. This wasn't how these arrangements were concluded – *a receipt*?

"I don't care what you write on it, just make sure it totals one hundred pounds," informed the colonel, handing him paper.

Barrett scrawled a few lines, signed the document and returned it to Wakefield.

"Translation fee!" Wakefield laughed after reading the receipt. "Just make sure it happens, Dickie," Wakefield said sternly.

"I will make sure it doesn't happen, sir," grinned Barrett.

"You'll need details, will you not?" asked the colonel.

"Don't worry about that, sir, I'll take care of everything," replied Barrett.

"Well, if you'll excuse me, I have some duties to perform before I depart to meet with Hobson."

"Good day, Colonel."

Illuminated by the flickering orange glow of an old oil lamp, Richard Barrett sat hunched over his small, shabby writing desk. He'd already formulated a plan to satisfy the colonel's needs and his own, and had begun outlining his instructions in a letter the previous evening.

Not long ago, a small shipping company in Van Diemen's Land had attempted to steal business from him at the whaling stations. He warned them to keep away, but still the ships came. Barrett's shipping agent in New South Wales arranged for two ships from the offending company to meet with an accident. As a result, both ships sank, and the shipping company wisely decided not to continue doing business in New Zealand. A satisfactory result, thought Barrett, and he could apply the same measures to the ship that would bring the commissioner for the land hearings to Wellington.

Of the one hundred pounds given to him by Wakefield, he would keep half and send the remaining fifty pounds to England, along with his correspondence and instructions. Barrett had many contacts and associates scattered across the globe and, over the years, had cultivated a complex network of people who aided him with any distasteful task requiring discreet handling.

As Barrett finished his instructions and folded the letter, he turned his thoughts to a loose end that still dogged him. Ngaiti. The only witness who could discredit him. He carefully addressed the envelope, added fifty pounds, and sealed it. Ngaiti's fate was like the envelope, thought Barrett with a grimace - sealed.

CHAPTER TWENTY

Kent, England.

The New Zealand Company's demands on George Whiting's time lessened over the past couple of months, and as a result, his work slowed considerably. The urgent need to fill emigrant ships with souls, as once demanded, tapered off, and George had more time on his hands. He decided it was time to begin looking for a more suitable form of employment that would assure him of the comforts and lifestyle to which he had grown accustomed. Until he could secure a new position, he would keep his eyes open and continue to please his masters at the New Zealand Company to the best of his considerable ability.

George arrived home after visiting friends and, to his surprise, found a letter from New Zealand waiting for him. He'd never met Richard Barrett in person, but over the years had helped him in a number of small ways, mostly by securing introductions and making recommendations. On Barrett's behalf, he'd occasionally offer a small bribe here or there to secure a contract, but nothing substantial. It was Barrett who'd initially suggested to George that he should seek a position with the New Zealand Company as an agent. Good advice, as it turned out, thought George. He owed Barrett a favour.

To George's astonishment, the envelope contained fifty pounds that tumbled out when he opened it. Pouring himself a generous glass of port, George sat down to read the letter.

Barrett's request was certainly unique, George mused. His own success was directly linked to the Company's. If the Company was doing well, then so would he. And perhaps now more than ever, this was a timely concern. The moral issue didn't bother George. He'd done much worse to provide for himself and put food on his table than what Barrett required of him. The letter's instructions were clear, and George needed to be resourceful to provide Dickie with what he sought.

George Whiting was owed favours from many quarters. He'd altered emigrant documents and made strong recommendations to the Company, urging them to accept a particular applicant. Usually, for a family whose daughter's reputation had been sullied, or for a son who needed to avoid a criminal conviction. There were others who'd offered him healthy incentives, which he'd readily accepted.

An idea already came to mind of whom he could have a quiet word with to obtain the information he needed to complete Barrett's request, and if that didn't work, the Company also had considerable resources at his disposal.

The fifty pounds sitting on his lap was the deciding factor.

Later that evening, George Whiting replied to Richard Barrett, informing him that he would accept the task, provide regular updates, and advise him on the final outcome as requested.

Within a day or so, George confirmed that the lawyer, William Spain, would head the land-hearing inquiry and would depart from Gravesend on April 20th aboard the barque *Prince Rupert*. George immediately sent another letter to Barrett.

As the departure date was still a few weeks away, George had time to learn who would prepare and fit the ship prior to sailing. After discreet enquiries and a few ales, George had all the information he needed, specifically the name and address of Charlie Swanson, a carpenter's mate who would be working on the *Prince Rupert* before departure.

CHAPTER TWENTY–ONE

London, England.

Edward Gibbon Wakefield looked out of the rain-splattered window and took in the dreary scene with a resigned sigh. Below him, people hurried to avoid the downpour and find adequate shelter from the inclement weather. Even a stray dog looked out forlornly from the shelter of a gloomy doorway as he scratched obsessively at a minor annoyance. Wakefield looked up at the smudge of greyness between buildings and blackened chimneys and saw no possibility of respite, only a bleakness that mirrored his mood. It made him want to scratch.

He rubbed the smoothness of his chin and returned his thoughts to the equally unpleasant business unfolding in New Zealand. He leaned against the window frame and thought again of William.

From frequent correspondence, it became clear that dear brother William was now encountering difficulties, and by appearances, much of it was of his own making. Initial reports from Jerningham indicated that William had enjoyed remarkable and rapid success, as the natives had been receptive to receiving gifts in exchange for their lands, but this was all changing. The servants of the church, the Wesleyans and the Church Missionary Society, opposed to the Company's business activities, continued to focus their protestations mostly on London, with tepid results.

According to Jerningham, Richard Barrett proved a valuable asset and served as translator with some skill. With modesty, Edward allowed himself a hint of a smile; the introduction of William and Barrett had been a splendid idea. He must remember to send a thank-you note to young William Fox for the recommendation.

However, it appeared William had failed the company - that much was plain. The instructions and orders William received made it clear that no land was to be purchased unless the natives fully understood the likely consequences of such a sale. Edward shook his head; by all appearances, William had not communicated this effectively. Furthermore, the natives claimed they had not received a fair share of the purchase money or goods.

There were a few other instances of minor wrongdoing that would incur the displeasure of the Board of Directors, but Edward felt there was nothing of real significance. He was confident he could deflect any criticism or admonishment directed at his younger brother. The land hearings, however, were a different matter.

Edward walked away from the window, seeking the comfort of the settee. The mounting charges filed against the Company could attract unwanted attention to himself. While William sought direction and instructions for the forthcoming land hearings, Edward thought it best to distance himself from any negative attention that could interfere with the advancement of his other interests outside the Company. Edward saw himself as an objective man, and with some frustration realised that the New Zealand Company may have reached the pinnacle of its success. His efforts at colonising South Australia had failed, not through any personal failings, he reminded himself. Now the Company's efforts to colonise New Zealand may have run their course.

Edward indulged himself with another generous pour of brandy to consider his immediate options and to draft a reply to William.

He returned to the window and saw the dog now sharing the doorway with a man, each respecting the other's space. Two entirely different creatures, each physically in the same place without fear or outward sign of aggression. Not dissimilar to colonisation, he thought with a wry smile. But if it were up to him, he'd have the dog relocated.

He certainly had a responsibility to ensure his younger brother was well advised. His own son, Jerningham, was still in New Zealand, and Edward felt a paternal need to ensure his well-being. Recent letters from William indicated that Jerningham was increasingly challenged by insobriety, a cause for concern. William also suggested to their youngest brother, Arthur, that, on completion of his naval duties, he too should embark for New Zealand and begin a career with the Company. Was New Zealand to be Arthur's destiny too? He was quite receptive to the idea.

Edward was repeatedly told that his past indiscretions prevented him from holding any significant office in England.

He would forever remain in the background, could never become a director of the Company or have a future in English politics; his future was thus limited. The only real opportunity he imagined for himself was with the 'North American Colonial Association of Ireland'.

Canada was the future, and with this realisation, Edward understood that Canada was where he would continue to focus his attention and disseminate his theories on Systemic Colonisation. A concept he had developed while incarcerated. Simply put, purchase affordable land from Indigenous people; land that men of superior intellect considered unused or wasteland. Sell the land to men of substance, character and means. Then send men to work the land and pay them in such a way that they were never able to purchase the land themselves. This would ensure dependence, social distinction and, of course, generate wealth for landowners. Yes, Canada would be where he would go.

Edward felt satisfied that his subtle disassociation from New Zealand Company business would preserve the reputation he had worked so hard to build. He refilled his glass and turned to his bureau to write to William.

Discredit and harass Spain and the commission, and employ delaying tactics where possible, wrote Edward. A potential change in the English Government will also see the Company's fortunes change, so create delays, he implored. He also knew the Board of Directors would advise William. John Ward, the Company's Secretary, would make recommendations that followed legal protocol and would absolve the Directors of any perceived improprieties. The rest was up to William.

Edward concluded his letter with family news and returned to the window. The man had departed, and the dog still remained, scratching in the doorway.

CHAPTER TWENTY–TWO

Gravesend, London.

Ships creaked and groaned, speaking to Charlie Swanson in a language only he could understand. He believed that ships could talk; in fact, he was convinced of it. Each ship was alive, possessed a soul, and had a story to tell. Some ships were happy, others were sad, and within a short time of being below decks in the hold, or sliding through the filth in the bilges, he would know what type of ship he was in.

Typically, because of his slight stature, Charlie could be found in the deepest, darkest places aboard a ship, creeping where others couldn't or didn't want to go. With a lamp and his awl, he'd crawl through the stinking bilges, looking for rot and stressed joints, or sometimes repairing leaks. The nasty odours didn't bother him; sinus problems had prevented Charlie from smelling properly for years. The rats were tolerated. As long as they left him alone, he ignored them. It was an unspoken truce between man and vermin.

Under the supervision of the ship's carpenter, Charlie would repair and replace wood on the ships he worked on. More recently, the carpenter wouldn't even go down into the bilges to check his work, preferring to trust Charlie's word on the task completed. Charlie believed there wasn't a better carpenter's mate in the whole of Gravesend. Most who'd worked with Charlie and seen his skills would agree.

Charlie didn't go out to sea on ships much these days. He belonged to a shore-crew gang who were hired to ready a ship prior to a lengthy voyage or to complete a refit. Occasionally, he'd go out if they were testing something, but Charlie preferred to stay close to land and the familiar surroundings of the public hotels and lodgings around Gravesend, where he knew almost everyone associated with sailing ships.

He didn't earn much money. When work wasn't available, he'd often go hungry. Normally, he earned only enough to feed himself, enjoy a tankard or two of ale, and sleep in a cheap room at Mother Mary's. A routine he'd followed for some time.

When a knock on the door woke him from his restless slumber, he sat up, startled. It couldn't be Roman, the aggressive manager at Mother Mary's Hotel, as his rent was paid until the end of the week. The persistent knock wouldn't let up. Charlie lit the stub of his last candle and rose from his bed, grumbling. With suspicion, he stood at the door of his squalid single-room home.

"Mister Swanson?" said the voice. "Open up, please, I have a matter to discuss."

Charlie carefully unlocked the door and opened it just enough to peer out. Not recognising the voice or the face, he tried to close it, but the man expertly thrust his foot into the small opening and pushed little Charlie back. Uninvited, the man entered the room and closed the door behind him.

"It's quite all right, Mr Swanson, I'm not here to cause you harm." The man looked around, his nose twitching at the reek.

Charlie stood uncertainly in the middle of the room, fidgeting in the soiled clothes he wore to work. A small cot with a straw mattress lay against the wall, a stained blanket offering the only warmth. At the foot of the bed, beneath a grimy little window, was a table piled with newspapers and sundries. An unfinished woodcarving of a ship's hull sat on the only available space; the man walked over and picked it up, turning it over in his hands.

"Whatcha want? I aint got nuttin'," said Charlie in a nasal voice, convinced the only reason a well-dressed stranger would call on him was to collect money.

The unknown man carefully replaced the carving back on the table and turned to face Charlie.

Feeling threatened, Charlie shuffled back.

"I think I'm in a position to make your life a little more tolerable Mr Swanson," said George Whiting.

CHAPTER TWENTY-THREE

Thorndon, Wellington.

Governor Hobson expressed his displeasure at the Company's recent land purchases in the Wanganui area. According to Hobson, the Company had exceeded the 110,000 acres it had been granted.

Wakefield challenged Hobson's assertion and decided to go to Wanganui to gather the evidence he needed to prove his case. According to Hobson, there were already over one hundred complaints lodged against the New Zealand Company, with more expected. This left precious little time for Wakefield to collect documentation and secure witnesses who would speak in his defence at the land hearings – if they were needed.

More than ever, Wakefield hoped that Barrett would honour his promise to delay the *Prince Rupert* and Spain's arrival. Barrett had assured him there was no need to worry; all would be taken care of.

Preferring order and method to chaos and clutter, Wakefield began organising his desk, making sure everything was in its place before leaving for Wanganui. During the process, he discovered a handful of receipts and invoices and left them on Andrew's desk. One receipt he'd found was for Barrett's exorbitant one-hundred-pound translation fee. The colonel knew enough about accounting practices to realise he needed to add more information to the document or risk Andrew's wrath. Without thinking, he quickly scribbled across the top, *'Prince Rupert'*.

The small stack of paperwork the colonel left for Andrew was waiting for him when he arrived at work that morning. Andrew didn't object to processing the invoices and receipts; it was the delay in receiving them that caused him grief. He would have another word with the colonel and his secretary to ensure they kept on top of it.

Andrew began entering each document into the journal and paused when he came across an unusual receipt. The only information on the receipt was a 'translation Fee' totalling one hundred pounds and the name 'Prince Rupert'. Andrew whistled. That was a significant amount of money, and who was Prince Rupert? He certainly wasn't aware of any visiting royalty. He recognised Barrett's signature, and, annoyingly, there was no date written on the document. He glanced at the dates on the other receipts and invoices and determined he could make an educated guess. He made a notation and put the receipt in a drawer of his desk. He would question Wakefield about it when he returned. He continued entering information into the journals.

Eleanor was at work today, cleaning Wakefield's residence. If she was not working, Andrew would go home during his midday break; otherwise, he would remain in his office, eat his lunch and read the newspaper.

Today, the newspaper held little interest for Andrew. He had no desire to attend an auction in Evans Bay for heifers and bullocks, and he couldn't see any need to purchase fifty tons of flour. He turned the page and began to read 'English News'. Again, there was little to pique his curiosity. If the Marquis of Westminster wanted to visit the Queen, it mattered not to Andrew, although Ellie enjoyed reading about what socialites and royalty were up to. Lastly, he turned to 'Police Notices'. Andrew took delight in reading about who had been up to mischief, but again, it appeared that everyone was sober and well-behaved. The only newsworthy event was the report on the death of an unknown Māori. The body of a male Māori had been discovered in Te Aro Flats, but no details or cause of death were mentioned. With a sigh, Andrew folded the paper, deciding it was time to return to work. He was looking forward to dinner that evening, as Eleanor had invited Isaac and his wife Bethia to share a meal with them.

Doctor Isaac Featherston was only a year or two older than Andrew and Eleanor. Although Isaac and Andrew had remarkably different backgrounds, Bethia was also a Scot and shared much in common with Eleanor. Both women enjoyed each other's company. In a small, growing community, it was only natural that people with similar interests would gravitate toward one another for the benefit of healthy social interaction.

Isaac and Bethia Featherston arrived with their baby daughter precisely on time, bringing a small bouquet of flowers for Eleanor. The Featherstons were warmly received, and while dinner was being prepared, Andrew and Isaac discussed local politics, arguing good-naturedly about social ills and, of course, the New Zealand Company, a topic sure to ignite friendly debate. Eleanor and Bethia discussed the exciting news that Bethia was with child again, a conversation both Isaac and Andrew chose to avoid.

Isaac asked after Ngaiti and recounted with a good laugh the fright he'd received from the Māori who'd accosted him when he'd come to visit that evening some months earlier.

"Andy, have you seen Ngaiti recently?" asked Eleanor from across the room.

"No, I haven't."

"We need to see him and make sure he is well. If you were a decent friend to him, you wouldn't need me to remind you," she said, giving him a wink.

Andrew wasn't listening and stared at a point on the wall.

"Andy? …Andrew!" repeated Eleanor.

"Where is the newspaper I brought home today?" Andrew asked, ignoring Eleanor.

"Where you left it, under your chair…"

Andrew rushed across the room and retrieved the paper. Isaac, Bethia and Eleanor exchanged puzzled glances as Andrew returned and opened it, running his finger down the narrow columns.

"What is going on Andy?" Eleanor asked, her voice giving way to concern.

"Here, read this," Andrew stabbed at the paper and handed it to Eleanor, who placed it on the kitchen table, nearer the lamp, to read. The headline jumped out at her. 'Body of Unknown Māori Found in Te Aro Flats'

"Oh Andy, no, you can't be serious!" Eleanor exclaimed.

Isaac read the few lines of text Andrew indicated after Eleanor finished.

"I pray to God I am wrong," said Andrew, "but something tells me this might be Ngaiti."

"No, Andy, how could you believe this is Ngaiti?" Eleanor questioned.

"I have to agree with Eleanor, Andrew. What makes you think this poor chap is Ngaiti?"

Andrew returned to his chair and sat with his hands covering his face. Eleanor came over and stood behind him, her hands on his shoulders.

"We all know that Barrett sees Ngaiti as the only witness who can prove his translations were outright dishonest, if not misleading," said Andrew, finally removing his hands from his head and looking at Isaac. "If Ngaiti testifies at the land hearings, he could ruin Barrett, not to mention the damage it would cause the Company. Ngaiti has told us he's felt threatened by Barrett for some time. Again, we know this to be true because he was attacked. We also know the land hearings will begin as soon as the commissioner arrives in New Zealand, so if Barrett were going to protect himself, he would do so now. The discovery of this body can only be Ngaiti's, I feel it," said Andrew. "Don't ask me how; I just know."

"Andrew, I hope you are wrong. Your feelings are not proof," cautioned Isaac.

They all remained quiet as they digested Andrew's claim.

"Isaac, perhaps you can go to view the body tomorrow?" suggested Bethia.

"Yes, that's a splendid idea," replied Isaac. "Tomorrow morning, I will go to view the body, if it's still at the coroner's office, and settle this once and for all."

Eleanor, upset, looked at Andrew, "What if you are right, Andy?"

He pulled her to him, "I hope I am wrong."

Isaac was scratching his head.

"There is something I'm unable to comprehend," began Isaac. "The *Tory*'s manifest states that Ngaiti was listed as a translator. Is this correct?"

"Yes, that is so," replied Andrew.

"In the book that John Ward, the Company secretary, wrote for the colonists, called *'Information Relative to New Zealand'*, he states that Ngaiti is a translator - he states that Ngaiti *is* the official Company Translator," said Isaac.

Andrew nodded in agreement.

"Then why was Barrett listed as the Company Translator for the Port Nicholson land sales?"

"Let me tell him, Andy," Eleanor said. "Ngaiti went to Colonel Wakefield and told him that what the Company intended to do was wrong, because they didn't understand Māori and their culture. If the Company went ahead with purchasing land, it would cause problems for both Europeans and Māori." Eleanor said, her voice rising with anger, "Colonel Wakefield told us during dinner aboard the *Tory* that the Company and Ngaiti did not share the same vision and interests!"

"And his services for the New Zealand Company were no longer required," finished Andrew.

"Ah, yes, now I understand," said Isaac thoughtfully. "Perhaps not that long ago, I would have sided unequivocally with the Company, but from what I have witnessed here first-hand and what has been recounted to me, I now see things differently and vehemently believe Ngaiti to be correct."

"And so you should," Bethia added. "Just because the New Zealand Company has support from rich Englishmen doesn't make them right."

"Spoken like a true Scot," laughed Isaac.

"That's how we both feel, too," replied Andrew, joining in.

Eleanor, still disbelieving that Ngaiti had come to harm, rose from her chair, walked into the storage room, and hung the Union Jack in the window, the signal for Ngaiti to visit.

True to his word, the next morning, Isaac went to the coroner's office and requested to see the body found in Te Aro.

"We were about to perform an autopsy on him, as there is no indication of the actual cause of death," the coroner informed Isaac. "So good timing on your part, doctor."

The coroner brought Isaac to where the body lay and removed the protective canvas sheet.

CHAPTER TWENTY–FOUR

Gravesend, London.

"Sit down, Mister Swanson," suggested George Whiting in a friendly manner.

Charlie warily sat on his bed.

"I'm told you are the best carpenter's mate in Gravesend."

Charlie looked at George and remained silent.

"I'm not here to harm you, Mister Swanson, far from it," suggested George. "Perhaps you are in a position to offer me some assistance, and I could, ah, reward your efforts with a small fee?"

Charlie licked his lips, his eyes darting around the room as he continued to fidget.

George lifted his eyebrows in question. He remained standing, unwilling to soil his clothes.

"I don't know ya," Charlie finally replied.

"No, I expect you wouldn't," he answered.

"What do ya want wif me?" Charlie finally asked.

"I need a carpenter's mate to do a job that requires some, er, delicacy."

"What type o'job?"

George looked at the slight man seated before him. Charlie was skinny, yet his muscles were corded, and his calloused hands were surprisingly large for a small man. George thought he was probably quite strong. Charlie's hawkish face looked at George, shifting from suspicion and fear to curiosity.

"There's a ship that you've just begun to work on, and -"

"The *Prince Rupert*," Charlie interrupted quickly, "bound for New Zealand, so I'm told."

"Yes, that's her," George replied. "I need you to make some, ah, modifications to the ship to ensure she founders and sinks when she is safely away from port and some distance from land."

Charlie raised his eyebrows in surprise.

"I think you'll be happy with the reward," offered George.

"Nah, don't reckon I'd be interested."

"No one would ever know, and you'll be recompensed for your effort." George Whiting kept his eyes fixed on the nervous little man. He could see indecision, and the lure of money was tempting.

"Who knows about this?"

"Just you and me, Mr Swanson. No one else, and so it will remain that way."

"Bugger me, that's a bloody big job! How much are you willing to pay, then?"

"I'll make it worth your while," George offered with a generous smile.

Charlie inclined his head in question. "How do I know I can trust ya?"

"Ten pounds," offered George.

Charlie was deep in thought, working out what he would have to do to sink this ship without getting caught. He had some ideas, but it would require a little preparation.

"Nah, not e'nuff."

Ten pounds was a lot of money for someone the likes of Charlie Swanson. George had anticipated that Charlie would leap at the chance to earn such a sum. Twenty-Five pounds was the maximum he would offer.

"Fifteen pounds!"

"Makes it twenty and y'aves a deal," instantly countered Charlie.

George pretended to look serious, as if giving the matter some consideration.

"I'm not sure. My employers may not approve of such a high fee."

"I'll do your job and do it proper-like. It will be done as you want, and she'll go down after seven or eight weeks or so," Charlie said with remarkable confidence.

George looked at Charlie for a moment and decided he had no option. He had to agree.

"It's a deal, but on one condition. I'll give you half now and the other half when the *Prince Rupert* has sailed and is no longer visible from port," George demanded. "If she starts to go down before she leaves harbour, you will not be paid the balance. Is this understood?"

"If she goes down in the bleedin' harbour, mate, I'll be in trouble," sniffed Charlie, his sinuses causing him some discomfort.

George wished he could withhold payment until the *Prince Rupert* actually sank at the correct time, well away from land, but there was little chance Charlie would approve.

"If she doesn't go down at all, I have some unpleasant friends who would enjoy making your acquaintance, Mr Swanson."

Charlie laughed. "Oh, I wouldn't worry 'bout that. If I tells ya, she's goin' down after a month, then that's what'll happen."

"Then we have a deal," informed George, avoiding the automatic response to shake his hand.

"Where's me money?"

Before he arrived at Mother Mary's, George divided all the money into equal amounts and placed each into a separate pocket. He made a show of extracting exactly ten pounds, giving Charlie the impression that it was all he had.

"Now tell me, Mister Swanson, how exactly will you make this happen?"

CHAPTER TWENTY-FIVE

Kaiwharawhara, Te Whanganui-ā-Tara.

With sadness, Chief Te Wharepouri stood alone at the shoreline, gazing out across the harbour of *Te Whanganui-ā-Tara*. With an angry roar, large grey waves relentlessly collapsed across the steep, coarse gravel beach of Kaiwharawhara, only to recede and begin again. Scattered by powerful gusts, clumps of foam that had collected at his feet tumbled away, eventually colliding with rocks and coastal scrub before disintegrating and disappearing. He shivered slightly as the late-afternoon chill found its way under the *kahu* he wore over his shoulders.

Across the harbour, beneath dark, ominous clouds, he could see big ships straining at their anchor chains, the same vessels that kept arriving, disgorging *pakeha*, ship after ship. This was not what he had expected when he and the other chiefs signed the land agreements with Wakefield. They told him *pakeha* would come - but not this many. They came in hundreds and immediately asserted themselves on the land. Few had tolerance for Māori; many treated them with disrespect and suspicion, certainly not as equals. The tension this created was dangerous, and he'd had to speak to many local chiefs, advising them to keep calm and not respond in anger.

Peace was precarious. The short-tempered Chief Te Rauparaha, who lived in the Kapiti area, wanted to fight the *pakeha*. He'd long since run out of patience and objected strongly to their presence and their insatiable appetite for land. Te Rauparaha was right, thought Te Wharepouri, as the colonists' self-righteous attitudes provoked animosity and distrust.

Te Wharepouri had only recently returned from Kapiti, where he'd urged Te Rauparaha to remain calm and exercise restraint in the face of the ongoing threat of being forced from his lands. He'd advised the older chief to use *pakeha* laws to question and challenge any wrongdoing. The last news Ngaiti had passed on from his friends, the young *pakeha* couple, was devastating. The New Zealand Company intended to focus on acquiring even more land in the northern area of the southern island. According to Ngaiti, Colonel Wakefield's youngest brother, Arthur, newly arrived from England, would soon find his way to the Nelson area and, on behalf of the Company, immediately begin searching for suitable arable land. As this region was controlled by Te Rauparaha, Arthur Wakefield's objective could only fuel further tensions.

Te Rauparaha was livid upon hearing the news, and it took all Te Wharepouri's persuasive skills to prevent the chief from setting out for Nelson immediately. Te Wharepouri knew his influence among Te Rauparaha's *iwi*, the Ngati Toa, was limited. He and Te Puni belonged to the Te Ati Awa *iwi*, and it was considered impolite to involve oneself in the affairs of another *iwi*. The Ngati Toa were a dominant force in this region, far more powerful than his own, and Te Wharepouri and his people lived in Kaiwharawhara at Chief Te Rauparaha's pleasure.

Chiefs Te Rauparaha and Te Wharepouri were grateful to Andrew and Eleanor for keeping them informed of Company plans. They also agreed that Barrett posed a very real danger and that he would certainly take steps to protect himself if he felt his position was threatened. In response, Chief Te Wharepouri ensured that, whenever possible, the young *pakeha* couple were watched and guarded. He didn't trust Barrett.

On returning from Kapiti, Te Wharepouri learned that the Stewarts had left a signal for Ngaiti, but no one had seen him for a few days. This, in itself, was unusual and worrying. Ngaiti had not informed anyone that he would be leaving, and Chief Te Wharepouri decided to pay a visit to the young couple once it was dark.

He turned his back on the angry ocean and slowly walked back up the path to the *pa*. Much concerned him, and more than anything, he needed to ensure that the settlement of Wellington remained free from hostilities. If killing began, Māori would lose any prolonged battle they fought with *pakeha* – of that he was certain.

The chief turned his attention to more pleasant thoughts. Tomorrow, he would continue working on the *waka* he was building. The hours he spent carving brought him pleasure and peace.

CHAPTER TWENTY–SIX

Doctor Featherston trudged up the steep path towards Colonel Wakefield's residence. He paused to button his coat and adjust his hat as the biting cold wind swept over Wellington's southern hills, further deepening his dismal mood. As the bearer of bad tidings, he took no pleasure in the news he intended to share with his friends and was reluctant to proceed.

With a frown, he pushed on, determined to deal with the unpleasantness as best he could. On reaching the New Zealand Company office, he paused briefly to collect himself before stepping inside the building.

Andrew was hunched over his precious ledgers, recording information, and didn't hear Isaac enter. Isaac stood quietly, fidgeting with his hat as he waited.

"Isaac! How long have you been standing there…?" Andrew's voice trailed off, aware that something wasn't as it should be.

After a moment's pause, "It's Ngaiti, Andrew, …I'm sorry."

"Oh no! What happened, Isaac?" Andrew rose from his chair and began pacing the room, shaking his head in disbelief. "I can't believe this … poor Ngaiti."

"There aren't many marks on his body, just a few scattered bruises, but the coroner hasn't officially determined the exact cause of death," Isaac offered. "Although we have our suspicions."

"I have to tell Ellie, she's here working today," Andrew said, rushing past Isaac. "Wait here."

Isaac walked around the small room, looking at the maps pinned to the walls and the ledgers and journals stacked in neat rows along the shelves as he waited for Andrew to return.

"I can't believe it, Isaac," said Eleanor between sobs as Andrew led her into the office.

"I'm so sorry, Eleanor. It saddens me to bring you this news. I wish it were different."

"Was it an accident?" she asked, dabbing her eyes.

Isaac looked at Andrew. "As I told Andrew, the coroner hasn't officially determined the cause of death yet, but he and I believe he was asphyxiated and died from lack of breath. The coroner intended to perform an autopsy on the body this morning, but I persuaded him to wait until Ngaiti's family could be informed. Māori aren't keen on having autopsies performed."

"How do you know that was the cause of death?" Andrew asked.

"There were contusions around his throat, bruises that indicate to me he was choked."

"Then it was murder!" cried Eleanor.

"It appears so."

"We don't know who his family is. The only person who would know is Chief Te Wharepouri," Andrew suggested. "We need to contact him."

"Andrew, you need to go to him as soon as possible. The body can't wait much longer."

"Yes, you should go, Andy," Eleanor agreed.

Andrew nodded, still offering comfort to Eleanor.

"Are there any suspects? Were there witnesses? Do they know who murdered him?" she asked, a flood of questions.

"No, apparently not. The body was found in Te Aro Flats, and no one who was questioned saw or heard anything, nor has anyone come forward with any information," added Isaac.

"I think Barrett was behind this," Andrew said.

"Andrew, you must be careful. There is no proof, and you cannot make public accusations unless you know this to be true, even if I do agree with you."

"I think it was Barrett," Eleanor said with finality.

Andrew finished his urgent work and quickly returned home to change before setting off for Kaiwharawhara. It was growing dark. The new winter season brought on the evening early, and Andrew was a little nervous about venturing to the Māori village unaccompanied.

He greeted a few workers returning home, and then he was alone. He felt vulnerable and exposed as he walked towards Kaiwharawhara, an inner sixth sense warning him that danger lurked, though he couldn't identify any threat. Perhaps it was just his imagination, he hoped. He continued north along the coastal path, using a lantern to light the way. Steep cliffs rose above him on his left, and a few scattered, wind-blown trees and low coastal bushes grew alongside the well-used track on his right.

Two men followed Andrew at a safe distance. The surf crashing on the beach drowned out any sound they made, and clouds obscuring the moon made it unlikely he would have noticed them in the darkness.

Slowly, the two men crept closer, narrowing the gap. It was easy to keep him in sight. The yellow glow from the lantern, like a beacon, kept him visible from some distance. Until tonight, the two men had only been following Andrew, tracking his movements and reporting who he met and talked to. Then their instructions changed. If he ventured to Kaiwharawhara, they were to kill him and dispose of the body near the Māori village by throwing it into the surf. The evidence would clearly point to Māori and a simple robbery gone awry.

Following the New Zealand Company accountant and keeping tabs on his movements was straightforward. Both men knew he posed no physical threat to them. Their biggest challenge was linking his death to Māori. They each carried a sharp knife and a small cosh, standard tools of the trade for men such as these, and, as professionals, they would obey their orders without question.

They patiently kept their distance, waiting until they were closer to the Māori village, then, as ordered, they would close in and make their move. One of the men stopped behind a bush, took a hip flask from his pocket and took a healthy swig of cheap rum.

"Keeps me warm," he whispered.

"Well, bloody hurry up, will ya," hissed the other. Then changing his mind, "Ere, pass it over, I may as well have a tot me'self."

Feeling its warming effects in the cold night air, the two picked up the pace and kept the man they followed close.

Andrew was remembering the good times he and Ngaiti had enjoyed aboard ship. The vigorous debates they had won and lost. The laughs they had shared and the closeness they had felt, almost like brothers. Even Ellie had taken to Ngaiti quickly and treated him like a sibling. Andrew smiled at the memory of the surprise on Ngaiti's face when Eleanor had cautioned him about his table manners.

His smile quickly vanished as strong arms grabbed him from behind and held him fast. He dropped the lantern and heard it shatter on the ground as a blinding flash of light engulfed him in pain. Everything went black.

"Cor, he's bloody heavy," said one.

"Just pick 'im up," replied the other

"I aint picking 'im up, just drag him. Grab an arm will ya," cried the first.

With an arm each, the two men dragged the unconscious body off the track towards the stony beach. Andrew's extra weight made the task more arduous.

"Stop, I need a rest," pleaded the first after dragging the inert body about twenty yards. He dropped the arm and retrieved his flask for another pull of rum.

"I don't have all bloody night."

Andrew slowly recovered consciousness and felt the gravel on the beach biting into his rump, he groaned as his senses began to register the pain on the back of his head.

"Aw look, it stirs."

"Knock it off and give him another whack, ya shoulda hit 'im harder th' first time."

He turned to his mate, who raised the flask to his mouth for another swig.

A hard blow drove his friend's head forward into the metal flask with a crack, the force breaking teeth. At the same time, he heard the sound of body blows, accompanied by the unmistakable crack of a bone breaking. A sound he knew all too well. His head whipped around, but there was nothing to see but darkness. In fear, he spun to defend himself against the surprise attack and felt the jarring impact as something hard slammed into his knee. His leg shot out at an unnatural angle, and intense pain shot through his body as he collapsed on the shingle beach beside his friend. Unable to defend themselves, both men continued to receive agonising blows to the head and body before finally succumbing and passing out.

Andrew was rubbing the back of his neck when he saw his two assailants crumple to the ground beside him. From the blackness, men appeared, and he watched in dazed confusion as the two fallen men were set upon and beaten unconscious. They carried spears, and some carried clubs. Even in the darkness, from what little he saw, they wielded their weapons with deadly skill. He recoiled in fear as a figure loomed over him, and he recognised the unmistakable figure of Chief Wharepouri.

Someone lit a torch, and in the flickering half-light Andrew saw the chief's heavily tattooed, unsmiling face. Without a word, he bent down and began to attend to him.

The Chief gently probed the back of Andrew's skull. Finding no blood, he grunted and knelt beside him. Warriors were moving around, each carrying weapons. There were men everywhere.

Surprising Andrew with his English, Te Wharepouri asked, "Can you stand?"

With the chief's help, he slowly stood, wobbled a bit, and remained upright. He began rubbing his bottom, which had taken some abuse while dragged across the track and the gravel beach. "What - what happened?"

"Bad men follow, they kill you and leave you in ocean," replied the chief in halting English.

Feeling dizzy, Andrew sat back down gingerly.

A break in the clouds left a small window of moonlight that shone over the beach.

Chief Te Wharepouri spoke a few words in *Te Reo*, and instantly, a couple of men appeared and began tying the hands and legs of the two injured thugs.

"Why?" asked Andrew.

The chief said nothing.

Remembering the reason for his outing, Andrew turned to face the Chief. "I came to find you. This is why I am out here this evening. Can you understand me?" Andrew asked, speaking slowly.

Te Wharepouri nodded.

"It's about Ngaiti," Andrew began, but paused, unable to continue for a moment. "Ngaiti... he, he's dead."

The only indication the chief understood was a tightening of his mouth; he betrayed no other emotion. He took a deep breath and swallowed. "Tell me... uh, what happen?" he asked after a moment of silence. He knew a Māori body had been discovered, but was unaware it was Ngaiti.

Sensing something important, the warriors, about ten in total, walked in from the darkness and stood in support of their chief.

Andrew spoke slowly and explained what little he knew; sometimes he had to repeat himself so that Te Wharepouri could understand.

"Can you tell his family for me?" Andrew asked. "Are they close to here?"

"Ngaiti is the youngest son of Chief Te Rauparaha," informed Te Wharepouri. "I will tell him."

Andrew was shocked. Ngaiti was the son of the famous chief! Yet, incredibly, whenever asked, Ngaiti had always avoided answering questions about his family.

Chief Te Wharepouri spoke again to his warriors. Assuming Ngaiti had died at the hands of men like those tied before them, they reacted with emotion. A warrior stepped out of the group, walked to one of Andrew's assailants, and, in anger, struck him again. He raised his club, about to deliver a final, fatal blow to the neck, but a quick word from the chief caused the warrior to stop.

Chief Wharepouri squatted beside Andrew and rested a hand on his shoulder. "Ngaiti is more than a friend, I know," he added simply, then removed his hand. "*Pakeha* not touch Ngaiti, no!"

Andrew presumed that the chief didn't want the coroner to perform any autopsy on Ngaiti. Of that, he was certain.

Again, Te Wharepouri spoke to the men who accompanied him, and four of them immediately ran off. He turned back to Andrew.

"I'm truly sorry, I told Ngaiti to be careful," Andrew said apologetically.

Te Wharepouri nodded. "We must go to Ngaiti and bring him to Kaiwharawhara," he stated.

"Yes, I understand," Andrew replied, not daring to tell the chief that it was unlikely the coroner would be available this late to hand over the body.

Andrew rested as the Chief addressed his warriors, waiting for the others to return. Andrew couldn't understand what was being said, but he could tell they weren't happy. The thugs chose a bad time to regain consciousness and immediately began yelling. He was thankful that silence was restored – his assailants were again unconscious.

Chief Te Wharepouri approached and held up the weapons the thugs carried. In the moonlight, Andrew saw a couple of lethal looking, very sharp knives and two coshes. "This was for you," he offered, the pale moonlight reflecting off the blades.

Andrew hadn't fully appreciated the danger he was in, and he began to shake.

The four warriors returned, bringing two handcarts normally used to transport vegetables. Te Wharepouri asked whether Andrew could walk or would he prefer to ride in the cart. Andrew replied that he would walk, as his rear end was in no shape to take any further punishment from a bumpy ride in a cart.

Both thugs were placed in separate carts, and they began the slow journey back to Thorndon. Andrew was curious about what would happen to the two men who had tried to kill him. Chief Te Wharepouri remained quiet; the news of Ngaiti's death had affected him deeply, but there was little evidence of despair or sadness on his impassive face.

As the group began the walk back to Thorndon, Andrew wondered whether Barrett had sent the two men. At one point, he'd gone to the thugs and asked them. Through their pain, even though they now had something stuffed in their mouths, they were defiant and said nothing. Not even a head nod.

Chief Te Wharepouri went to the two men – the sound of the nearby surf was drowned out by an ear-piercing scream.

"Yes, it was Barrett, stop, please!" cried one. Another scream broke the stillness of the night. "We were gonna kill him, … no, please, no more!" the thug pleaded. "We were told to leave 'im in the ocean near your village," he hurriedly finished.

Te Wharepouri removed his hand from the broken knee joint and stood facing Andrew. No words were spoken. Andrew was in shock - Barrett.

As they approached the first buildings and dwellings in Thorndon, Chief Te Wharepouri untied the thugs and threw them, none too gently, onto the track; their cries of pain filled the night, which was sure to attract attention and deliver its message to Barrett. Te Wharepouri indicated to Andrew to hurry as best he could as they made their way home.

Eleanor waited anxiously for Andrew. Earlier, she had demanded to go with him to Kaiwharawhara, but he had firmly insisted she remain at home. Unable to sleep, she paced backwards and forwards in their home, waiting for his return.

Something was wrong. She knew it and feared for his safety.

There was some relief when the door finally opened, and Andrew slowly walked in, accompanied by Chief Te Wharepouri.

This sight of her dishevelled husband confirmed all was not well.

"Oh my God! What happened, Andy?" She rushed over and hugged him, simultaneously checking for injuries.

Despite the sadness this evening had brought to Chief Te Wharepouri, the corners of his mouth twitched ever so slightly. Nothing was more powerful than a woman's love.

CHAPTER TWENTY–SEVEN

The three-hundred-and-twenty-two-ton barque *Prince Rupert* was careened. Taking full advantage of low tide, the ship was beached so that her sides, normally beneath the waterline, were now dry and exposed. This allowed the carpenter's mates, under the strict supervision of the ship's carpenter, to attend to repairs and maintenance. Heeled over, the *Prince Rupert* looked ungainly and helpless as workmen clambered over her sides and addressed her needs. When all tasks were completed and the ship was floated with the aid of the incoming tide, she'd be nearly ready to begin her voyage to the far side of the world.

Charlie Swanson was pleased that the hull of the *Prince Rupert* was not sheathed in either copper or the new 'Muntz' metal recently introduced. It would have interfered with his plan and inconvenienced him considerably. Sheathing ensured the submerged wooden planks would last longer when covered by a protective, non-corrosive metallic coating and provided some protection against shipworm, which ate into the wood. As the *Prince Rupert* would be spending most of her time in colder waters, it was less of an issue, and, of course, the decision not to sheath the ship would save the ship's owners considerable expense.

During the previous evening in his dingy room at Mother Mary's, Charlie had spent hours cutting and shortening the copper zinc bolts used to attach the wooden planks to the side of the ship. It was a laborious and tiring task that left his hands a little sore today. Shortening the wooden dowels, or *treenails,* took him only moments.

Charlie had carefully selected an area on the port side near the ship's stern and promptly found a few planks that were conveniently rotten and needed replacing. By all outward appearances, Charlie was diligent in his work, and when the carpenter came to inspect, he found nothing untoward to arouse his suspicions. Had the carpenter examined the replacement planks and their attachments more closely, he would have discovered something horribly wrong with Charlie's work.

The straight planks Charlie replaced were well below the waterline. Accessing them from inside the ship required a visit to the stinking bilges in an area few people had any reason to go. Charlie had chosen wisely. When he attached the replacement planks to the hull, he'd taken from his pocket the bolts he'd cut in half, inserting each into the holes he'd drilled. He did the same with the modified treenails. Returning to the bilges, he then extracted the other, shortened half of each bolt and inserted them into the holes. It now appeared that each plank was firmly attached and secured by bolts. He completed the task by carefully caulking and sealing each plank, so it appeared normal. When the ship's carpenter came for the final exterior inspection, he showed his pleasure to Charlie with a broad smile and a compliment, saying the job was well done. Of course, he inquired how everything was inside the hull, apologised to Charlie for being unable to review his work due to time constraints, and trusted that all was satisfactory.

The new planks were held in position only by caulking; even a gentle outward push from inside the ship would dislodge them.

Once the *Prince Rupert* set sail, the planks would eventually absorb water and swell. As Charlie had ensured the planks were loosely fitted, any swelling would force them to move, and the path of least resistance would be outwards. Within a few weeks, the constant flexing of the ship in the southern oceans, combined with the battering of heavy waves, would weaken the caulking's tenuous hold on the planks. They would finally break free and disappear, and tons of seawater under immense pressure would rush into the opening. As she filled with more and more water, the *Prince Rupert* would become unresponsive to commands from the rudder and would sink quickly. This is what he explained to the well-dressed man who had offered him the money, and the man appeared satisfied.

Under the orange glow of his lamp in the fetid bilge, Charlie admired his handiwork and was pleased. The only way his sabotage could be detected was if the planks were pushed outwards or the bolts were turned, neither of which was likely to happen.

As all passenger ships departing port, well-wishers, family and friends gathered on the quay and waved farewell to loved ones. Women flourished flimsy handkerchiefs and occasionally dabbed at their eyes. Husbands remained stoic, if not a little envious of the possibilities of adventure and fortune in far-off lands. Children, quickly bored and restless, tugged at their parents' arms, impatient to return home and receive the treats they had been promised. Passengers lined the deck and waved frantically, emotional at the thought of leaving behind the familiarity of an orderly life they knew so well, and anxious about the uncertain dangers of a long sea voyage and a destination they knew so little about.

Officers barked commands, and sailors, under the captain's watchful eye, cast off shorelines and, with a slight groan, the Prince Rupert, finally free from constraint and no longer attached to land, eased away from the pier. Clouds of black smoke spewed from her single funnel, threatening to envelop anyone on the quay as she slowly turned.

William Spain, the lawyer appointed by Lord John Russell as Land Claims Commissioner to investigate the New Zealand Company's land purchases, stood beside his wife, Mary, and their brood of nine children at the rail. All waved vigorously at relatives and acquaintances who had come to see them off. As the heavily laden *Prince Rupert* slowly departed from Gravesend, they remained on deck until the figures on the pier could no longer be seen.

From across the bay, two men watched the *Prince Rupert* manoeuvre out of the harbour. Trailing a cloud of smoke and gaining speed, she eventually disappeared from view.

George Whiting took ten pounds from his pocket, which he'd promised Charlie, and without fuss handed it over. "Let's hope you are correct and she goes down in the middle of the ocean," said George, with no thought for the welfare of passengers and crew.

"Like I told ya, she'll go down in rough weather, more'n likely."

"Then there's no reason for us to communicate any more. You will not acknowledge me if our paths cross in future, understood, Mr Swanson?"

Charlie turned and began walking away, his response to George was a casual wave of his arm.

CHAPTER TWENTY–EIGHT

Wellington,

It was a well-turned-out event, another opportunity for ladies to look their finest, catch up on local gossip and make new acquaintances. For gentlemen, it was a chance to share a laugh, gripe about this or that with their friends, and feel comforted that they had supported their wives in their latest diversion, all for the good cause of promoting the common interests of horticulture within their community.

It was the second meeting of the 'Port Nicholson Horticulture Society', and Dr Isaac Featherston had just been elected Secretary of the newly formed club. Enthusiastic applause filled Barrett's Hotel as Isaac modestly stood and acknowledged his support with a bow and a dramatic sweep of his arm. Bethia, seated beside Eleanor and Andrew, glowed with pride and clapped loudly. It mattered little to her that the role of Secretary was uncontested in the election.

Dickie Barrett stood at the back of the room and shared an anecdote meant only for the ears of men. No women stood near Barrett, so it was unlikely he had offended anyone. Typically, his cheeks glowed a healthy pink, and his infectious laugh never failed to bring a smile to those nearby. His jolly demeanour added to the amiable, harmless publican he portrayed so well.

When the opportunity presented itself, he watched Doctor Featherston carefully. Dickie had noticed the hostile looks Featherston had given him earlier, glances that spoke volumes. Barrett made a mental note to pay closer attention to Featherston; he'd been seen visiting the young Stewart couple more often. Since the accountant and his lovely wife had been on friendly terms with Ngaiti, this little group continued to prick at Barrett's sense of comfort.

Barrett grew increasingly concerned about the approaching land hearings, where he would undoubtedly be required to appear, and his translating abilities tested. The unfortunate death of Ngaiti was most timely. He allowed himself a smile. It removed the only English-speaking witness who could testify against him. The repercussions, as were bound to happen, would likely come from Māori and Te Wharepouri. They would suspect that he had been involved in Ngaiti's death, but there was no evidence to prove his involvement. The man who had actually committed the murder was safely back at the Te Awaiti whaling station with his debts all paid.

A few people in Wellington required watching; certainly, Chief Te Wharepouri had made a mockery of him. Dickie had a long memory, and he would deal with anyone who interfered with his business operations. Both the Stewarts and the Featherstons were a worry as well, particularly since their association with Colonel Wakefield meant he would have to exercise extreme care in how he dealt with them. His attempt to deal with Andrew Stewart had failed. The two men assigned the task were severely injured and, if they were lucky enough ever to walk again, would do so only with the aid of a cane. Oh yes, he knew the chief was protecting the Stewarts, but there were still other ways to deal with the bothersome accountant.

"Dickie, is the game still on tonight?" asked a passing gentleman, interrupting his musings.

"Why, Mister Harrington, I didn't know your interests extended to horticulture. I thought they were more directed towards the adult kind of entertainment enjoyed by gentlemen such as your good self," replied Dickie with a laugh.

Harrington leaned closer to Barrett. "I'm only here to keep Mrs Harrington happy; I don't care for weeds," whispered Mister Harrington in reply.

"Then we shall look forward to your company at the conclusion of tonight's activities," replied Barrett with a smile, clapping Harrington on the shoulder in a good-natured way.

"Yes, I shall return once I've seen Mrs Harrington safely home," winked the gentleman.

Barrett enjoyed a good game of cards, especially when he was winning. However, recently his fortunes appeared to have deserted him. A temporary run of bad luck, nothing more, he surmised.

Harrington wandered off to rejoin his wife, and Dickie cast his thoughts to the *Prince Rupert* and the impending disaster of William Spain's fateful voyage. George Whiting had proven to be a reliable asset, and Dickie hoped that George had successfully ensured that the *Prince Rupert* never arrived in New Zealand. If George failed, Barrett's own position and esteem with Colonel Wakefield and the Company would be adversely affected.

Life for Dickie Barrett was becoming more complicated. As his wealth and influence over Colonel Wakefield and the New Zealand Company grew, so did the problems. Land purchases he'd made as a New Zealand Company agent in Taranaki were now being challenged, and Wakefield, although naïve, would soon tire of mounting disquiet as a reckoning with the Company became increasingly likely.

Doctor Featherston moved to the table where his wife and the Stewarts were seated. Barrett noticed the envious glances the men cast towards Mrs Stewart. She was undoubtedly the most beautiful woman in the room, and her natural poise and elegance attracted considerable attention. Dickie watched her closely, his mind calculating and assessing. With a smile, he turned and ordered another drink.

"Barrett's been watching us," whispered Andrew, trying to find a more comfortable position on the chair. His backside still ached from the previous evening's battering on the beach.

"Yes, I know. I saw him looking over here," replied Eleanor. "Do you think we are still in danger from him?"

"We have done nothing to threaten him; he has no reason to harm us," Andrew replied with a confidence he didn't feel.

"And that didn't prevent you from being attacked, did it?"

"No, but why does he think we are a threat to him?" Andrew replied.

"Probably because he feels you've been sharing Company information with Chief Te Wharepouri," Isaac replied.

"Yes, but only since Ngaiti was attacked, and it hasn't been anything you would call secret."

"Yes, of course," said Isaac, looking thoughtfully at Barrett. He leaned towards Andrew and whispered, "I have half a mind to confront Barrett and ask him point-blank about Ngaiti."

"Do you think it's possible he will admit to his involvement? I doubt it," Andrew replied.

They both watched Barrett from across the room as he spoke with a gentleman.

"He has a lot to lose, doesn't he? If the land hearings draw attention to his failings and the Commissioner rules in favour of Māori, Barrett's future is bleak," said Isaac.

"I think so," agreed Andrew, "He is earning a considerable amount of income from the Company, not to mention the gifts he's received."

"I'm increasingly disappointed by William and the outright lies he's been telling colonists and settlers. By the way, did you feel the earthquake today?" Isaac asked.

"Oh yes, it was horrid. I didn't know what was happening," replied Eleanor, then turning back to Bethia and the topic of babies they were discussing.

"Yes, well, that's just another lie. The New Zealand Company said New Zealand had no earthquakes," Isaac volunteered.

"I didn't feel anything; I was walking at the time," said Andrew, continuing to watch Barrett.

"It was a very disagreeable experience, let me tell you. What other lies has William spread, I wonder?" mused Isaac. He raised his glass and emptied it. "I'm going to make a promise - here and now," he added, waving his arms.

Once he had the attention of Andrew, Eleanor and Bethia, he said, "I will become editor of a newspaper very soon, and I will expose frauds, cheats and liars. I shall make a public spectacle of those who persist in causing adversity to the good people of this fair town."

Bethia rolled her eyes. "He always gets like this when he's had one drink too many, and he won't remember a thing in the morning. It's a good thing he hasn't any patients to see tomorrow."

Andrew and Eleanor laughed.

"Don't you be drinking any more tonight, Andrew Stewart. We have Ngaiti's funeral to attend at Kaiwharawhara tomorrow," warned Eleanor. "And I will not spend my day listening to you moan about your sore head. Having to hear you complain endlessly about your bottom is bad enough," she laughed.

"Does your injured posterior require my attention, Andy?" Isaac asked, sporting a wide grin.

CHAPTER TWENTY–NINE

Kaiwharawhara, Wellington

"Whiro is the lord of darkness, and he lives in the underworld. He also represents death," Aroha quietly told Andrew and Eleanor. "His followers live amongst us, ready and waiting to strike and take us."

Andrew and Eleanor listened carefully as the young girl explained the *waiata*, the song sung to honour the passing of Ngaiti. Chief Te Wharepouri invited Andrew and Eleanor to attend the *tangihanga*, the funeral, for Ngaiti. As suggested, they arrived at the Kaiwharawhara *pa in the* late morning and were immediately met and welcomed by Aroha outside the village. Eleanor immediately took a liking to the young Māori girl who spoke English so well and learned that she had been taught English by the wealthy family for whom she worked.

A woman began a high-pitched wailing call. This was the *houkainga*, the invitation for guests to enter the Marae. Aroha instructed them both to hang their heads in respect for the ancestors and the dead as they slowly walked through the gates.

Eleanor was taken by Aroha's looks and demeanour. She had beautiful, unblemished dark skin, flawless and radiating warmth, glowing with natural youthful vitality and energy. Her large brown eyes were liquid pools of innocence and naivety. She spoke clearly, with a crispness that suggested confidence and poise, and she held her chin just right, as if defying anyone to challenge her. As she'd explained, Chief Te Wharepouri was her father, and it was plain to see he doted on his fourteen-year-old daughter. The

Chief had instructed Aroha to stay at Andrew and Eleanor's side, to ensure they were treated as honoured guests, as *whanau*, family, and to translate when needed.

Now seated on mats, Eleanor and Andrew watched the formal proceedings with curiosity.

"Hine went to battle Maui, who lost the fight. Maui was light, and Hine was the lady of the night, so light was overcome by darkness," Aroha continued.

"It's all confusing to me," Andrew said, easing himself into a more comfortable position.

Eleanor gave him a disdainful look.

A line of people, some acquaintances, others relatives, slowly approached Ngaiti's body. Immediately, the women began to wail and weep.

"It's so sad," said Eleanor, referring to the women who were crying.

"They are saying farewell, Miss Eleanor. They want Ngaiti to journey safely to where his ancestors and elders will greet him."

"Similar to our heaven," Andrew suggested in a more respectful tone.

As his body began to decompose, Ngaiti was wrapped tightly in a blanket. Over the blanket, he wore a *kahu-moteā*, a cloak of mourning. His knees were drawn up and tied to his body, allowing him to be seated. His face was painted red, and feathers hung from his ears as adornments. Around his neck he wore a pounamu[6] pendant, and his hair was neatly combed - he could have been alive.

It felt very unreal. Both Andrew and Eleanor were still deeply shocked and upset by the death of their dear friend.

"It could have been you," Eleanor said, her eyes filling with tears. "If it hadn't been for Chief Te Wharepouri, you'd be dead too, Andy."

That very thought had been on his mind constantly since the failed attack. His reminders were a bruise on the back of his head and a sore bottom - he repositioned himself on the uncomfortable mat they sat on. Eleanor seemed quite at ease, enjoying the winter sunshine and observing the culture and rituals so unfamiliar to them.

On the other side of the *marae*, Andrew noticed a small but growing group of older men. They sat together, talking amongst themselves,

---

[6] *Pounamu – New Zealand greenstone*

occasionally sharing a spirited laugh. As people arrived and were welcomed, younger men would drift over to the older men, offer a polite greeting and pay their respects before moving on. The older men who arrived would join the group, greeted with heartfelt, genuine welcomes. Aroha explained that these men were elders and earned the respect they now received.

People continued to enter the marae. Nearly all were Māori, and the young *pakeha* couple stood out. They received curious looks from some but were accepted and treated with warmth and friendliness by all. The couple's initial nervousness had long since departed. Despite the reason for being there, they now felt relaxed and welcome.

A small commotion caused heads to turn. The mournful call from the *houkainga* added drama as a small procession slowly made its way into the Marae. In answer, another call was heard. This was the *manuhiri*, the response call from the visitors. Recognising the status of the new arrivals, Te Wharepouri politely moved away from the people he had been talking with and respectfully waited for his guests to walk in.

"Chief Te Rauparaha has arrived," Aroha informed them.

"He's much older than I imagined him to be," Andrew said, looking in awe at the famed chief.

"Yes, he is no longer a young warrior."

Te Wharepouri greeted Te Rauparaha with the traditional Māori *hongi,* and then the two chiefs, heads bowed, walked side by side solemnly towards the lifeless body of Ngaiti. Te Rauparaha raised his hand slightly, indicating to Te Wharepouri that he intended to take the last few steps alone.

"I don't think parents should outlive their children," Eleanor said, her voice heavy with sadness. "I can't imagine what that poor man is feeling right now. He looks so alone and sorrowful."

Aroha turned to look at Eleanor, her big eyes moist.

Eleanor realised she was in love with Ngaiti. She reached forward to grasp Ngaiti's hand, offering comfort and understanding.

The marae settled into a steady rhythm of visitors and relatives who trickled in to honour Ngaiti. The chiefs gathered to discuss matters of importance, re-establish bonds and strengthen relationships, and, to the joy of some, even arrange a marriage or two.

Aroha continued to explain the workings of the marae and what was happening around them when, suddenly, she stood and stepped out of the way. Unsmiling, Chief Te Rauparaha stood over them. He looked closely at Andrew, then at Eleanor. Unsettled, Andrew took Eleanor's arm and went to stand. Te Rauparaha spoke quickly to Aroha.

"Chief Te Rauparaha asks that you remain seated, you have nothing to fear," Aroha translated.

Releasing Eleanor, Andrew continued to stand and faced the chief. "It's a pleasure to meet you, Mr Te Rauparaha. My wife and I are deeply sorry for your loss. Ngaiti was a dear friend to us, and we will miss him terribly. We can't possibly imagine the grief you must feel."

Aroha duly translated Andrew's formal greeting and condolences.

Chief Te Rauparaha nodded thoughtfully and held eye contact with Andrew before he again spoke.

"Thank you for your kind words," Aroha translated for Andrew. "Ngaiti spoke of you often, and we all know your *mana* is strong. We welcome you as family. I hope to get to know you better so we can become friends."

Chief Te Wharepouri approached and stood beside Te Rauparaha as Aroha finished translating.

Te Rauparaha continued, then waited for Aroha to translate.

"He hopes you will stay and enjoy the spirit of these good people, so you can learn and begin to understand us. May you enjoy the fine food, which will be ready soon."

Te Rauparaha rubbed his belly and said "*puku*," pointing to Andrew's slight paunch. Both Te Wharepouri and Te Rauparaha laughed good-naturedly, easing the tension from the earlier formalities. Eleanor and Aroha joined in the laughter as the two chiefs walked away. Andrew's face turned pink.

The afternoon wore on, and the smell of cooking food from the *hangi* was overpowering. It was an unusual smell, unfamiliar and very earthy.

"They are preparing food for us now. Soon we can eat. Are you hungry?" asked Aroha.

Before she could reply, a couple of warriors ran past them towards the entrance of the *pa*, each carrying a spear. Aroha's face showed concern as she watched.

"What's happening, Aroha?" asked Eleanor, seeing the look of worry on her face.

"I'm unsure. It looks as though *pakeha* men wish to enter the marae, but they are not permitted," she said.

Andrew stood to watch. "I've seen these men, they work for Barrett."

"Yes, I think you are correct, Mister Andrew. My father has asked that they not come here."

"I wonder what they want?" said Andrew with suspicion.

Other people had stood, curious about what was taking place at the gate. The two men heaved a large object from a wagon, placed it on the ground after saying a few words to the warriors, and then quickly left. Te Wharepouri was making his way to the gate.

"If Barrett is involved, then I don't trust him," Andrew said.

"I will ask for you," Aroha said, and quickly ran to her father.

Eleanor turned to her husband. "Barrett's up to something, Andy. Why would he even send people here when Chief Te Wharepouri suspects his involvement in Ngaiti's murder?"

"That's what I'm thinking Ellie."

With youthful energy, Aroha returned, wearing a big smile. "My father says Barrett offers us *koha,* a gift to help feed family and friends during the *tangihanga,* er, funeral."

"That's a thoughtful gesture," said Andrew with sarcasm.

"Yes, we will be eating pork tomorrow, my favourite," said Aroha.

"It's Andrew's too," said Eleanor poking Andrew in his *puku.*

Andrew wasn't listening.

"I'll be back in a moment. I need to move around a bit. I'm still a little tender," he said, and immediately began walking towards Chief Te Wharepouri, who was inspecting the pig.

Chief Te Wharepouri was talking with the men who were about to carry the pig away to begin cleaning and cutting it up. He wasn't happy. While the gift of a pig was always welcome, the motive behind Barrett's gift bothered him. He saw Andrew approach and was about to comment on it when Andrew stopped. Andrew's face betrayed his anger.

Pork-Chop.

"Andy?" yelled Eleanor as she walked quickly towards him, with Aroha at her side.

"Oh no!" she exclaimed, putting both hands to her face. "Pork-Chop!"

Te Wharepouri looked on in puzzlement. He turned to Aroha, questioning her.

Eleanor stood beside Andrew and looked in horror at the carcass before them. It was their pig, their Pork-Chop.

"Are you offended by pig meat?" asked Aroha.

"No… no, we are not," replied Andrew, trying hard to regain his composure, his voice shaking with fury. He pointed to the carcass. "This was our pig! Barrett's men must have gone to our home and slaughtered her while we were here."

Aroha translated for her father. His curiosity turned to anger as he understood what had happened. "Do you want to take the pig home?" he asked, without needing Aroha.

After a moment's pause, Eleanor said, "Please accept this pig as our gift. As our *koha*?" She looked to Aroha to confirm the correct use of the word *koha*.

Chief Wharepouri immediately ordered his men to remove the pig quickly. He turned back to Andrew. "Come, we must talk."

Eleanor had tears in her eyes. She was visibly upset, and Andrew looked on as Aroha slipped her arm through Eleanor's and led her back to the mat. Chief Te Wharepouri took Andrew to the small group of chiefs discussing a marriage agreement. Te Rauparaha had seen the activity at the gate but didn't know what had transpired. The expressions on Te Wharepouri's and the *pakeha* faces told him something serious had happened. He waited patiently with the chiefs as Te Wharepouri approached.

Once seated on mats, Te Wharepouri explained to the gathered chiefs the circumstances surrounding Ngaiti's death. He then explained how

Barrett had taken Andrew's pig, killed it, and offered it as *koha*. He waited for their comments, sure they would come.

Te Rauparaha cleared his throat, and all heads turned expectantly. They waited.

"Barrett dishonours us," he began. "He brings us koha, koha that was not his to give."

Voices murmured in agreement. Andrew watched and could not understand the conversation. It looked serious, and no one dared to interrupt the chief as he spoke. Andrew observed in fascination; this was as disciplined as he imagined any meeting of generals.

"Barrett dishonours us because he stole from us!" Te Rauparaha raised his voice and pointed at Andrew. "He is part of our *whanau*, our family. Does anyone disagree?" Again, the chief raised his voice to drive home his point, and heads turned to look at Andrew.

Te Rauparaha waited, no one challenged him.

"My youngest son was killed. We know it was *pakeha*, and we know Barrett was behind this," Te Rauparaha's voice was unsteady with emotion. "Barrett's hands may not have touched my son, but my son was taken from me by the hands of Barrett!"

Te Rauparaha finished, and the group fell silent. Out of respect, junior chiefs would not speak until more senior chiefs had spoken first.

"Te Rauparaha is wise." Te Wharepouri nodded in agreement. "We can take Barrett's life," he suggested. A few heads nodded in agreement. "Will the *pakeha* allow such a thing to happen? They will not be happy and will seek to impose their laws on us. They will bring soldiers and more will die - *pakeha* will turn against us!" He paused, formulating his thoughts.

"Barrett enjoys his power, his riches and his greed. We can take them from him and cast him out of these lands." Te Wharepouri looked at the chiefs around him. "We can do this, and the *pakeha* will not point their finger at us. We can take his *mana*, his honour and his *pakeha* money. And we will protect our *whanau*!" Te Wharepouri looked at Andrew. "I have a way!"

Te Rauparaha said nothing more. He listened to Te Wharepouri and watched the other chiefs' reactions, assessing them carefully. He was deeply troubled and saddened by all that had happened.

When younger, Te Rauparaha reflected that retribution would be swift and unforgiving. Injustice was dealt with quickly, without remorse or pity. As he listened to Te Wharepouri, he realised how times had changed. The old days were gone. *Pakeha* came, and their influence and power affected his people, changing them forever. It was as if they had taken something from Māori.

He understood the reasoning behind Te Wharepouri's thinking and, to a certain degree, supported it. He made himself a promise that he would not roll over like a tamed dog, waiting to be scratched by its master. No, he would show *pakeha* his teeth.

Andrew eventually returned to his relieved wife and explained what he thought had happened during the meeting. Te Wharepouri occasionally said a few words to him, but for the most part, he had no idea what had been decided.

They were eating food that had been cooking all day in the ground. It was as tasty as anything Andrew had ever eaten, a fusion of flavours and smells that were unique and distinctive. Andrew wanted more, but reluctantly accepted Eleanor's urging not to have a second helping. Aroha laughed and explained how rocks had been heated by fire, then placed into a large pit dug in the ground. Meat and vegetables were then placed in baskets on top of the rocks, and everything was covered with earth to cook for hours. This was a *hangi*, she said proudly.

Andrew noticed that after the chiefs had eaten, Te Rauparaha and Te Wharepouri went to visit the elders. Aroha told Andrew that her father and Chief Te Rauparaha sought advice and counsel. No decisions would be made unless there had been discussion and all points of view had been considered fairly.

"It can't be all serious," said Andrew, as another bout of laughter came from the group.

"You have much to learn about Māori," said Aroha with a laugh.

CHAPTER THIRTY

Prince Rupert, Table Bay, Cape of Good Hope, South Africa.

The captain reluctantly cancelled the evening's entertainment. Orders were given to a junior officer to ensure that all passengers remained in their berths due to deteriorating weather and a rising sea. It would be dangerous to have passengers wandering around on deck in such conditions. The weekly Saturday night dance was popular and broke the tedium of shipboard life for passengers and crew alike. Everyone would be disappointed.

The ship crested another large swell and plunged down the far side, her hull slamming into the oncoming wave, sending sheets of seawater cascading over the deck. Large, violent seas were normal in these southern oceans, especially as they approached the Cape of Good Hope. The captain wasn't overly concerned, just disappointed. He, too, looked forward to the music and enjoyed watching the ladies pirouette across his deck on Saturday nights. Instead, prayer services would be held below decks for the passengers in steerage, and a separate service would be held for cabin passengers.

The *Prince Rupert* made excellent time on her voyage to New Zealand, and the weather was mostly agreeable. Passengers enjoyed the ever-changing sights and the variety of aquatic life that appeared, which was always exciting. Most entertaining were the flying fish, which skimmed from wave top to wave top. Passengers enthusiastically recorded new sights and experiences in their journals and diaries. In particular, the children were always excited, shrieking with joy when dolphins were spotted leaping playfully out of the water. Of course, there were also turtles, and even the odd shark was seen.

William and Mary Spain worked hard to keep their nine children amused and occupied. No easy task. Both Mary and William continued their children's education by holding classes, playing games and creating other activities to hold their attention. Needless to say, tensions rose in the Spain family from time to time, as they did elsewhere on the ship. Family disagreements were resolved with a stern word and a minor punishment, often leaving a tear and a frown.

If only it were as easy with the land hearings, thought William Spain with a smile. He imagined ruling on a claim only to see the defeated party sit in the corner, pouting.

He placed the documents he'd been studying back into his case. The ship's motion always made him feel rather ill, especially when he was reading in their cuddy. William reviewed and studied all the land court documents he'd received and was familiar with all the parties involved. He also knew that even more complaints awaited him upon his arrival, and he was eager to begin determining the validity of each claim and achieve a fair and satisfactory resolution.

On deck, Captain Ramage assessed the weather conditions and decided to turn in for a few hours. As the outlook wasn't promising, he would be needed on deck later in the evening and probably wouldn't sleep after that. He checked with the helmsman before going below.

The *Prince Rupert* cleaved her way through another large wave, crested the top, and smashed down into the trough, shaking the ship violently. She slowly began the agonising climb up the next steep wave, starting the process all over again.

If it were possible for Charlie Swanson to observe his handiwork, he would have been disappointed. The *Prince Rupert* was still afloat after considerable time at sea, and until this evening, the planks he'd replaced remained in position and did not threaten the safety of the ship.

However, tonight it was different. The ferocious seas began to strain the *Prince Rupert*, and she flexed and twisted in minuscule amounts as huge seas relentlessly battered her. The caulking that held the planks in position began to break free, allowing additional moisture to seep into the planks and surrounding wood. The wood swelled as it absorbed more seawater, slowly forcing one plank outward.

Inside the ship, the one hundred and sixty passengers were unaware of anything untoward. The Captain was in his cabin, attempting to sleep, and the helmsman was thinking of the women who'd soon be enjoying the pleasure of his company. His experienced hands kept the ship safely on course.

As the ship shuddered from the impact of another mighty wave, the last piece of caulking holding the upper plank of the two Charlie had replaced finally gave way, and the plank moved outwards. The seawater rushing past the hull immediately sucked the plank from its position, sweeping it away and beginning to flood the ship. The breach was well below the waterline, and instantly the second plank was also torn from its position, just as Charlie Swanson had anticipated. Under immense pressure, even more water was forced into the ship. The bilges began to flood, and the water level rose at an alarming rate.

The helmsman, trying to control the *Prince Rupert* in the turbulent seas, felt nothing at first. The first indication that something was amiss was the pull to port. The ship began to turn to the left, and he dutifully corrected at the wheel, thinking it was the current or a rogue wave.

As tons of seawater continued to flood into the ship's hold, the *Prince Rupert* began to founder and settled lower in the water. The ship's weight increased, and the waves she'd been able to ride over easily now launched themselves at her sides and over her deck. The wind, waves and current began to force the *Prince Rupert* off course. The water taken aboard made the ship heavy and unresponsive, and any course corrections attempted from the helm were ineffectual; she was now completely out of control and headed directly for Mouille Point in Table Bay, South Africa. The only good news for the captain was that Table Bay was sheltered. The waves and wind eased considerably as the out-of-control ship was thrust into the bay and towards the rocks.

There was little anyone could do; the *Prince Rupert* was helpless and at the mercy of the elements. The captain was almost asleep when he felt a change in the ship's motion and, realising something was drastically wrong, rushed on deck. The engine failed, and he knew the ship was doomed. All he could do now was ensure the safety of his passengers and crew.

"Fire the signal cannon!" he screamed to a seaman.

Ship's officers began preparing the lifeboats as panicked passengers rushed on deck in confusion. Children were crying, and passengers shouted, demanding to know what was happening. Some unwisely brought possessions on deck, clutching suitcases, bags and sundry items. Crewmen were equally uncertain, turning to officers for direction and orders. If things weren't brought under control soon, people would begin jumping overboard.

Boom! The signal cannon fired. The surprise report brought a moment's respite and a pause for confused passengers and crew, like a signal to remain calm and orderly. Without warning, the *Prince Rupert* shuddered. Everyone felt it, and then the ship's motion stopped. The *Prince Rupert* ran firmly aground on Mouille Point.

Captain Ramage's decision to fire the signal cannon probably saved the lives of many people that night. Only two miles away, further into Table Bay, the Indiaman *Bucephalus* was at anchor and saw the flash of the cannon from the stricken *Prince Rupert*. Immediately, a boat was launched to come to her aid.

William Spain and his family huddled on deck amid the disorder and fear. The captain had quickly briefed his assembled officers and told them what was required of them. Crewmen finally began to respond to commands, and order was once again restored as they informed passengers and issued instructions. Everyone was to leave the stricken ship. Amongst the clatter of winches and pulleys, boats were slowly lowered, and passengers prepared to disembark.

"Women and children first!" yelled a seaman over the noise.

Within moments, others echoed the cry as men began ushering their wives and children closer to the rail. William followed suit, helping his family over the side. Before long, the first boats were full. He watched as oars dipped into the water and the boats slowly pulled away, taking his family with them. He wondered if he'd ever see them again – but at least they were safe. He offered a small prayer of thanks and began assisting others, helping them into the boats and lowering crying children into the raised arms of fretful women below, seated in tiny bobbing boats.

The *Prince Rupert* was stuck fast. As water continued to flood into the ship, she settled immovably, sinking further onto the point of land that held her so tightly.

The *Bucephalus'* long boat made three trips, rescuing about thirty people in total. On the last trip, believing everyone had been rescued, someone thought they had seen people still aboard the *Prince Rupert*. After unloading the survivors, the boat, with a crew of seven, immediately headed back out. On arriving at the *Prince Rupert*, they manoeuvred nearer to the stern, where the reported people had been last seen. Moving in close, a large wave caught them unawares, swamping them. No one saw the very next wave that lifted and flipped the rescue boat, causing it to capsize. All went overboard, and three men lost their lives. All were crewmen from the *Bucephalus*.

CHAPTER THIRTY–ONE

Wellington.

The cold wind whistled through the cracks in the building, rain smeared the windows, and water drops splashed onto the rough wooden floor from a leaky roof. Occasionally, the building would shake as a powerful gust gripped the hotel, as if deliberately trying to shake it loose from its foundations. In concern, Richard Barrett looked up, expecting the roof to lift and be torn away. He was sure he could see the windows bending as the wind assaulted them. He turned the collar of his coat up, a cold draft chilling him as he sat in his small upstairs office.

His contact in London, George Whiting, had sent another letter, his last, informing him that all had gone according to plan, that the *Prince Rupert* had sailed from Gravesend, and that she should encounter difficulty one month into her voyage. Barrett did the calculations. It had taken sixteen weeks to receive this letter, and the *Prince Rupert* had sailed at the same time. If George was correct, news of the mishap should reach Wellington fairly soon. On the other hand, if George was wrong and his man had failed to sabotage the ship, the *Prince Rupert* would be sailing into Wellington any day.

Thankfully, Colonel Wakefield had not mentioned the arrangement since the day he handed him the money. To have done so would only have added more stress and tension to his life. He had more than enough mounting pressures as it was. The colonel was expecting a delay in the arrival, while Barrett wasn't expecting William Spain to arrive at all. Much hung in the balance, including his own reputation, income, and the influence he had with the Company and settlers, all of which were in jeopardy. So far, so good. Another week or two, and news should arrive of the fate of William Spain and the *Prince Rupert.* Or so he hoped. He placed Whiting's letter amongst the clutter on the desk and turned his attention to other matters.

Dickie felt like a trapped wild animal, yes, like a whale being hunted. He gave them a fleeting moment of sympathy. Enemies were coming at him from different quarters, seeking his blood and wanting his head - harpoons at the ready, waiting for him to surface. He admitted that he had erred, making a grave mistake in slaughtering the Stewarts' damn sow. At the time, it seemed a good way to threaten the Stewarts, a subtle hint encouraging them to distance themselves from Māori and stop interfering in his business. Now Māori welcomed the Stewarts as if they were family. Wherever the Stewarts went, Māori lurked in the shadows nearby, and two of his best men were now crippled and useless. Things would have been considerably different if they had succeeded in throwing Andrew Stewart's body into the ocean that night.

How was he to know that Chief Te Rauparaha would have attended Ngaiti's funeral, and that, of all things, Ngaiti turned out to be the chief's son? He could kick himself.

He allowed himself some joy and laughed out loud. How he would have loved to have witnessed the Stewarts' reaction when they saw their slaughtered pig. But now he had incurred the wrath of both Chief Te Rauparaha and Chief Te Wharepouri. There was little he could do against the older chief; he was far too powerful, but Te Wharepouri was a different matter.

It would serve more than one purpose to have him taken care of. Te Wharepouri would testify against him at the Land Court hearings; he was sure of it. And now, whenever he needed Māori help, they went out of their way to make life difficult for him. They deliberately delayed his deliveries and shipments, and broken agreements cost him dearly. Also, with Te Wharepouri out of the way, the Stewarts would no longer be protected.

It would have been perfect to have the Stewarts dismissed from Colonel Wakefield's service, but the young man had proven himself too good at his job. Already, he'd saved the New Zealand Company considerable expense by performing the work of more than two men. The colonel was always glowing with pride and never failed to remind everyone how fortunate he was to have such a skilled and dedicated accountant.

The moment he spoke to Wakefield about the Stewart man, it would draw attention to his other enterprises and commercial activities in Wellington that the colonel would neither support nor tolerate. Wakefield was a naïve and gullible fool, thought Barrett with disgust. There is nothing worse than the superior moral convictions of a reformed felon.

Everyone took advantage of the colonel; they'd pulled the wool over his eyes and used him. Even the esteemed Company Board of Directors had practically deserted him. Not wanting much more to do with the Company, Wakefield's own brother had fled to Canada. As long as there was money to be made and opportunities to follow, he would avail himself of them and remain indispensable to the New Zealand Company and Colonel Wakefield. Barrett sat back in his chair, smug, the rain and wind temporarily forgotten. If it hadn't been for him, the New Zealand Company would not have achieved the financial successes it had already realised.

With a sigh, Barrett stood and walked out of his tiny office, his thoughts turning to other things, such as how to prevent Chief Te Wharepouri from destroying everything he had worked so hard to achieve. … He had an idea…

CHAPTER THIRTY–TWO

Wakefield Office and Residence, Thorndon.

Andrew looked up from his work at the commotion at the entrance. Colonel Wakefield's private secretary was arguing with someone. Not an unusual occurrence these days.

The outer office door flew open, and Dickie Barrett strode in.

"Colonel Wakefield has left precise instructions not to be disturbed, Mister Barrett. I implore you to desist from your unannounced visits and make an appointment like everyone else," pleaded the secretary.

Barrett was grinning and ignored the secretary, who followed close behind, flapping his arms in indignation.

"Ah, Mister Stewart, how are you today?" said Barrett with a smirk. "And how was your lovely sow?"

Andrew was stung.

"It's difficult to tell you both apart," replied Andrew quickly.

Barrett's smile vanished as he strode past Andrew, knocked once on Wakefield's door and walked in.

The secretary turned to Andrew for help.

"It's quite alright, Mister Simpkins, carry on," called the colonel to his secretary through the open door.

"That man is intolerable," whispered Simpkins to Andrew as he returned to his desk outside.

Dickie threw a folded newspaper onto Wakefield's desk.

"Have you seen this?" Barrett asked, jabbing his pudgy finger at an article. "Read it, sir."

Warily, the colonel picked up the South African newspaper, '*The Cape Government Gazette*'. As always, the colonel checked the date. It was a recent edition and must have been brought over on a packet ship, he thought. He looked down at the article Barrett indicated as Dickie sat down, smiling. The earlier rebuke from Andrew forgotten.

> *WRECK OF THE PRINCE RUPERT.*
> *On the 4th September (1841), the Prince Rupert, from London, with one hundred and sixty passengers and cargo for New Zealand, in entering Table Bay, about nine o'clock in the evening, ran aground on Mouille Point, stuck fast, and be-came a total wreck. When the Prince Rupert struck, about fifteen minutes past nine o'clock, she was, on firing a gun, observed from the Bucephalus, Indiaman, at anchor about two miles from the point, within the Bay.*

"The *Prince Rupert* met with a mishap!" Barrett said smugly, his hands folded across his ample belly and his short legs stretched out before him.

The colonel looked up from the newspaper.

"How many people on the *Prince Rupert* lost their lives, Dickie?" asked the colonel, concern creeping into his voice.

"I don't know, sir. It was an unfortunate accident, and I hope all passengers were rescued. However, sadly, I may add, three crewmen from the rescue ship lost their lives. It says so right there, sir."

"What of Spain and his family?"

"I have no news of their well-being. Let's hope they survived the ordeal and are being taken care of."

Colonel Wakefield lowered his head in thought. After a moment's reflection, he looked up. "If the Spain family survived, when is it likely they would arrive in New Zealand?"

"I'd be guessing, but I reckon it's perhaps in late November or December. Does this unfortunate delay ease the burden somewhat, Colonel?"

Andrew was listening intently. Amid the excitement, Barrett had forgotten to close the door, and Andrew moved closer to better overhear the conversation.

"Let's hope so, Dickie, let's hope so," said the colonel, deep in thought. "Oh yes, and good work. As always, you came through as promised." The colonel smiled.

"I hopes you never doubted me sir?"

"No, no, of course not, Dickie. Now, if you'll excuse me, I have to attend an engagement of some importance. I mustn't be tardy," said Colonel Wakefield as he led Barrett from the office, past a very busy accountant who did not look up from his work. On reaching the outer door, Wakefield turned back to look at Andrew.

"Do you need me for anything, Mister Stewart? I shan't return until later this evening."

"Uh, oh no, sir, all is well," said Andrew.

Colonel Wakefield closed the door, and Andrew immediately opened a drawer on his desk and began searching for a document. After a brief search, he found what he'd been looking for. It was a rather peculiar, basic receipt listing translation fees of one hundred pounds, written and issued by Barrett, with *Prince Rupert* scrawled across the top in the colonel's handwriting.

Andrew waited a few minutes to ensure the colonel did not return, then hurried to Wakefield's office and found the newspaper. He returned to his desk and began searching for the article Barrett had referenced.

"It doesn't prove anything, Andrew," Isaac Featherston said. "And what you have isn't enough to seek any form of recourse from a magistrate or anyone else, for that matter."

"I believe it's likely that both of them are involved, Isaac. And I wouldn't put it past them to cook up a scheme to prevent the land commissioner from doing his duty," said Bethia as she fed their youngest.

"Bethia's right, you know. Barrett has every reason not to want to see the Commissioner arrive in New Zealand," Eleanor responded.

"I agree with you all, but this is still not evidence," Isaac said. "The most you can gather from what Andrew's discovered is that Barrett and William will do anything to safeguard their own interests – and you can't prove a thing."

"So, what can I do?" asked Andrew. "I know what I heard in his office. Somehow, both of them were involved in that wreck."

"Be bloody careful," replied Isaac.

They sat in the cramped living room of Isaac and Bethia Featherston's small cottage, which stood at the foot of a large hill overlooking Thorndon.

"Look at the people who have been or are in a position to harm Barrett," Isaac said thoughtfully. "Ngaiti, William Spain, and Chief Te Wharepouri!"

"What about Andy?" asked Eleanor.

"Andy's a nuisance, nothing more," Isaac replied.

"Thank you very much," Andrew feigned, looking hurt.

"But Ngaiti is dead, Te Wharepouri is alive, … and Spain? We don't know yet. I think the chief needs to be concerned. If something were to happen to him, that would help Barrett and the Company tremendously."

"Then I will go to the chief and tell him to be careful, in case Barrett wants to harm him," Andrew said.

"Yes, but this time, have him come to you. Last time, you almost ended up going for a swim," Bethia said.

CHAPTER THIRTY–THREE

Te Awaiti Whaling Station, Marlborough Sounds

The smell hit Dickie like a brick. He'd been away from here too long and was no longer accustomed to the stench that pervaded everything. It repulsed him more than at any time before. Perhaps it was age, he thought. As a younger man, the stink had not bothered him much at all - no, he decided, he wasn't old, just getting soft.

"The two men accompanying Dickie, his associates, had never been to a whaling station and looked uncomfortable. The smell assaulted the newcomers to this land with the subtlety of a right cross – something they were familiar with."

"Harden up, lads. Better get used to it. We'll only be here a couple of days at most," said Dickie, trudging up the beach, laughing.

Richard Barrett spent many years living in Te Awaiti. He was not a man of superior physical ability and therefore was not suited to the rigours and lifestyle of whaling. To survive, he relied entirely on cunning and intelligence, having accumulated his modest but adequate wealth through productive investments, buying cheap and selling high, and exploiting whalers' needs. In the early years, he'd received his share of beatings and endured hardship, but quickly realised that as long as he never posed an obvious threat or openly challenged the hardened whalers, he could make his life more tolerable. This was why Dickie was seen as a jovial and agreeable gent, always willing to share a laugh, tell a story, and offer a smile. From time to time, he'd even helped people.

As a trader, he supplied goods and merchandise to those who could afford them. To those who couldn't, he would extend credit, and his terms were always fair. If he were perceived as a scoundrel, his stay here would have been short-lived, and he would most likely have been dumped unceremoniously in a *trypot* and boiled.

He sold rum cheaply and other necessities at higher prices, claiming that shipping expenses raised his costs. When whalers spent most of their hard-earned money on rum and women, there was little left to buy other slightly overpriced essentials, namely food, which he also sold. Dickie, being a generous fellow, provided credit, which ensured the debtor remained in the area, working and continuing to purchase rum and other merchandise from him. The cycle continued.

This was one of the reasons Dickie decided to pay a visit to Te Awaiti.

Claude Arnoult, known locally as Claude de Fraud, had been whaling at Te Awaiti for about five years. No one could really remember when he first arrived, but it was suggested his ship departed in haste, deliberately leaving Claude marooned. At first, Claude proved hard-working and likeable. He held his own in a few brawls, gained some respect, and worked as hard as anyone could expect. In whaling, a man was paid according to his yield. Shares of the whaling station's profits were divided among all the whalers according to experience and productivity. Hard work was rewarded, and everyone was paid fairly.

Like many whalers, Claude took a lay wife, a young Māori woman named Kaia. She cooked his meals, provided comfort, washed his clothes occasionally, and enjoyed cheap rum as much as he did. In return, Claude provided her family with a small stipend, ensuring her loyalty and devotion.

The problems for Claude began innocuously. After another night of heavy drinking, Kaia suggested, on a cold morning, that he stay in bed, continue drinking and not go to work. Influenced by intoxication and a warm body beside him, he couldn't think of any good reason to disagree. It didn't take long before this routine and intoxication became habitual. His productivity fell and his debts mounted. When Kaia's family arrived for a friendly social visit and to be paid, they returned home empty-handed. This didn't bode well for Claude or Kaia.

Because Claude was reasonably well-liked, he was able to borrow a little money here and there, always with a sincere promise to repay the small loans promptly. Sadly, for Claude, he failed to honour his promises, favouring inebriation over slaughtering whales. Kaia's family insisted she return home or find another, more suitable and financially secure man to love. She left Claude wallowing in self-pity and despair, which earned him the moniker Claude de Fraud.

More recently, Claude had turned over a new leaf and begun working again, slowly repaying his debt, but still leaving a considerable sum of thirty pounds owed to his major creditor, Dickie Barrett.

It was Claude that Dickie had decided to pay a visit to.

Claude was near the beach, stirring the boiling whale blubber in one of the *trypots,* a physically exhausting and demanding job. He wasn't too happy when Dickie approached him. Barrett's two associates loitered close by, ensuring the discussion remained friendly and that Dickie wasn't mistaken for a whale and disposed of in a similar fashion.

After considering various options, it was decided that Claude would offer a cow he owned as partial payment toward settling the debt. He also had a little money in his pocket, which he handed over. It was agreed that he could expect Dickie to return to the whaling station in the near future to receive the balance. Dickie bid farewell to the scowling whaler with a friendly wave and headed away from the beach towards the cluster of huts to inspect his new cow. His associates, hoping for some olfactory relief, eagerly followed.

Dickie followed Claude's instructions on where he could find the cow, and, stopping occasionally to offer a friendly greeting to the locals, he eventually located the animal. To the amusement of onlookers, who doubted Dickie Barrett could tell one end of a cow from the other, he performed a reasonably thorough inspection of the beast and declared her healthy. Satisfied with his new acquisition, he decided it was time to attend to the other important matter that brought him to Te Awaiti.

As Barrett wearily struggled up the track and into the hills surrounding the whaling station, he considered his priorities. He had to avoid suspicion, safeguard himself against anyone who could be a witness and point a finger at him, and, more importantly, prevent the public from seeing him display any open hostility or animosity towards his target. To accomplish this, he needed to use guile and cunning, dealing with each problem from afar – one at a time. This was how he had achieved previous successes, and he would do so again.

Taking a moment to catch his breath, he stopped, removed his jacket, and wiped his brow. It wasn't hot today, but for the decidedly unfit and overweight man, the exertion posed an unpleasant physical challenge.

"How much further, Dickie?" asked one of his companions, who followed about ten yards behind.

"For you two, not far," replied Dickie. "See that tree up the track? Wait there for me until I return."

"How long will ya be?"

"As long as it takes!" Dickie muttered obscenities under his breath, questioning the man's lineage and his mother's occupation.

"Righto," the man yelled back.

With a heavy sigh, Dickie turned and continued on his way, leaving his two associates beneath the tree.

"Think I'll take a wee kip while we wait for his lordship to return, eh," whispered one of the men to the other with a grin.

"Think I'll do the same," snickered the other, already making himself comfortable.

Dickie continued up the track and looked back. He could see his associates settling down under the tree, which suited him perfectly. He didn't want anyone seeing where he was going or whom he was going to visit.

The person who posed the greatest danger to Dickie was Chief Te Wharepouri, and he was the reason Dickie was here now.

Dickie stopped, looked around carefully to make sure no one was following him, then turned off the main track onto a small, almost hidden path that could easily have been overlooked. He decided to rest for a moment or two in the shade of a large tree and collect his thoughts.

He hated physical exertion and would have taken a horse, but doing so would have raised questions he didn't want to answer. The fewer people who knew where he was going, the better, and so far, no one did. Small rivulets of sweat trickled down his back, and he reached around to scratch.

He was doing this to preserve his name, reputation, and, of course, business interests. The Governor was forcing his hand, and, like a cornered wild animal, he would defend himself. You could be certain of that. George Whiting had saved him, at least temporarily, and although the attempt to prevent Spain from arriving in New Zealand had apparently failed, Colonel Wakefield was thrilled by the delay he had desperately desired. There was little chance of reaching Spain now, so the next best thing was Te Wharepouri.

Crouched behind some flax about twenty yards away, a young Māori watched Barrett as he sat and rested. He'd followed Barrett and his companions from the moment they arrived at the whaling station. There was no chance anyone would see him; he was an expert in bushcraft and stealth. Afterwards, when Barrett returned to Wellington, he would send a message about Barrett's movements to Chief Te Wharepouri, who, in turn, would pass any relevant information on to Chief Te Rauparaha.

The young Māori considered killing Barrett, which he could do easily and quickly, but he'd only been told to watch and follow. Had both chiefs known Barrett would expose himself like this, they might have taken advantage of the opportunity and had him slain. There were plenty of *pakeha* at Te Awaiti with motive, and Māori would never have been suspected or blamed.

Feeling rested, Barrett eased himself to his feet and resumed his slow pace along the path towards the valley floor.

The young Māori following him stopped, his stomach tightening in knots. He would go no further. He knew where Barrett was going and was frightened. Rather than continue, he would find a safe position and wait for his return, but he would not go where Barrett was headed.

Barrett was apprehensive, his mouth suddenly dry.

"You're late!"

Barrett almost jumped, surprised by the voice.

"How can I be late when you didn't even know I was coming here?"

Birds scattered at the sound of laughter, shrill and unnerving.

"I knew you were coming before you had even made up your mind," she said, stepping from the shadow of a tree. She turned away from him and walked towards a low hut nestled in the floor of the tiny hidden valley. Barrett followed tentatively.

Her name was Missy, no last name - just Missy. As far as Dickie could remember, that's what she'd always been called. It was difficult to assess her age; she was somewhere between thirty and fifty. A few times, Dickie had seen her looking young and almost attractive; other times, she looked old, frail and haggard. As with many Māori women, it was difficult to tell her age.

A young girl, perhaps about fifteen, crawled out of the low opening of the hut. She spoke briefly to Missy in *Te Reo*, then went back inside. Missy walked to a large log, worn smooth by constant use, that served as a seat near a fire pit, and sat down; she turned her attention to Barrett.

Her English was good. She had learned the language from the whalers and European visitors. Some said she could also speak French, which wouldn't have surprised him; actually, nothing this woman did surprised him, as a witch, she could do anything. Not normally superstitious or a believer in the occult or black magic, Dickie was a logical man and therefore everything had a rational explanation. But with Missy, she defied that reasoning. Most people at Te Awaiti treated her with respect or fear and kept their distance unless, of course, they needed her skills – and they frequently did.

Māori called her a *tohunga makutu,* an expert in the underworld and magic, and she was also a priestess in the cult of *Io.* Whenever a Māori died, she would prepare the body and provide spiritual cleansing – she would even do it for *pakeha*. Missy's young apprentice reappeared with a bowl of food, sat in front of Missy, and began to feed her. Because she handled the dead, Missy wouldn't touch the food she put into her body.

Dickie watched, feeling unsure and very uncomfortable.

"Sit, Dickie," she said between mouthfuls, pointing to a nearby mat.

Gratefully, Barrett lowered himself, sat awkwardly, and watched her carefully as she finished her meal.

After a few moments, the young apprentice returned to the hut, and Missy reached behind her and gathered a handful of slender sticks, each about six inches long. She placed some in the ground and balanced others on top. Some sticks fell to the ground, and Missy peered closely, bending forward to see how they fell. This was the *Niu* divinatory rite, and she used it to obtain knowledge and answers. The sticks' fall and position told Missy what she wanted to know. With a cackle, she gathered the sticks, returned them behind the log where she sat, and looked at Dickie, who was nervously licking his lips.

"You were foolish to come here today," she admonished him.

Barrett said nothing, surprised at her assertion.

"You don't want anyone to see you come here, yet you were followed." Missy looked from Barrett into the bush surrounding them, her eyes fixed, moving slowly across the small, bush-covered valley.

"Oh, those two men are with me," said Dickie somewhat relieved.

"Those fools sleep," she said dismissively, "there is another, but wisely he keeps his distance."

Barrett quickly stood, following Missy's gaze.

She laughed. "Do not worry. If he were going to harm you, he would already have done so. He is too clever for you to see him. He waits in the shadow of a Rata tree for your return."

Barrett sat back down with a grunt, concerned about Missy's claim.

She turned and spoke over her shoulder. Within seconds, the young apprentice appeared with a cup of water, which she handed to Barrett. Immediately, he held the cup to his lips and drained it in one gulp.

He wiped his mouth with the back of his hand and looked at the peculiar woman. "I, uh, have a small problem that I believe you may be able to help with." He paused, looking towards the hut where the young girl was.

"She will say nothing," cackled the witch. She kept her eyes fixed on him, her own searching, probing, unblinking and intense.

"I wish to have someone killed in a way that looks natural, so that I cannot be blamed or even suspected of involvement in his death. I need this done as soon as possible." He couldn't meet her gaze and looked away.

"You are not a brave man; do you fear to do battle with him whom you wish to meet in death?"

Stung by the accusation, Barrett turned to her. "You have the knowledge to make this happen. I know you do. You worship that God of yours, *Io,* and even you have a price, as does everyone."

With fury, Missy stood and pointed a bony finger at him. "You will not speak of Him! You will not blaspheme his name with your mouth, and you will show respect, or I will not help you! You know nothing of this - and so it should be! Never, ever utter those words again," she warned. "Perhaps I should just leave your carcass for the dogs and rats who feed at the beach!" she spat. She slowly returned to her log, her eyes locked on Barrett's as her anger subsided. "You're a fool."

"I haven't come here to cause you any offence, Missy. I came because I hoped you could help me," Barrett offered in a conciliatory tone, flashing his trademark smile.

"You dishonour me if you think you can hide your nature and your *wairua*[7] from me. I see who you are, Dickie Barrett. You cannot hide behind your white teeth and false smile."

"I apologise, again, I meant you no offence."

Missy remained quiet, continuing her assessment. After a brief pause, she shifted her position on the log. "Why do you wish to see this man killed?"

Having anticipated the question, Barrett replied quickly, "He poses a threat to my future in the town, to my name and my business. He seeks me ill fortune."

Missy nodded, pulling a loose thread from the old dress she wore, considering Barrett's request.

"I can do this for you, but as you said, I have a price, and what you ask is not easy and will be expensive."

---

[7] *Wairua – Spirit or soul*

Barrett nodded.

"Can you get close to him?"

"No, I cannot, but I have someone who can."

"This is good, Dickie."

"Then you will help me?" he asked. "What do you want in return?"

"Causing this person's death as you wish will not be easy and will take some time. For this, you will give me your cow."

Barrett had only just acquired the milking cow. How could she possibly know about it? His expression must have given away his thoughts.

Missy laughed, the piercing sound only making him more uncomfortable. "Do you believe I don't know what goes on around here? You underestimate me."

Barrett turned and looked down at the ground at his feet. She wanted his milking cow. He thought about it quickly, an easy decision. What was he going to do with a milking cow, anyway?

"Yes, I agree, you can have the cow. And how will you cause this man's death?"

"*Kōpī.*"

"Talk to me so I can understand," pleaded Barrett.

"The man you wish to die will be poisoned by the seed of the Karaka tree. It is a slow death that will appear natural, just as you desire, and no one will suspect poison. Not even the *pakeha* men who treat the sick will know."

"Poison! I don't want him to die of poison. The moment he complains of any stomach cramps, they will cure it. It won't work."

"This poison will not affect his stomach much; it will affect his mind," Missy said with easy confidence. "You will need to add the poison to his food over time. He will begin to have problems walking and moving, and eventually his mind will go."

"Good, then give me the poison and I will be on my way," said Dickie, eager to be gone.

"You will come here in one month, and I will have your poison for you," she said. "The Karaka tree I seek is not close by, and I must travel some distance to obtain it."

Dickie was about to interrupt when Missy raised her hand, stopping him.

"Some Karaka trees contain more poison than others, and I know of a tree whose poison is more potent than most. I must dry and crush the seeds, and then you can have your poison," she said.

"One month?"

Missy pulled an old clay pipe from the folds of her dress. She slowly packed the bowl and lit it, enveloping them both in a cloud of smoke. It didn't smell like ordinary tobacco, he thought.

"Yes, one month," she replied once her pipe was lit.

"Will it take effect quickly?"

"Oh yes, as long as you follow my instructions. Come back in a month, Dickie," said Missy with a smile, gently rocking backwards and forwards on her log.

It wouldn't take anywhere near a month to prepare the poison, but having her customers wait a month allowed time to cool off, and often they changed their minds.

Barrett stood, easing his joints after lying on the uncomfortable mat. "Do you know where the cow is?"

"I do."

"Good day to you, then, Missy. I shall return in a month."

Feeling a chill, Dickie put on his coat and walked slowly back up the path. He could hear Missy's laugh following him out.

"What did *Niu* say?" asked the apprentice, who had come out from where she had been quietly observing just inside the shadows of the hut's doorway.

Missy exhaled a cloud of smoke before she replied. "Like the smoke, it goes where it wants. Sometimes we can't foresee the direction we want it to take. Just like Dickie's life, he is planning for it to go this way," Missy swept her arm across her body. "*Niu* showed me it will go that way," she swept her arm in the opposite direction.

"He spoke of *Io*. Can you tell me more about this?"

Missy's anger began to rise. Remembering that the young girl was a student eager to learn, she took a deep breath and spoke calmly. "There will come a time when this becomes known to you. Until then, you must never speak that name again, not to me or anyone."

The young girl nodded, her eyes wide.

"And never speak that name under the roof of a building, do you hear me?" insisted Missy, her eyes fixed on the innocent face before her.

She nodded again.

Missy patted her head in understanding, "Come, we have a journey to make, we must prepare."

Dickie was pleased to leave Missy. She unsettled him; indeed, she frightened him and made him feel very exposed. But he did have faith in her skill to deliver him a powerful poison, and if what she said was true, it was worth a milking cow. He looked around, hoping to catch sight of the person the witch had said was following him, but he could see or hear nothing. Just a crazy old woman, he thought.

Within ten minutes, he was kicking his two associates awake and continued down the track back to the small whaling community.

CHAPTER THIRTY–FOUR

Thorndon, Wellington.

Andrew knocked once on Colonel Wakefield's door and paused.

"Enter," came the response.

He saw the colonel was absorbed in a letter he was writing.

Wakefield was frustrated and again corresponded with the Board of Directors about the latest developments. Governor Hobson had decided to make Auckland the capital of New Zealand. What a preposterous notion, thought Wakefield. Its location in the North was entirely unsuitable, and the only reason Hobson had not chosen Wellington was his personal animosity towards the New Zealand Company - Wellington should have been the capital.

His frequent letters amounted to nought. The last letter of real significance had been from prominent colonists, on Wakefield's urging, who wrote to Her Majesty, Queen Victoria, protesting Governor Hobson's behaviour and the unrest caused by his meddling. The colonists who had invested heavily in New Zealand were now in danger of losing title to the lands they had purchased because of Hobson's insistence that the land had been obtained illegally. The reply from Her Majesty had been unwelcome and stated that Hobson would remain as Governor and that the Crown had the utmost faith in the appointment of Lord Russell and stood behind his decisions.

Andrew looked around the room casually as he waited for the colonel to finish what he was doing. Maps and plans cluttered the walls, and a few ornaments sat on a credenza alongside a sabre. Andrew wondered how many men the colonel had slaughtered with it and whether any had been accountants. He'd seen all these items many times before, but his curious mind always looked for what was new and different when he entered the colonel's office. Wakefield's pen continued to scratch as Andrew patiently looked on. With a flourish, Wakefield signed the letter and returned the stylus to its holder. He pushed the letter aside and looked up for the first time.

"Mister Stewart, how may I help you?"

"I apologise for disturbing you, sir, but I need clarification on this receipt. I need a date."

"Let me see," said the colonel, thrusting his hand out. "Oh, …ah, yes."

Andrew noticed the briefest flash of concern pass across Wakefield's face as he handed the document over.

"No need to concern yourself with it, just use any date that comes to mind," replied Wakefield with a smile, hoping to mollify his accountant. "It matters not."

"Excuse me, sir, but it does matter. It's a considerable sum of money, and I need to register the precise date on which that money was debited from the company's accounts. Failure to -"

"Yes, yes," interrupted Wakefield. He turned to his personal journal and flicked back through the pages. "December 4th, 1840, I believe," he said after a few moments.

"Are you sure of this?"

"Yes, of course I am. Do you doubt my powers of recollection, Mister Stewart?"

"No, sir, this receipt represents a considerable amount of money. If an error is made, this will have severe consequences for reconciling the ledger," Andrew replied.

"December 4th, 1840, as I said, Mister Stewart," replied the colonel dismissively. "Anything else?"

"Actually sir, there is."

Wakefield waved his hand repeatedly, impatiently urging Andrew to continue.

"I have yet to encounter a receipt that lists such a substantial amount for services described as translation fees. Could this receipt have been written in error?"

"Unlikely, seems accurate to me," Wakefield replied, becoming more uncomfortable by the minute. "That will be all."

Andrew's natural gift for recalling numbers had now become evident.

"Sir, since the Company has retained the services of Mister Barrett as a translator," Andrew paused briefly to verify the figures in his head. "He has submitted invoices totalling three hundred and forty-one pounds over a period of twenty-four months. That's an average invoice total of approximately fourteen pounds and change. This receipt is unusual in that respect, is it not?"

Wakefield was shocked by Andrew's ability to recall these numbers at will. This conversation was heading in a direction he did not want to go, and he was certainly discomfited by his accountant raising this issue.

"Mister Stewart! May I remind you of your responsibilities to this company? It is not within your station to question or comment on confidential matters. I don't care whether you approve of this transaction. If this receipt is for one pound or one thousand pounds, it is, frankly, not your concern!" Wakefield's face had turned scarlet, and his outburst surprised him as much as Andrew. He glowered at Andrew, who remained standing.

Not intimidated by the colonel's demeanour, Andrew continued pressing his point. "Why would Mister Barrett be translating for a ship that had yet to depart from England, and why would he be translating about it at all? It's not possible for Mr Barrett to have been acting as a translator or to have had anything to do with the Prince Rupert long before she ever departed England. He was here in New Zealand. Sir, it is my opinion that this receipt is incorrect or false, and as a Company accountant, it is my responsibility to bring this to your attention." Andrew kept his voice respectful and waited for the colonel to respond.

Wakefield's knuckles were white as he gripped the arms of his chair. He glowered at him, unsure how to respond. Deep down, he knew his bookkeeper was correct, but he could not allow this conversation to escalate into more questions he was unwilling to answer and could not answer without implicating himself. He was caught out.

"Return to your desk. I will double-check my records to verify everything is as it should be," Wakefield said curtly.

"Yes sir," replied Andrew taking the receipt with him and returning to his desk.

A few moments later, Colonel Wakefield left his office and walked past Andrew without saying a word. Andrew couldn't help but grin.

William Wakefield returned to his private residence and paced the drawing room. He was in a spot of bother and wasn't sure how best to resolve the issue. A simple receipt and a mere accountant challenging its validity were outrageous. The facts recounted by Stewart were accurate, and his reasoning was logical, demonstrating an inquiring mind that Wakefield could only be impressed by. Certainly, his uncanny ability to recall dates and numbers at will from memory was astonishing.

Wakefield knew he had erred in having Barrett write that receipt. It should never have happened, and he had underestimated his bookkeeper. Should he simply order Stewart to enter the receipt information into the Company records and leave the matter alone? Certainly, the obvious solution. However, if Stewart pushed the issue, this could expose his involvement and the true purpose of the one hundred pounds he had funded Barrett with. What information could he give Stewart to satisfy him that the receipt was genuine?

Or perhaps there was another way. Something he should have done from the beginning, when Barrett first proposed delaying that confounded ship. Perhaps it would be wise, and before he did anything rash, he should talk to Dickie first.

Doctor Isaac Featherston, his very pregnant wife Bethia, and their daughter were in the company of Andrew and Eleanor. They were all spectators at an informal game of cricket being played on one of the rare patches of flat ground in Thorndon. The sun shone, but a crisp, mild southerly wind kept the temperature fresh. While far from a manicured cricket oval they were used to, the Thorndon pitch had received some attention when a few people with shovels had made a reasonable effort to improve it. They smoothed divots, filled puddles, and chased away the sheep that had eaten the grass to an acceptable height for a spirited game of cricket, one that demonstrated more fervour than flair, as Andrew observed.

They arrived a short time ago and settled on blankets, far enough away that the odd ball coming their way would not interfere or pose a danger. Andrew again, with his usual tact, suggested that it was unlikely any batsmen had the necessary skills to hit a 'six', let alone belt the ball in their direction.

They burst out in laughter as Andrew told of his meeting with Colonel Wakefield the previous day.

"Andy, I can't believe you provoked the colonel. You were fortunate you weren't dismissed," said Eleanor, shaking her head at Andrew with a smile.

"Do you truly believe the receipt you mention implicates Wakefield and Barrett in the *Prince Rupert*'s grounding?" asked Isaac.

"Yes, I do. That receipt was never meant to be questioned. It was created purely to account for the debit of one hundred pounds. The colonel was beside himself and was struggling to explain it to me," laughed Andrew. "I almost felt sorry for him."

"Does it prove anything, Andrew?" Bethia asked as she and Eleanor played with the child between them.

"No, it doesn't prove a thing," Andrew replied dejectedly.

"Do you not have a responsibility to tell someone about it?" Eleanor asked.

"Who would he tell, and who would listen?" added Isaac.

"I will tell Chief Te Wharepouri," Andrew said.

"Does this put you at greater risk? What if Wakefield finds out and tells Barrett? This may prompt him to take further action against you," Bethia suggested.

"Yes, I had considered that," said Andrew, looking at Eleanor. "Perhaps it is safer to do nothing, and perhaps more information may come to light that could prove something if we wait."

"Perhaps when Spain arrives, you could at least tell him. He should be informed of this if people are plotting against him."

Andrew nodded in agreement.

"I may have a quiet word with William. As friends, I can talk with him, and he may say enough to me that I can warn him to be careful." Isaac said.

"He won't say anything to you, dear," Bethia said. "He'll try to sell you another piece of land, as he did last time. We still haven't been able to sell that piece of swampland in Britannia, which we first bought when we arrived. Remind him of that!"

"I fear Colonel William Wakefield is less of a man than I thought he was," Isaac said glumly. "I succumbed to his silky overtures and polished rhetoric; he misled us with shallow promises and lies, all in the guise of friendship." Isaac paused, thoughtful. "Is not a true friend one who genuinely cares for your well-being and enjoys your company?" Isaac turned to look at the faces around him. "Someone who uses friendship to advance his own self-interests is not a friend."

Andrew and Eleanor looked at each other.

"I agree, Isaac, they are not friends, just someone you know, an acquaintance," Andrew volunteered.

"I feel William Wakefield exploited us." Isaac turned to his wife.

A mis-hit ball tumbled along the grass towards them, its progress slowed dramatically by the uneven pitch. The umpire signalled a 'four' to the derision of the fielding team, who began protesting loudly.

"Ah, the sport of gentlemen," Isaac said, laughing as the game halted temporarily while players on both teams separated the batsman and the bowler, who were about to come to blows.

"Speaking of gentlemen," said Eleanor, watching the umpire make a hasty retreat, "We received a letter this week. My uncle Charles will be relocating from Van Diemen's Land to Wellington soon. He will come alone, and once he has bought a home and a business, he will send for my aunt."

"That's wonderful news, Ellie," said Bethia. "You must be thrilled. Do you have a good relationship with him?"

Andrew laughed. "If you saw him, the mountain of a man he is, and spent a few minutes with him, you couldn't help but be drawn to him."

"What's his profession?" Isaac asked.

"Captain Charles Suisted owned a small shipping company but has fallen on hard times. I don't believe he wants to continue in that line of work any longer," Andrew replied.

"He's a lovely, caring man and I adore him," said Eleanor with a smile.

"And he is very protective of Ellie," volunteered Andrew.

Isaac nodded, "How fortunate." His interest piqued.

Order had been restored to the cricket match. The batting team had been denied the 'four' previously awarded to them by the umpire, who returned cautiously to his position. Play continued, though not without jeers and colourful comments questioning his eyesight and sobriety.

CHAPTER THIRTY–FIVE

Bay of Islands, Northern Island, New Zealand.

The William Spain family were all reunited after that fateful evening three months earlier, when their ship, the *Prince Rupert*, ran aground in Table Bay, South Africa. During their rescue, they were transferred by ship to Algoa Bay, where plans were made to continue their journey to New Zealand. Some possessions were lost, some were salvaged, but by the grace of God, the entire family was spared.

Eventually, the two-hundred-and-eighty-three-ton brig *Antilla* was chartered to transport the Spain family and others who had been displaced to New Zealand. A few passengers decided they'd had enough and would not continue their journey, instead choosing to remain in South Africa. To the immense relief of many, the *Antilla* arrived in Auckland on December 24th, 1841, nearly nine months after they first departed from Gravesend in London. The cause of *Prince Rupert*'s disaster was never fully ascertained, although initially the captain was held responsible. After an official inquiry into the accident, Captain Ramage and crew were acquitted of intentionally running the vessel aground. It was just a coincidence that Captain Ramage's previous ship, on which he was first mate, had also run aground in Table Bay exactly one year earlier.

William Spain arrived in Russell, northern New Zealand, eager to begin work after meeting Governor Hobson and being briefed on the New Zealand Company and the pending disputes and claims filed against it.

He sat anxiously in Hobson's outer office, waiting to be seen. Spain's wife, Mary, remained in Auckland with their children, resting and recovering from the perils of their long voyage. Lord Normanby had previously told Spain he might receive a tepid welcome from the Governor, as Hobson had insisted that any Land Claim hearings be settled internally, without interference from the Colonial Office in England. "Your appointment certainly ruffled Hobson's delicate feathers," the Lord told him. "Tread carefully, William."

Finally, Spain was admitted to see Governor Hobson. After polite pleasantries and a chat about the latest news from England, Hobson turned to the business at hand and informed Spain of the latest developments in the land claim disputes while he'd been in transit.

Spain observed Hobson, and while Hobson appeared alert and attentive, he could see the man was unwell and that the apoplexy he had suffered a year ago had taken something from him; he looked frail, but not without spirit.

"Are you aware, Commissioner Spain, that I was against your selection for this position?" stated Hobson matter-of-factly.

Surprised by the bluntness of the question, Spain was momentarily taken aback. He kept his expression neutral as he considered his response.

"Lord Normanby mentioned it in passing, sir."

"I see," said Hobson, rubbing his chin. "Did he also tell you that I had selected two exceptionally qualified gentlemen to represent the Crown at the hearings?" It was Hobson's turn to watch Spain, gauging his reaction.

Spain knew the Governor was testing him, assessing his loyalty and his ability.

"Are you questioning my attitude towards working in collaboration, sir?"

Now it was the Governor's turn to be surprised.

Spain continued, "Allow me to be more specific in my response." He leaned forward in his chair, meeting Hobson's gaze. "If the gentlemen you have chosen are as capable as you suggest, there is less likelihood that three proficient Commissioners will fail to serve the best interests of the Crown and the people of this fair country." Spain leaned back, maintaining eye contact with the Governor.

Hobson said nothing. Spain could see a vein pulsing in the Governor's neck as he chewed his bottom lip.

After a long, uncomfortable pause, Hobson placed both hands on his desk and stood. "I think we should have a refreshment, Mister Spain, or may I address you by your first name, William? Come," he ordered, gesturing with his arm and walking from the office through the door into the sunshine and warmth of the garden overlooking the bay.

Astonished, Spain followed to find the Governor already seated in a comfortable chair, his feet stretched out, his hands behind his head, looking out at the splendid view.

"My dear friend James Busby, an intolerable Scotsman, by the way, fancies himself a vintner, and he hopes I'll slowly succumb to his poison by leaving me with copious amounts of wine I can't possibly drink," said Hobson with a straight face. "Don't just stand there, man. Take a seat. You're putting me on edge."

Spain slowly eased himself into a comfortable chair and, for the first time in nine months, began to feel at ease. An attendant brought two glasses and a bottle of wine.

"So, William, how are we going to clean up the mess Colonel Wakefield has left us with?" Hobson said, flashing Spain a friendly smile.

"Very cautiously, sir. I understand that Māori are less than happy and quite volatile."

Hobson nodded thoughtfully, his glass of wine held to his lips as he pondered his reply.

"Perhaps I can offer some insights and background to aid your understanding of these rather delicate and infinitely complicated affairs."

Spain reached into his jacket and extracted a notebook.

"You can put that notebook away, William. The moment you stepped through that garden door, our official interview was over. We are now two friends enjoying the spectacular scenery and a quiet chat."

"Of course, sir," replied Spain, understanding that what the Governor intended to tell him was unofficial. He returned the notebook to his jacket.

"William!"

"Yes, sir?"

"No, damn it, address me as William," Hobson laughed, joined in by Spain.

Both men sipped their wine and gazed across the bay, enjoying the peacefulness.

"Māori do pose the biggest challenge for you, as they have for me too. Heaven knows I've upset them enough through silly errors on my part," began Hobson. "But all is not always as it first appears. The complex relationships of tribal allegiances and power among chiefs have complicated the issues before us. Look, let me explain it this way," Hobson repositioned himself as Spain listened closely.

"Wakefield purchased land around Wellington from a senior chief who claimed he controlled it. Wakefield never questioned whether that chief had the right to sell it, and he probably should have. However, within the Māori community, this wasn't so cut-and-dry. Lesser chiefs questioned the validity of the deed of sale and the senior chief's right to transfer ownership and control of large tracts of land to the New Zealand Company."

"I see, then the question is, who was the rightful owner of the land?" asked Spain.

"Yes, but it's not that simple. Just because a chief and his people live on a piece of land doesn't necessarily mean it's his to sell. He may have been granted permission by a more senior and powerful chief to live on that land, much like a landlord-tenant relationship. Another factor to consider is how long they have controlled and lived on the land. Perhaps it's not their ancestral lands, and another *iwi* has a claim on it."

"*Iwi*?" asked Spain.

"Tribe."

Spain nodded.

"So, ownership is not quite so obvious. Do you follow?"

"Yes, carry on."

The two chiefs pivotal to the Wellington land claim purchases are Chief Te Wharepouri of the Te Ati Awa *iwi* and Chief Te Rauparaha of the Ngati Toa *iwi*. Te Rauparaha is older, more powerful and a highly respected warrior. He lives about a day's ride from Wellington, outside the boundaries outlined in the Port Nicholson deed. He allowed Chief Te Wharepouri to take up residence in the Wellington area. It was Te Wharepouri and some other chiefs who live within those boundaries who sold the land to the New Zealand Company.

"If this is the case and Te Wharepouri knew the land wasn't his, why did he sell it? Was he greedy and tempted by gifts, or just stupid?" asked Spain.

"Ah, a good question, William. No, he isn't greedy, and as I've come to discover, he's not stupid, perhaps far from it. Actually, it wouldn't surprise me if Te Rauparaha and Te Wharepouri cooked up the whole damn scheme." Hobson turned to look closely at Spain. "Don't underestimate these men, William. They are not imbeciles."

Spain nodded thoughtfully.

"I'm led to believe that Chief Te Wharepouri wanted Europeans to live amongst his people because it would bring him peace. Other warring *iwi* would be less likely to attack Wellington if the land was inhabited by colonists and settlers protected by soldiers. So, Te Wharepouri was willing to sell large areas of land to the New Zealand Company if he could achieve this peace by allowing some Europeans to live there. And it appears he has succeeded, as no other Māori have since attacked Wellington."

"Then Te Wharepouri is an ally of ours?"

"Not entirely, William," said Hobson, emptying his glass. "Te Wharepouri is unhappy about the number of colonists and settlers who have settled on the land. He claims he was misled and that the New Zealand Company misrepresented the extent of the land sales to him. I believe Chief Te Wharepouri may actually have a legitimate grievance."

The attendant must have been observing closely as he brought another bottle of wine, filled both glasses, and removed the empty bottle.

"Surely, the terms of the land sale were made clear to him at the time of purchase," Spain suggested after taking another sip of Busby's wine. He found the rather bold flavour slightly unpleasant but was surprised to see how much the two of them had drunk in such a short time.

"You are correct, and Wakefield believes the same. The issue may lie in how the terms of the land purchase were explained to Māori through an inferior translation," offered Governor Hobson.

Spain nodded in understanding. "And what of the other Chief, Te Rauparaha, where does he stand in all this?"

"He's not thrilled at all; he has refused to sell any more land to the New Zealand Company. My understanding is that Te Wharepouri, who is doing his best to keep him from rising against us, is mollifying him. I believe Te Rauparaha's anger stems more from frustration than from abject hatred of Europeans, which is why Te Wharepouri has been successful so far, but that could change. However, I do believe we need to keep a close eye on Te Rauparaha and his nephew, young Chief Te Rangihaeata."

Hobson stood, stretching his back and legs.

"And what of the surveying?" William Spain asked, rising from the chair to stand beside the Governor.

"This is where Wakefield's impetuous behaviour has caused friction between the colonists and Māori." Hobson turned to Spain. "This concerns me greatly, and we have taken steps to bring in our own surveyors to sort this out."

Spain looked puzzled, "I'm not sure I totally understand."

"Wakefield acted with haste; he'd been under immense pressure to provide land to the colonists who had paid for it in advance. On arrival, the colonists were promised land in the township and in the country, where they could build their estates. Wakefield couldn't purchase land quickly enough, and his surveyors were pressured to hurriedly define boundaries so the colonists could take title and possession. It appears that many of these boundaries are now being disputed, causing tension between the colonists and Māori," informed the Governor.

"Yes, and presumably between the colonists and the New Zealand Company," offered Spain.

"Exactly! And this has caused friction and generated a great deal of animosity towards me as Governor. Some colonists oppose the land hearings, while others fear the Crown may rule in favour of Māori and that they'll lose title to the land they purchased. Wakefield has been a confounded pest, deflecting the colonists' wrath from himself and the New Zealand Company and turning it on me." The Governor was becoming visibly angry. "Were you aware that a group of Wellington colonists, encouraged and supported by Wakefield, attempted to form a republic? I put an end to that very quickly, let me tell you."

"No, I hadn't been informed of that."

Spain returned to his chair, and Governor Hobson followed.

"Do you also realise that if the crown hadn't secured sovereignty over this land when it did, the New Zealand Company would have divided this island and forced Māori to live in the extreme north, on land the Company didn't want? Can you imagine what we'd be facing today?"

Spain remained silent and looked on with interest.

"William, if the New Zealand Company had had its way, we'd be fighting a war with Māori rather than resolving these issues through a fair and legal process. I feel the New Zealand Company's philosophy towards the indigenous peoples of this land has been harmful and dangerous. Left to their own devices, with Colonel Wakefield enthusiastically following Company directives, Māori would have been exiled to the far north and left to suffer in squalor as unwanted tenants on land that is rightfully theirs."

Spain listened attentively.

"But let me offer you another perspective." Hobson turned to face Spain directly.

"What if the Imperial Government has shackled the New Zealand Company's efforts, not for the goodwill of Māori, but so that it itself can lay claim to the land?" Hobson raised an eyebrow as he gauged Spain's reaction.

Spain remained quiet and fidgeted.

"I see! Then you *are* familiar with the Imperial Government's motives!" It wasn't a question and put Spain in a delicate position.

Spain looked down into his glass.

"I've put you in an awkward spot. No doubt you've been briefed on exactly that and can't elaborate. Don't worry, dear chap, it's not your fault, our masters pull the strings, and we obey."

Hobson placed his glass on the table before him and turned back to Spain.

"As Commissioner, your responsibilities will be to deal with the land disputes arising from the purchase of land by the New Zealand Company alone. You needn't occupy yourself with non-New Zealand Company land disputes; you'll have more than enough to handle. The other two Commissioners who will work with you are Captain Mathew Richmond and Colonel Edward Godfrey. I'm sure you'll find their assistance more than useful, William," offered Governor Hobson as he leaned towards Spain. "You will hold court at such places as may afford claimants the greatest facility for producing native witnesses, and you will be guided by the real justice and good conscience of the case, without regard for legal solemnities. Do you understand, William?"

"Yes, sir, absolutely."

Despite the cautionary advice offered by Lord Russell, Spain found Governor Hobson to be a most agreeable fellow, and, much to his surprise, Hobson had ratified his appointment as intended by the Colonial Secretary and even provided assistance.

"You are very well informed and have a thorough understanding of current affairs. I am grateful for your consultation," Spain said politely.

Hobson laughed. "William, you will come to learn that no man can fully understand Māori or the actions of the Imperial Government. I'm not sure that Māori fully understand themselves, let alone Europeans. James Busby has been very forthcoming in sharing his local knowledge with me, and I am grateful. But I have also been fortunate that a Māori chief has seen wisdom and has faith that we can resolve these disputes equitably. He has been useful and has consistently provided me with information so that we can assess the land disputes justly, without being swayed by the individual authority of New Zealand Company board members or their influential advocates."

Spain raised his eyebrows. "I take it that Chief Wharepouri is the man you speak of?"

Hobson smiled, "Indeed, he is, but may I suggest you keep that to yourself?"

"Of course."

Hobson turned away from the bay to look once again at Spain.

"Another matter of importance has come before me that concerns the safety of you and your family."

"Oh? …please continue."

"While I do not support malicious rumours and gossip, I've been given information that leads me to suspect that the incident that befell the *Prince Rupert* was not an accident, but wilful sabotage.

"To what end?" asked Spain in surprise.

"To prevent you from arriving in New Zealand, I can only surmise."

"Who would do such an appalling thing? What evidence do you have?"

"If I had evidence, I would act on it; however, it seems unlikely that any proof will be offered unless someone were to confess, and that is highly unlikely."

"Is my family in danger?" asked Spain, leaning forward in his chair.

"I think steps should be taken to ensure you and your family remain safe, but in all honesty, I think the danger has passed. Someone did not want you to arrive in New Zealand, and now you are here, so it is too late. Yes?" Hobson smiled.

Spain considered Hobson's warning and agreed with him. "Would Chief Te Wharepouri have been the source of your information?"

Now it was Hobson's turn to look surprised. He turned away to resume looking at the bay.

"I thought so," said Spain after a moment. "How would a Māori chief come by this information?"

Hobson remained quiet for a moment, deciding how much he should disclose. Considering what Spain and his family had endured, he thought it was only fair to tell him.

Hobson took a deep breath. "An accountant in the employ of the New Zealand Company in Wellington suspected sabotage after coming across irregular paperwork, overhearing conversations, and making an elementary deduction. Apparently, Te Wharepouri holds this young man in the highest regard. The accountant thought it best to pass that information on to me through the chief, although he has no definitive evidence."

"And do you believe this?" asked Spain, shaking his head in wonder.

"I have no reason to disprove it, do you?"

Spain shook his head and leaned back in his chair, scratching the back of his head. "Well, I never... This Chief Te Wharepouri, he is quite supportive of the Crown, I take it."

Hobson laughed again. "I suspect Chief Te Wharepouri is supportive only to the extent that it serves his people's best interests."

William Spain and William Hobson looked over the bay in silence as each contemplated the challenges they faced. Perturbed by news that his family might be in imminent danger, Spain decided that at the first opportunity, he would make the acquaintance of the accountant in Wakefield's employ and glean any information to ensure his family's safety. The thought that *Prince Rupert* had been deliberately sabotaged to prevent his arrival in New Zealand was horrific; he shuddered at how close they'd come to death that night.

As if reading his thoughts, Hobson asked, "Tell me about your family, William?"

CHAPTER THIRTY–SIX

Te Awaiti Whaling Station, Marlborough Sounds.

Dickie Barrett never found his sea legs and detested the voyage across the Cook Strait from Wellington to Te Awaiti. The body of water was often rough, and during such crossings Dickie could often be found at the rail, emptying his stomach, as he was today.

He stepped back from the rail, wiped his mouth on his coat sleeve, dabbed his watering eyes, and took a deep breath before condemning his misfortunes. He cursed the whales for their slow disappearance from these waters; he damned the whalers who owed him money; he swore at the Wakefields and the New Zealand Company. Then he launched himself towards the ship's side, hanging over the rail and retching again. Today was not a good day.

Barrett's associates looked on with just a little pity, and, as usual, the ship's crew ignored him. They'd seen this a hundred times and took no pleasure in watching anyone suffer from seasickness. There was little they could do, and it was best to leave the afflicted alone to suffer in their abject misery.

The last of the Cook Strait's large waves tossed the ship into the Queen Charlotte Sounds, where a flat, mirror-like seascape greeted them. Framed by steep hills, lush vegetation and bush grew to the very water's edge. The calm and peace of the Sounds stood in stark contrast to the savage ocean that knocked persistently at its door. The Te Awaiti whaling station at Ship's Cove was only minutes away, and Dickie felt better already; he wiped his mouth on his sleeve yet again, held his face to the breeze, closed his eyes, and breathed deeply. A small gust of wind carried the hint of rotting whale carcasses to his nostrils.

"Claude, Claude!" shouted Tommy as he ran towards the small hut that Claude Arnoult called home.

Breathless, Tommy banged on the crude door, "Claude, are ya there?"

"Go away, leaves me," Claude's muted voice responded from inside.

"A ship! A ship is arriving. You wanted me to tell you if Barrett was coming, well, he's coming, but if you don't care, then bugger off!" yelled Tommy as he began to walk away.

The door creaked open and Claude de Fraud stepped into the sunlight, blinking he held his hand to his eyes, shading them from the afternoon sun.

"Vhat sheep? Za one Barrett alvays uses?" asked Claude, his voice croaky. He swayed a little and had to hold onto the door for support.

Tommy walked back towards the door, careful not to get close to the foul-smelling Frenchman.

"Yes, the same bloody ship," he said.

"*Putain!*" exclaimed Claude, still holding on to the door for support. He was worried because he knew Barrett was coming to collect on his debt, and he had no money to give him. Barrett had told him that next time he came, he would have Claude beaten within an inch of his life if he didn't pay up. Claude wasn't partial to being assaulted, certainly not to within an inch of his life as Barrett had threatened, but as other men also owed money to Barrett and were unable to pay their debts, they had hatched a plan over a few rums.

The scarcity of whales and reduced income meant they had incurred even more debt to Barrett, and no one wanted to face him or his thugs. It was time to disappear.

"Get za others Tommy, quickly, hurry. I veel vait here," Claude finally said.

Tommy ran off, and Claude returned to the gloom and filth of his windowless hut. He scrambled through the mess and found the vicious, long, very sharp knife he was looking for. He pulled it from its sheath and tested its edge against his thumb. His unsteady hand drew a thin line of blood.

"*Imbecile*," he cursed himself, returning the knife to its protective sheath and putting it in his pocket.

After wiping his bloody thumb on his grimy trousers, he searched for his hat and wobbled outside to wait anxiously for his friends to arrive. Across the bay, he could see the ship that Tommy had warned him about, and even as he stood watching, he could make out a longboat pulling towards the shore, no doubt carrying Barrett and his thugs.

Before long, two men ran up the path, breathing hard, and stopped in front of Claude.

"Got your jammer, Claude?"

Claude patted his pocket, looked at his thumb and again wiped the blood on his trousers.

"Bloody fool," said the whaler to Claude, seeing his injury.

"Ve must go now," Claude said irritably, then set off, stumbling up the path into the hills. His two friends followed close behind, both in no better shape.

Dickie's mood hadn't improved when he discovered that Claude had vanished. Feeling the financial pressures of hard times, Barrett had taken four burly men with him. They were either to extract payment or to deliver a severe beating to Claude and the others, who also owed him. Dickie soon discovered that Claude and two others had been seen heading into the hills only minutes earlier.

"Burn it," said Dickie outside Claude's home.

With a grim expression, he began the labour of trudging up the hill, leaving his men to incinerate Claude's home and the meagre possessions within. He didn't want to be seen in the vicinity as small flames began licking through the gaps in the walls. He crested the first low hill and turned to look back, not far behind, his men raced to catch up. Flames and thick smoke belched upwards as the squalid hut became engulfed in fire. Dickie allowed himself a smile of satisfaction as he waited for his men. Let that be a lesson to those who choose not to pay me, he thought.

Just as last time, he'd come to Te Awaiti, Barrett and his men were followed. The same young Māori lay hidden in the bushes, watching every step Barrett took. He'd watched with surprise as Barrett's men torched the whaler's hut. He knew the French whaler who lived there, and he felt a little sympathy as he watched the flames destroy the small home. He also knew Barrett was searching for Claude and the other two men who had run with him. They had passed this way not long before Barrett arrived, and from a snippet of conversation he'd overheard, he suspected they would find a suitable place to lie in wait and attack Barrett if he followed them. As he watched the little round *Pakeha* man carefully, he wondered whether Barrett would return to the *tohunga makutu,* the evil lady who lived in the small valley not far away. He remained out of sight and followed Barrett quietly through the bush.

Even though Barrett's stomach began to return to normal and the queasiness disappeared, his day was not improving. Claude de Fraud was somewhere ahead of them, and he and his friends needed to be found. Up ahead was the large tree where he would have two of his associates wait, while the other two continued searching for Claude, and he went in the other direction to visit Missy.

Dickie was thankful he had taken two extra men with him today. He knew things could turn rough and wanted the extra muscle for protection. They carried pistols concealed under their jackets - a wise precaution. He issued instructions to his men, then, once he was sure he wasn't followed, continued over the hill alone, veered off the path, and headed towards Missy's hut on the valley floor.

"Death follows you Dickie," said a voice from the bush.

This time he did jump as Missy stepped from the shadows and walked away from him towards her hut.

"Do you always hide in the bush and frighten your visitors?" he asked.

He couldn't hear her mumbled reply and assumed it wasn't polite.

"And why does death follow me?" he asked, speaking to her back.

Missy stopped and turned to face him. "You bring death with you today," she laughed. "That is the price you pay for your greed." She turned away and walked on as Barrett followed. Arriving at her home, she sat carefully on the log by her fire pit and looked Barrett over. Dickie saw the cow nearby, chewing grass.

"I haven't come to discuss my disposition; I want what you promised me."

Missy continued to stare at Dickie, as if considering what to say. She chose to remain silent and turned her head towards her hut as the young apprentice appeared, carrying a small bottle.

"This is what you want, Dickie. Now you can leave."

The apprentice handed the bottle to Dickie without a word and returned inside.

"Be gone, Dickie Barrett. Walk with your arms spread wide, for today you meet death. Greet death with respect, for after today you will pay the price," she laughed.

"What do I do with this stuff and how do I use it?" he asked, uninterested in her cryptic ramblings.

Missy bent down and scooped up a small amount of dirt from the ground. She held out her hand. "This much! Put this much in his food every day, until he is overcome by death."

"How long will it take?"

"A week before he feels something, a couple of months before he dies." She looked closely at Dickie. "Do not fear. No one will know you are behind this. Now go!" she shouted.

Barrett turned and slowly walked back up the path, where the thick bushes either side of the track cast long shadows as the late-afternoon sun sank lower.

"Why were you in such a hurry for him to leave?" asked the young apprentice as she reappeared outside the hut.

"He has the shadow of death over him; today, men will die by his will. I do not want the darkness to fall here."

Missy remained seated on the log. She lifted her head slightly, as if listening, and with the infinite patience of the elderly, she waited.

Three men stepped out of the shadows, surprising Barrett for the second time that day. Two stood threateningly in front of him, and one stood behind him. They had him surrounded, and there was nothing he could do. He was unarmed and vulnerable. He never put himself in a position where he needed to protect himself; he hired other men for that unpleasant task.

"Dickie, fancy meeting you out 'ere then," said the largest whaler, with an unkempt beard and a broad smile that failed to hide his rotting black teeth.

"Thoughtful of you to consider my welfare and to escort me back to the station," said Dickie in his cheeriest voice.

"I don't zink vee have come to help you," said Claude from behind. "*Non, non,* you will not be leaving here, *mon ami.*"

Dickie placed the bottle carefully in his pocket, turned to the side so he could see all three whalers, and raised both hands to placate them.

"You burn my house!" accused Claude, the first note of anger creeping into his voice. Earlier, he had watched from the hill as his house was consumed by flames.

"No, Claude, I wasn't there. It had nothing to do with me." Dickie licked his lips, his mouth suddenly dry.

"Wot ya got in your pockets then?" asked the big whaler, stepping closer and drawing a knife from his boot. He waved it in slow circles in front of Barrett, inches from his face and stomach. "Empty 'em!"

Barrett gulped and took an involuntary step back. A tree prevented him from going any further.

The smallest whaler also drew a slender knife and held it with the confidence of an experienced street fighter. He stepped forward in a low crouch, and with unbelievable speed, the knife slashed across Barrett's stomach, cutting through the fabric of his coat. He stepped back and laughed. The others joined in.

In fear, Barrett grabbed at his stomach, and the knife nicked him.

"Oh, poor Dickie, are you frightened?" mocked Claude. He lunged forward, slashing down, his knife slicing through the side of Barrett's jacket.

"Wots it feel like, then, to be on the other side for a change?" the big man asked, savouring the moment.

The large whaler feigned a slash with his knife towards Dickie's midriff. As Dickie moved in reflex, the big man struck him squarely on the chin with a powerful left-handed punch. Dickie stumbled and fell to his knees, clutching his face, his stomach forgotten.

The three whalers were enjoying tormenting Barrett. They intended to humiliate him, then slowly carve him up, a gradual and painful end they had all dreamed of. Afterwards, his corpse would be abandoned in the bush, left to rot.

All three men owed money to Barrett, and Claude owed the most. The other two were notoriously lazy and, as a result, earned less. Barrett was facing his own financial hardship and, as a result, had been pressuring those who owed him to cough up. He also knew that many whalers hid valuables. It was those assets he now sought. Shake the tree hard enough, and the fruit would fall.

For the three desperate whalers, disposing of Barrett would solve all their immediate problems.

"Stop, stop!" Dickie wailed. "We can talk this through. Please don't hurt me!"

Claude lifted his foot, ready to kick Dickie. Still feeling the effects of a night of inebriation, he was off balance and fell heavily to the ground. His two friends laughed. The laughter ended abruptly with a gunshot. The big whaler stumbled, his knife falling from his hands as he looked down in surprise at the spreading red stain on his chest. He toppled forward with a grunt as the single shot reverberated around the hills. He lay unmoving on the path, his blood pooling beneath him.

Suddenly sober, Claude rolled away. Dickie threw himself forward, hands over the back of his head, eyes tightly shut. The smaller whaler charged the shooter, his knife moving faster than the eye could follow. He almost made it when another shot rang out, spinning him around. The big ball from the musket hit him in the shoulder. Before he could react, one of Dickie's associates sprang forward, plunging his own knife deep between the whaler's ribs, piercing his heart. He fell, blood draining from his lifeless body.

Claude had crawled into the thick undergrowth lining the path. He was no bushman and had no skill in evasion. His instinct was to flee, and he panicked. He rose from the ground and ran, crashing through the ferns to evade Barrett's hired thugs. Another of Dickie's henchmen stepped a few paces into the bush, then, with confidence, raised his pistol, sighted on the fleeing Frenchman, and pulled the trigger.

With a fizz, the powder in the pan ignited with a flash. A split second later, the powder in the barrel exploded. The rapidly expanding gases had nowhere to go, and the mounting pressure propelled the shot outwards down the length of the barrel. The accelerating round ball didn't travel in a straight line and wouldn't reach the target area the shooter intended. Affected by its imprecise shape and air currents, the shot veered from its intended trajectory. It didn't even have much range, and such a pistol was usually only deadly at very close quarters. Had Claude de Fraud remained still, the erratic flight of the shot would have easily missed. But Claude had one thing on his mind, survival, and he ran directly into the path of the fast-moving projectile. The round shot entered the back of his head and passed clean through, exiting just below his left eye. Claude felt no pain; he was dead long before his body hit the ground near the feet of the young Māori who, in total astonishment, witnessed the entire scene.

Honi recoiled as blood and grey matter splattered across his face. Slowly, he stood, taking a step backwards, transfixed on the corpse in front of him.

"There's another– a Māori!" yelled the man who had just shot Claude.

Tossing the useless single-shot pistol to the ground, he rushed towards Honi, who remained paralysed by shock.

"Don't let him get away!" cried Barrett, regaining his voice and rising to his feet. "He saw everything!"

The other three men quickly spread out, trying to prevent Honi from escaping.

Honi watched the onrushing man and saw the knife appear in his hand. In dawning realisation, he knew that if he didn't get away, he would die here.

Honi moved quickly and ducked under a fern, its broad leaves fanned out like a wall. He rushed through the leaves, disappearing for a moment, then turned left and headed deeper into the bush-clad valley. Like Claude and his whaler friends, Barrett's men weren't bushmen. They were more comfortable in towns and dark alleyways, where they normally plied their trade. They were at a disadvantage and knew it. They had to move quickly, or the fleet-footed Māori would vanish.

"I saw him, this way!" the man who had been closest to Honi pointed. He caught a brief glimpse of the young Māori's back as he disappeared down a bank.

Honi stopped running and planned his route out of the bush. With infinite care and patience, he crept back towards the men, hoping to pass them on their flank. Moving upwards was the only way to evade them. The afternoon sun was setting behind the hills, and the bush grew darker. It became Honi's friend.

Dickie remained on the path. The earlier experience had frightened him, and he needed a few minutes to compose himself. He could hear the voices of his men as they called to each other, the distance widening as they searched for the Māori.

Barrett's four associates spread out in a long line, blocking any escape back up the path to safety. They were herding Honi towards open ground and Missy's hut, and they knew that once he was visible, they would have him.

Honi used low-growing ferns and bushes to hide, keeping away from the tall trees that formed a canopy over the bush and left open spaces. He crawled from bush to bush, then waited and moved again the instant one of his pursuers turned his head. He was being forced lower into the valley, where the bush had been cleared, closer to the place he feared to go. The place where the *tohunga makutu* lived. He could see two of the men; the closest was only yards away, yelling and taunting him.

The man turned his head away and shouted to his friends. Without making any sudden movements, Honi quietly eased away, his body blending into the shadows. On a signal, the line of four men began to swing, pivoting around the man closest to Honi. They knew he was close, and the move forced him even further down the hill. Taking advantage of the shouting to mask any noise he made, Honi bolted from cover, bent low, and ran down the hill, away from the men. He couldn't run to the path, as Barrett still stood there, blocking his escape.

A small hand with a powerful grip grabbed his arm. He gasped in surprise. Missy's apprentice stood behind a tree and pulled him close. With her free hand, she held a finger to her lips, signalling him to stay quiet. As if he didn't know.

She pulled him away from the tree and from danger; he had no choice but to follow her. She led him around the far side of the clearing towards the low hut, the home of the *tohunga makutu* that frightened him so much. He could see the figure of a woman sitting on a log, oblivious to the events unfolding around her. Honi paused, unsure.

"Come, follow me, you will be safe," whispered the girl.

"Where are you taking me?"

"Where you will be safe, the *taiwhetuki* will protect you," she replied.

Honi knew of the *taiwhetuki*. It was the house where black magic and knowledge of evil and death were kept. Perhaps no other place was more feared. But death at the hands of *pakeha* wasn't a pleasant thought either. The sound of the four men searching and fast approaching was encouragement enough. With apprehension, Honi reluctantly followed. She took him to the rear of the hut, lifted a small hatch in the wall, climbed in, and urged Honi to follow.

The inside of the hut was tidy and clean. There were no dead bodies hanging from the roof as he expected. Along one wall were jars, pots and bottles containing various items, while another wall held clothing and some kitchen-type utensils. Two sleeping mats were rolled up in a corner, but as it was poorly lit, it was hard to make out detail. The only light came from the partly open door. Honi was scared and breathing hard.

"You will be safe here. Just keep calm and trust us," said the young girl, her voice reassuring.

She pointed up to the dark recesses of the roof, to the wooden beams that provided strength and support to the structure.

"Climb up and lie across that beam, you will not be seen, hurry," she urged.

Honi paused, unsure whether to trust his fate to these women. Through the partially open door, he could see the *tohunga makutu,* the woman who frightened him. She had a pipe to her lips and sat calmly, looking out towards the bush.

"Hurry, boy, they will be here soon," Missy suddenly said, without turning her head, her lips hardly moving, spurring him to obey.

Reaching up, Honi grabbed the wooden beam the young girl indicated and hoisted himself into the darkness. He crawled to the gloomiest corner and lay across the wooden support, blending into the shadows, almost invisible. Illuminated by the light from the doorway, dust motes drifted down like magic powder. Otherwise, there was no sign he was in the hut.

Honi watched the young apprentice as she sat on the floor by the door, breaking leaves apart. He wondered whether it was for some evil magic potion or ritual. He'd never been so scared in his life and knew in his heart that the witch would turn him into a green lizard at the first opportunity. He shuddered.

Barrett was the first to appear, and soon after, his four associates emerged from the bush. Dickie rubbed his jaw where he had been struck. Even through his beard, a red welt was evidence of the blow. His jacket hung awkwardly, shredded by knives, and a thin smear of blood stained his shirt from his abdomen. With suspicion, the men approached the hut. Missy, who sat on her log, puffed away on her pipe with calm and unconcern as Barrett walked towards her. His eyes blazed with anger.

"What do you know of this?" he yelled. "Where is he?"

Missy turned and spat on the ground. "The man you seek is long gone. He is back at Te Awaiti," she replied.

"You knew this would happen. You said as much when I was here. How did you know?" He pointed a stubby finger towards her.

Missy laughed, her shrill cackle unnerving. "You came here with the shadow of death over you, Dickie. You came here, and *Whiro* followed you. That is how I know." She turned her head slightly to look up into Barrett's eyes. The dark, mystical pools of her eyes made Barrett uncomfortable.

"Where is *Whiro* now? Where did he go?"

One of Barrett's men began walking slowly to the hut.

Missy laughed again, causing the man to stop and look towards her.

"*Whiro* is a spirit, Dickie. *Whiro* is darkness and lives in the underworld. *Whiro* is death, and he came with you today. That is how I know." She replied with contempt.

Dickie's man continued to the hut, curious about what lay inside, while Barrett looked around, hoping to catch sight of the man he was pursuing.

"Have you no thought for a frail old woman? The death you have brought here has created much work for me. Go and fetch me the bodies of the men you have slain," Missy ordered.

Unsure, Barrett paused. *Perhaps she is right*, he thought. This is what she does. The sooner she gets the bodies, whatever it is she does, the sooner they will disappear. The man who had escaped probably would not be found. He turned to the three men who had remained standing.

"Bring the bodies back here."

They stood, unmoving.

"Now!" he yelled.

Grumbling, they turned and headed back up the path to do as instructed.

The other man was bending down, looking through the hut's doorway.

"There is someone inside!" he yelled.

The young girl pushed open the door, bent low, and walked past the surprised man to stand beside Missy. He continued to look inside the dark interior, preparing to enter.

"Tell your man, Dickie, that if he goes inside, I will not be responsible for what happens to him," she paused. "Or to you!"

Dickie feared Missy, though he would not admit it to anyone. He'd lived amongst Māori long enough to have both respect and fear for the *tohunga*. That was why he had come here for her help in the first place.

"Check around the back," Dickie ordered the man.

Relieved he wasn't required to go inside, Dickie's man walked around the back of the hut, looking for signs.

Honi lay in the rafters, holding his breath. He was petrified, afraid of discovery and of what Missy would do to him, although the pretty apprentice seemed quite friendly and unthreatening. Honi pushed his lustful thoughts of the girl aside and closed his eyes, listening intently to the conversation outside.

Dickie looked around, ignoring Missy and the apprentice. It was quickly growing dark, and they needed to leave here very soon. He rubbed his sore jaw again.

"If you are lying to me, I will come back here. Your spells and witchcraft won't protect you from what I will do. If you have anything to say to me, say it now."

The man returned from walking around the back of the hut and stood, leering at the young apprentice. Missy watched with an amused expression.

"Your men return with three bodies, Dickie," she said with a smile. "Who will pay me for preparing them?"

Dickie knew what she was referring to. If he gave her money, the bodies would disappear quickly. He reached into his pocket, withdrew a few coins, and threw them on the ground.

"Put the bodies over there," Missy instructed the men. She didn't want them near the *taiwhetuki*. Their *tapu* was not good and would infect the area if they came too close.

As requested, the men obeyed, and everyone was eager to leave.

"Remember my warning," said Barrett. Turning to his men, "We should leave."

Missy's haunting laugh followed them out.

Missy and her young helper watched the five men walk away, and she let out a sigh of relief. She had been frightened. The unpredictability of *pakeha* men always bothered her, and she usually made them wary and cautious by acting aggressively towards them. But the men with Barrett were hard and evil men. She would have been powerless to prevent them from doing whatever they chose.

"Tell the boy to come out. He is safe now."

Honi stooped through the door and walked outside, timidly. The apprentice was lighting the fire, and he approached nervously, convinced his time had come and that he was about to be turned into a lizard.

"Come here, boy," Missy ordered, reverting to *Te Reo*, the language of her people.

Honi hated being called a boy. He wasn't a boy; he was a man, a warrior. Perhaps only a young warrior, but a warrior none the less.

He shuffled over, afraid to look the *tohunga* in the eyes, and kept his head low.

"You were foolish to follow the *pakeha*. You could easily have been killed," she admonished him. "What did you see today?"

Unsure how to respond, Honi considered lying, but she would know if he did. "I saw whalers waiting for Barrett. When he walked from here, they attacked him with knives. One man hit him in the face."

"Go on."

"Then Barrett's men arrived. They had guns and shot all three men. One man didn't die, and his heart was pierced with a knife. One of the men ran towards me, where I was hiding. Then I was seen and ran. You know the rest."

The flickering orange light from the fire danced across Missy's face as she looked at the young man before her. She was a little troubled at how much the boy had seen.

"What did you see of Barrett when he was here?"

"I, I, never came down this far. I, umm, I was a little frightened," admitted Honi. "I waited for him to return near the big tree on the path, so I don't know what he did here."

Missy looked closely, studying Honi carefully, trying to tell whether he was telling the truth. Deciding he was, she asked, "Were you the one following Barrett a month ago when he came last time?"

"Yes, that was me. How did you know?"

"I know everything," she stated emphatically.

Honi considered her reply and decided it was best to ask the *tohunga* about his future while he still could. He raised his head and looked at her bravely. "Will you turn me into a lizard now?"

Missy suppressed a smile. "I'm not sure yet. I will decide later," she said slowly.

Honi looked up at the sky. Thinking about running away into the darkness.

Seeing his look, she said, "It is not safe for you to return to Te Awaiti. You will sleep here tonight."

The young apprentice who sat near the fire smiled. Honi was a handsome warrior, brave and clever, having shown it by outsmarting the *pakeha* who were looking for him. It would be pleasant to have the young man sleep here.

Honi looked worried.

"Who saw your face? Did Barrett see you?" she asked.

"Only one of his men saw me; Barrett didn't."

Missy nodded, obviously pleased. "Rest. We will eat soon, and you can return in the morning."

The last rays of the day's sun filtered down onto the path as Dickie wearily headed back towards Te Awaiti. He walked slowly, favouring his left leg, his knee painful after taking the full weight of his fall when he dove to the ground during the attack. Two men walked behind, and the other two walked in front, offering protection against another incident.

Barrett's associates retrieved their spent pistols, reloaded them, and kept them within easy reach, hidden under their jackets. Dickie was pleased. They had acquitted themselves well and had done exactly what he paid them to do. No one had suffered any injury, other than a minor nick to his stomach. They had taken the initiative to come to Dickie's rescue even after being instructed to remain behind. The oldest and most experienced later told Dickie that the two men had returned to the tree after failing to find any trace of Claude and his friends. They realised that Claude and his friends must have gone in the same direction as Dickie and immediately set out to find him when they came across the ambush. Barrett was thankful. If his men hadn't come for him, he'd be dead, cut to pieces and lying on the path as a bloodless corpse.

As the small group approached the outlying huts of the whaling station, they could see the smouldering ruins of Claude's hut. At risk of being burned, someone had already picked through the wreckage, taking any items of worth. The few remaining possessions Claude owned lay scattered around the smoking ruins, discarded and deemed worthless.

CHAPTER THIRTY–SEVEN

Wakefield Office and Residence, Thorndon

"Open wide," coldly instructed Doctor Isaac Featherstone. "Tongue out, please."

William Wakefield obediently did as he was told, as Isaac used a tongue depressor and peered over his spectacles, studying the inflamed throat of his patient closely.

"Jacket off and undo the top four buttons of your shirt, please," ordered Isaac, his tone less than friendly.

"What's got into you, Isaac?" asked William

"Hush," admonished Isaac as he placed his stethoscope on William's chest.

It wasn't lost on Wakefield that Isaac hadn't warmed the instrument before touching the cold metal to his skin.

Doctor Featherstone moved the scope to a new location. "Big breath in… good, …now out."

Isaac stepped back, removing the scope from his ears, extracted his fob watch from his pocket, and grabbed Williams's wrist to check his pulse. Wakefield remained quiet, allowing Isaac to perform his diagnosis.

"You're ill!" stated the doctor coolly.

"I know that, damn it, Isaac, that's why I called for you," said William, breaking into a wet, hacking cough.

Isaac turned away from Wakefield and began placing his instruments back into his bag.

"What's wrong?" asked William between ragged breaths, his face red and watery.

"Don't fret. You're not dying, not yet, anyway," replied Isaac unsympathetically.

William sat on the edge of his bed, fastening the buttons on his shirt, and looked over at Isaac, who stood with his back to him.

With his medical bag repacked, Isaac turned to Wakefield, "*cattarhus acutus!*"

"What?"

"You are afflicted with *cattarhus acutus*. I don't believe your temperature is elevated to the point where I will perform a bloodletting. However, if your symptoms persist and your fever worsens, then I shall."

Wakefield looked on in puzzlement. "What is cat – ir – us? Is it curable?"

Enjoying the moment, Isaac looked solemnly at William. "No, there is no cure. However, I urge you to stay warm, avoid the cold, and drink water. Try steam to clear your congestion. Your symptoms will pass in seven to ten days, and then you can go about your sordid business!"

William continued to sit on the bed, disturbed by Isaac's prognosis. "What is this, this thing I have, Isaac?"

Isaac walked towards Wakefield, stopped in front of him, and leaned over. "You have a cold, William. That is all."

The relief was evident on Wakefield's face. "Why is it that I get the distinct impression you are unhappy with me, Isaac? What have I done to earn your displeasure?" Colonel Wakefield returned to another bout of coughing.

"To earn my displeasure?" Isaac cupped his chin, as if in thought. "Let me recount some of the things you have done to EARN MY DISPLEASURE!" Isaac shouted. He strode to the far side of the room as Wakefield finished hacking. "Do you even realise what you've done? How you've deceived people into immigrating to this country, offering them a life and opportunity that don't exist," Isaac stared accusingly at Wakefield.

"You're overreacting, Isaac. I cannot be held responsible for those who fail to take advantage of the opportunities this wonderful country offers. Why, let me-"

"You've tricked Māori into selling you land," Isaac interrupted as Wakefield began coughing again. "You have a responsibility to conduct your business ethically and honestly, and you have failed in this, William. In so doing, you have destroyed the dreams of many and negatively impacted the natives who live here, the same people who were here long, long before you ever came to seduce them with your trinkets," Isaac shook his finger reprovingly. "The radical policies of the New Zealand Company have not sown pastures on rolling, productive fields. No! You've sewn false hope and are reaping discontent. And you, yes, you, Colonel, are too smitten with wealth and greed to see the harm it's creating." Isaac was pacing the room in anger.

Colonel Wakefield held a handkerchief to his nose, unable to respond.

"You hoodwinked Bethia and me into coming here. You lied to us. We thought you were our friend. We trusted you!"

"Now hold on a minute-"

"No, William, I will not hold. You misrepresented everything about this country to us. All you really cared about was selling land!" Isaac spun, grabbed his bag, and headed for the door. "Yes, I can treat your ailments and maladies as your physician, but if I had been as deceitful as you have been, could you possibly conceive of the consequences? Look how you felt moments ago when you thought you had an incurable illness. But I didn't lie, did I? No, I was just being deceitful. How does it feel to be deceived?"

Isaac reached for the door handle and, over his shoulder, said, "Good day, sir!" He stormed from the room, leaving the door ajar.

"Isaac, Isaac!" spluttered Wakefield, walking towards the open door. In anger, he swept a vase of flowers against the wall as he bent over the dresser and coughed.

Eleanor was in Wakefield's kitchen. A pot of soup simmered over the range, and she was placing another log on the fire when Isaac stormed in, his face betraying the rage he felt. The sound of the vase crashing against the wall made her wince as she looked up at Isaac.

"I'm sorry, Eleanor. There's no need to be alarmed," Isaac said, rubbing his thinning hair. "That dreadful man irks me, and he can't even see what he's doing. He had to be told, and I'm pleased I finally did."

Eleanor had heard the exchange between Isaac and the colonel, as had most of Thorndon. She wiped her hands on her apron and turned to the soup. "You certainly made your point, Isaac."

"Will it make any difference? That's what I wonder," said Isaac, heading towards the kitchen door. "I apologise again, Eleanor. You didn't need to hear that. Now I must leave to attend to Bethia. She is suffering considerably from this latest pregnancy. Good day, M'dear."

"Give Bethia my love. I will call in to see her later. Good afternoon, Isaac," Eleanor responded.

Doctor Isaac Featherston pulled up his coat collar and stepped out into the cold southerly wind.

As did Eleanor, Andrew also heard the fiery altercation. He was at his desk with Wakefield's secretary, Simpkins, when they heard the crash as something broke against the wall.

"Do you think it would be a good time to see Colonel Wakefield about these accounts?" Andrew asked with a straight face.

Simpkins ignored the question and scurried fearfully back to his desk.

The thin walls of Wakefield's residence offered little privacy, and Andrew digested what he'd heard. He knew Isaac's anger had been brewing for quite some time and was in total agreement. However, he doubted it would change the colonel's or the Company's actions. Colonel Wakefield firmly believed that everything he had done was acceptable.

CHAPTER THIRTY–EIGHT

Port Nicholson, Wellington

Easily heard from shore, the three-hundred-and-sixty-nine-ton brigantine *Patriot* dropped her anchor with a resounding splash, accompanied by the clatter of chains. Immediately, the newly arrived ship began to swing slowly and settle, rocking gently and content to point her blunt bow towards the northwest, in the direction of the prevailing wind. Sailors, motivated by the promise of shore liberty, quickly began furling sails, stowing lines and lowering the ship's boats. Wellington's Collector of Customs had already been aboard and had recently departed, allowing the *Patriot*'s Master to begin offloading passengers and stores. Larger tenders were already making their way towards the ship and were greeted by the movement of a crane as it prepared to hoist her consignment of general cargo to the shipping agents eagerly waiting on shore.

Watching from a small pier where passengers would arrive, Eleanor hopped with excitement as she sought to catch a glimpse of her Uncle Charles. Andrew firmly held her hand, lest in her enthusiasm she hopped one hop too far and fell off the pier.

As a dashing young officer with dreams of sailing the world, Charles met his wife, Mary, after a lengthy layover in England and married her shortly afterwards. Uncle Charles, or Carl Eberhard Sjöstedt, as the Swedish birth register recorded his name, found his name unpronounceable in English. He promptly changed it to the friendlier Charles Suisted, making it more acceptable to English society. Amidst a huge farewell and much sadness, the newly married couple immigrated to Van Diemen's Land, where stories abounded of fortune and prosperity.

Mary, the younger sister of Eleanor's mother, brought the popular and dashing Swedish Captain to visit numerous times, and Eleanor grew very fond of him. Andrew met Uncle Charles and as expected, the two enjoyed each other's wry sense of humour and healthy wit. Andrew looked forward to his arrival as much as Eleanor, though in a more restrained, subdued manner. It would be difficult to miss the man; he towered above everyone at an astonishing six foot six inches tall.

The first boatload of passengers arrived to heartfelt welcomes from friends and relatives gathered; once ashore, they began to drift away, making it easier for Eleanor to see. The next boatload of disembarking passengers approached, and Eleanor could hear his distinctive loud laugh long before she saw him. Andrew smiled and shook his head. How typical, he thought. He watched as passengers leapt onto the dock, revealing the imposing figure of Uncle Charles, laughing with a sailor as the hapless young fellow handed over some coin to Uncle Charles. He responded by clapping the sailor on the back with a mighty paw, almost knocking him overboard, before lightly stepping onto the dock, where he saw Eleanor beaming.

"Ellie, my vonderful beautiful Ellie!" he yelled as she leaped into the wide expanse of his outstretched arms.

Enveloping her in a massive embrace, he effortlessly lifted her and kissed her on the left cheek, then the right, then the left again, and, for good measure, the right, before he remembered to put her carefully back down.

"Oh Ellie, is so good to see you again. You look beautiful as alvays, ya?"

Uncle Charlie turned his attention to Andrew, who had his hand outstretched in greeting.

"You are looking good, Andrew. I see Ellie is cooking good food for you, ya?" he said, beginning with a smile that ended in a laugh as he looked at Andrew's belly. He shook Andrew's hand, then gathered him up in one arm while he still held Eleanor in the other, giving them both a loving squeeze.

"It's so wonderful to see you, Uncle. It's been forever," Eleanor said, finally free from his grasp.

"Welcome to New Zealand. We hope you had a pleasant voyage," said Andrew.

"It vas a good sailing and ze sailors on ze ship had deep pockets, ya?" laughed Charles.

"You weren't gambling, Uncle?" asked Eleanor, attempting to look stern.

Charles winked at Andrew. "I had a small vager vis a young sailor. I bet him that I would arrive and be on the dock on the afternoon of December zerteenth. He said, no, no, it would be the next day, on the fourteenth," Charles laughed. "I am very happy to be here and to see you, ya?"

A sailor deposited Charles's travelling holdall on the dock and, with a friendly wave, headed back out to the *Patriot* to pick up another load of disembarking passengers.

They all sat comfortably around the table, enjoying their second cup of tea. Eleanor caught up on the latest family news from Van Diemen's Land and from her home in England, and in turn shared news of their own adventures in New Zealand, while Captain Charles Suisted listened quietly, with more than casual interest.

Uncle Charles told them that Mary and their two children would be following him here once he had determined that opportunities existed for them and had found a suitable home and a business to purchase. Life in Launceston had been good for the Suisted family, but his business suffered when two ships he'd owned were shipwrecked in the turbulent waters between Van Diemen's Land and the mainland. Then the economy experienced a downturn, and the burden of recovering from the financial loss proved too great. Charles insisted that uprooting the family and immigrating to New Zealand to begin again was their only real option.

Charles had acquaintances in Wellington and was eager to renew them at his earliest convenience. The following morning, he set out to familiarise himself with the lay of the land and the streets of Wellington.

While Uncle Charles cut an imposing figure and possessed immense strength, his greatest weakness was gambling. Unable to resist the lure of a deck of cards and a willing adversary, Captain Charles Suisted would seldom shy away from a quick wager and felt no compunction about relieving the unwary of their pecuniary burden. Andrew and Eleanor knew that Uncle Charles would eventually track down a game, drink to excess, and make many friends while emptying their pockets. He wasn't a charlatan; he was lucky. It was the way of the man. Those who had tried to stop him from gambling had failed, and only Mary partially succeeded in tempering his vice.

Next morning, as Uncle Charles walked away from the cosy cottage and his loving niece and nephew, his smile quickly vanished. He realised that his plans might put Eleanor and Andrew in some jeopardy.

CHAPTER THIRTY–NINE

Barrett's Hotel, Lambton Quay, Wellington.

Dickie needed to purchase alcohol. As yet, no one had begun to brew ale locally in Wellington, but it was being brewed further north in Russell, though not in sufficient quantities, which made it difficult to obtain. As a result of the shortage, he continued to buy his ale and rum from established contacts in New South Wales.

The Secretary of State for War and the Colonies, Lord Normanby, who would later be replaced by Lord Russell, had instructed Governor Hobson to impose an excise tax on alcohol. Much to Barrett's delight, beer was exempt. However, six months later, the law changed, and a levy was imposed on the importation of all alcohol, including beer. This didn't sit well with Dickie at all, so he chose to circumvent the law by becoming a part-time smuggler.

To avoid detection and payment of taxes to the Collector of Customs, it was easier to have his stock of rum and beer quietly shipped directly to Te Awaiti and then sent to Wellington in barrels labelled Whale Oil. He was expecting such a shipment this evening.

He'd sent a handful of men to the docks, where, under cover of darkness, they would unload alcohol in barrels from a ship newly arrived from Te Awaiti and, over the short distance, deliver it to his hotel on barrel carts. Dickie was alone in his storeroom, performing a last-minute inventory of his remaining supplies and waiting for his men to return, when he sensed someone nearby. Adjusting his lantern to peer into the dark recesses of his storeroom, he was shocked to find two rather stout men watching him.

"What are you doing in here? Out, get out!" He yelled with authority and some bluster.

Blocking access to the door, both Māori slowly approached. To free his hands and out of fear of fire, Dickie placed the lantern securely on a barrel and cautiously began to back away, seeking safety behind the barrels as he warned the intruders away.

"I have men coming here any minute now, so leave now while you still can!" he cautioned.

The two men remained silent, steadily approaching the frightened publican. Realising he was in imminent danger, Dickie quickly scrambled to put as many barrels as he could between himself and the intruders.

"Help! Someone help!"

Dickie climbed over one barrel, evading a hand that reached for him, and began climbing over another when he felt his leg caught in a firm grip. Unable to pull it free, he kicked with his other leg, catching one of the men squarely in the head. The sound of his boot striking flesh did little to dampen his attackers' enthusiasm. The man fell back with a grunt, clutching his face, and Dickie clambered as fast as he could over the barrels to escape.

"Help! Help!" The pitch of his voice rose in fear as he continued yelling. "What do you want from me?"

Ignoring his appeals and warnings, one of the men blocked the only exit from the room, while the other, rubbing his jaw where Dickie's foot had struck, approached from the other side. Dickie had nowhere to go; he was trapped. The man who'd been kicked leaped forward and grabbed Dickie around the shoulders, pulling him back towards the open space. Fighting with all his strength and yelling the entire time, he was no match for the muscular Māori, who threw him to the floor, where they began to brutally assault him. Barrett succumbed to a barrage of blows from both men. He was struck around the head and kicked repeatedly; all he could do was curl into a foetal position and take the beating. His attackers were merciless and without pity.

"Do you remember Ngaiti?" asked one of the men in halting English as he delivered another painful kick.

The realisation dawned on him that these men had come to avenge Ngaiti's death and that he was going to die here tonight – they had come to kill him. He screamed as hard as he could, hoping someone would hear him, but received a jarring blow to the back of his head for his effort.

"You like having others do your dirty work for you, and you pay men to beat up others?" the Māori asked, not really expecting a reply.

Another kick landed squarely on his chest, the sharp pain indicating that at least one rib was broken.

"You steal from innocent people and kill their animals?" came another question, followed by a powerful blow to his thigh.

Barrett found it painful to breathe. He knew he had some loose teeth and some broken bones, and his mouth was filling with blood - they weren't finished with him yet.

Then, as suddenly as it began, the kicking stopped. One of the men drew a knife, a nasty-looking weapon, one of the many knives given to Māori in exchange for land.

"Do you see this?" yelled one of the men, waving the knife in front of Barrett.

Barrett opened his swollen eye and saw the gleaming blade. In response, his bladder let go and he soiled himself. A puddle pooled on the floor beneath him as he lay in its comforting warmth.

"What were you doing with the *tohunga* at Te Awaiti?" asked the man, the first question he'd asked for which he expected an answer.

Barrett groaned, unwilling to reply. He was kicked again in the side.

"Tell me!" shouted the man. "What were you doing with the *tohunga*?"

Suddenly, there was a knock on the wall. It came again with more urgency. It was a signal telling the two men it was time to leave. One of the guards posted outside saw Barrett's men approaching and, as arranged, issued his warning.

"*Pepeke*!" yelled the muffled voice from the other side of the door, a warning to leave quickly.

The plan was to extract information from Barrett and have him confess. Killing him was the preferred option, but Chief Te Wharepouri insisted he wasn't to die - not yet. It was too late to finish the interrogation, as Barrett's workers were returning to the hotel with the barrels.

Leaning forward, one of the Māori grabbed Dickie by the hair, pulling his head up.

"I will come back for you, and you will tell me," he said, releasing his head and delivering a parting kick to Barrett's groin, emphasising his statement.

As silently as they had come, the two men departed, closing the door behind them. Dickie felt the intense pain creeping up and spreading outwards. He then began retching before passing out.

Barrett's men found him unconscious, lying in a pool of urine, blood and vomit. His eyes swelled almost shut, and blood smeared his face where his teeth had bitten through his lips. Dickie's unknown assailants had come and gone, and no one had seen or heard a thing.

Chief Te Wharepouri decided that Barrett's antics had gone on long enough and intended to visit Dickie himself – it was time to even the score. It was only fitting that he personally administer the punishment and take Barrett's life, but recently, he'd not been feeling well and was a little unsteady. However, there was another reason Barrett wasn't killed. An unexpected visitor had politely appealed to him to spare Barrett's life temporarily. After some discussion, the chief agreed and would honour the unusual request.

Concerned for his health, his trusted warriors insisted he stay behind while they dealt with Barrett. Chief Te Wharepouri reluctantly agreed – on the condition that they not kill him. The warriors returned to the *pa* and recounted what had happened at Barrett's Hotel.

Everything went to plan. Te Wharepouri's spies informed him of the incoming alcohol shipment and the expected routine of Barrett's men as they unloaded the illicit cargo.

It had been easy for Te Wharepouri's men to sneak into the storeroom to wait while others loitered unseen outside. After leaving Barrett to his misery, they stayed nearby and watched. Dickie's men had made only a half-hearted attempt to search for the assailants and, as predicted, never reported the incident to the town magistrate. No one saw the shadow of a very large man watching the hotel. As Te Wharepouri's men disappeared into the night, so did Charles Suisted. Te Wharepouri's main concern now was to wait and see whether and how Barrett would retaliate. As arranged, he would speak to the big man again.

The chief turned to Honi. "Tell me, what happened when Barrett visited the *tohunga* at Te Awaiti?"

"I don't know," Honi repeated. He looked at the ground, ashamed that he had lacked the courage to follow Barrett when he went to see Missy.

"Did Missy say anything? What about her apprentice? Did she give any clues?" asked the Chief.

They'd already gone over the details a few times since Honi returned from Te Awaiti, and no one was any the wiser about what Barrett was doing there.

Honi shook his head.

The warrior with the bruised face spoke up. "If Barrett had not been doing anything wrong, he would have answered my question. Why don't we go and visit Missy or the young apprentice?"

Everyone looked at the warrior as if he had just been turned into a lizard, which was what they all believed would happen to them if they visited the *tohunga* and threatened her.

"Would you go to her?" Te Wharepouri asked with a hint of a smile.

The brave warrior, the victor of countless battles and slayer of many, licked his lips. His tongue darted out, a sure sign of unease. "Perhaps I spoke too soon, …without thinking," he replied.

The others laughed at his retraction.

"I will watch Barrett closely; I won't let him out of my sight," volunteered Honi, hoping to redeem himself in Te Wharepouri's eyes.

The chief looked to Honi and studied the young man closely. "Yes, go, Honi. Just make sure Barrett's man, who saw your face at Te Awaiti, doesn't see you. Take someone with you, go now, and be careful."

To the warrior with the sore face, Te Wharepouri said, "Go to Te Rauparaha and tell him what happened, that we failed. Understand?"

The Warrior nodded and stood, relieved that his offer to go to the *tohunga* had been rejected.

Te Wharepouri's stomach was a little upset, and he was tired. It was time to sleep. As he slowly walked towards his hut, he was puzzled by why his face had begun to twitch a little, and his arm felt numb.

Dickie Barrett was taken upstairs to his hotel room, and a doctor was called to attend to him. The assault wasn't reported.

The injuries were severe. Dickie had two cracked ribs, a concussion, multiple contusions, one broken tooth and a few loose ones. Both eyes were almost swollen shut, and his nose was broken. He was in pain and stayed in bed and out of sight for a few days before he felt able to move around. Even then, he did so gingerly and with help.

He knew who was behind the attack and felt no need to retaliate. With some satisfaction, Barrett knew that Chief Te Wharepouri was already feeling the effects of his poisoning.

The seeds of the Karaka tree are highly poisonous, and, as promised, Missy collected them, dried them, and ground them into a fine, toxic, ingestible powder. There was a woman at Te Wharepouri's *pa* whom Barrett paid handsomely. She would do as asked. She had no alternative. On returning from Te Awaiti, he arranged to meet with her, handed over the bottle containing the powdered seeds, and indicated how much poison should be mixed with his food. Too much powder would affect the taste and be detected; too little would have minimal effect. She was instructed to administer the poison to the chief's food daily until it was all gone.

Fearing the poison would be detected, she had mixed only small amounts into his food, and as a result the Chief began to experience only mild symptoms. The discomfort Te Wharepouri felt was a long way from the dramatic effects of Karaka poisoning Dickie had envisaged. A powerful neurological toxin, Karaka poisoning manifests as tremors, seizures, coma, respiratory problems and even permanent brain damage. Sustained ingestion would be fatal, and death would be painful.

What Barrett hadn't allowed for was Chief Te Wharepouri's constant travelling. He would often be away for days at a time, visiting family and checking on lands he controlled far from Wellington. During those times, the effects of the poisoning lessened. The woman could only poison his food when the chief was home. There were days when the chief felt unwell and days when he felt fine. If Dickie Barrett expected Chief Te Wharepouri to be poisoned and die within a short time, he'd be disappointed.

CHAPTER FORTY

Office of the Commissioner, Land Court Hearings, Manners Street, Wellington.

William Spain was genuinely upset by the news that Governor Hobson had died from a second attack of apoplexy. He fondly recalled his visit with the Governor in Russell and the afternoon spent drinking wine while looking out over the spectacular scenery of the bay, as Hobson dispensed advice. Spain believed Governor Hobson was an honourable man, motivated to do the right thing for New Zealand and all who lived here. The news also informed him that he must now report to acting Governor Willoughby Shortland, whom he had yet to meet.

Rumours circulating in Wellington suggested that Shortland wasn't exactly popular and that he had an embarrassing experience the first time he faced a Māori *haka*, a synchronised war dance. He naively assumed the Māori were about to attack him and ordered his soldiers to raise their rifles, ready to defend. Spain put little credence in malicious gossip and would judge the man fairly based on its own interactions with him.

On establishing his office in Wellington, William Spain immediately began his responsibilities to investigate the New Zealand Company's land purchases. The task was becoming more complex by the day.

Spain set down the latest correspondence he was reading and rubbed his forehead. This Land Commission was nothing more than political manoeuvring and posturing. Hobson instructed Spain to return to Māori the land that was unjustly held. As Hobson correctly assumed, others in political office saw the situation quite differently. Colonial Secretary Lord Normanby was more concerned with avoiding future wrongs than with putting matters right in accordance with the Treaty of Waitangi. The Colonial Secretary also informed him that much of the Wellington land, presently in dispute, had been more or less guaranteed to the New Zealand Company, apart from some token areas where Māori were permitted to live. The Imperial Government made no secret of its desire for prime land. Further, Spain had no powers other than to make recommendations on his findings. In coming to a decision, Spain immediately decided he would seek the authority to award grants.

From his desk, William Spain removed his jacket and began pacing the confines of his office. The Commission's recommendations and subsequent judgements would win him no favours, he thought. After considering the evidence presented to him at the land hearings, he was sure that, no matter how he ruled, he would incur the displeasure of many. A knock at the door interrupted his deliberations.

"Enter," ordered Spain.

"Excuse me, sir, you have an unannounced visitor, a Mr Stewart, from the New Zealand Company, requests a moment of your time," informed Spain's Secretary, Robert Yates.

"I'm busy at the moment; have him schedule an appointment like everyone else," instructed Spain, frustrated that the Company always felt they could intrude and have their way.

"Very well, sir," acknowledged the secretary, closing the door.

Spain resumed pacing, feeling a nagging sense. Then it dawned on him who Mr Stewart was, and he rushed to the door.

"Mister Yates, wait. Perhaps I can spare a moment. I will see Mr Stewart now, if you please," said Spain, closing the door, putting on his jacket, and returning to his desk.

After a polite knock on the door, Spain's secretary entered the office, with Andrew following. "Mr Spain, may I introduce Mr Andrew Stewart?"

"That will be all," said Spain to his secretary, who quietly left the office, leaving Spain and Andrew alone.

"How can I be of assistance Mister Stewart?"

"Thank you for seeing me without an appointment, sir. Colonel Wakefield asked me to bring this to you. It's called the Plan of Lands." Andrew handed over a tube containing a large map.

Spain unrolled the map from the tube on his desk. As its name suggested, it detailed the areas of land the New Zealand Company purchased from Māori around the Post Nicholson area and highlighted the boundaries as interpreted by the Company. Spain immediately placed it back into the tube. "I will look at this later, thank you. Please have a seat, Mr Stewart." William Spain gestured to a chair, indicating that Andrew should be seated.

"Why is a New Zealand Company accountant delivering messages?" Spain asked with a smile. "Surely you have more important things to do?"

How does he know I'm an accountant, wondered Andrew.

"Yes, sir, I'm normally quite busy, but there wasn't much to do this afternoon, so I offered to deliver this to you, as the colonel felt it important that you receive it at your earliest convenience."

"I see," said Spain, pondering his next question. "Why did you want to come here, Mr Stewart?" William Spain rested his elbows on the desk and leaned forward.

Andrew felt awkward at Commissioner Spain's directness, and suddenly it didn't seem quite so important to tell him about his suspicions. "It's a lovely afternoon for a walk, sir," offered Andrew, feeling uncomfortable.

Spain nodded, pausing for thought. "Yes, it is nice weather. In contrast, it reminds me of the inclement weather we had on our voyage over here. I'm sure you also endured unpleasant weather on your journey?"

The silence was awkward.

"I, I really need to return to the office, Mister Spain. Do you wish me to pass on any message to Colonel Wakefield?"

"No, but thank him for his, uh, map. I shall give it due consideration." Andrew stood and reached out his hand. "Good day, sir."

Spain stood from his desk, shook Andrew's hand, and walked to the door. Andrew didn't move.

"Is there something else Mister Stewart?"

Andrew looked at Spain and thought of Spain's wife and children, and of what they had endured. How close they had come to death. He owed it to this man to tell him what he knew, even if he could prove nothing.

"Yes, sir, there is."

"Sit." Spain walked back to his desk and again directed Andrew to the chair.

Andrew sat as requested and began fidgeting, uncertain how to proceed. Finally, he decided to come right out with it.

"Mister Spain, I have reason to believe that the *Prince Rupert* was intentionally sabotaged. I can't prove it, but I have my suspicions," began Andrew.

Spain remained quiet, reflecting on how Andrew's revelation supported Hobson's claim. "That is quite an accusation," he said after a brief pause. "Please, Mr Stewart, tell me what you know. I do appreciate your coming forward to share your knowledge with me, and I can promise you that your name will not be disclosed should anything eventuate. You have my solemn word on this."

Andrew told William Spain what he had overheard in Wakefield's office between Barrett and the colonel. He then took from his pocket the original invoice issued by Barrett, which had alerted him to Barrett's involvement. He handed it to Spain.

"The date has been written by someone else, as have the words *Prince Rupert*, which have been written again by another hand," stated Spain.

"Yes, sir, you are correct. The *Prince Rupert* was written by Colonel Wakefield, and the date of December 4th 1840 was written by me shortly after I questioned the colonel about it, which he confirmed."

"That is peculiar indeed," said Spain, rubbing his chin in thought. "That means Wakefield made payment to Barrett before the *Prince Rupert* even left Gravesend. And you say Colonel Wakefield confirmed that date?"

"That's what I believe too," said Andrew. "And yes, Colonel Wakefield was insistent that the date was correct."

"One hundred pounds is an unusually large sum of money, especially for translation services. Does that seem odd to you, Mister Stewart?"

Andrew inclined his head in agreement.

"As you suggest, this proves nothing; it's merely circumstantial. But it does tend to arouse suspicion about Barrett's actions, doesn't it?"

"I agree. That's why I felt you should know about it."

"It also implicates Wakefield"

"That's my belief too, sir."

"While I'd welcome the opportunity to question Barrett, I don't believe he would answer honestly, and apparently he is incapable of answering anyone's questions at the moment," offered Spain.

"Why is that, sir?"

"Have you not heard? It seems someone took to Mister Barrett and gave him a rather severe beating. I understand it was quite a savage attack."

Andrew was shocked. "Do they know who did this?"

"No, Barrett is tight-lipped and won't say anything."

Andrew was considering the possibility that Chief Te Wharepouri had something to do with it. Spain must have noticed, because he was looking at him intently.

"Why, do you know something?"

"No, sir, this is the first I've heard of Barrett's misfortune. I don't know who it could have been."

Spain watched Andrew carefully and surmised that Andrew knew more than he was letting on.

"What can you do about the information I have given you?" asked Andrew, changing the subject.

"Not much, I'm afraid. Unless further information comes to light, there is little I can do. But I am very grateful to you all the same."

"You are very welcome, sir," said Andrew, replacing the receipt in his pocket. "I had better return; the colonel will be anxious."

"Very well," replied Spain. "Should you come across any other relevant information, I hope you feel comfortable bringing it to my attention."

"Of course, Mister Spain."

William Spain rose from his chair to open the door for Andrew, then paused, turning to face him. "Why did you feel it important to share this information with me? Surely this conflicts with your loyalty to the Company?"

Andrew knew this question was coming and had expected it, and he had rehearsed his answer with Eleanor. "I am under contract to the New Zealand Company, but that does not mean either my wife or I condone the Company's business activities or objectives, sir," said Andrew with confidence.

"Can I ask what changed your mind? I am sure you didn't always feel that way."

This question was not what Andrew expected, and he was unsure how to respond. Spain waited patiently.

"Ah, no, we didn't," Andrew said slowly, as he formulated his response. "We -"

"We?" interrupted Spain.

"My wife, Eleanor, and I."

"Please continue."

"Eleanor and I believe that Māori have been taken advantage of, and that the Imperial Government and Company principals have an agenda to obtain as much land as possible, with Māori be damned! – They are fighting amongst themselves, the Government and the Company, like scavengers, to wrest as much as they can, with no thought of consequences or respect for the people who lived here before we came."

Andrew looked directly into Spain's eyes, gauging his reaction, the unintended outburst surprising himself.

Spain said nothing, folding his arms and slowly nodding. He watched Andrew as Andrew looked on. "Spoke with real passion, Mister Stewart. I applaud your conviction."

"When you have been here a little longer, Mister Spain, perhaps you will see for yourself, and may your judgments and rulings in the Land Court reflect that. Good day, sir," said Andrew, offering his hand again.

Spain shook Andrew's hand and opened the door, watching him as he left the office. *An interesting fellow* thought Spain.

Andrew walked down Manners Street, away from William Spain's office, unhappy with himself for speaking his mind. It wasn't his intention to be so forthcoming, and he hoped he hadn't said too much.

More surprising was what had happened to Barrett. Who was behind the attack? He didn't feel any empathy for the man. He had it coming, and if Barrett had received a beating, it was well deserved. He thought of Ngaiti, his best friend.

"Andrew! You valked past us. Is everything alright, ya?"

Looking back, Andrew saw Uncle Charles walking briskly towards him, with another man following closely behind. He grinned. "I'm sorry, Uncle, I didn't see you."

"You are thinking of food, ya," said Charles with a hearty laugh, giving Andrew a pat on the shoulder that almost knocked him over.

"No, far from it."

"Please forgive me. Andrew, this is my friend Tom Steward, a good man, ya?"

Tom took a step closer to Andrew and held out his hand, offering a smile.

"Tom, this is my nephew Andrew Stewart, almost za same name, ya?"

"Nice to meet you Mr Stewart."

Andrew looked at the face. He looked familiar. He'd seen him before, but couldn't place him. He shook hands and noticed his steel-grey eyes. They were cold and hard, not reflecting the warmth of the smile. Andrew took an instant dislike to the man.

"What have you been up to, Uncle?"

"Ya, ve have had a good day, and I met a business man, a nice mans," said Charles, turning to Tom, who nodded in affirmation. "Very funny mans and good head for business."

"I'm pleased you are meeting the right people in Wellington, Uncle."

"Yes, I sink so. But he vas not vell. He had injuries. I vill see him again in a day or two vhen he feels better, ya?"

Tom nodded and remained quiet, watching Andrew carefully.

Andrew knew of only one man who had apparently been recently injured. "What's his name?"

Charles felt a stab of guilt. It pained him to do this to Andrew and Eleanor. "Mr Barrett, ya?" he replied, hiding his discomfort.

CHAPTER FORTY–ONE

Thorndon, Wellington

"Calm down, Andy. Tell me slowly what happened?"

"Uncle Charles, he's made the acquaintance of Barrett! What is he thinking?" Andrew paced the small living room as Eleanor sat watching.

"We told him. He knew about the bad things Barrett has done. So why is he now making friends with the man?"

"I don't know Andy. Seems peculiar to me, too. Come and sit down."

"So now Uncle Charles has become best friends with Barrett. Next, he'll be down at the hotel drinking and gambling…" Andrew froze in mid-stride.

"What is it, Andy?"

"Him, the man Uncle Charles was with. Now I know where I remember his face. He was at the door of Barrett's Hotel."

"What are you talking about?" Eleanor asked, becoming frustrated.

"Earlier today, Uncle Charles was with a man. He introduced me to him. His name was… Steward, Tom Steward. Yes, it was almost the same as our name. He had cold eyes, Ellie, a little unsettling. But he looked familiar, and I couldn't remember when I had seen him. Now I know. It was the evening we went to the Settlers' Association meeting at Barrett's hotel. You became ill that night. You remember, Ellie, don't you? That man, Steward, was at the door. He's one of Barrett's men. I clearly remember him because of the way he was looking at you."

"Yes, of course, I remember. It is strange that Uncle Charles would associate with Barrett and his people after all we told him."

Andrew finally sat down in frustration. "We'll have to talk to him."

Charles Suisted wasn't thinking about his niece or nephew; he had just passed on another hand of Loo. More disconcerting was that he had a considerable sum invested in the pot, and with the way the cards were being dealt, it seemed unlikely he would win it back, he thought with a wry grin. He noticed others weren't playing particularly well either.

As usual on most weekend evenings, once the last inebriated patron had stumbled from his premises, Dickie Barrett hosted card games. More often than not, there were about twelve keen participants; on other occasions, as few as five. All were gentlemen with means. One thing was certain. Barrett won frequently, and he did so with graciousness, providing liberal amounts of alcohol that kept everyone happy, more or less.

Dickie sat in a comfortable chair, a rug draped over him, his battered body still recovering from the beating he'd received. He sucked on his pipe and watched the game, his swollen eyes darting quickly over the cards on the table with the experience of a seasoned player. Luck had deserted him on the last hand, and again he'd passed. He watched the newest member of their card-playing group, and even if he was a likeable oaf, the big Swede couldn't play Loo and was in danger of losing his purse.

When the next hand was dealt and the trump card turned over, Charles was happy. He knew the cards he held were good and would probably win the entire pot. He risked a casual glance at Barrett and immediately saw the familiar twitch of the pipe, indicating Barrett had also been dealt good cards. Tonight, Charles Suisted was only interested in winning back the money he'd laid on the table, as he had on each of the other few evenings he'd played. He didn't want to appear to be a good player, so he played his hands accordingly. He lost hands he should have won, played the wrong card at times, and appeared distracted and unfocused on the game.

Charles was tired and wanted to go home, but first he wanted to recoup his losses, and he quickly calculated he could do so on this hand. To vociferous laughter, he finished his tale about a particularly lithe young woman of questionable virtue from Valparaiso. While the story wasn't particularly amusing, it was the way Charles recounted it that created the mirth. With everyone distracted, he quietly won the first trick, allowed Barrett the second, took the third, and let Barrett win the fourth and fifth. Had anyone been observing closely, they would have assumed Charles Suisted was an enthusiastic gambler who showed little skill but was favoured with some good fortune from time to time. Barrett was grinning from ear to ear at his three-trick win, his eyes almost hidden by the swollen black-and-blue bruises that still marked his face. The other players lost considerable money and showed their displeasure by teasing Barrett in good-natured banter for winning yet again.

Slowly, Charles stood from the table, pushing his chair back and patting his pockets as if lamenting his losses. "Gentlemen, it's time for me to return home, ya?" He bowed his head formally to the remaining players, thanked Dickie, and headed for the door.

Disappointed that he didn't take Charles for more money, Dickie shouted to Charles's back as he strode away, "I'll get you next time."

Dickie didn't see Charles smile.

Tom Steward, also a keen gambler, decided to end his night before he lost any more money and yelled out for Charles to wait.

Once outside, they walked in the quiet of the evening, sharing a laugh at an unfortunate gambler who had lost badly again.

Within days of arriving in Wellington, Charles purchased a cottage, conveniently close to Lambton Quay, where Barrett's Hotel was located. Tom lived nearby, and it suited them both to walk home together, as they'd done since Charles became a regular at Barrett's.

When the two men saw a man lying in the deserted street, they immediately rushed over to offer assistance. Bending over the prone figure, Charles inquired about the man's condition but received no response. As he turned to comment to Tom, he noticed a fleeting dark shadow move behind them. Charles ducked as an axe swung viciously over his head, missing him by a scant inch. The man on the ground rose quickly, grabbed Tom, threw him to the ground, and attempted to launch a flurry of vicious punches.

The axe man, caught off balance, attempted a reverse swing, but Charles quickly rose and stepped back. The axe hissed past, narrowly missing his chest. The assailant staggered as he tried to regain his footing, and Charles calmly stepped forward and, with his right hand, delivered a stunning blow to the axe man's face. Immediately, the axe fell to the ground, and the man cried out, spitting broken teeth and blood. He stood for a moment, holding his face, cursed, and then ran off into the night.

Tom's attacker was receiving a brutal thrashing as Tom threw him onto his back and now crouched over him, savagely delivering punch after punch to the man's torso and face. Charles walked over and gripped Tom's shoulder.

"I zink he is done now, ya?" suggested Charles.

Tom straightened and watched the man curl protectively into a foetal position. "Who are these men? I've never seen them before," said Tom, breathing hard and rubbing his bloody knuckles.

"Ya, they want money," replied Charles.

They both looked at the man on the ground, who was now scooting back, trying to put distance between them.

"What did you want from us? What's your name?" yelled Tom, still showing signs of anger.

The would-be assailant cowered and remained silent.

"Let's go, Tom. They von't bother us again, will they?"

Tom landed one final brutal kick, then reluctantly stepped back at Charles's urging.

"They don't know who they are dealing with," stated Tom, as the two men resumed their walk home.

"I see you have fought before. You are a good fighter, Tom."

"I've been known to win a few, more than I care to remember," he replied, looking back over his shoulder to make sure they weren't being followed.

Charles was deep in thought. He knew Barrett had told Tom to keep a close watch on him, and from the way Tom pummelled the man, the attack didn't seem staged, though with Barrett, you never knew. Was it just a random attack, a robbery gone awry?

"A penny for your thoughts."

"Huh?" Charles looked around.

"You looked like you were miles away," said Tom.

"Ah, ya," laughed Charles. "I vas sinking, vhy ve vere attacked. It is strange, ya?"

"My thoughts too," said Tom, who was thinking almost the same thing as Charles.

They continued walking up Willis Street and were about to go their separate ways when a shout made them stop.

"Who is that?" asked Charles.

They waited together for the man to approach. As he drew nearer, Tom recognised him.

"That's Major Richmond, one of the Police Magistrates," Tom said in surprise.

"Good evening, sirs. I'm Richmond, the Police Magistrate. Please keep your hands out of your pockets, sir," the magistrate told Charles.

"It didn't take you long to get here, and we weren't even going to report the incident," said Tom. "Was there a witness to what happened?"

Charles looked on curiously.

"I just received a complaint that two gentlemen fitting your description attempted to rob an individual. When he refused to hand over the money, one of you beat him, then robbed him," said Richmond, speaking arrogantly. "I'd like you both to come with me to the courthouse, where I will take your details. I'll have your names now. You first," he pointed to Tom.

"Wait one minute. We were walking home when we came upon a figure lying on the road. It was nothing more than an ambush. Another man with an axe took a swing at Mr Suisted, while the man on the ground attempted to assault me."

The Magistrate showed little interest in Tom's version of the incident. "What is your name, sir?"

"Thomas Steward."

"And yours," Richmond looked to Charles.

"Charles Suisted."

"Let me look at your hands?" Richmond stepped closer to Charles, who held up both hands. Even in the moonlight, there were no marks, blood, or evidence that Charles had been in an altercation. Turning to Tom, who also held his hands up, Richmond could easily see scraped knuckles and blood. "Very well, sir. Both of you will accompany me."

The Crown Prosecutor sat down and studied his fingernails intently as the Chief Magistrate continued his tirade. Both Tom and Charles sat and listened as the magistrate berated the prosecution for wasting the Police Court's valuable time by presenting an alleged robbery case with insufficient evidence. Police Magistrate Richmond studied a point on the far wall, hoping to remain inconspicuous. The Chief Magistrate, satisfied that the officers of the court were aware of his less-than-friendly feelings towards them, looked to Charles and Tom and apologised for the imprudent police work and the imposition on their time. They were free to go.

Mr William Woods, the so-called aggrieved party, sat near the disinterested prosecutor and sported a bandage over his nose, matching black eyes, and felt less inclined to press his flimsy and ludicrous claim. He kept glancing towards the door, hoping to make a swift exit at the appropriate time.

Andrew and Eleanor were waiting near the entrance to the Police Court for Uncle Charles to appear. They'd not spoken to him and had only learned of the incident through Colonel Wakefield, who, after hearing about it from Barrett, made a rather desultory comment that cast doubt on the good name of Charles Suisted.

The door finally opened, and they watched as a man wearing a bandage over his nose quickly departed and disappeared. Tom was next to leave, followed by Charles. Seeing Eleanor and Andrew, Charles paused for a moment as if he was about to say something to them, then turned away, clapping Tom on the back and striding off. Tom also saw the young couple waiting and, seeing Charles's reaction, was surprised that he did not speak to them. Both men headed towards Barrett's Hotel.

"Uncle Charles!" yelled Andrew, but he received no response.

Eleanor looked on, surprised at the unexpected behaviour of her uncle.

"What's wrong with him? Why is he doing this?" queried Andrew.

"Let's go home, Andy," said Eleanor quietly, grabbing Andrew's arm.

Dickie Barrett was sitting in his favourite chair, still feeling the effects of his beating, when Charles and Tom entered the hotel, accompanied by Charles' booming laughter.

"I see you avoided gaol," said Barrett, grinning.

"Yes, the charges against us were dropped. Insufficient evidence, and it appeared the Chief Magistrate did not believe the allegation was even legitimate. He was none too happy," said Tom, bellying up to the bar.

Charles shook his head, "I cannot believes dis man vanted to press charges against us, ya?"

Tom laughed. "The cheek of the man. I wonder what happened to the other fellow. No sign of him."

"He is still hurting, ya?" Charles laughed.

"Have a drink," invited Dickie, "on me."

"Yes, a quick one, den I must go home, ya?" smiled Charles.

Toasting the judicial system, Charles downed his drink in a mighty swallow, bid Barrett farewell and thanks, and left the hotel with the intention of returning home.

Dickie nodded to one of his men, who quickly left, following Charles at a discreet distance.

"What happened?" asked Dickie in a serious tone.

"Not much, really. The magistrate dismissed the case, and we left. That annoying Stewart lad and his woman were waiting outside for Charles when we came out. He disregarded them and avoided all contact."

"Doesn't appear that Charles is on the best of terms with his niece and nephew," said Barrett, smiling.

"That's right, it doesn't appear so," replied Tom.

"Good." Barrett looked thoughtful for a moment. "When he first showed up here, I thought he'd be trouble."

Tom laughed. "I'd hate to be on the wrong side of him. You should have seen what he did with a single punch to that fellow who attacked him. I think we can trust him."

Dickie, sucked on his pipe and nodded.

"Ah, Dickie?"

Barrett turned to face Tom.

"Did you put those two blokes up to have a go at us?"

Barrett returned Tom's look and said nothing.

Charles was walking home, heading up Willis Street. He took his time, stopping to greet the odd person and chatting to merchants along the way. He loved nothing more than socialising and took every opportunity to be friendly and outgoing. He saw the man following him and knew Barrett had sent him. Identifying him was easy. He smiled. Everything was coming together nicely – except for the unfortunate incident the previous evening, the attempted robbery.

His smile vanished as he thought about Eleanor and Andrew. He hated doing this to them, but he had no choice. It was unfortunate that they were both involved and that they knew Barrett, something he had not counted on when he formulated his plan. But he had no other option. Neither his niece nor his nephew must be involved in what he was planning. If they knew what he intended to do, they could be in even greater danger. Since Barrett had already attempted to harm them once, he would probably do so again. It was best that he be seen to have no association with them. He took a deep breath and looked forward to the time when this unpleasant task was over.

CHAPTER FORTY–TWO

Land Court Hearings, Wellington

Colonel Wakefield was in a trance, sitting at his desk, staring into nothing. A housefly buzzing around the room broke the spell, and with a resigned sigh, he returned to the present and the unpleasantness of his mounting challenges. He was under constant pressure from immigrants, increasingly upset and more vocal about the lack of work available to them. They'd been promised jobs, and under the strategy outlined by his brother Edward, wealthy colonists who had purchased land would need the services of skilled workers. Company agents based in England were not as successful as first envisioned in luring the wealthy to New Zealand in sufficient numbers, and the publicised ongoing land disputes obviously contributed to the unease.

Communications between Company Directors and New Zealand were failing to address the worsening problem, and revenue from the sale of land to colonists was well below anticipated figures. Profits from land sales were used to bring immigrants to New Zealand, and the growing imbalance was a major cause of concern. Cash reserves were alarmingly low, especially given the Company's promise to build schools and churches.

Commissioner Spain's land hearings would begin later this morning, and Wakefield was keen to move on and put the ordeal behind him. The New Zealand Company Directors decided that Doctor George Evans would act as counsel for the New Zealand Company. A skilled barrister and gifted orator, Evans was a fair choice, although Wakefield was nervous about the strategy he intended to employ. Evans would undoubtedly challenge Spain and handle technical legal issues with ease. Still, Wakefield wasn't entirely convinced that the success of defending his land purchases hinged on legal jargon and the letter of imperial law. The complexity of legal documents was far beyond the comprehension of many, let alone of uneducated natives, whose understanding was at a childish level. As far as he was concerned, this was a moral issue, and he believed he'd acted with integrity and treated the savages with respect.

Against William Spain's wishes, Colonel Wakefield sent his younger brother, Arthur, to the Nelson area to acquire land and to pacify mounting disquiet among three thousand newly arrived colonists. The exuberant Captain Arthur Wakefield assured them they would receive all the land as promised, including one acre of urban land, fifty acres of suburban land, and one hundred and fifty acres of rural land. He enthusiastically insisted that land *would* be available and that the Company was taking every conceivable measure to satisfy its obligations. This proved somewhat challenging for Arthur, as land was scarce and the colonists' collective voice was strong.

Nelson's Chief Magistrate, Henry Thompson, sent a letter to Colonel Wakefield offering support and encouragement, and confirmed that his office would help ensure the Company's objectives were met and that colonists were mollified. It mattered not to Thompson that Chief Te Rauparaha had no desire to part with the rich and arable land he controlled in the northern region of the South Island. Even Edward Wakefield suggested that perhaps the Company should proceed cautiously rather than risk upsetting the Governor and volatile Māori.

Wakefield allowed himself a smile. This Land Court hearing was pure nonsense, and any irregularities would be dealt with easily and promptly. The real reason for this commission, he reasoned, was that the Imperial Government wanted the land the Company had purchased, and this was their perfidious way of obtaining it. To hell with Spain and its interference. The colonel gathered his papers and prepared to walk the short distance to the Court, where he would meet Dr Evans again before the hearing commenced.

Located on Lambton Quay, Wellington's Court House building was known to locals as the 'Barn of all Work'. It also housed a post office, a police station and a church. Not only could an individual be apprehended and sentenced for their criminal behaviour, but they could also presumably send a letter notifying loved ones of the reprehensible deeds they'd committed and then pray for atonement – all without stepping outside.

This morning's activities in the building were more secular in nature, and the appointed Land Claims Commissioner, William Spain, would finally begin the public phase of his investigation to determine the legality of the New Zealand Company's Port Nicholson land purchase. All available seating was taken, and those who came to observe looked on with curiosity, hoping for a spectacle. While some were here to witness the New Zealand Company receive its comeuppance, others came to see Māori put in their place. Newspapers sent reporters who stood lazily at the rear of the courtroom to chronicle the proceedings. The room was a buzz with chatter and noise.

Commissioner William Spain glanced around the room at all the interested parties. Of particular interest was Richard Barrett, who'd just entered and was warmly greeted by those he knew. Judging from the uproar, it appeared he knew most of those in attendance.

Once things had settled, all the preliminaries were dealt with in accordance with procedure, and everyone was sworn in. Commissioner Spain delivered a brief speech outlining the purpose of the hearings and immediately began addressing priority issues. The morning progressed smoothly, and after a brief break for luncheon, Spain continued with the intention of calling the first witness. Not all witnesses he'd summoned to appear before the court were available, notably Chief Te Wharepouri, who was ill. First to testify would be Colonel Wakefield, who would clarify a few points. Then the first major witness would be Dickie Barrett.

"Was it explained to the natives before they signed the deed that they were selling their villages, burial grounds and cultivated lands within the boundaries of the deed?" asked Spain of Wakefield.

"The expression made use of, was that they were selling all the land within those boundaries, but that reserves would be made for them; there was no special mention made as to their villages, burial grounds and cultivated land," replied Wakefield confidently.

There were a few other elementary questions, and Wakefield was stood down.

Richard Barrett was called, and Spain watched him with more than casual interest. Barrett appeared haughty and joked with the people seated near him. By outward appearances, it was plainly obvious he wasn't taking the hearings seriously at all.

Dickie's heart pounded. He was adept at showing the public his relaxed, jovial and amenable side, but inwardly he felt stifled in the crowded room, which didn't help his nerves. He waited with some trepidation for the commissioner to begin.

Once Commissioner Spain had established Richard Barrett's official role within the Company, he quickly focused on what he believed was the real and contentious issue.

"Mister Barrett, please tell this court exactly the terms in which you explained the deed of purchase to the gathered chiefs – in Māori!" requested Spain, holding up a copy of the original Port Nicholson deed of sale. With a flourish, he waved the handful of documents in the air for all to see, then handed a copy to Barrett.

Barrett's expression slowly changed. As he feared, his abilities as a translator were now being questioned. This was the moment he dreaded.

"Um, of course," Dickie paused, recollecting his thoughts and shifting in his seat, which had grown increasingly uncomfortable.

Spain secured the services of George Clarke, a long-time resident of New Zealand who was fluent in *Te Reo* Māori, sympathetic to their well-being, and familiar with their culture. He sat beside Spain and, as arranged, would transcribe Barrett's words and then translate them back to the court. Chief Te Puni looked on, waiting for Barrett, with a neutral expression. His response to questions about Barrett's translation would be crucial.

"Do you require more time, Mr Barrett?" asked Spain, peering over his spectacles.

Barrett nervously licked his lips and began to recount what he had told the chiefs. After a short time, he stopped.

"Carry on, Mr Barrett," asked Spain pleasantly.

Barrett turned his chair towards Wakefield, seeking support. Wakefield looked back and nodded for him to continue.

"That's it. That's what I told them," said Barrett.

"Perhaps I did not make myself clear, Mr Barrett. I asked whether you would convey to this court your translation of this entire deed and all its numerous pages - in the Māori language." Again, Spain held up his copy of the Deed-of-Sale, with all the pages, for everyone to see.

"Yes, sir, that's what I just did."

Wakefield's mouth opened as the realisation dawned on him.

It began with a short snicker from a single onlooker, and within moments, the entire gallery was laughing. Barrett, feeling humiliated, had nowhere to go and nowhere to hide. William Spain let the disruption continue longer than was normally acceptable; he was enjoying the moment.

"Order, please!" he finally demanded, looking at the red-faced Barrett.

Once things had settled, Spain requested that the court interpreter translate Barrett's latest remarks from Māori into English.

Colonel Wakefield leaned forward – his mouth agape.

George Clarke finished transcribing Barrett's recollection and stood. He cleared his throat and in a clear voice, began. "Listen, natives, all the People of Port Nicholson, this is a paper respecting the purchasing of land of yours, this paper has the names of the places of Port Nicholson, understand this is a good book, listen the whole of you natives - to write your names in this Book and the names of the places - are Tararua continuing on to the other side of Port Nicholson to the name of Parangarahau; it is a book of the names of the channels and the woods, the whole of them to write in this Book People of children the land to Wairaweki when the people arrive from England they will show you your part- the whole of you."

The court was deathly quiet as the spectators waited for Spain's response.

"Explain what Wairaweki is," Spain asked once Clarke had finished translating and resumed his seat.

"That is what some Māori call Colonel Wakefield," replied Barrett.

"Do you agree with Mr Clarke's interpretation of what you said?" asked Spain. A hint of a smile flickered at the corners of his mouth as he looked at Barrett.

Barrett swallowed hard, unsure how best to respond. He turned to the Colonel and received no look of support or encouragement.

"Mr Barrett?"

Again, the onlookers threatened to start laughing until Spain held up his hand.

The court waited for Barrett.

"Um, yes," Barrett replied softly.

"I'm sorry, Mr Barrett. Please speak up and clarify."

"Yes, I agree with George's version of what I said!"

This time, the commissioner was unable to prevent the laughter directed at Barrett. The uproar continued for a short while before order was finally restored. He looked with contempt at the man who had tried to kill him and his family, feeling no pity. Colonel Wakefield looked straight ahead, refusing to meet anyone's gaze, his anger clearly visible. He didn't understand …

Young Jerningham Wakefield, who would testify on the Company's behalf, wrote glowingly of Barrett's interpreting skills … Colonel William Wakefield was in shock. He tried to hide his embarrassment by looking down at his feet.

"Thank you, Mr Barrett. You may return to your seat. Would Chief Te Puni please come forward?"

Barrett walked slowly back to his chair amid sniggers and pointing fingers. Isaac Featherston sat at the rear of the court and shook his head in amazement. A short time later, Charles Suisted appeared and decided to sit beside Featherston in a reserved seat. Isaac slowly reached into his pocket and extracted a small, folded note. He casually lowered his hand to rest on the seat, and Charles reached across and took the note from Isaac and placed it in his own pocket. No one saw the exchange.

Everyone in the court was listening attentively. What Isaac heard only reinforced his belief that the New Zealand Company and its activities were nothing more than a ruse to extract money from the wealthy, with no regard for anyone who stood in their way. Noticeably Māori.

Mr Clarke translated, and Chief Te Puni slowly rose from the chair and, with a dignified air, walked to the chair Barrett had just vacated.

Through George Clarke, the court's official translator, Chief Honiana Te Puni-Kokopu, speaking to the best of his recollection, affirmed that Richard Barrett's account was a close approximation of what had been translated to himself, Chief Te Wharepouri, and the other chiefs on the *Tory* two years earlier. He kept his eyes on William Spain throughout. No one could doubt the sincerity or honesty of Chief Te Puni as he spoke to a hushed room.

Realising the implications of Barrett's translation, a voice from the back of the room shouted, "Is the title on my land valid?"

Other voices rose in question, which Spain quickly quelled.

Commissioner Spain adjourned the court for the day, and as people began to file out, Wakefield turned to Barrett and demanded to see him at his office immediately.

Without speaking a word and in a contemptuous mood, Wakefield returned to the New Zealand Company office and slammed his office door shut.

Andrew was at his desk, tidying up before he left work for the day, when Wakefield's private secretary, Simpkins, led Dickie Barrett through the office. Andrew looked up, expecting the habitual jibe that Dickie normally flung at him, but Barrett walked by without saying a word.

He entered the colonel's office as Wakefield's booming voice ordered Simpkins to get the hell out. Obviously offended, Simpkins said nothing as he scurried back to his desk in the outer office.

Andrew decided to loiter a little longer and learn a little about what was happening.

"I trusted you and paid you a fortune for your expertise, and what do I find out?" boomed the colonel. "I find out you are inept and incapable of speaking Māori! What a fool I've been." Wakefield shook his head. "By your deceit, you may have ruined all this Company has tried to achieve, not to mention the financial implications."

Wakefield was standing, leaning forward with both hands resting on his desk for support, glowering at Barrett.

"Good God, man, what were you thinking? Did you honestly believe you could hide this from me? The colonists already believe their land titles may be worthless, all because of you!"

Wakefield's face was red, his rage threatening to overwhelm reason.

"And as I've come to find out, you advised me to purchase land, knowing it would have disastrous effects on the stability of Māori tribes. I paid you for expert counsel, and through your greed, you have made a mockery of the New Zealand Company and its principals!"

Wakefield pointed an accusing finger at Dickie, who sat impassively, picking at his fingernails.

"You are worthless! You are worthless to me and a liability to this Company. I no longer have need of your services!" spluttered Colonel Wakefield. "Now get out!" He waved his arm towards the door.

Andrew had no need to move from his desk; he could hear every word clearly. He was grinning, enjoying the fact that poor old Dickie was finally receiving what was due.

"You have absolutely no idea what I've done for you, do you?" Barrett responded, his usually friendly demeanour with the colonel now absent. "If it wasn't for me, you'd still be sailing in circles, looking for land to buy!"

Barrett stood and faced William Wakefield, his eyes blazing with anger. "I've put money in your pockets when you deserved to fail. I bribed, cajoled and threatened on your behalf, and now, because you're facing some obstacles, you turn on those who helped you."

This time, Barrett raised a thick finger and pointed at Wakefield, "You are so naïve... Even those closest to you have taken advantage, and -"

"Totally preposterous," interrupted Wakefield.

"Oh, really? Then perhaps you should ask him!" shouted Barrett, pointing to the door.

"Who?"

"Your meddling accountant," laughed Barrett. "He's been scheming and plotting against you since the day you first arrived here, and you've been too stupid to see it."

Andrew's grin vanished.

Wakefield strode from behind his desk and opened the door. "Get out and don't let me catch sight of you again. People like you disgust me!" he shouted in derision. "Out!"

Colonel Wakefield neither saw nor heard the outer office door close as Andrew made his hasty departure.

Seething, Wakefield returned to his desk. The loss of Barrett was acceptable, and one that the Company could endure. Wakefield rubbed his chin, curious about the allegations made against his accountant, another matter to look into.

CHAPTER FORTY–THREE

Thorndon, Wellington

Andrew hurried home as quickly as possible to tell Eleanor what had happened at work. There was little satisfaction in knowing that the New Zealand Company no longer employed Barrett, as they both knew that if Wakefield believed Barrett, their employment and housing, both provided by the company, were in jeopardy.

Eleanor was distraught, and Andrew's attempts at reassurance offered little comfort, for he believed strongly that they were in a precarious position. They'd eaten their dinner in silence, each lost in their thoughts and worries, having realised that they were entirely dependent on the Company and at the will of their master, Colonel William Wakefield.

Since arriving in New Zealand, they had discussed on numerous occasions the possibility that Wakefield could dismiss them from service, but the prospect seemed so distant and unlikely that neither had been unduly concerned. Barrett's revelations to the colonel changed the picture considerably, but as Andrew pointed out, they could deny any accusations as nothing more than a weak attempt to ruin the relationship between the Company and them. Andrew decided that, if confronted, he would deny everything. After all, what had they really done?

Andrew looked over at Eleanor, who was dabbing her eyes.

"What will you do, Andy?" she asked, looking up.

"What can I do, Ellie? For heaven's sake, we can't do anything unless the colonel challenges us. I'm not going to do or say anything until he does so."

"We can't do nothing; we can't just sit here and wait for the axe to fall."

"Ellie!" Andrew raised his voice in frustration. "There is nothing I can do at present!"

"Well, perhaps you should give it some thought!"

Andrew stood in anger. "Why don't you remind me of all the options we have so I can think about which one is best? You're not listening to me!"

"What do you expect me to do, Andrew? Sit here like the dutiful wife and wait while you have a flash of inspiration? Sitting and doing nothing doesn't help us at all!" Eleanor stood and stormed past Andrew into the bedroom, slamming the door behind her.

"Perhaps running and hiding in the bedroom is a good solution for you, but it isn't for me!" shouted Andrew as he grabbed his coat and hat and left the house, slamming his door considerably louder than hers.

Andrew wandered aimlessly through the night, the smell of wood smoke and the distinctive call of New Zealand's native owl, the 'Morepork' (known to Māori as the 'Ruru'), echoing across the hills, deepening his loneliness. He'd never fought with Eleanor or raised his voice to her before, and he felt terrible. He continued his solitary walk, lost in the confusion of guilt, worry and love.

Before long, he found himself at the Featherston's home. The lights were still on inside, and Andrew paused, deciding whether to talk to Isaac. He was angry with Eleanor, but her actions weren't typical. She had never raised her voice at him before. Was this what being married was like? Without consciously being aware of it, he found himself knocking on the door.

"Andrew!" exclaimed Bethia, "What brings you out this late? Come in."

Once inside, as Bethia made a pot of tea, she told Andrew that Isaac had been called to Kaiwharawhara. Apparently, Chief Te Wharepouri was very ill, and his daughter Aroha had hoped Isaac might be able to help him.

"Is his ailment serious?"

"We'll have to wait for Isaac to return home. I don't really know."

Andrew lowered his head.

"What brings you by at this hour, Andy? Where's Ellie?"

Andrew held the teacup in both hands and stared into the fire. His expression gave him away.

"You've had a quarrel with Ellie, haven't you?"

Andrew didn't respond.

"Let me guess, you exchanged unkind words, she is pouting, and in a huff left the house with her pride wounded?" Bethia said, rocking slowly backwards and forwards with her youngest daughter in her arms.

"Yes, something like that."

Andrew went on to explain what caused the disagreement while Bethia sat quietly and listened.

"I can't tell you what you should or shouldn't do about your situation with the Company, Andrew, but I can tell you that if you go home to Ellie, tell her you love her, and you're sorry for leaving her, then she'll apologise, all will be well, you'll see," she offered reassuringly.

The sound of Isaac returning interrupted their conversation. "Andy, what on earth are you doing here at this hour?" Isaac inquired as he kissed his wife and baby after putting his doctor's bag on the floor.

"That is not your concern, Isaac Featherston. All has been resolved," warned Bethia with a smile and a wink at Andrew.

Andrew looked sheepishly at Isaac, prompting a laugh.

"Yes, ah, well, I think I understand," said Isaac, sitting down with a sigh. "Andy, my boy, I'm pleased you are here; it saves me a visit to see you. But I do have some rather distressing news."

"Bethia told me you'd been called to see Chief Te Wharepouri. Is it about him?"

Isaac fell silent for a moment as he formulated his reply. "Yes, it is. Chief Te Wharepouri is very unwell. I'm deeply concerned for him."

"Did he have an accident?" Andrew asked.

"No, no, nothing like that. It appears to be considerably more serious than a basic injury."

Andrew looked to Isaac.

"The prognosis for the Chief isn't good, I'm afraid. It appears he has a nervous disorder." Isaac sat down and faced Andrew. "He is experiencing seizures and tremors, the frequency of which appears to be worsening. His coordination has been affected, and his condition is deteriorating almost by the day. It doesn't look hopeful for him."

After a moment's pause, Andrew asked, "Is he in pain?"

"Yes, very much so."

"What can you do for him? Surely you have medicine that can cure it?"

"It's not quite that simple, Andrew."

"Is he likely to die?"

This time, it was Isaac's turn to fall silent for a moment. He looked down at the floor. After a moment, he looked up. "Yes, at his present rate of decline, I believe it is terminal. I'm sorry, Andrew."

"This is dreadful news." Andrew hung his head as Isaac and Bethia looked on.

"Does Eleanor know you are here?" asked Isaac.

"No," replied Andrew self-consciously.

"Then you should go to her, Andrew, hold her in your arms, and tell her that you love her," Bethia suggested.

"Yes, it is late; I should go home." Andrew eased himself out of the chair, walked to Bethia, gave her a peck on the cheek, and patted Isaac on the shoulder. "Thank you so much; you are both truly dear friends."

His walk home was lost in the confusion of Te Wharepouri's illness and the love he felt for Eleanor. He felt guilty for raising his voice to her.

When he arrived home, a blanket and a pillow were on his chair. The bedroom door was closed. He stood, staring at the door, deciding whether to go in and apologise. Perhaps Ellie would open it and come out. He desperately wanted to be with her. Instead, he settled into his chair, wrapped in his blanket, and spent a fitful, uncomfortable night alone with his thoughts.

CHAPTER FORTY–FOUR

Barrett's Hotel, Lambton Quay, Wellington

He began filling his pipe with methodical slowness, packing the tobacco firmly in the bowl, but not too hard. It had to be just right. He placed the stem in his mouth and gave a couple of experimental sucks before lighting a match. With a grimace, he slowly dipped his head, still feeling the odd twinge from the beating he'd received. With the flaming match held above the bowl, he sucked noisily, drawing the flame down. Within seconds, the smouldering tobacco enveloped him in a cloud of blue smoke. With a vigorous wave of his hand, he extinguished the match before he burned his fingers, then flicked it into a can at his feet. Dickie exhaled a long, drawn-out breath.

He was tired, sore and humiliated; he'd had enough. His life and dreams were crumbling around him. There was little future for him with the New Zealand Company – that much had been made perfectly clear to him by Wakefield. A shortage of whales meant that Te Awaiti offered little hope as a sound business venture; its days as a whaling station were numbered, and now people were finger-pointing and laughing at him. Yes, he had heard the off-handed comments directed at him, mocking his translating skills. Now he had to watch his back, as Māori probably wanted him dead. In fear for his life, he needed protection at all times; the threat made to him that evening in the storeroom was still vivid and one he took seriously. Since he'd testified at the Land Claim Court, he'd remained indoors and away from the public. Some people were even holding him responsible for their misfortunes and the worsening situation here in Wellington.

It was time to leave, and he wouldn't be sorry to go. He'd begun quietly by looking for a buyer for the hotel. Advertising its sale would suggest he was desperate and that he was running away to hide, and they'd offer him less. But subtle hints he'd dropped here and there would draw out any interested and potential purchasers with money.

Many people were unhappy in Wellington. Work was scarce, and there were no jobs. Rumours were rife that Colonel Wakefield was not responding to settlers' pleas, their cries for help going unanswered. Some even suggested he'd suffered a nervous illness. He was accused of abandonment, and now there were predictions that even food would become scarce. They couldn't blame him for that, although they'd probably try, he mused.

Perched on a stool at the back of the room, he surveyed the bar and looked around as people began to filter out. It was closing time, and the barmen were encouraging everyone to leave. Even the inebriated were carried outside and deposited on the beach to sleep it off. Order was being restored, and Dickie was looking forward to the evening ahead.

Normally, the game of Loo was played on weekend evenings at Barrett's Hotel. Small sums were won or lost, and those evenings were usually fun, informal gatherings where laughter and good-natured banter created a friendly yet competitive atmosphere. In the past year, every few months or so, Dickie would host a special evening of cards, during which they played a new game. The game was called poker and was familiar to most sailors, especially those who had been to America, where it had become increasingly popular. But here at Barrett's, they played with fifty-two cards instead of the twenty cards favoured by Americans.

Tonight was such a night, and Dickie extended invitations to select people only. It would be the usual group, influential gentlemen with deep pockets, plus the newcomer, Charles Suisted. He'd demonstrated a fondness for wagering, was agreeable and not prone to anger. By all accounts, he was a man of wealth and, based on his card-playing ability, was more enthusiastic than skilled. It wasn't friendship that prompted him to invite the Swede; it was his money. Tonight would likely be the last evening he hosted his poker evenings, and he was ready and prepared.

The man at the door admitted the players one by one, and with cheerful welcomes, they headed to the bar for drinks. With their thirst slaked, they lit cigars and chatted. Laughter preceded Charles' entry, and as usual, his huge presence drew all eyes. Some looked in question, as they were not acquainted with the giant Swede, but soon everyone was spellbound, to their ribald amusement, as Charles told another of his improbable tales, this time about a salacious oriental encounter. There was little risk of offence, as no women or clergy were in attendance this evening. Caught up in the merriment, even Dickie had to wipe his eyes.

Once everyone had settled down, Dickie assumed the role of host and directed all the players to take their seats. The rules and expected behaviour were explained, and everyone acknowledged understanding them.

Charles watched the other players carefully. He'd made a few discreet inquiries about the gentlemen he wasn't as familiar with and was reasonably comfortable with their card-playing talents, or lack thereof. Barrett was the dangerous one; Charles recognised and respected his skill, but he wasn't overly worried. He had faith in his own talents to best him. Since arriving in Wellington, it had been Charles Suisted's sole desire to bring about the downfall of Richard Barrett and take from him everything he deemed of value. Tonight was the final step, the night he'd been waiting for.

Charles Suisted and his family had lived in Van Diemen's Land, where he owned and operated a small flotilla of ships that plied to New South Wales and back, delivering merchandise and general goods. The struggling economy meant Charles needed to expand his operations. Looking further afield, he'd secured new contracts and ventured across the Tasman, beginning to deliver essential supplies to the whaling stations that lined New Zealand's Cook Strait. Fearful that competition would erode his lucrative profits, Barrett warned visiting ships away, his threats clear. Obliged to fulfil his existing contracts, Suisted had little option but to order his captains to ignore the illegal warnings and continue their delivery schedules to the whaling stations.

The first ship foundered and sank off the coast of Van Diemen's Land, which Charles attributed to pure bad luck. A short time later, another ship went down in similar circumstances. With suspicions aroused, Charles began an exhaustive investigation and soon discovered the culprit – a carpenter's mate who confessed and reluctantly admitted that a shipping agent in New South Wales had paid him to sabotage both ships. Charles paid the agent a friendly visit, and without much prompting, the agent quickly volunteered that his instructions had come from Dickie Barrett in New Zealand.

Charles came from a wealthy family in Sweden, and after his parents' deaths, he'd invested wisely in shipping. The loss of two valuable ships was just too much to bear in the failing economy of Van Diemen's Land; they were losses he couldn't sustain. It wasn't difficult to make some subtle inquiries about Dickie Barrett and to learn a lot. Among other things of interest, he learned about the regular card evenings and the occasional special poker games Barrett hosted. Seeking revenge, Charles devised a plan, which almost came unstuck when he discovered that Andrew and Eleanor were already acquainted with Barrett and were not thought highly of by him. Charles realised that if he wanted access to the card games, he'd need Barrett's trust. By distancing himself from the young couple, he ensured they would not be implicated or suspected of being active participants in his scheme. This would also protect them if things didn't work out. Although painful to do, it was why Charles avoided all contact with his niece and nephew. Barrett had seen evidence of it. As a result, Dickie trusted Charles, and before him lay an evening of poker – and the ultimate revenge.

The first few hands went as predicted. A couple of men, in their eagerness, wagered senselessly and lost, the recipients being both Charles and Dickie. Occasionally, Charles lost a hand or two and was only out of pocket by a paltry amount, while Dickie continued to slowly increase his purse. Barrett's boisterous nature increased in proportion to his winnings, while others remained surly as they contemplated their losses. So far,

Charles had yet to be dealt a hand in which he could place a reasonable bet. He knew that, with patience, good cards would eventually fall for him.

Finally, with some satisfaction, a hand dealt to him had potential. He turned in two cards, and the cards he received gave him a full house, three tens and two sevens. Much better, he thought. Charles tried to keep a tally of the other cards on the table. It sometimes proved useful, especially if someone was bluffing. But with this hand, Charles hoped to win.

Dickie removed his pipe, and Charles lost the advantage of the tell-tale signs of pipe twitching, always an indication that he held favourable cards. This wasn't helpful to Charles. He tried desperately to remember the cards he'd seen to confirm he had a winnable hand and then raised the stakes considerably. Dickie smiled. Favouring his own luck, he met the bet and, much to everyone's surprise, increased it.

Other players who'd been bemoaning their ill fortune stopped their chatter and looked on with curiosity. Seldom had they seen this much money on the table.

Charles kept his face impassive and raised his bet again. In response, Dickie increased the stakes. A deathly hush fell over the room as everyone turned to Charles, waiting to see how he would respond. Charles still had money in his pocket, but the money on the table was an impressive sum. Combined with everyone else's contribution, the pot must have been in excess of three hundred pounds.

Charles looked at Barrett's face as he again raised the bet.

Dickie licked his lips, feeling unsure. A flicker of doubt crossed his face. It would cost him about twenty pounds to see the Swede's hand, or perhaps he should count his losses and fold. It was too late now, decided Dickie. He had far too much money on the table to give up. He took a hefty swallow of rum and placed twenty pounds on the table – he wished to see his opponent's cards.

The other players leaned forward as Charles laid his cards down, revealing his full house. Barrett offered no grimace or smile and slowly fanned his cards on the table for everyone to see. A collective gasp went around the room. Barrett had laid down four of a kind – and won.

Charles was devastated. He'd been sure he held the better hand. He'd just lost around one hundred and fifty pounds, a small fortune.

Dickie was ecstatic, relishing the attention from the other players as they congratulated him. Charles offered a warm smile, downed an entire glass of rum, then stood to go to the toilet outside.

"You're not going home yet, are you? Let's play another. Give you a chance to win your money back," laughed Barrett.

"Ya, ya. Ve, play another," shouted Charles over his shoulder as he walked out, enjoying the fresh air.

The small waves lapped at his feet as he relieved himself. It felt good to be standing, especially after sitting cramped on a small, hard wooden chair for a couple of hours. He thought about the money he'd lost. It was a significant amount. If he went back inside to play more, he risked losing everything, and the thought of explaining to his wife what he'd done was not pleasant. Walking away now was the sensible thing to do. With a grimace, Charles buttoned himself up and decided to end this now and go home. He'd go back inside, say goodnight, and leave while he still had some dignity and some money. He'd find another way to get back at Barrett.

All the players stood to stretch. On seeing Charles return, they sat down expectantly, looking forward to continuing. Charles slowly walked towards the table to retrieve his coat and bid goodnight to everyone. Dickie sat down and immediately reached for his pipe and began packing it. Seeing Dickie with the pipe in his mouth gave Charles a rush of hope. He sat down with a laugh and rubbed his hands together, his desire and need to return home forgotten.

"Shall we begin, gentlemen, ya?"

Charles lost a little more money, as did Barrett, the cards failing to fall kindly for either. Dickie still had his pipe in his mouth when it began to twitch a little. A subtle movement, but enough for Charles to notice. His own hand also had potential. Deciding which cards to discard, Charles decided this was the moment and took a big risk. He had a pair of kings and decided to discard one. The dealer flicked him a replacement card, and Charles stared at it. Slowly, he thumbed the corner of the card as it sat on the table and had a quick peek.

Dickie's hand was good. He also threw out one card, and when he looked at his new card, he could hardly contain himself. With the pipe held firmly between his teeth, he flicked the end of it with his tongue ever so slightly. Charles saw the pipe move and knew Dickie had a good hand, but how good? This could go two ways, thought Charles. If Dickie had a bad hand, he wouldn't bet, but if he had a very good hand, he would most likely bet a lot. Were Barrett's cards better than his own?

The other players soon folded, leaving about fifty pounds on the table. Only Dickie and Charles remained in the game. Dickie increased the betting considerably. He added one hundred pounds to the pot and hoped Charles would fold or run out of money. Charles raised the bet by an additional fifty pounds, causing the other players to whistle in surprise.

Seeking confirmation, Dickie risked a glance at his cards. Two kings and three queens stared back at him. The pipe twitched again, and, with confidence, Dickie placed another hundred pounds on the table.

Charles was running out of money and couldn't maintain this high level of betting. He looked at the growing pile of money before him. All the money Dickie had won earlier, plus more now, lay on the table. Charles risked another look, carefully lifted his cards from the table, fanned them out before him, stared long and hard, and came to a quick decision. He met Dickie's bet and raised it by another one hundred pounds. He had no more money left; this was it – he hoped Dickie would not raise his bets further.

Dickie was now unsure. Could Charles have a better hand than he did? He looked at the table; in the middle sat more than £550 pounds. The other players remained quiet, occasionally exchanging glances and shaking their heads. Dickie wanted that money; he needed that money; his future depended on it. He placed his pipe on the table and licked his lips.

"That's uh, a lot of money, Charles."

"Ya, a little," replied Charles, appearing unconcerned.

"Uh, my hand will beat yours. Are you sure you want to continue?"

"Ya, but of course," said Charles with a big grin. "But you have to place a bet to find out, ya?"

Dickie paused, took another healthy gulp of rum, and looked at his cards again, just in case they had changed since he'd last looked.

"But I seem to have a slight problem. I didn't bring enough money with me this evening," said Dickie.

"Ah, ya, I zee," nodded Charles in sympathy.

Fearing that they would be called on to lend Barrett money, the other players seemed suddenly preoccupied and disinterested.

"And vat do you suggest?"

Barrett's mind was racing. He couldn't walk away from all that money on the table. "I tell you what, I will put this hotel on the table – actually, the lease."

Everyone was shocked and gasped at Dickie's offer.

"Are you sure you want to do that Dickie?" asked someone.

Dickie ignored the question. "But you see, the hotel lease is worth more than the hundred pounds I need to see your cards…"

"Ya, ya, I see. How about I put my house on the table? Your hotel and my home, ya?"

"And that makes our bets even?" asked Dickie, seeking confirmation. "I get to see your hand?"

"But of course, ya," said Charles, inclining his head in acceptance.

Dickie looked at his cards again, giving him time to think. "Very well." He went to turn his cards over.

"Ah, no, Dickie," laughed Charles. "Ve must first sign the paper, our agreement. Ya?"

"Yes, of course," said Barrett, nervously.

One of the players, William Brannagh, was a local Wellington barrister, and he quickly drew up a document for both men to sign. The other players enthusiastically signed as witnesses, and then Dickie and Charles both signed. One of the two men would win a sizeable sum of money this evening, either a cottage or a hotel and substantial cash.

Charles was feeling uncomfortable, his nerves beginning to take their toll. He looked over at Dickie, who was now sweating profusely; his pipe lay on the table.

"I think we should have a toast, eh?" Barrett suggested.

"Ya, vhy not."

Once the glasses of all the players had been filled, Brannagh raised his glass and said, "To the winner!" He then downed it.

"Hear, hear!" The others replied, following suit and draining their glasses with grimaces.

The signed agreement was placed in the middle of the table, on top of the money, where it sat, waiting for the winner to lay claim.

Charles' heart was pounding frantically; he was sure others could hear it. He looked again at Barrett, who was wiping his brow with a handkerchief.

Neatly folding the cloth and putting it back in his pocket, he looked up and said, "Charles?"

Swallowing hard, Charles took a deep breath and carefully turned his cards over, revealing his hand to everyone. A couple of men gasped and immediately looked to Barrett, who hadn't reacted. He sat, staring at the cards Charles laid out before him.

"Dickie?"

To sounds of astonishment, and with infinite slowness, Barrett flipped his cards. The five cards lay on the table, exposed. Everyone craned to see. Charles dropped his head and said a quick prayer, stunned and disbelieving. He looked up at Barrett, into his eyes, savouring the moment; his king-high straight flush beat Dickie's full house.

The other players were in shock. Everyone was staring at Dickie, who'd not said a word. Charles placed his head in his hands. He'd done it. Dickie had not only lost a fortune tonight – he'd lost his hotel!

Inside the hotel, it was quiet. All the men were still looking at Barrett, who remained silent. Scraping his chair back, Dickie slowly stood, carefully put his tobacco pouch and pipe in his pocket, and turned to Charles.

"Come back tomorrow at midday. Good night, gentlemen." He wasn't smiling as he walked away with a slight limp.

CHAPTER FORTY–FIVE

Wakefield Office and Residence, Thorndon

Unable to focus on his work, Andrew stared at the far wall, hoping for clarity and answers. Colonel Wakefield would be returning soon and, no doubt, would have questions. As if life couldn't get any more complicated, he thought. Uncle Charles had been acting strangely, as had Ellie, who remained cold and distant. The cosy, comfortable life he knew so well was falling apart. Even Chief Te Wharepouri was seriously ill; perhaps he should pay him a visit to see how he was doing. Andrew's reflections were interrupted by the intrusion of Wakefield's secretary, Simpkins, who informed him he had a late visitor.

Charles Suisted strode into the office with a smile that matched his presence – enormous. His mop of untidy curls only seemed to add to his height as he spread his arms wide, ready to squeeze the life out of Andrew. As Andrew stood to greet him, he was immediately enveloped in an affectionate embrace that threatened to cause permanent damage.

"Uncle!" exclaimed Andrew, before the breath was squeezed from him, "What a pleasant surprise."

"It's good to see you, ya?" said Charles, lowering Andrew to the floor.

"We've been worried about you. What's been going on? You've ignored us, and Ellie has been very upset."

"Ya, ya. I must apologise to you. I wanted to speak with you to explain. I know Ellie is upset. Can we talk here, ya?" Charles raised a single eyebrow in question.

"Yes, Colonel Wakefield is not here at the moment, and I will be going home soon, so we can talk. But you have been quite impolite." Andrew pointed to a chair, indicating for Charles to sit.

Charles looked around the office. "So this is the office of the great man Wakefield, eh?"

Andrew remained silent waiting for Charles to begin.

"And you do all za accountings?"

"That's correct."

Charles looked intently at Andrew, his smile replaced by genuine contrition. "I am sorry, Andy, to you and Ellie. But it vas necessary – to protect you both, ya?"

"To protect us, why, for heaven's sake!" responded Andrew testily.

Charles explained the loss of his two ships, the discovery of sabotage, and how the trail led to Wellington and Dickie Barrett.

"And you want revenge on Barrett?" asked Andrew.

"Ya, but I haves already taken revenge," said Charles, his customary smile returning.

"What?"

"Ya," laughed Charles. "I played cards vis him and won much."

Andrew couldn't hide his smile. "What did you win?"

"His hotel and abouts three hundred pounds, ya?" smirked Charles, threatening to destroy the chair as he leaned back, his thumbs hooked into his jacket lapels.

"His hotel! Barrett's Hotel?"

"Ya. But I could not haves Barrett sink you were involved, or he's not trust me. This is vhy I keep aways from you and Ellie, ya?"

Andrew began to laugh, "How wonderful is that, Uncle?"

Charles joined in the laughter.

"I can think of few reasons why, in the course of fulfilling his duties, an accountant should be amused or find a reason for frivolity," said Colonel Wakefield coldly, standing in the doorway, his expression less than friendly.

"Colonel Wake…" greeted Andrew.

"I can only surmise that you are not working and just wasting valuable company time?" admonished Wakefield, walking towards his own office.

Andrew swallowed. "Colonel Wakefield, this is my uncle, Captain Charles Suisted."

"Your reputation precedes you, Captain. I understand that, having escaped a robbery conviction, you are now the licence holder of Barrett's Hotel."

"Forgive me Colonels, I wanted to talk quickly vis my nephews, ya?" Charles extended his hand in greeting to Wakefield as he walked past. "But's I vill go now, ya?"

"It matters not; it appears Mr and Mrs Stewart are no longer in the employ of the New Zealand Company." He replied, ignoring the outstretched hand.

"What!" exclaimed Andrew in horror.

Wakefield stopped and turned. "I am no longer in need of your services, or those of your wife, Mr Stewart. Please ensure you remove your possessions from this office at your earliest convenience."

"For what reason?"

Ignoring the question, Wakefield continued, "I believe you have satisfied your obligations to the Company and will not be required to pay any bond. Of course, you will be required to vacate your home – by the end of the month, Mr Stewart." Wakefield entered his office and bellowed for Simpkins.

"Mr Simpkins, please see Mr Stewart and Mr Suisted to the door," he ordered as his secretary arrived.

Andrew was mute in shock, his mouth hung open. He took a step towards Wakefield's office, his anger beginning to boil over.

Charles latched on to Andrew's arm and held it in a vice-like grip, pulling him towards the door. With his free hand, he grabbed Andrew's coat.

"Do not worry, Andrew," said Charles as he propelled Andrew outside.

"You can't just dismiss me!" Andrew yelled over his shoulder to Wakefield.

Wakefield returned to his office doorway. "Mr Stewart, I can do anything I choose!"

Ellie knew something was amiss when Andrew unexpectedly arrived home with Uncle Charles, a little earlier than usual. The look on Andrew's face was a clear indication that all was not well. She looked disdainfully at her uncle, wondering at his part.

Once inside, Andrew explained that they had both been dismissed from the Company, and then it was Charles' turn. Ellie sat quietly as both men told her of the unfolding events; she said little, toying with the dish towel as Charles finished.

She blinked back her tears as she scolded Uncle Charles, admonishing him for his unacceptable behaviour. She added that he had no right to pretend they didn't exist, even if he was protecting them. The reprimanded uncle looked distinctly guilty. She then turned her attention to her husband, who couldn't meet her gaze.

"I've let you down, Ellie. I'm sorry. You deserve better than this," he finally said, looking up at her.

Eleanor stood and threw the towel onto the chair. In three quick steps, she ran to him and, from behind, wrapped her arms around his shoulders. "Andy, there isn't another person I could love as much as you. You've done nothing to disappoint me." She kissed him on the cheek and buried her face in his neck, hiding her tearful eyes.

Charles looked awkward, unsure where to look. Wanting to give them some privacy, he stood and quietly walked to the door.

"And you can sit yourself down, Charles Suisted!" said Eleanor, disengaging herself from Andrew. "Now we need to decide what we will do."

"I can ask around to see if any local businesses need an accountant," offered Andrew.

"And I should be able to find some housekeeping work," Eleanor added.

"Perhaps I can helps, ya?" beamed Uncle Charles. "Sit, please, ya?"

Charles waited for Eleanor to be seated. "I hope you both don't mind, but I have invited a friend to come here. He will be here soon, ya?"

Eleanor and Andrew exchanged looks, her eyes still brimming with tears. "Who, Uncle?"

"We should wait a little, Ellie. You'll see. And you do make good tea," Charles hinted.

"Not that Tom Steward fellow you introduced me to?" asked Andrew, some concern in his voice.

Charles laughed, "No, no, not him."

Eleanor went to make some tea while Charles recounted his evening playing poker at Barrett's and how he had come to win the hotel and money. Despite losing his position with the Company and being upset at the unfair dismissal, Andrew couldn't contain himself and laughed.

"Andrew, vis your head for numbers, you should play cards, ya?" Charles laughed. "Is good money."

"Over my dead body," retorted Eleanor, trying to look stern but failing.

A knock at the door interrupted their laughter as Eleanor went curiously to see who their visitor was.

"Good evening, Ellie."

"Isaac?" She stood and stared.

"Will you invite me in, or should I just sit on the step?"

"Excuse me, I'm sorry, Isaac, of course, please come in."

Andrew stood and greeted Isaac warmly, and then introduced Isaac to Uncle Charles.

"Ve haves already met, ya?" beamed Charles.

"I think there needs to be some explaining here," said Eleanor, her hands on her hips, the look on her face indicating that no one should argue.

"Some time ago," began Isaac, "Not long after the attempt on your life at Kaiwharawhara, Ellie told us at the cricket match that her uncle would be coming to Wellington. I took the liberty of finding Mr Suisted and sending him a letter."

"What?" cried Ellie.

"Now, just hang on a moment, Ellie," replied Isaac, holding up his hand to placate her. "In that letter, I expressed my concerns about your safety. Bethia and I had very serious apprehensions. We agreed to write and inform your uncle of what had happened to you." Isaac turned to Eleanor. "For goodness sake, Ellie! Andrew was nearly killed, Ngaiti was killed, your pig was killed, and both of you seemed quite oblivious to the potential for harm to befall you."

Eleanor reached for Andrew's hand, her expression softened.

"But there is more," Isaac turned to Charles, who had remained unusually quiet. "I'd also been attending to Chief Te Wharepouri during his illness, and he asked after you both. He was the one who suggested I contact a family member. It was his idea. He felt that, because of his illness, he couldn't keep watch over you as much as he wanted and thought it best to seek help from family. Bethia and I discussed it, and we agreed."

"But things have quietened down considerably," said Andrew.

"Ah, not quite, ya?" said Charles. "Chief Te Wharepouri had decided to take some sort of revenge against Barrett. It wasn't going to be pleasant, ya. He wanted Barrett to admit to having ah… Nut…"

"Ngaiti?" interrupted Isaac.

"Yes, … Ngaiti was killed, ya? But instead, Barrett received a bad beating. He thought that perhaps Barrett would come after Andy and Ellie."

"Thankfully, that never happened," finished Isaac.

"So you've been deliberately keeping away from us, watching Barrett while watching us?" asked Andrew.

"Ya, all of us," smiled Charles.

"And you met Chief Te Wharepouri?" Andrew asked.

"Oh, ya, many times, he may be sick, but he's a good drinker," Charles laughed.

"No, he shouldn't be drinking alcohol in his condition!" interjected Isaac.

Once the laughter had subsided, Charles continued. "But I also discovered that Barrett was responsible for the sabotage of two of my ships. I knew this before I came to Vellington, and I wanted my revenge - his hotel."

"Were you involved in this, Isaac?" asked Eleanor.

"Only to introduce Charles to Chief Te Wharepouri and pass messages between the two. You see, Charles was scared Barrett would be killed before he exacted his revenge, and that very nearly happened."

Charles nodded. "When I first came here to Vellington, I wanted to buy a business, other than to take my revenge on Barrett, ya?" Charles grinned. "Mary and I, ve talk abouts buying a hotel, and now I have a hotel," Charles shrugged his shoulders. "Then Chief Te Wharepouri told me about a hotel near his village. He says to me it would be perfect for Andrew and Eleanor. So, I talked with the owner, ya? With Mr Futter. Do you know James Futter? Mr Futter is the proprietor of the Vhite Horse Inn, which is in Kaiwh… uh, Kai…"

"Kaiwharawhara, the White Horse Inn is in Kaiwharawhara," offered Andrew.

"Ya, ya. Vell, Mr Futter is not happy, he wants to sell his hotel. But because I won much money from Barrett, I can afford to give you both money to buy this hotel?" Charles looked to both Eleanor and Andrew.

"Uncle, we can't…" began Eleanor.

"Ellie, this is goods for you both. Yes, I have money, plenty, so it's not problem, ya?" He spread his arms and grinned. "Let us go to the hotel and look, ya? And Chief Te Wharepouri, and Isaac and his wives want this for you."

The next day, Isaac, Charles, Eleanor and Andrew took a carriage and headed along the coast towards the village of Te Wharepouri, which bordered the White Horse Inn in Kaiwharawhara. The Inn sat on sections numbered eight and nine. It was a small hotel, with a few guest rooms, a dining room, a bar and a little land. It was nothing like Barrett's hotel, but as Uncle Charles explained, the Inn had the potential to provide a stable income if it was well managed. Andrew could easily manage the finances, Eleanor understood the hospitality side, and Charles was always available to help if they had problems.

James Futter was a small, fussy man who made no secret of being only too happy to leave Wellington with his family. After a little haggling over the value of the Inn, they finally agreed on a price, and Mr Futter sold the White Horse Inn to Andrew and Eleanor Stewart. Charles handed over a sizeable deposit, and Futter would receive the balance when Andrew and Eleanor took possession at the end of the month.

Andrew and Eleanor were ecstatic. Colonel Wakefield had unknowingly done them a favour, and now their future held promise for the young couple. Uncle Charles made it clear to them both that the money he used to purchase the hotel was not a loan; it was a gift. Charles was adamant and would not accept no for an answer. As Charles kept saying, "It was like Barrett bought the White Horse Inn for you, ya?"

Aroha came bounding up with youthful exuberance and launched herself into Eleanor's outstretched arms. Isaac, Uncle Charles and Andrew watched, all smiling broadly at the genuine display of affection. After separating herself, Aroha embraced Andrew, then Isaac, and, to everyone's surprise, she flew into the arms of Uncle Charles, who picked her up and held her tightly. Once she was safely back on the ground, Charles dug in his pocket, pulled out a small box tied with a red ribbon, and handed it to her. Surprised to receive the gift, she held it carefully with both hands as she looked into the eyes of Uncle Charles.

"Opens it, Aroha, it's a gift, for you, ya?"

Aroha looked to Eleanor for confirmation.

"Go on open it."

Aroha had tears in her eyes and turned back to Uncle Charles. "I've never received a present like this before. May I open it in front of Father?"

"Yes, of course, where is he?"

"Come, this way," she said over her shoulder and led them into the Marae.

At first, Andrew didn't recognise the chief. As they approached, Andrew saw an old man sitting in a chair outside a low hut, a cloak draped over his shoulders. With the aid of a stick, the man attempted to rise from the chair but failed, sitting back down awkwardly. It was only when the man looked up that Andrew realised it was Chief Te Wharepouri.

Afflicted with tremors, his hands shook, and occasionally an arm or a leg would spasm. He clutched a small cloth tightly in his fist and, now and then, used it to wipe the corners of his mouth, where spittle collected. His head seemed to shake ever so slightly, but his eyes shone brightly, sparkling with intensity. Both Andrew and Eleanor were astonished and didn't know what to say. The Chief looked like an old man, frail, weak and vulnerable.

With Aroha's help, Chief Wharepouri stood and welcomed his guests with the traditional *hongi*, then reached out with a trembling arm to shake their hands. Forgoing protocol, Eleanor leaned in and kissed the chief on the cheek. From his reaction, he didn't seem to mind. He returned to his chair and smiled at his guests, indicating with a trembling hand that they should sit. Once seated on the flax mats, he asked after their health and welfare as Aroha stood beside his chair, hopping from one foot to the other in impatience.

He finally turned to his beaming daughter. "What have you there, Aroha?"

She held out the box to him, the ribbon so bright in the afternoon sunlight. Speaking English, she told her father it was a gift from Uncle Charles. Te Wharepouri looked up from his chair towards Charles.

"Open it, Aroha." Even his voice shook.

She pulled the ribbon gently and the bow neatly unravelled. Curious, she lifted the small lid and peered inside. Wrapped in special paper lay a delicate white lacy handkerchief embroidered with a single gold thread. The thread was sewn into the finely woven cloth in an intricate, unbroken pattern of leaves and swirls, ending with a flourish. Aroha pulled the cloth from the box, feeling its softness and holding it to her face, her eyes closed as she breathed in the fine lavender fragrance. Eleanor turned to look at her Uncle Charles, touched by the thoughtfulness of his gesture. He seemed to have some dust in his eyes and didn't notice her glance.

"I have never received a gift such as this before, thank you very much," said Aroha with formal politeness to Uncle Charles. "Why have you brought me this?"

All heads turned to Charles.

"Is this not what we do for families?" He cleared his throat. "When I first came here, Chief Te Wharepouri told me how he and his people had accepted Andy and Ellie as family. Well then, is not Aroha, Chief Te Wharepouri and the people here also part of our family? Aroha has shown much kindness and love. A handkerchief is a small token to bring a smile to the face of a beautiful young lady, ya?"

Unused to such attention, Aroha blushed and thanked Charles again for the present.

Chief Te Wharepouri looked carefully at the faces of those gathered around him. He knew he was dying and had little time left. Each day, his condition worsened, and, as any loving father, he was concerned for his daughter's happiness and future. He was a good judge of character, which had helped him remain alive all these years, and from this small group of friends, he felt a genuine familial warmth that transcended race or culture.

He raised a trembling, unsteady hand and, with some difficulty, slowly dabbed at the drool that ran from his mouth onto his chin.

He felt reassured that Aroha would be cared for, not only by her immediate family but also by the *pakeha* who sat here with him. He looked into Eleanor's eyes, then into Andrew's. Yes, he trusted them implicitly. He turned his attention to Charles, the giant, soft-hearted man. It was obvious he loved Aroha as a daughter. Even the righteous Doctor Featherston, with so many children of his own… Aroha would be well looked after.

The frail chief raised a trembling hand again to wipe his mouth, but couldn't find his face. Aroha came to his aid, gently taking the cloth from his hand and softly wiping his chin. With his dignity restored, Chief Te Wharepouri focused on the group and saw Eleanor watching him, her tears glistening in the warm afternoon sunlight.

Aroha blushed and thanked Charles again. After a word from her father, she ran off to show her gift to others.

With his voice a little unsteady, Chief Te Wharepouri looked to Eleanor and Andrew, apologised for his ill health, and thanked them for visiting. He asked of their latest news.

Andrew spoke slowly so that the Chief could understand. Although his English had improved considerably, understanding the odd word still posed problems.

"Ellie and I are no longer employed by The New Zealand Company," Andrew began. "The cottage we live in belongs to the Company, so we must move elsewhere." Andrew couldn't hide his smile. "With Uncle Charles's help, we have purchased the White Horse Inn, and it seems we will be neighbours."

"This is how it should be," replied the chief slowly. "We can live here in peace, without fear of our enemies." He looked at Charles. "Your uncle is a good man, and I am proud to call him a friend." Te Wharepouri shook his head as he finished.

"I think both Ellie and I are fortunate to have special friends and family. We both feel truly blessed." He looked closely at each person. "We thank you so very much for all you have done for us."

The Chief sat quietly and nodded his understanding.

"What of Barrett?" asked Isaac. "Does anyone know what he is doing? Do we need to fear him?"

"Dickie said he vas moving from Vellingtons, ya? But that is all I knows."

"He has begun making plans to leave here, but we hope to make it difficult for him," said the Chief.

"Barrett is out of favour with Wakefield. I heard the colonel shouting at him, telling him he was no longer employed by the Company," added Andrew.

"Will he try anything against any of us? Are we still in danger?" Eleanor asked.

Everyone looked thoughtful, but no one had an answer.

Isaac stood, walked to the Chief's side, and spoke to him quietly. Te Wharepouri nodded, and Isaac began to check his pulse and perform other basic tests. The others stood and stretched their legs as Aroha came running back.

Colonel Wakefield sat at his desk, reviewing correspondence from England. He had instructed Simpkins not to admit any visitors and to turn them all away. He had no patience for mundane trivia today and certainly had had enough of colonists and settlers demanding that the Company pay for new buildings and facilities. The New Zealand Company had promised colonists and settlers that it would build and pay for schools and churches and provide public amenities as the township prospered. At present, there were more pressing matters to deal with. Cash reserves were down, and he needed money to purchase land and find jobs for the mounting number of unemployed.

The ever-increasing concerns from the New Zealand Company Board of Directors were becoming a nuisance. They had sent a letter informing him that they were sending an accountant to Wellington to conduct an audit and review the financials, and that the accountant would arrive in Wellington within the next few days. In light of Barrett's disclosure about Andrew Stewart's meddling, terminating his employment had been very convenient and timely. Regardless of what Barrett had told him, Andrew Stewart had served his purpose.

William Spain was taking his time with the Land Court hearings, and any hope of a quick resolution seemed very unlikely. Wakefield picked up a letter he had received from the Land Court. Until all disputes were settled, Spain had urged Wakefield not to pursue any land purchases in the Nelson region. Māori filed a claim over a land title dispute in the Wairau Valley, near Nelson, and, as advised, decided to place their trust in the legal process and would wait for the court's adjudication. Wakefield thought it was pure nonsense; it was nothing more than prevarication and delaying tactics.

He placed the letter back on his desk and leaned back in his chair. He felt tired, bone-weary and exhausted. At every turn, it seemed they were all out to get him – it was a battle, and he would emerge the victor. Wakefield grimaced as he thought of Barrett and what he'd done. How was it possible the man had deceived so many people about his language skills? Didn't anyone know? Surely someone must have had an inkling. Perhaps replacing Ngaiti with Barrett had been the wrong thing to do, he mused.

Simpkins knocked on the door again. "Go away, leave me in peace, damn-it," shouted the colonel.

PART THREE

CHAPTER FORTY–SIX

Kaiwharawhara, Wellington.

They'd been waiting impatiently for him, and three pairs of eyes now watched carefully as he slowly approached. They jostled for position, hoping to gain an advantage by pushing each other aside as he drew near. Usually, the sound of his voice indicated he was coming, but not today. No words were heard, and the speed at which he walked was different. His steps were unusually slow and measured. With squeals of delight, the small pigs were indifferent to his mood and temperament, caring only for the delicacies that would soon be presented to them. As expected, the bucket was upended and the treats spilled out, splattering the enclosure with a kaleidoscope of colour and texture, and a medley of complex, delicious flavours.

Andrew placed the bucket on the ground and sat on a nearby tree stump, his elbows resting on his knees as he slumped forward, watching the small pigs enjoy their breakfast. At that moment, the pigs had no interest in Andrew or his disposition; they cared not that he was distressed or for his sombre mood.

Eleanor stood at an upstairs window, the pale powder-blue of her dress standing out against the shadows of the room behind her. She looked down at her husband, her eyes red with tears. Seeing his slumped shoulders, she felt an upwelling of emotion that threatened to overwhelm her again. She flicked back a loose strand of hair, wiped her eyes, left the window, and moments later appeared on the path, heading towards him.

He shifted his legs slightly, opened his arms, and she sat on his knee, burying her head in his neck. Her arms reached around his shoulders, holding him tight. They sat this way for a while as the pigs snorted and grunted, oblivious to the couple's despair. Borne on the light morning breeze, the woeful sound of a *waiata* washed over them like a cloak of sadness, enveloping them with the memory of a man they had respected and loved.

Only a hundred yards away, the Kaiwharawhara Marae was in mourning. For many days, they'd been celebrating the life of Te Wharepouri, or Te Kakapoi-o-te-Rangi, as some knew him, as they said farewell and wished him a safe journey to meet his ancestors who had journeyed along that much-travelled path before him.

Wracked by spasms, tremors and seizures, his last weeks had been very unpleasant. Family remained at his side throughout his ordeal, and his older cousin, Chief Te Puni, was summoned when the Chief grew noticeably weaker. After his arrival, they had talked briefly. Te Wharepouri asked his cousin to assume the role of chief, and they'd reflected on their past deeds and lives together. Te Puni held his hand in comfort as they talked of happy times and the uncertain future ahead.

Chief Te Wharepouri's last words were to Te Puni, and he said, "*Muri nei ki aku taonga Māori ki aku taonga pakeha*", meaning "Care for my Māori and European people when I am gone". The pain and suffering were too much for the ailing chief, and he closed his eyes for the last time, passing into unconsciousness before his heart finally stopped. He was diagnosed as having succumbed to a brain tumour. Adhering to Māori custom, no autopsy was performed.

As a memorial tribute to Chief Te Wharepouri, Te Puni buried his body along with part of an unfinished *waka* he had been building, in Pito-one.

The *tangihanga* for Chief Te Wharepouri was a special event; people came from far and wide to honour the chief, celebrate his life, and remember the times they had spent with him. The sense of loss and emptiness was profound for Andrew and Eleanor, and the vibrant man would forever remain in their hearts.

Dickie was staring at the mountain that rose majestically from the fertile plains around New Plymouth. Covered in snow, Mount Egmont was bathed in sunlight, with the blue, cloudless sky providing a picturesque backdrop, a sight he never tired of. Nearby, cows grazed on the lush green grass, and birds flitted by, chirping and twittering as they tracked insects and called to each other in warning or greeting.

The warning shriek of a pair of plover drew Dickie's attention to a patrolling harrier hawk. As he watched, an aerial battle commenced, pitting the territorial plover against the larger bird, lazily swooping around trees and low hills in search of prey. With incredible speed and acceleration, the plover dived to strike the hawk. With a graceful flap of its enormous wings, the hawk dodged the oncoming missile and continued its hunt, almost oblivious and seemingly in contempt of its angry squawking attacker.

Dickie imagined himself as the plover in a contest against a bigger, stronger adversary. Again, the plover swooped low across the grass, then swept up with astonishing speed, rising above the hawk and beyond. At the apex of its climb, it turned with agility and, with a flash of its white wings, began gathering speed and momentum on its descent. The hawk, unperturbed and largely ignoring its noisy adversary, continued to hunt. From high above, the plover rocketed down. A collision seemed inevitable, and again, with a single powerful flap and a warning, the derisive hawk dropped its lethal talons in defence and, with precise timing, jinked away as the plover raced past. Dickie urged the plover to strike, willing the smaller bird to make contact and kill the arrogant hawk. Content to search elsewhere for food, the hawk lethargically altered course to patrol over another clump of bush on a low hillock not far away, while the plover returned to its mate on the grass below, satisfied it had defended its territory to the best of its ability.

Dickie spat on the grass. No longer welcome in Wellington, with his life threatened, his hotel taken from him, and his businesses all but ruined, Dickie was left with the scraps and had resorted to raising cattle hundreds of miles from Wellington. Taranaki would be his new home. He would leave his mark here, and people would remember Richard 'Dickie' Barrett for all the good things he had done and would still do. Dickie picked up his pipe and tobacco pouch and began filling the bowl.

Once his pipe was lit and he was settled, leaning back in his chair, his gaze returned to Mount Egmont, the immovable fixture that towered above the lowlands. Small wisps of cloud were forming near its summit, and before long the mountain would be hidden beneath a thick blanket of dense clouds, not unlike himself – hidden but still very present, an immovable force.

The news of Te Wharepouri's death travelled fast, and within a day or so Dickie heard that the Chief had died of a suspected brain tumour. Missy *had* delivered! Evidently her powerful poison was potent, and an adversary had been satisfactorily dealt with. He was pleased, though it was a little late. He wondered whether the Wakefields were safe from harm.

CHAPTER FORTY–SEVEN

Wairau Valley, Nelson Region

Sailors bent their backs and pulled, straining to propel the heavily laden longboat to shore. Grunting with the effort, the cox'n yelled, urging the sailors to pull in time to the cadence he'd set. The oars dipped into the water, and the sailors straightened their legs, pulling back as the boat slowly angled towards the beach.

Three surveying crews were already ashore, impatiently waiting for the rest of their equipment to arrive. They watched as the longboat approached and, with a clatter of oars, finally grounded on the beach. Immediately, chainmen and labourers rushed into the water to begin unloading the heavy cargo. Once unburdened, the longboat quickly returned to the anchored ship, *Victoria*, where it was loaded again for the last time and, ponderously, made its way back to the beach. After the last load was safely ashore, the surveyors meticulously checked and accounted for all their equipment before signalling to the ship that all was well.

The light breeze offered no respite to the men as they laboured in the hot sun. Sweat ran freely down their faces and backs as they hauled supplies and equipment from the beach to the base camp.

Chief Surveyor Frederick Tuckett watched the activity for a few moments before other surveyors, Mr Cotterell, Mr Parkinson and Mr Barnicoat, joined him on the small rise that gave them an expansive view of the large valley before them. Unfolding a rough map, he indicated the areas each would work in and discussed technical issues, emphasising safety. They scribbled notes in their field books as the Chief Surveyor droned on.

Of some concern to Mr Tuckett were local Māori who'd been observed watching them from a distance. Although no communication passed between them, Tuckett knew they were unhappy to see the surveyors here. On obtaining the title to the land, and with support from Henry Thompson, the Police Magistrate and Native Protector, Captain Arthur Wakefield gave Tuckett precise instructions. With expedience, survey and carve up the land into suitable plots for the waiting colonists. Somewhat apprehensive, Tuckett knew that Chief Te Rauparaha had contested Arthur Wakefield's assertion that the New Zealand Company had a valid title to this land and had lodged a protest with Commissioner Spain at the Land Court. Spain promised to visit Nelson and resolve the dispute as soon as he had concluded business in Wellington, instructing all parties to wait until then. With arrogance, Magistrate Thompson assured Tuckett that they were operating within the law, to ignore Commissioner Spain and any protests made by Māori, and to begin surveying as soon as possible. As Arthur Wakefield ordered, surveying would begin the next day.

Surveyor Cotterell and his team headed up the Wairau Valley, some distance from the base, and began setting up camp. The area became a hive of activity as men immediately began collecting rushes and necessary wood to build a thatched hut to store their equipment. Using canvas from an old sail, they gathered nearby wood to build a frame and erected a tent for sleeping. There was a lot of land to survey, and these men expected to be here for some time.

Two other surveying teams, led by Mr Parkinson and Mr Barnicoat, moved further down the valley to the areas they'd been instructed to survey. The three teams were now widely dispersed, separated by many miles. Each team built thatched storage huts and erected tents similar to Mr Cotterell's.

As the sun began its ascent, its warming rays taking the chill from the morning air, Cotterell's chainmen began carrying the long Gunter chains and laying them out in preparation for the arduous day ahead. Mr Cotterell was obsessively wiping his valuable theodolite, removing any dust and debris that may have accumulated since the last time it had been cleaned, while labourers created piles of arrows and pegs and tried to avoid the often grumpy surveyor, who was only too quick to deliver a rebuke, whether it was deserved or not. Slothfulness wasn't tolerated in Cotterell's team; he was only too willing to reproach anyone who didn't carry their weight. To anyone unfamiliar with surveying, the activity seemed chaotic and disorganised – to the surveyor, it was just another day.

Easily visible on the hillside, bright white boundary pegs marked the newly laid-out plots. The Gunter's chain rattled out, and Cotterell was busy waving his arms or shouting precise directions to the chainmen. They responded by moving in small increments left or right until Cotterell was satisfied. Labourers hauled stacks of pegs, moved the arrows used by the chainmen, and were kept busy. Boundaries were marked, and progress was being made. Cotterell was reasonably happy, as the Company should be, he thought.

In Wellington, William Wakefield was troubled, and not just by ill health. Arthur had been aggressive in his search for suitable land in the Nelson area and had obtained a large tract of land from the widow Blenkinsopp in the Wairau Valley. The authenticity of that deed of sale was now in question. Mrs Blenkinsopp claimed her husband, Captain John Blenkinsopp, had purchased the land directly from Chief Te Rauparaha, who controlled the area – the Chief claimed he had never received payment. Unwisely, Arthur pushed the issue by offering the Chief cash for the land. Te Rauparaha refused. He had no interest in selling any more land and quickly contacted Commissioner William Spain in protest.

Sources close to Wakefield informed him that Chief Te Rauparaha and his nephew, Chief Te Rangihaeata, had recently departed Kapiti and were heading to the Wairau Valley for a confrontation. Now more than ever, the impetuous Arthur needed to demonstrate calm and take positive steps to de-escalate a potentially volatile situation. Even Edward in England had urged caution. Arthur responded by writing that he would not be intimidated by travelling bullies and would forge on regardless.

Cotterell removed his hat and wiped his brow as a labourer came up the hill, running towards him, breathing hard and clearly out of breath.

"They be comin, they're comin!" yelled the young man as he pulled up panting.

"Who is coming?" growled Cotterell.

"Māori, sir. A whole lot of 'em, over there in the bay, in canoes!" He waved his arm to point into the distance.

Shading his eyes, Cotterell scanned the area. Just as the young labourer had stated, there were a number of canoes heading towards the mouth of the river.

"Get back to work, boy, I'll deal with it."

The labourer ran off to rejoin his crew.

Replacing his hat, Cotterell looked again. He counted eight canoes and a whaleboat. Although too distant to count the men, there was clearly a significant number, he thought. He hoped this was nothing serious and that he could warn them away if they came this way. Seeing something was amiss, the survey team stopped working, and all watched nervously.

"C'mon, back at it, lads," he barked.

There was little, if anything, he could do.

Chief Te Rauparaha urged calm on his nephew. Chief Te Rangihaeata wanted to storm the surveying sites and attack the *pakeha* invaders. He had little tolerance for European ways, especially in the face of the disrespect shown to Māori.

With the assurance that *pakeha* laws were fair and just to Māori, Te Rauparaha tried to settle this problem the *pakeha* way by taking his grievance directly to the Land Court.

Ignoring Spain's instructions and before Spain adjudicated on the protest, the New Zealand Company surveyors, under Captain Arthur Wakefield's orders, swarmed over his land and arrogantly assumed they had rightful possession. As far as Chief Te Rauparaha was concerned, this was an insult and demonstrated a clear lack of respect for both his people and the Land Court.

Te Rauparaha and his nephew, Te Rangihaeata, were riding in one of the many *waka* now heading towards the mouth of the Wairau River, which flowed into Cloudy Bay. The beach was rapidly approaching as large surf propelled the swiftly moving *waka* towards the shore. The accompanying whaleboat lagged, unable to match the speed of the narrower-beamed *wakas*. With expert handling, all the *waka* arrived without mishap, and the heavy craft were quickly hoisted and brought safely onto the beach. The whaleboat ground onto the stony shore, disgorging its occupants before large waves could flip it. Once under control, the boat was dragged up the beach alongside the *wakas*.

"We will stop here," said Te Rauparaha to his weary warriors. "Later, we will go up the river. Rest now."

"This is where we will build a *pa*," Chief Te Rauparaha said in the morning gloom. He pointed to a few landmarks, sweeping his arm to outline the area where he wanted the *pa* built.

A few men began to study the ground and issued instructions to begin construction immediately.

"Now I will visit the *pakeha*."

A murmur of approval rippled through the assembled warriors.

"We will bring only slaves; warriors will stay here," he added, looking sternly at the faces of the men gathered around him.

Before Chief Te Rangihaeata could question his uncle's decision, Te Rauparaha spoke.

"We have not come here to fight a battle," he said loudly for all to hear. "We have come to remove the *pakeha* from our land. This is my word – I have spoken!"

Without pausing for comments or questions, he moved away from the group and walked a short distance before stopping to stare up the hill towards the distant surveyors' camp.

The sun had not fully risen when the people of the Ngati Toa began erecting a stout fence, a palisade that would encircle a group of huts yet to be built. Chief Te Rauparaha chose this site well; it was easily defensible and offered a fine view of the Wairau Valley before them.

Thinking about the day ahead, Cotterell wondered about the large group of Māori. From his vantage point on the hill, he kept a close eye on them. During the night, they had moved and were now camped about six miles from the beach, near the Tuamarina Stream. He could see activity and correctly guessed they were constructing a *pa*. He expected a visit from them soon, probably this morning.

As his team prepared their equipment, Cotterell was amending notes in his field book when he looked up and saw a small group of about thirty Māori walking up the hill towards him. As they approached, he saw they were led by an older man whom Cotterell recognised as Chief Te Rauparaha, with the younger Chief Te Rangihaeata at his side.

Cotterell carefully put his notebook away and ensured his theodolite was safely stored and out of harm's way.

As the group approached and stopped, Surveyor Cotterell stood and stretched his back.

"You should not be here; this is not your land. You must leave!" ordered the warrior known as Chief Te Rangihaeata.

"I have a legal right to be here; it is you who are trespassing. Now clear off," Cotterell responded dismissively, waving his arm. His tone of voice was typically gruff and unfriendly.

Agitated by the demeanour of the *pakeha*, the younger chief toyed with his musket; he felt the touch of his uncle's hand on his arm, a reminder to exercise self-control. Turning, he spoke to his uncle. Unable to hear the exchange, Cotterell anticipated something dramatic was about to happen. Chief Te Rangihaeata spoke quickly, issuing instructions to the other men, who immediately ran into the surveyors' hut and began removing items stored inside. Others went to the tent and began emptying it of its contents.

"Hey, what are you doing?" shouted Cotterell. "The New Zealand Company owns this property. You have no right…"

All the equipment and chattels collected from the hut were placed on the ground some distance from the hut. Cotterell could only watch helplessly.

His protests were met with an icy stare from the young chief.

"There will be serious repercussions from this!" he warned.

The other members of the survey party were rounded up, and everyone stood anxiously together, wondering about their fate.

Cotterell smelled smoke and turned back to the hut, where he saw it had been set ablaze. The canvas from the empty tent was ripped from the wooden framework and placed with the other items, safely out of the way.

The wooden tent frame was dismantled and set alight. Pulled boundary pegs were added to the fire, but none of the surveyor's possessions were destroyed or damaged.

Feeling helpless, Cotterell was powerless to prevent the destruction, as Chief Te Rangihaeata kept a close watch on him. Chief Te Rauparaha stood with arms folded, a little apart from the group, watching the events with a scowl.

"Are we in danger, Mr Cotterell?" asked a timid voice.

"Shut it, will ya," responded Cotterell unpleasantly, also unsure of his future.

"But Mr Cotterell…" whined the young labourer.

"Quiet," hissed a chainman as he delivered a cuff to the nervous lad.

"You will leave now. To the *pa*!" ordered Chief Rangihaeata.

The surveyor and his team had no choice but to obey. The Māori began to gather the surveying equipment, stores and bedding. Cotterell ordered his men to help. Carrying all their possessions, they began the trek down the hill to the *pa,* still under construction, as the hut, fully engulfed in flames, collapsed in a shower of sparks.

"Will they kill us?" whispered the young labourer to another in a shaky voice, his fear evident.

"That's enough!" spat Cotterell.

As they arrived at the bottom of the hill and approached the *pa,* Cotterell could see a *waka* lying on the riverbank and a whaleboat tied to a tree, floating in the river.

All the equipment was carried to the river and loaded into the whaleboat.

"Where are you taking us?" asked Cotterell.

"You will be taken safely to Whites Bay," replied Chief Te Rangihaeata.

"I don't want to go there. Take us to Ocean Bay. That would be more convenient," insisted Cotterell.

Te Rangihaeata conferred with Te Rauparaha, "Yes, we will take you to Ocean Bay," he replied.

"What will you do now?" asked Cotterell, curious as to their intentions.

Chief Te Rangihaeata pointed up the valley, "Remove other *pakeha.*"

"This will sort the buggers out once and for all, eh, Captain?" said Police Magistrate Thompson as he handed over the arrest warrant for Chiefs Te Rauparaha and Te Rangihaeata.

"Arson!" exclaimed Wakefield. "That's it? That's all you can charge them with?"

"That's plenty. The courts won't look favourably on their behaviour, and the charge is serious enough for us to have them removed and detained," replied Thompson.

Arthur drummed his fingers on his desk as he thought through the next step. "You realise they won't come willingly. You'll need a sizeable force, and you don't have the resources."

"Already thought of that," smiled Thompson. "I'm going to swear in Special Constables, who'll be granted powers of arrest."

Arthur continued tapping his fingers. "We're going to need more than press-ganged constables, Thompson. Make sure you enlist the Crown Prosecutor's help. What's his name?"

"You mean Prosecutor Richardson. I've already spoken to him and to Justices of the Peace, Captains England and Macdonald. They're on board, Captain. All we need is to arm everyone."

The tapping continued. "Very well," finally said Arthur. "How many men will you bring?"

Thompson thought for a moment. "I reckon forty-seven constables, plus you and me. Chief surveyor Tuckett is keen to come along, and then the others. Ah, that's about fifty-three."

"Hope that will be enough, Thompson," said Arthur, looking up at the Magistrate.

"Shouldn't be a problem. According to Cotterell, Te Rauparaha didn't have much of a fighting force, and many were slaves."

"Hmm, we shall see," muttered Arthur.

Captain Wakefield instructed his secretary to locate the Company storekeeper, James Howard.

"I've commandeered the government brig *Victoria,* which is anchored in the harbour. She will take us in the morning if that is suitable, sir?"

"Very well, Thompson, tomorrow morning it is."

A knock at the door alerted Wakefield to Howard's presence. "Mr Howard, are you acquainted with Magistrate Thompson?"

"Yes, sir, we've been introduced," replied the diminutive storekeeper. His eyes darted around the office before settling on the Magistrate.

Thompson barely nodded in greeting.

"Mr Howard, I'll need you to provide weapons and ammunition, including cutlasses, muskets and pistols, to arm approximately fifty-three men. Please ensure you prepare this afternoon and be ready to distribute them early tomorrow morning."

Howard raised his eyebrows at the unusual request. "Of course, sir, if you'll excuse me, I will need a requisition." Again, his eyes flitted around Wakefield's office.

"You'll receive it this afternoon, Howard, that will be all."

Once James Howard had departed, "Anything else you need, Thompson?"

"Fair weather, Captain."

CHAPTER FORTY–EIGHT

Barrett's Hotel, Lambton Quay, Wellington

Since Charles Suisted became the proprietor, money was spent wisely to improve the hotel. Paint, comfortable chairs, and a welcoming, friendly atmosphere had done wonders for the place. Mrs Suisted and the children arrived from Van Diemen's Land, and she immediately went to work, cleaning, scrubbing and adding curtains. Her contribution added warmth that the ladies of Wellington gratefully appreciated.

Gone were the men of dubious character who always loitered in the shadows or stood at the door, suspiciously observing patrons. The sound of Charles' booming laughter now resonated throughout the establishment, as did his vivacious personality.

The Horticultural Society was holding another well-attended meeting at the hotel, and most of the seating was taken, although a few men still preferred to stand at the bar, allowing their wives to chat freely about matters only women discussed amongst themselves. Amidst friendly rivalries and much bravado, the results of the latest horticultural competition had been announced, and the lucky winners were all congratulated and prizes bestowed.

Isaac Featherston was beaming. He'd had the honour of receiving first prize in the vegetable category for the fine English potatoes he'd grown from seed, and he was then awarded another first prize for his peas. With smug satisfaction, he took particular delight in having bested Francis Molesworth, who had only received second prize for his collection of motley spuds. Although Molesworth, between mouthfuls of beer, boasted of winning first prize for his lovely cauliflower.

Andrew pointed out to Isaac, who'd just returned to his seat, that if all the prizes were tallied, Molesworth would be the undisputed champion, having received more prizes than anyone else. Isaac politely asked Andrew to keep those findings to himself, as making them public would serve no purpose for the community or for humanity. Not content to let things lie, Andrew reminded Isaac that he should enter the fruits category and begin growing berries. Colonel Wakefield won second prize with his cape gooseberries and was ripe for the plucking from his perch. He received an elbow in the ribs from Eleanor.

"Perhaps the boundaries of Colonel Wakefield's garden should be challenged by Spain!" offered Andrew, the effects of alcohol beginning to show.

The table erupted into laughter.

"I can see it now," said Andrew, tears streaming down his face. "Mr Wakefield, the Court has ruled that your gooseberries were in fact grown on Māori land. Therefore, you must forfeit any and all awards and recompense you have received."

Isaac howled with laughter. Even Eleanor, determined not to fall victim to Andrew's irreverent wit, couldn't contain herself. Bethia, not gifted with a developed sense of humour, joined in, which made Isaac laugh even harder.

"Do you have a problem with my cape gooseberries, Mr Stewart?" interrupted Colonel William Wakefield, standing over Andrew.

The laughter ended abruptly.

"Good evening, Mr Wakefield," offered Andrew, still smiling. "We were having a little fun at the Land Court's expense."

"I see… I fail to understand how you could find anything about the Land Court amusing. Would you care to enlighten me so I can share in your mirth?" Wakefield's eyes blazed with anger.

"Mr Wakefield, the conversation I was enjoying was with my friends and was private and…"

"Then perhaps you were mocking the Company?" interjected the colonel. "That *is* my concern."

"I don't find anything humorous in what the Company has done – far from it. So, if you'll excuse us…"

Eleanor leaned over, "Andrew," she whispered. "Leave it."

"It's quite all right, Ellie," he whispered back.

"And therein lies the problem. Your lack of understanding of Company activities is astounding to me. I'd prefer you keep your uninformed opinions to yourself and not share them in a public house for all to hear. Am I understood, Mr Stewart?"

Isaac stood, angered by Wakefield's aggressive behaviour. "You've gone too far, William!"

"Please, Isaac, sit down. I can deal with this," Andrew said quickly, rising from his chair to face Wakefield. "Colonel, you've given me a wonderful opportunity to tell you how I feel about your beloved Company. You," he pointed at Wakefield, "and all the Directors should feel ashamed of how you've exploited Māori. You've treated them unfairly and unjustly, with no thought for or understanding of them as people. And, sir, I shall share that opinion with anyone I choose."

Wakefield smirked. "Oh dear, you are so naïve. This is business and commerce, and as an official of that business, my responsibility is to return a profit to its shareholders and investors. And…"

"And," Andrew jumped in, "with no thought for how your business activities affect others. Your plan of Systemic Colonisation…" Andrew laughed. "Is nothing more than an invasion by any other name! You bring good, hard-working people to this country with promises of work and a future you can't provide, and, if the truth be told, they really aren't in a position to better themselves at all, are they, Colonel?"

Andrew allowed no time for Wakefield to respond.

"In fact, under the New Zealand Company's plan, they don't want workers to earn enough money to eventually purchase land." Andrew glared at Wakefield. "Do they!" he shouted.

Nearby conversations stopped as people began to listen to the argument.

"You've treated Māori like cattle and failed to show the decency or civility to treat them as people."

The colonel opened his mouth to interrupt.

"I have nothing but contempt for you and for anyone who supports the New Zealand Company's unethical pursuits." Andrew looked at Wakefield with disdain.

"They are savages; we've brought them prosperity, civilisation and laws!" Wakefield countered.

Hearing the commotion, Charles made his way to the table.

"You've brought them grief, and you should be ashamed of yourself!" Andrew retorted.

"He's absolutely correct, William. I agree with everything he's said. Now go and leave us in peace," Isaac stated emphatically.

"Gentlemen, gentlemen, please," said Charles as he arrived. "Please, Colonel, sit down and have some refreshments, ya?" He grabbed Wakefield's arm and led him back to his table at the other end of the room.

Wakefield's face was scarlet.

Andrew was shaking, his hands trembling with rage.

"I think he has had a little too much to drink," Bethia said after the colonel was out of earshot.

"I didn't realise he was close to us when I made that joke," Andrew said.

"No, I didn't see him either," Eleanor said.

"Well, you certainly told him," laughed Isaac. "I thought he was going to attack you."

"So did I," replied Eleanor. "In anger, he looks capable of anything."

Isaac looked thoughtful, and after a moment's silence, he said, "Let me tell you all something. William just doesn't understand. He has no idea what he's done and the impact the New Zealand Company is having on New Zealand and the Māori. Just because he is conducting business within the law, although that is debatable, he believes he is in the right. But there is a moral issue here and a humanitarian one that continues to be ignored. He's blinded – the man's a fool."

"I couldn't agree with you more," Andrew replied, shaking his head in wonder.

Uncle Charles returned, having ensured the colonel was calm again, and said quietly to Andrew, "Be careful, Andy. He is an angry man, ya?"

Andrew apologised to Uncle Charles for causing an incident, and the table returned to its previous good humour.

"What's the matter, Andy? You look concerned. Are you worried about the colonel?" inquired Isaac.

"No, I was thinking about Chief Te Wharepouri."

"Yes, and…?"

"You said it was a brain tumour that killed him, am I correct?"

"As Māori won't allow *pakeha* to perform an autopsy, then that is our best guess. Why?"

"Could it have been something else that killed him?"

"Like what, Andy, a numen or devil spirit?" Isaac laughed.

"I don't know… I was just thinking, that's all."

CHAPTER FORTY–NINE

Wairau Valley, Nelson Region

The New Zealand government brig *Victoria* set sail on the morning tide from Nelson, heading for the Wairau Valley via Queen Charlotte Sounds. On board were forty-seven Special Constables, sworn in by Police Magistrate Augustus Thompson, and a handful of others in their official magisterial capacities. On oath for this mission only, many of the constables showed little inclination to bear arms, especially given the possibility of a confrontation and the dangers ahead. They'd received no special training, and many were ordinary labourers, unfamiliar with military procedure and reluctant to put their lives on the line. The New Zealand Company opened its stores and provided the men with an assortment of well-used pistols, muskets, bayonets and cutlasses. Some men, now suitably armed, swaggered on deck with the confidence of pirates, while others looked uncomfortable and frightened.

As Magistrate Thompson informed everyone, the purpose of this mission was to execute an arrest warrant to remove and detain Chief Te Rauparaha and his nephew, Chief Te Rangihaeata, for wilfully setting fire to the surveying huts. They'd been charged with arson, and once apprehended, the trial would be held aboard the *Victoria*. This exercise, he explained with the vigour of a battlefield general, was simple and straightforward.

Captain Arthur Wakefield stood at the ship's rail as she approached the calm waters of Cloudy Bay towards the river mouth at the Wairau valley. In the distance, he could see the expanse of land he believed the New Zealand Company held title to. He hoped this unpleasantness would be resolved quickly so his surveying crews could return to work immediately.

With a resounding splash, the ship dropped her heavy anchor, and longboats were quickly released, settling onto the calm waters and expertly secured to the ship's side by the crew. Unused to disembarking in this manner, men clambered over the rail and lowered themselves awkwardly into the waiting boats. Avoiding mishaps, and once full, seamen began ferrying them to shore, where they assembled, waiting for Police Magistrate Thompson's final instructions.

With the confidence of the position he enjoyed, Thompson hoisted his trousers, puffed out his chest, and addressed the men.

"No one, no one, will discharge his weapon without an order to do so, is that understood?"

"We'll be bloody lucky if these things even fire!" came a voice. His tone emphasised the poor condition of the weapons everyone carried.

"Settle down, men. We've an unpleasant job to do, and we'll do it to the best of our ability!" responded Thompson.

With his hands on his hips, he regarded the diverse group of men standing nervously before him. Some nodded in response; others looked blankly back at him or uncomfortably at the ground at their feet.

"All we are doing here today is executing a warrant of arrest!" Thompson waved the document for all to see. "By the powers granted to you and to me as newly sworn Special Constables, we will remove from this land and detain two men, Te Rauparaha and Te Rangihaeata!" He paused for dramatic effect, underscoring the seriousness of their task. "Any questions before we begin?"

"When's lunch? I'm hungry," asked one voice, prompting a bout of laughter.

Another voice yelled, "Where's the privy? I need to go," causing more unruly reactions.

Ignoring the comments, Thompson picked up his musket, slung it over his shoulder, and, with Captain Arthur Wakefield at his side, began walking towards the Wairau Valley. Spread out in a long, untidy line, the others followed less enthusiastically on the six-mile trek.

Chief Te Rauparaha watched the *pakeha* as they slowly trudged towards the valley entrance. He could see they were armed, but he wasn't concerned. His warriors outnumbered them considerably.

He gave instructions for two groups of men to disperse and remain hidden, covering each flank, as a precaution should the situation turn violent. He would attempt to resolve the situation fairly and without bloodshed, and had made this clear to his armed warriors. His men were disciplined and would follow his instructions without question; many had fought alongside him in past battles, and he trusted them implicitly. To demonstrate his peaceful intentions, he agreed that women and children should not be sent away; they now mingled with his warriors. His nephew, Te Rangihaeata, had married his daughter, and he'd brought both her and their baby to watch. She sat near her husband, the child in her arms, and keenly observed the approaching *pakeha*.

"Come no closer!" yelled Chief Te Rangihaeata as the first Pakeha approached the stream that divided the two groups.

On hearing the command, Thompson and Captain Wakefield stopped. Arthur nervously repositioned his loaded musket, while Police Magistrate Thompson removed his hat and wiped his brow. It was hot and he was sweating. Ahead, on the other side of the Tuamarina Stream, he could see a large group of armed Māori. This didn't look good. Over his shoulder, he could see his constables standing anxiously behind him.

The Magistrate pulled the arrest warrant from his pocket. "I have a warrant for the arrest of Te Rauparaha and Te Rangihaeata for the crime of arson!" he yelled, waving the document for all to see.

Chief Te Rangihaeata and Chief Te Rauparaha conferred quietly.

"Only five men may cross the stream; the rest must wait!" shouted Chief Te Rangihaeata in reply.

It was quickly decided that Thompson, Wakefield, Cotterell, Captain England, the Justice of the Peace, and the Crown Prosecutor would cross the stream. Thompson ordered the other men to stand ready. They unshouldered their muskets and shifted their feet nervously. Many had their weapons loosely aimed at the Māori, a short distance away.

The small five-man group, led by Thompson, warily crossed the stream, the treacherous wet rocks making each step uncertain. Once across, Chief Te Rauparaha, with his hand extended in greeting, welcomed them.

Thompson ignored the gesture, repositioned his musket, and again held the arrest warrant directly in front of Chief Te Rauparaha. "We have come to arrest you and Te Rangihaeata for arson. You will come with us and stand trial."

Te Rauparaha scowled, offended by this man's lack of respect. He looked closely at the faces of the men standing before him, then turned back to the Magistrate. "How can I be arrested for burning wood that grew on my land?" he laughed. He recognised surveyor Cotterell. "Was not your equipment unharmed?"

Cotterell nodded.

"Come and sit with me. We can discuss this problem and talk so we can agree," offered Te Rauparaha.

"No, there will be no discussion!" yelled Thompson. "I'm required to arrest you – you must come."

Te Rauparaha shook his head slowly.

Thompson drew a pair of handcuffs from his pocket and clumsily reached for Te Rauparaha's hand. Seeing the aggressive move, warriors nearby stepped forward, their muskets at the ready. Offended by the lack of respect, a low growl rippled through their ranks. The chief stepped back as his nephew, Te Rangihaeata, tensed.

Sweating profusely and with his mouth suddenly dry, Arthur Wakefield was uncomfortable, frightened and unsure. Around him, heavily armed warriors glared with open hostility at the small group. Arthur risked a quick look over his shoulder. The sight of almost fifty poorly trained armed men in support now offered little comfort.

"Perhaps we should leave?" he suggested to Thompson quietly. "There may be a better way to serve the warrant at a later time."

Shaking his head and muttering under his breath, Thompson turned to the constables still waiting on the other side of the stream.

"Fix bayonets, and advance!" he yelled.

Wakefield looked up in surprise. *What was he doing?*

Chiefs Te Rauparaha and Te Rangihaeata exchanged looks of disbelief.

Scared and ill-trained, many men stood motionless and didn't respond, frightened to take aggressive action against such a feared and respected warrior as Chief Te Rauparaha.

"You heard me!" yelled Thompson. "Move!"

"We can talk, discuss this like men," repeated the older chief, opening his arms in appeal for restraint.

Again, Magistrate Thompson tried to reach for the elder chief's hand.

A flash of anger crossed Chief Te Rauparaha's face as he avoided the feeble attempt.

Reluctantly, some of the constables responded, attaching bayonets to their muskets, while the eager ones, with bayonets already affixed, began to cautiously cross the stream, the slippery rocks making it hazardous. A misplaced foot would result in a sprained ankle, or worse, humiliation at the expense of friends. Holding muskets at the ready while stepping on wet rocks was challenging. As instructed earlier in the day, the constables held their weapons horizontally and aimed forward, directly at their intended targets. One constable, eager to cross first, slipped. As his body teetered and threatened to tumble into the stream, he tightened his fingers in reflex, inadvertently squeezing the trigger and discharging his musket.

The ball travelled the short distance across the stream, almost hitting Arthur, and struck the chest of a Māori warrior. Mortally wounded, he collapsed with a grunt. Te Rauparaha saw the constable slip on the wet rocks and knew he'd accidentally fired his musket. He'd hoped the *pakeha* would see reason and stop – they didn't. The report of the weapon's discharge galvanised other men into action. Fearing they were being attacked, the constables began to shoot. Arthur watched in horror as his own musket seemed to fire of its own accord – the ball from his musket striking Te Rangihaeata's wife, instantly killing her.

"Retreat, retreat!" Thompson screamed above the din.

Yet no Māori retaliated; they'd not fired a shot.

Te Rangihaeata was in shock as he witnessed his wife's death, blood already seeping from beneath her still form. Men were shouting, and within seconds, more shots were fired, and another warrior fell.

Time seemed to stop for Te Rauparaha as he stared at his daughter's lifeless form. Unable to tear his eyes away from her, he roared in fury, ordering his men to fire their weapons and attack.

Constables were panicking and retreating across the stream as fast as possible.

Arthur, realising the situation was completely out of control, sought to return to the relative safety of the far bank. He saw Magistrate Thompson, who'd been very quick to retreat, running for cover.

The fusillade continued, and some shots missed their targets completely. Hit by a musket ball, another warrior fell to the ground, followed quickly by two more.

Constables began to fall, shot by enraged warriors. In fear, those looking back saw Māori warriors charge at them in an uncontrolled rage. Many carried a *patu,* a club raised above their heads, ready to strike the unwary on the head. Warriors ran through a cloud of blue smoke that hung suspended above the stream, firing their muskets and pistols and killing in unrestrained, vengeful fury – men fell screaming and died. Some warriors descended on the retreating constables, striking with carefully aimed blows to the neck and head with their clubs. Even the wounded were indiscriminately set upon. Māori warriors smashed bones and skulls with ease as the constables fled.

Incredibly, Arthur Wakefield was unhurt and tried to evade the oncoming warriors, but he knew it was pointless. They were killing everyone.

"Stop, stop, we surrender!" he cried, stumbling back from the onrushing warriors. "Ceasefire, ceasefire!" His pleas for the carnage to end went unheeded.

Intent on revenge, Māori spared no one.

"Lay down your arms! We surrender!" Wakefield threw down his musket and pistol and raised his arms.

Arthur Wakefield felt no pain when struck by the first shot. It felt like a powerful punch, and he stumbled. Recovering his footing, though unsteady, he was barely able to remain standing. He tried to yell for everyone to stop, but no sound came from his mouth. The second shot knocked him down, killing him instantly. He lay facing Police Magistrate Thompson, also on the ground, staring skyward with unseeing eyes, the back of his head caved in.

On hearing Wakefield's early cries for a ceasefire and surrender, some constables, including surveyor Cotterell, threw down their weapons and stood motionless. The pursuing warriors, incensed by the brutal and unprovoked attack on them, killed the constables without hesitation.

The first constables to cross the stream were all cut down, their blood tinting the water red. Devoid of life, other bodies littered the banks. Like red ribbons, their blood trickled between the rocks, a tributary of life that eventually fed the hungry stream.

Men lay wounded, some screaming in agony, others calling for mercy as warriors fell on them, silencing their cries with a quick thrust of a *taiaha* or a brutal club to the head.

Fortunate to be alive, some men ran for their lives and eventually reached the safety of Nelson. Five constables were wounded, leaving twenty-two *pakeha* bodies scattered across a small area.

Surprisingly, Chief Te Rauparaha came through unscathed, as did Te Rangihaeata. Both men surveyed the aftermath with heavy hearts. Four Māori had died, and their bodies were already being transported back to the newly built *pa*. Three wounded warriors were being tended to.

Chief Te Rauparaha walked amongst the dead and decided to leave the bodies for *Pakeha* to bury. He stopped at the corpse of the Police Magistrate who had tried to arrest him. Still clasped in the Magistrate's unmoving hand were the handcuffs he had tried unsuccessfully to place on the chief. Chief Te Rauparaha pried them from the Magistrate's fingers and held them high above his head for all his people to see.

With an aching heart, Te Rauparaha looked over at Te Rangihaeata, it was time to leave.

Newspaper editors wrote that retaliation would be swift and merciless, and that there were even rumours the Imperial Government would send warships to New Zealand to exact revenge on the marauding savages. Few were sympathetic to Māori, believing they stood in the way of progress. The newspapers called it the 'Wairoo Massacre', and many were confident that New Zealand's newly appointed Governor would take immediate and severe punitive action.

The newspapers did little to quell rumours and unsupported speculation. By embellishing the incident with published accounts of exaggerated Māori brutality, the papers incurred the displeasure of the newly appointed governor, Robert Fitzroy, and riled nervous colonists and settlers. Few dared to apportion blame to the New Zealand Company and to the actions of irresponsible officials who had zealously attempted to enforce the unlawful arrest warrant.

Colonel Wakefield was unwell. The news of his younger brother's death affected him deeply and contributed to his poor health. Both Edward and William repeatedly urged their younger brother to proceed with caution, but their sound advice was blatantly ignored. William claimed that he was no doubt persuaded and encouraged by the impetuous Magistrate Thompson.

Due to ill health, William Wakefield was unable to perform his duties as Principal Agent of the New Zealand Company and recommended that Francis Bell assume his role. The New Zealand Company Board of Directors readily agreed.

Recently vacated by Colonel Wakefield, Mr Bell now sat at his new desk, wondering what he'd got himself into. Land sales had ground to a halt, the country was virtually bankrupt, and the Company had little or no funds to purchase land. Even immigration to New Zealand had come to a virtual standstill, and many people, frightened by the prospect of outright war, chose to leave.

He picked up a glass of water, gulped down its contents, and rose from his chair. Walking to the window, he wiped condensation from the glass with his sleeve and looked out at the bleak, oppressive weather. The persistent drizzle settled in, and he expected it to last a day or two longer. A perfect welcome for the governor, he thought.

The turmoil following the Wairau incident simmered, threatening to escalate. To the disappointment of many, neither chief was arrested, and both remained at liberty in the Kapiti area. Recent reports indicated that

Chief Te Rauparaha was consolidating his forces and intended to attack Wellington. Other Māori returned to their iwi strongholds, fearing *pakeha* would seek vengeance against them.

Throughout the townships of Nelson and Wellington, groups of armed militia were formed, practised daily with weapons, and, in defence of their homes and families, began to dig trenches and fortify buildings. Curfews were imposed, currency was scarce, and the New Zealand Government was in debt. It was paramount that Governor Fitzroy resolve the situation quickly, appease the colonists, and prevent Māori from going to war. With a degree of hope, Bell had complete faith that Fitzroy would succeed when he visited the old Chief to complete his investigation of the Wairau tragedy. Governor Robert Fitzroy would arrive in Wellington tomorrow from Nelson, then travel to Kapiti and meet with Chief Te Rauparaha. He and William Spain would accompany the Governor. Their mission was urgent and of the utmost importance. They must seek a resolution and prevent further unnecessary killing.

CHAPTER FIFTY

Wakefield Residence, Thorndon

"The affront of the man," yelled Colonel William Wakefield, hurling the *'Wellington Independent'* newspaper to the floor in contempt. "How dare he! Do you realise who will read this? Do you?"

Wakefield immediately bent down to retrieve the offending newspaper from the floor and passed it to Doctor John Dorset, his closest friend. "Read it. What conclusion can you possibly draw from this nonsense?"

"Yes, William, I've already read it, more than once, may I remind you. And may I also remind you that your current disposition and annoyance are not conducive to your good health, for which I am responsible."

Ignoring the doctor's advice, Wakefield snatched the paper from Dorset's hands and poked at the article, stabbing it viciously with his finger. "I have never in my entire life been so insulted." He walked back to the fireplace, retrieved his brandy from the mantel, and emptied the glass with a shudder as he felt the burn. He looked again at the article.

> *Little Lessons for Local Politicians–No.1.*
> *An old woman had a stall, on which were plums and*
> *pears for sale.*
> *A sharp lad asked the price of all the plums and pears*
> *she had. She was deaf, and told the lad a price, which*
> *was in fact the price she would take for the plums.*
> *The lad wrote down the price, and that it was for the*

plums and the pears both, and got the old woman to set her mark to it, as she could not write. He then began to take up the pears, but the old woman said, she did not sell them.

He would go on to take them. The old woman cried out to the Policeman.

When he came up, the lad put the paper into his hand, but he saw from the old woman's mark that she could not write, and he thought she could not read.

So he said, "What did you sell the young man?"

Then the old woman told him, she had sold the plums, and the price at which she sold them.

"And a good price too," said the Policeman, "What more can you want for them?" Then he said to both of them, "What do you say to the pears?" And they did not speak. So he said, "The lad should have the plums, and not the pears."

Then the lad said, "Blind Bay and Cloudy Bay bought at the same time by the same deeds, with the same goods. Blind Bay acknowledged by the Commissioner himself to have been better bought than any other land in New Zealand, must not Cloudy Bay have been so too?"

Can anything be more conclusive? Why should the sharp lad have made any difference. Pears must have been thought then worth more than plums. Can we doubt that the Policeman should have said the pears have been bought as well as the plums. If the case of the New Zealand Company rested upon such shallow reasoning, it is time for the shareholders to dissolve it.

"The man has declared to the entire world that I am a liar and a thief!" In disgust this time, he threw the newspaper into the fire with finality and watched the flames hungrily consume it.

"William, you're going to have to let this go, or it will cause you even more harm. It's just a weak analogy about pears and plums. There's nothing you can do. You're not the editor of the newspaper, so you have no real opportunity to offer a rebuttal or retort."

"And herein lies the problem, John," said Wakefield, both hands on the mantelpiece as he stared at the dancing flames before him.

Dorset sat and watched as his best friend tormented himself over the critical editorial piece Isaac Featherston had written. The emotional and fiery Isaac, an ever-present thorn in William's side, finally overstepped the bounds of graciousness and civility, causing serious public offence to the esteemed Colonel William Wakefield by challenging his character in a most scurrilous manner.

Deep in thought, Colonel Wakefield tried to make sense of his predicament. "It's my honour and reputation that's been slighted," he said, walking away from the fire's heat and returning to his chair.

"Yes, I would agree," said Dorset helpfully.

Wakefield grunted. "Well, that's settled then."

"What's settled?"

"Irish Rules John."

"Irish Rules? Are you out of your mind?" said Dorset, leaping from his chair to stare incredulously at Wakefield. "What on earth would prompt you to choose that course of action? You've gone crazy!" spluttered Dorset. "Have you been self-medicating again, William?"

"My honour and reputation have been offended, and I will not sit by and allow that fool Featherston to continue slandering me. It has to stop! Failure to respond can be seen as nothing more than an admission of guilt and highlights a weakness of character, neither of which I possess."

"Well, that's not what I'm questioning, William–"

"Damn it, John, it's exactly that!"

"You're taking this to extremes and overreacting."

"Over-reacting! What do you suggest I do? File a motion with the Horticultural Society, or, better yet, do what Dickie Barrett would probably have done and have him beaten in a dark alley?"

"And look what good that did Barrett. It had him chased out of town to hide in the backwoods of Taranaki - forever in fear for his life," said Dorset, returning to his seat with a dramatic wave of his arm.

The two men sat in silence.

"Irish Rules John. There's no other option," said Wakefield decisively.

The insistent pounding at the door made Eleanor look up in alarm.

"Who could that be?" she asked, setting her knitting on the floor.

Andrew rose from his chair and peered through the curtains. "It's Isaac!"

He hurried down the stairs and greeted his friend.

"Isaac, what's the matter? You're winded," enquired Andrew, holding the door open for Doctor Featherston to enter.

"I wish you lived closer to town," he gasped as he climbed the stairs and entered the Stewarts' living quarters at the back of the Inn. "Eleanor, how lovely to see you."

Eleanor rose with some difficulty from her chair to greet Isaac.

"No, please, don't get up on my account." Isaac strode over to kiss her on the cheek. "As always, Eleanor, you look wonderful. Being with child suits you," he offered, helping her back to the chair.

"Isaac Featherston, what have you done?" Eleanor asked. "Do you think I will succumb to your flattery so easily?" she admonished him with mock sternness. "I know you, and you've done something. Is everything all right?"

"What's happened, Isaac?" queried Andrew, indicating for him to sit.

"Have you seen today's paper?" Isaac asked.

"Only briefly," Andrew replied. "Why?"

"I wrote an editorial highlighting the mendacious activities of William Wakefield. The article, er, could be perceived as a personal attack on his character."

"Good," Andrew responded. "And about time, too."

"He's taken offence at the article and accused me of ruining his reputation and of offending his honour."

"That doesn't surprise me," Eleanor replied.

Andrew handed Isaac a glass of wine, then returned to his own seat. "And?" Andrew asked cautiously.

Isaac turned to look at Eleanor, then at Andrew. "Duello!"

"What!" shouted Andrew. "Surely this is just a prank?"

"No, it's not Andrew."

"What's a duello?"

"A duel, Ellie. It appears the colonel has challenged Isaac to a duel. Am I correct?"

"Oh no, Isaac!" Eleanor cried, her hand clamped over her mouth in shock.

"Tell us what happened, Isaac."

Isaac took a deep breath, followed by a healthy sip of wine, and began. "About two hours ago, Wakefield's man, John Dorset, came to see me at home. He informed me that Wakefield felt his honour as a gentleman had been questioned and challenged me to a duel. Apparently, he has appointed Dorset as his second," Isaac said, shaking his head and laughing.

"What's a second?" Eleanor asked.

"He ensures the duel is conducted fairly and assists his man by making sure the rules are understood and adhered to. If pistols are used, he loads the weapon. He also attempts to solicit an apology when relevant - Isn't that correct?" Andrew said, turning to Isaac.

"And you want Andrew to be your second?" Eleanor asked, her anger beginning to show.

Isaac looked at Andrew sheepishly, "Would you?"

"Isaac Featherston, you have no business duelling when you have a lovely wife and such wonderful daughters," reminded Eleanor.

"Did you accept?" asked Andrew.

Isaac looked down at his feet, not responding.

"You accepted, didn't you!" cried Eleanor. "What did Bethia say? Isaac Featherston, if I wasn't in this condition, I'd knock some sense into you – how could you?"

"I accepted because I have no alternative," Isaac said quietly. "What I wrote in the paper, I believe, was the truth. If I declined to duel or apologised, that would admit what I wrote was untrue, that I lied." Isaac looked up at Eleanor. "Don't you see? I have no choice." Isaac placed his head in his hands, now visibly upset.

After a moment of silence, as Andrew and Eleanor exchanged glances, Andrew asked, "What weapons did you choose?"

"Pistols, I'm no swordsman."

"And you're no pistoleer either," Andrew added.

"Dear God!" cried Eleanor.

"Andrew, will you be my second?"

Andrew looked again at Eleanor. "Yes, Isaac, I'll be your second."

"When will this duel take place?" Eleanor asked, shaking her head in disbelief.

"Tomorrow morning at dawn, on the hill near the cemetery on Thorndon's south side," replied Isaac. "And it's Irish Rules, Andy."

"What are Irish Rules?"

"That's where the entire duel follows a strict procedure. Isaac, did Dorset seek an apology from you when he came to see you?"

"Yes, he did, and of course I declined."

"And what of the pistols, where will you obtain them?"

"Wakefield has a pair of duelling pistols, I agreed we can use them."

"Oh, Isaac, what have you done?" asked Andrew sadly.

Dawn was slow to break. Dark, black clouds raced across the hilltops, preventing the sun's first rays from shining on the small group of men gathered in the early-morning chill on the hill overlooking the township of Wellington. Large trees swayed in protest as their leaves eerily rustled to and fro. Long grass lay flattened by the powerful gusts of unseasonably cool, windy weather. Even the birds had yet to begin their optimistic dawn greeting. It wasn't a beautiful morning, and this was reflected in the sombre mood of the four men who stood bundled in coats and scarves in the melancholy grounds of the cemetery. They all waited anxiously for sufficient light, so that two of them could uphold and restore their aggrieved honour and pride.

Seeking privacy, Isaac and Andrew stood a short distance from Wakefield and Dorset as they discussed tactics.

"The wind will be coming from your right and will have a considerable effect on your shot, so make sure you aim slightly to the right and a little high, as it will drop and veer off target," reminded Andrew.

"How come you know so much about this?" Isaac asked.

"I grew up on a farm, and as a young lad, I'd often go hunting with a pistol. I used to be quite a good shot."

"You should be the one facing Wakefield," Isaac said with a smile he didn't feel.

"Perhaps in the new light of day, cooler heads will prevail," said Andrew as he turned to look at the dark shadow of Wakefield, bathed in the dull yellow glow of a lantern. "He may have reconsidered and realised that his wounded pride is nothing more than a slight scratch."

"I doubt it. Wakefield is a pig-headed, obstinate fool," said Isaac, following Andrews' gaze.

"I'm going to ask if he has reconsidered," said Andrew.

As Andrew walked over, Dorset saw him coming and walked to meet him, carrying the lantern.

"Has the colonel changed his mind and decided this duel is ridiculous?" asked Andrew.

"No, I believe he intends to restore his honour this morning, Mr Stewart," said Doctor Dorset coldly.

"Is this your guess, or have you actually asked him?"

"I asked him, and he's determined to see this folly through," Dorset replied, a little more warmly. "And Isaac, has he changed his mind?"

"As reluctant as he is to be here, he refuses to apologise or change his mind."

"So this duel will go ahead, then?"

"Unless either one has a change of heart, it will," replied Andrew sadly. He turned and looked to the East, seeing the bleak greyness of dawn approaching. Dorset saw it too.

With a heavy sigh, Dorset shook his head. "Wait a moment, please."

The doctor walked away and returned, reverently carrying an ornately engraved wooden box. "Make your selection, Mr Stewart," he said, lifting the lid to reveal perfectly matched duelling pistols.

It was one of the second's responsibilities to select and load the weapon. Andrew picked up the first pistol and inspected the barrel carefully. He then checked the trigger mechanism to ensure it wasn't loose or too tight, placed it back into the box, and picked up the other pistol. He inspected it with equal care and was satisfied that both weapons were suitable, in good condition, and safe to use. There was very little difference between the two, as Doctor Dorset knew, but Andrew favoured the first pistol over the second, as the trigger action felt firmer.

"We'll take this one," Andrew said, replacing the second pistol and lifting the first from its red velvet cradle.

Andrew's familiarity with the weapons and the ease with which he handled them surprised Dorset. "Very well, Mr Stewart," he said, handing Andrew the powder and shot to load. He held the light so Andrew could see.

"I used to be a good shot with these once," said Andrew with confidence as he expertly and quickly loaded the weapon.

Dorset looked at Andrew's face. From the way he handled the pistols, Dorset believed him.

Once finished, Andrew held the lantern and watched carefully as Dorset awkwardly loaded the remaining weapon. Both pistols were now loaded to each other's satisfaction and ready to fire. Andrew turned again to the East, hoping dawn would never arrive.

"Won't be long now," said Dorset, uneasy.

Andrew sighed and looked back at Isaac. Unable to hide his nerves, he kept his head down and paced backwards and forwards, using gravestones as markers. Andrew looked in the other direction. Wakefield stood unmoving, his hands buried deep in the pockets of his coat. With his back to the wind, he stared out across the darkness of Wellington and the harbour beyond. One of these men may be dead soon, he thought.

The Featherston's house was considerably closer to the cemetery than their own home, and Eleanor and Andrew had spent a restless night as their guests, listening to Isaac and Bethia's tearful arguments. As Isaac faced the harsh realities of his decision at the cemetery, Eleanor was consoling his distraught wife. As the dawn's first rays began to lighten the room, Bethia sobbed, fearful she'd never see her husband alive again.

"I told him his temper would get the better of him one day," said Bethia between sobs. "He insisted that, because he was morally right, it was perfectly acceptable to write about it."

"Maybe one of them has changed his mind, and Isaac and Andy will come striding through the door, laughing about it, without a care in the world," Eleanor offered, with some hope.

Bethia wiped her nose and dabbed her eyes with her handkerchief, then carefully placed it in her sleeve and held out her arms for her baby. Eleanor returned Bethia's youngest daughter to her mother's loving embrace.

"I don't think that is very likely, Ellie, do you?" she said gently, rocking backwards and forwards.

Isaac was struggling to light his cigar in the uncooperative wind. "Andy!" he called.

Andrew came quickly, thinking Isaac had changed his mind.

"Stand there and unbutton your coat," Isaac instructed.

Andrew did as asked while Isaac bent down and struck a match in the shelter provided by Andrew's coat. Within moments, he was sucking furiously and blowing the small smouldering tip of his cigar into life.

"Much better," he said, giving Andrew a friendly smile. "Thank you."

"You don't seem to be concerned about this anymore."

"No point in worrying about it, Andy. It's all in God's hands now."

"No, Isaac, it's in Wakefield's hands."

Isaac puffed at his cigar with pleasure. Satisfied that the glowing end was as it should be, he reached into his jacket and extracted a sealed envelope. "Take this, Andrew. Please ensure you give this to Bethia in the event that I am deceased. It's my Last Will and Testament."

Unsure what to say, Andrew took the envelope and looked at it in the growing light. Finally making up his mind, Andrew looked up at his friend. "Isaac, you don't have to go through with this. You have the freedom to walk away and return to your wife and daughters."

"And have to listen to him gloat and crow over my cowardice." Isaac pointed his cigar at Wakefield. "No, Andrew, one way or another, it ends here." He patted Andrew on the shoulder and looked towards the sky, taking a long, deep breath.

"You realise, Andrew, we are surrounded by death, and someone will likely die here this morning–"

"Isaac, don't talk about this, please."

"Let me have my say. Even this location where we stand, a cemetery, is a place of death." Isaac shook his head sadly. "Look above you at the beautiful tree. As an enthusiastic horticulturist, I can inform you with certainty that the majestic leafy Karaka tree towering high above will kill you."

"Yes, I imagine that if it were to topple, it would kill many people," replied Andrew dryly.

"No, Andrew, it has seeds which are highly toxic."

"Toxic, what do you mean–?"

"It's time!" yelled John Dorset, walking towards Andrew. "Are we going ahead with this?" he shouted.

Andrew left Isaac to his morbid thoughts and walked over to Dorset. "It appears so. He hasn't changed his mind."

"So be it. We've gone over the rules, Mr Stewart. May I remind you that both parties will stand back-to-back over there," he pointed to an earlier-agreed mark on the grass, "and each party will walk ten paces on my count. At the end of ten paces, I will drop my handkerchief, and they may, at will, turn and shoot. Is this understood and agreed?"

"Yes, doctor, Isaac is aware of the rules," said Andrew, suddenly growing angry at the foolishness of the duel.

"Very well, let's begin, said Dorset, walking away.

"Oh, doctor?" called Andrew.

Dorset stopped and turned.

"Just confirming – we are abiding by Irish rules, are we not?" enquired Andrew.

"Of course."

"And *you* have agreed to these rules, Doctor Dorset?" Andrew asked, his voice beginning to betray his anger.

"Yes, what of it, Mr Stewart?"

"May I remind you, sir, that Code Duello, or Irish Rules, state that Seconds can resolve this issue in the same way as the principals!" Andrew shouted.

Andrew was too far away to see John Dorset's face turn deathly pale, but he didn't fail to notice the doctor nervously begin to lick his lips. Dorset remained frozen, unable to move in abject fear. Andrew didn't move and continued to stare down at Doctor Dorset.

Unable to hear the exchange between Andrew and Dorset, Isaac walked over. "Andy, what is going on?"

"Nothing, Isaac. I think it's time," Andrew said quickly, turning away from John Dorset.

Dorset was horrified. He slowly walked towards Wakefield.

"What happened, John? Has that fool Featherston finally decided to apologise?"

"Ah, no, William. Mr Stewart just asked me whether we were abiding by Irish Rules and –"

"Of course we bloody are," Wakefield interrupted testily.

"He reminded me that, under those rules, seconds have the right to duel."

Wakefield quickly turned to look at Isaac and Andrew, who were waiting. "Is he serious?"

"I believe he is absolutely correct, William," said Dorset, swallowing hard.

"Dear God, what have I done?" muttered the colonel. The implications of another possible death were striking home.

"We have no option but to continue," said Doctor John Dorset. He now felt distinctly unwell.

Wakefield was taken back, unsure of what would happen if he wounded or killed Featherston. What would Andrew do?

"Did you see the way he handled those pistols?" timidly asked Dorset. Wakefield shook his head.

"Like an expert, he claimed he was once a fair shot."

Both men looked over to Andrew, who was talking to Doctor Featherston, who was calmly smoking a cigar.

"We must carry on, John. I have my honour to defend," said Wakefield, clearing his throat and feeling more than a little apprehensive.

Colonel William Wakefield and Isaac Featherston walked towards each other in the growing watery light. As instructed by Dorset and keenly watched by Andrew, they stopped, turned, and stood back-to-back.

"Under Irish rules," gulped Dorset, "I must ask both of you whether there is any chance of reconciliation or an apology. Colonel Wakefield?"

"No!"

"Doctor Featherston?"

"Absolutely not!"

"On my count, begin pacing. Are you both ready and willing to proceed?"

"Just get on with it, John!" yelled Isaac.

"One!"

Both men immediately took a slow step forward, holding their loaded pistols vertically.

"Two – Three - Four – Five!"

Looking up, Andrew offered a prayer, he wanted nothing more than for this to end now and avoid unnecessary bloodshed.

"Six – Seven!"

Andrew thought of Bethia and their beautiful daughters. He hoped she was coping.

"Eight – Nine!"

Isaac pulled the cigar from his mouth.

"Ten!"

Dorset released the white handkerchief, which immediately blew away. Both men clearly saw the signal and turned to face each other, pistols levelled.

Time slowed for Isaac. He looked down the barrel and adjusted its position as Andrew instructed, slightly high and to the right. He could clearly see Wakefield standing twenty paces away, pistol raised and aimed directly at him.

Andrew stood directly behind Dorset to avoid obstructing the line of sight to the handkerchief and to ensure Dorset remained impartial, but he couldn't watch and hid his eyes with his hands. He noticed that Doctor Dorset was looking down, unwilling to watch as well.

Wakefield was having trouble keeping the pistol steady; he'd extended his arm and immediately felt his hand begin to tremble. It was difficult to sight.

Isaac's heart was pounding, resonating through his entire body. He looked at Wakefield down the length of the wavering barrel. He closed his eyes.

The wind swallowed the report of the single shot—the smoke from the gunpowder dispersed in an instant. No one spoke. The contestants made not a sound and remained still. Andrew looked up nervously and saw that both men were still standing, unmoving. Both men had their arms and pistols lowered. Who had fired? He checked Isaac, who appeared to be unharmed. A quick look at Wakefield revealed he too had not a mark on him. No one appeared to be hit, so whoever fired must have missed. One of them had a free shot, but who? The expressions on both Isaac's and Wakefield's faces were of shock.

Other than the wind, there was not a sound, and neither man moved. Succumbing to temptation, John Dorset lifted his head. Equally puzzled, he looked from one man to the next, uncertain. Three men waited; one man expected to be shot.

Wakefield moved first. He slowly raised his arm and pointed his pistol at Isaac. He held it steady, then quickly tilted the weapon upwards into the air. With a fizz, a crack, and a cloud of smoke, he discharged the weapon.

"I will not shoot a man who has seven daughters!" he shouted and walked away.

Isaac and Andrew left the cemetery just as the sun's rays began to cast long shadows over the grey headstones on the hill. After retrieving the pistol from Featherston, Dorset chased Wakefield, who said nothing to his best friend about his change of heart.

Isaac had remained silent as he and Andrew walked. The tremors and shaking he felt immediately after the duel began to wear off, and the realisation that he had survived the duel affected him deeply. Isaac wanted nothing more than to go home to his wife and hold his children close, the thrill of being alive almost overwhelming.

They arrived at the Featherston home, and Isaac paused, turning to Andrew and holding out his hand. "Thank you, Andrew. I deeply appreciate your support. You are indeed a true friend."

"You are most welcome," Andrew replied, shaking his hand warmly.

Isaac turned to walk through the gate, with Andrew at his side. "What did you say to Dorset to cause him such consternation?"

Andrew didn't respond immediately and walked into Isaac's garden before replying. "I asked him whether we were all abiding by Irish Rules. He replied that we were, so I asked him whether he was also agreeing to these rules. He confirmed that he was."

"What does that have to do with it?" asked Isaac, puzzled.

"I then reminded Dorset that, under Irish Rules, the seconds also had the right to duel."

"So you suggested to Dorset that you were considering duelling him?" Isaac asked.

"Yes, but I had made a deliberate show of handling the pistols and loading them in a way that could only indicate I was something of an expert," Andrew began to laugh, further confusing Isaac.

"What's so funny about that?"

"Dorset thought that if Wakefield won the duel against you, I would duel with him," Andrew replied, still chuckling to himself.

"And?"

"And the rules say no such thing. What the rules do say is that both seconds can duel, but only at exactly the same time. Not afterwards. So, Dorset told Wakefield, who must then have wondered what would happen if he won. He thought I'd shoot his best friend, Dorset."

Isaac began to laugh, releasing all his accumulated tension and stress. The sound of genuine, heartfelt laughter gushed out into the street and the surrounding neighbourhood as tears ran freely down the faces of both men as they walked up to Isaac's home. Still unable to contain themselves and gasping for breath, Isaac and Andrew were laughing as Isaac opened the door and both men stepped inside the Featherston home.

On speaking before the New Zealand Legislative
Assembly about the decline and fall of the New
Zealand Company,

*"The Company was founded by men with great souls
and little pockets, and fell into the hands of men with
great pockets and little souls."*
– Edward G. Wakefield

End

AUTHOR'S NOTES

As I discovered, New Zealand's early colonisation is complex and difficult to understand. Researching *'Boundary'* was an education, and I soon realised how little I knew about that era. It's not surprising, as many reference books contain contradictory information, and early historical accounts paint a remarkable picture that is often far from accurate when compared to witness statements, letters and books. It is also interesting to note that even newspaper articles published 170 years ago were heavily weighted by the personal agendas and politics of editors and publishers – not much has changed in that regard.

I had to frequently remind myself that *'Boundary'* is not a textbook; it is a work of fiction, and I gratefully resisted the temptation to write endless pages of historical background. As I will clarify here, many events depicted in this story were very real and did happen. While scholars and historians will appreciate that I have been selective about the events I have chosen to write about, I'm sure they'll also understand that, in some situations, I have interpreted subjectively and exercised creative licence by altering and condensing the timeline to create a more compelling story.

I hope the reader found this novel thought-provoking and that it fuelled a genuine desire to learn more. The actions of the Imperial Government and the New Zealand Company should be brought to public attention and openly discussed. Only then can we begin to understand the people, both Māori and the immigrants, who endured the injustices and lasting effects of Edward Gibbon Wakefield's plan for Systemic Colonisation.

The prologue highlights men whose names have been immortalised and glorified in street names, towns and places of interest throughout New Zealand. For many of those prominent places, I'm unable to understand why we have retained their names and why we don't choose to honour the names of men and women worthy of remembrance and acclaim. The Wakefield brothers are a prime example; as I have described, both William and Edward Wakefield were found guilty of kidnapping and incarcerated for three years, and Arthur was largely responsible for a senseless battle that resulted in the loss of almost thirty lives. Even poorly documented records misrepresent William, implying he obtained his officer's commission in the service of England, when in fact his five years of military experience were gained in the service of Brazil and later Spain.

The politically conservative New Zealand Company Board of Directors held some astounding beliefs. Incidentally, those who hold conservative political views are often labelled 'Tories' – hence the ship the Company took delight in naming *Tory*. Certainly, the Directors' beliefs were precisely reflected in Company Secretary John Ward's book, '*Information Relative to New Zealand: Compiled for the use of Colonists*', which, as I wrote, he never visited New Zealand. Supported by the Board of Directors, his book is a published representation and endorsement of Company philosophy that, even in 1839, was probably considered somewhat extreme – in the 21st century, it is despicable.

Tory's manifest lists a passenger named Nayati; other historical documents refer to the names Nayti, Neti, Nahiti and Naiti. I have assumed they all refer to the same person, who was probably named Ngaiti. More than any other character in this novel, he is a true enigma. A young Māori is tricked into sailing to France on a French whaler, befriends Edward Wakefield, who introduces him to English culture, and is groomed as a gentleman. He is popular and intelligent. After returning to New Zealand on the *Tory* some years later, he more or less disappears. Had I created the persona of Ngaiti from my imagination, his story would have seemed far-fetched and implausible. The Ngaiti I write of is based on a very real person.

The New Zealand Company Secretary, John Ward, wrote of Ngaiti –

'We shall be particularly anxious about the fate of Nayati. He is no longer a New Zealander in manners, habits or tastes but has acquired those of a well-bred Englishman.'

Other than offer insult to New Zealand,, I can conclude that Ward, through constant name misspellings, also wrote that Ngaiti might have been Chief Te Rauparaha's younger son –

'He is a younger son of a chief of the Kapiti tribe, who settled on both sides of Cook Straits; his immediate family residing on the island of Mana, in Queen Charlotte's Sound. Rauparo, the chief of his tribe, was notorious for his cruelty, but Naiti, his young kinsman, abhorred his ferocious habits and always spoke of him as a very bad man. Naiti is about twenty-five years of age, five feet eight inches high, and of a stout, well-made figure; he is slightly tattooed.'

All other historical documents I have seen suggest that Ngaiti was from the Ngati Raukawa iwi, but the iwi mostly controlled lands to the north of Kapiti and Mana, in the Manawatū and Horowhenua regions. The Ngati Toa iwi, with Chief Te Rangihaeata, made his home on Mana Island, and Chief Te Rauparaha lived on Kapiti Island, which are the areas that Ward refers to. Also, I don't believe the Raukawa iwi controlled lands at the top of the South Island. Where would Secretary Ward have obtained his information but from Ngaiti?

Edward Jerningham Wakefield wrote (New Zealand Gazette, 9 May 1840) that on March 15th 1840 he visited the community of Mana (Ngati Toa land on the Kapiti coast), where Ngaiti greeted him. Curiously, he had discarded his European garments in favour of traditional Māori clothes. Against the accepted belief, I can only assume that if Ward and E. J. Wakefield were accurate in what they wrote, then Chief Te Rauparaha must be Ngaiti's father.

Tory's manifest lists Ngaiti's occupation as 'interpreter', which makes sense to me and, no doubt, to New Zealand Company officials. However, why was Richard Barrett employed as interpreter when the Company already had a capable translator they knew, liked and respected? Richard Barrett may have had adequate knowledge of New Zealand, and Colonel

Wakefield most certainly assessed his language skills before appointing him as a translator. However, undisputed historical records clearly state that Richard Barrett was the interpreter at the initial Port Nicholson land purchases. Why wasn't it Ngaiti? Again, Secretary Ward provides confirmation –

'When the New Zealand Company dispatched their preliminary expedition in May last, Naiti was selected for the office of interpreter to the expedition, which he gladly accepted, as an opportunity of returning home in an honourable station in the English service.'

I can only surmise that Ngaiti departed England aboard the *Tory* as the Company translator/interpreter, but during the voyage to New Zealand either Colonel Wakefield changed his mind or Ngaiti did. What happened? Perhaps Ngaiti disagreed with Company ideology and the European lifestyle, which would explain why he chose to return to wearing traditional garments.

When the *Tory* first arrived and anchored in Port Nicholson, Ngaiti left the ship and, apart from Jerningham's report, was almost never mentioned again. I found a brief newspaper paragraph describing the discovery of an *unknown* male Māori body in Te Aro. On hearing this, Chief Te Wharepouri was deeply upset and claimed that *pakeha* were responsible for the death. As was Māori custom, the Chief insisted that the coroner must not interfere with the corpse to perform an autopsy. It was convenient for the development of this story to link Ngaiti with the Te Aro body and provide closure on the life of a perplexing young man, but there is no factual basis for the notion that the body discovered in Te Aro was actually Ngaiti.

I believe that Pito-one chief, Nga Pakawa's poignant question to the assembled chiefs was very insightful when he asked –

"What will you say when many, many White men come here, and drive you all away to the mountains? How will you feel when you go to the White man's house or ship to beg for shelter and hospitality, and he tells you, with his eyes turned up to heaven, and the name of his God on his lips, to be gone, for that your land is paid for?"

There are many conflicting accounts of what Nga Pakawa actually said. What I have written is the most accurate and detailed version I could find.

It shows the depth of concern he, and I believe, many Māori felt about the land acquisitions sought by the New Zealand Company. Perhaps the missionaries planted the seeds of doubt; I wonder whether they had taken root and whether Nga Pakawa's question had been taken more seriously.

I couldn't find any documentation offering insights into who replied to Nga Pakawa. As Te Puni was about sixty years old and probably the oldest chief of the assembled group, then I make the presumption he responded in support of Te Wharepouri's plan. In '*Boundary*' Chief Te Puni's response to Nga Pakawa's question is my interpretation and purely fictional.

Surveyors during the time period of this novel must have been extraordinary men. Often isolated, working in remote, hostile country and exposed to extreme weather, while confronting threatening or confused locals, must have been challenging.

Due to their exceptional navigational skills, many Māori were employed by surveyors as guides and chainmen. Although they recognised that the theodolite was a powerful instrument, Māori were suspicious of its use and considered it *tapu*. In this context, I presume *tapu* refers to *forbidden or restricted*. Many surveyors were sympathetic and treated Māori with respect. They learned to communicate effectively and thus remained alive. Others were less than friendly and had limited understanding or empathy for Māori, who could do little to prevent surveyors from carving up their land. I attempted to capture both sides in '*Boundary*', the understanding Mr Parks, who surveyed Te Aro Flats, and the abrasive Mr Cotterell in the Wairau Valley. Although they really were surveyors, there is no historical evidence to support the way I have described their respective personalities.

Many historical accounts of Chief Te Wharepouri are less than glowing, suggesting he may have been a shallow man, intent only on trinkets, guns and money, and that he became a drunk. I don't believe this is entirely true, and supporters of the New Zealand Company spawned those accusations to discredit him.

Firstly, I doubt Chief Te Rauparaha would have tolerated or trusted a superficial man; he was too astute for that. Te Wharepouri played a pivotal role in the Port Nicholson land purchases, and his motivation for agreeing to allow immigrants to live amongst Māori may have been nothing more than a desire to secure a peaceful and safe place to live.

Chief Te Wharepouri was also an accomplished warrior who fought and survived many battles. He forged strong inter-iwi relationships and successfully maintained the status quo in Wellington. While he was alive, apart from a few minor, isolated incidents, there were no significant conflicts in Wellington; it was a safe place to live. His relationship with Chief Te Rauparaha must have been interesting, and, based on cautious mutual respect and trust, perhaps even friendship.

I believe Chief Te Wharepouri was very perceptive, intelligent and knew far more about *pakeha* than he was given credit for. How could he not? He'd visited New South Wales twice, had strong relationships with Europeans, including Richard Barrett, and, over the years, had been in contact with many missionaries. Christian teachings may also have played a significant role in shaping his understanding of Europeans and their behaviour. Any derogatory writings about Chief Te Wharepouri may have originated with the New Zealand Company, who must have felt he was a thorn in their side – discrediting him served a purpose. It seems unlikely a shallow, uncaring drunk would utter on his deathbed –

"Muri nei ki aku taonga Māori ki aku taonga Pakeha"

"Care for my Māori and European people when I am gone"

It's interesting to note that he said, 'Care for my Māori *and* European...' and not just Māori.

It has been written that Te Wharepouri became a drunk. While this may be possible, it is also likely that, due to a neurological illness, he exhibited symptoms that affected his motor skills and made him appear intoxicated. Records state that Chief Te Wharepouri died of a brain tumour, not as a result of poisoning from the sustained ingestion of ground Karaka seeds, as I have written.

Could he have been poisoned? Was there a motive, and who would have benefited from his death?

Unless an autopsy had been performed, it may have been very difficult to distinguish between the symptoms of a brain tumour and the effects of neurological poisoning, as I wrote. Other conflicting reports state that he had an abscess on his head that resulted in his death. It is unlikely we will ever know.

Of all the characters in this book, few have attracted more attention than Richard 'Dicky' Barrett. Often contradictory, the biographies do share one thing in common: they do not portray the man as I have. It is likely that Barrett was involved in some shady dealings from time to time. He may have associated with people of a dubious nature and might have broken the law on occasion, but there is no factual basis for the character Richard Dickie Barrett I created. The Dickie Barrett in this novel is purely a character of fiction. With respect to Mr Barrett and his descendants, I considered altering his name, but that would have caused difficulties and confusion with historical references to the character.

Barrett's Hotel was a central and important venue in early Wellington; it hosted many events for organisations such as the Horticultural Society and Settlers Association meetings, among others. Here again, I was confronted with inaccurate historical records. One account suggests Richard Barrett sold the hotel licence to recover financial losses from whaling. You can imagine my joy when I discovered another record stating that Charles Suisted won the licence from Richard Barrett in a game of cards. For an author looking to develop the plot, losing the hotel licence in a card game offered more exciting opportunities to advance the story. One thing is certain. The giant Swede, Captain Charles Suisted, did become the licence holder of Barrett's Hotel, which he went on to develop with remarkable success.

Before relocating to New Zealand, Suisted lived in Van Diemen's Land, where he operated his shipping company. Economic hardship forced him to move, and his wife, Mary and their children arrived in Wellington about a year after Charles. While researching, I found a brief newspaper article reporting the court appearance of a, *C. Suisted*, at which the Magistrate, due to a lack of evidence, dismissed a charge of robbery against him.

In reality, Samuel Revans may not have quoted from John Ward's book at the Republican meetings held at Barrett's Hotel, but the excerpt from the book is very real.

Annexing Māori to the north, beyond Cape Kidnappers, and proclaiming land in the south as the republic of 'New Victoria' were part of a legitimate plan that was thankfully quelled by Lieutenant-Governor Hobson. Colonel Wakefield must have felt humiliated by being ordered to swear allegiance to Queen Victoria after Shortland's visit. By all accounts, Shortland wasn't a popular man and was disliked by many. His visit to Wellington with the 80th Regiment, during which he made the proclamation, actually happened.

William Spain and his large family must have suffered. Surely there were times when he questioned his decision to come to New Zealand as commissioner for the land court hearings. George Whiting, a New Zealand Company recruiting agent in England, did not conspire with Barrett to employ Charlie Swanson to sabotage *Prince Rupert*.

As an author, real historical events sometimes unexpectedly fall into your lap and can truly enhance the story. You can imagine my delight at discovering that the *Prince Rupert* was in fact wrecked en route to New Zealand with the Spain family aboard. The newspaper article that William Wakefield read in his office describing the incident was an actual word-for-word extract from '*The Cape Government Gazette*', which reported it. The *Prince Rupert,* with the Spain family aboard, foundered in Table Bay, off the coast of South Africa, as I wrote and described. However, there must have been numerous people who were not looking forward to Commissioner Spain's arrival, and any delay would have been advantageous to their cause. Certainly a thought to ponder.

I can't begin to understand Commissioner William Spain's politics or his decisions. I expect he was influenced by the Imperial Government, Governor Hobson, Acting Governor Shortland, Governor Fitzroy, the New Zealand Company, and his belief that he was doing what was right. I deliberately did not write about the Court's rulings. Instead, I defer to those who truly understand the complexities and decisions of the Land Court Hearings, who can offer informed opinions on its findings and judgments.

One thing the Wellington Land Court Hearings did determine was Richard Barrett's poor translating skills. Commissioner Spain requested that Barrett orally translate the Port Nicholson deed-of-sale documents into the Māori language, exactly as he had done on the *Tory*. Unable to do this accurately to the Court's satisfaction, Barrett's understanding of the Māori language was shown to be nothing more than 'pidgin' Māori. On that revelation, I'm sure Colonel Wakefield regretted not having Ngaiti as his translator. In this novel, Barrett's oral Māori translation of the Port Nicholson deed was, incredibly, the actual word-for-word transcript taken from historical court records.

I can only feel for the families of all those who suffered and needlessly died at Wairau. The event was certainly tragic and should never have happened. The outrage expressed by colonists and settlers in the aftermath gave rise to erroneous stories and inflated accounts that have since pervaded our documented history and altered public perception of the event. Often misleading, contradictory and inaccurate, these accounts made it challenging to determine what really happened that fateful day. In the end, I relied on eyewitness accounts published in June 1843 by the *Nelson Examiner* and *New Zealand Chronicle*. Within the framework of this novel, I have closely followed those witnesses' reports and largely ignored contemporary writings, which I believe are inaccurate. I also accept that those eyewitness accounts may have been embellished and/or inaccurately reported.

Some historical records lay the blame squarely at Arthur Wakefield's door for his misguided enthusiasm, which set in motion the events that culminated in such tragedy. Others imply that Police Magistrate Henry Thompson's arrogance was the cause. In all my research and reading, one thing was made clear. Thompson was determined to arrest Chief Te Rauparaha, and nothing would stand in his way, even when common sense should have prevailed. It is likely he felt humiliated by Chief Te Rauparaha, and pride wouldn't allow him to back down. Certainly, Arthur was initially confident that Thompson could fulfil his duties and accompanied him to arrest the Chief, but when faced with a superior number of armed and capable warriors, Arthur probably did, or should have, had second thoughts. As a military man, Captain Arthur Wakefield would have known it was a fight he could not win and may well have suggested to Magistrate

Thompson that he back down, leave, and return another day. He certainly had the authority to terminate the mission.

Chief Te Rauparaha was never arrested for what happened at Wairau, and the new Governor Fitzroy wisely and accurately absolved the chief of any blame.

Andrew and Eleanor Stewart did not exist; they are fictional characters. Any similarity to real people is purely coincidental. James Futter did not sell the 'White Horse Inn', and the hotel remained in his possession for many years. No trace of it remains today, and commercial developments now occupy its original site on sections eight and nine in Kaiwharawhara.

Disillusioned and disappointed upon arriving in New Zealand, Doctor Isaac Featherston wrote that Wakefield had promised so much and delivered so little. Over time, those feelings never diminished and must have simmered malevolently. Featherston took opportunities to voice his opinions and opposition to the New Zealand Company, which must have been awkward at times, as Wakefield and he presumably shared friends and saw each other frequently at social gatherings and events. Perhaps it was ironic that Wakefield did not shoot and kill Dr Isaac Featherston when they faced off in the duel. About a year later, William Wakefield suffered a stroke at a Wellington bathhouse. Featherston, along with two other physicians, came to his assistance. He would die four days later on Sept 19th, 1848.

Featherston was Secretary of the Horticultural and Botanical Society, and Wakefield was a member. They both competed in competitions exactly as I described. Eventually, Isaac Featherston, who became editor of the *'Wellington Independent'* newspaper, took the opportunity to write an editorial that deeply offended William Wakefield. Much has been reported about the aberrant story, but not the article's context or what it actually contained. It must have been an atrocious editorial for Wakefield to risk his life by challenging Featherston to a duel. I wanted to know what Featherston wrote that was so terribly offensive. I searched high and low; I read the papers backwards and forwards and checked past issues. The only article I found was – *'Little Lessons for Local Politicians–No.1.'* The story of the old woman in the stall, which I copied verbatim from the newspaper.

'Wellington Independent' Newspaper, Volume II, Issue 152, 27 March 1847, Page 3.

Printed and published by William Edward Vincent, Thomas McKenzie, James Muir and George Fellingham. Lambton Quay, Wellington, Port Nicholson, New Zealand.

Wakefield must have been so enraged by that editorial that he was willing to place his life on the line by challenging Featherston to a duel – and duel they did. Historical records disagree on the exact location of the duel, but I believe it took place at the Bolton Street Cemetery in Wellington. Doctor Dorset was Wakefield's second, and Francis Dillon Bell, who replaced Wakefield as Principal Agent for the New Zealand Company when Wakefield became ill, was Featherston's second – it was the last recorded pistol duel in New Zealand history.

As I wrote, William Wakefield reportedly told Featherston, '*I will not shoot a man with seven daughters*', and walked away. I find this astounding and thank him posthumously for providing a wonderful ending to this novel.

Paul W. Feenstra
I welcome positive feedback.

INTO THE

SHADE

by

PAUL W. FEENSTRA

Sample Chapter

CHAPTER ONE

Saturday evening, June 27th, 1914, Sarajevo.

A barking dog announced the presence of a stranger, an intrusion into the mundane territory of a bored animal. Seconds later, another joined in, quickly followed by a third. Had the stranger been inclined to curse, he would have. Instead, he glanced anxiously over his shoulder, shifted the dirty canvas bag on his shoulder, and quickened his pace. Anyone watching closely might have noticed him clutching a relic—a small wooden cross, scarred and darkened with age.

Doors remained shut. Curious children were ushered away from windows lest they see something they shouldn't. It was best this way; the less anyone knew, the safer it was for everyone.

The dogs eventually lost interest and fell silent—but not before alerting others to the stranger's approach. From the shadowed interior of a neglected, nondescript two-storeyed house, two pairs of eyes scanned the darkened street, searching for a threat or a sign of pursuit.

With relief, the lookouts recognised the approaching figure—then looked beyond, praying he had not been followed.

The man paused in the middle of the street, gently lowered the heavy bag to the ground and began rummaging in his pockets. After a moment, he extracted a small tin, nimbly flicked open the lid, pulled out a pre-rolled cigarette, placed it in the side of his mouth and lit it. The sputtering flame illuminated his face and confirmed to the two watchers that the man was Father Stevan Belic, the man they expected. The lit match was a signal, confirming to the watchers that all was well. If his appearance in the neighbourhood concerned its residents, they didn't show it. Curtains remain closed, and no one questioned his presence.

From a window on the upper floor of number fourteen, an answering match was struck, then quickly extinguished. Father Stevan did not acknowledge the prearranged return signal, indicating it was safe to proceed. Instead, he picked up the heavy bag, hoisted it onto his other shoulder, and turned toward the dilapidated gate of number fourteen.

He slowed and casually glanced down at the brick gatepost. It was difficult to see, even in the generous moonlight, but it was there—another precaution. A simple horizontal chalk line, faint yet stark against the aged red brick. He exhaled quietly in relief. It was a signal, confirming it was safe to continue.

The old, freshly oiled gate swung silently open as the priest pushed through. Ahead, an overgrown path wound through a neglected garden toward a tall concrete step and a heavy wooden door. Still lit by moonlight beneath a clear sky, Belić followed the path. As he reached the two-storey house, the door opened.

He dropped his cigarette, ground it into the dirt, and looked back one last time before stepping inside.

The interior was damp, heavy with the smell of mould and stale tobacco. Even the warmth of a Sarajevo summer could not fully banish the residue of a harsh winter. Without a word, the man who had opened the door turned and climbed the stairs. Father Stevan followed close behind, his bag banging softly against the wall—an unmistakable signal of his long-awaited arrival.

Light spilt from an open door at the top of the stairs, revealing a wall lined with yellowed wallpaper that may once have been floral. In places, darker patches hinted at a long-forgotten water leak. No one presently inside the house cared; according to the authorities, the building was abandoned—ideally suited to the needs of the secretive nationalist Black Hand organisation. Number fourteen was a refuge. It was a safehouse.

As the priest creaked up the stairs, he heard subdued, muffled voices drifting from the room above. With a respectful nod, the man leading the way stepped aside and allowed him to enter before returning downstairs to resume his watch at the door.

All conversation ceased.

Eight men of varying ages occupied the smoke-filled room. Most were familiar to Father Stevan, but the three young Bosnians seated together on a threadbare sofa were strangers. He had never seen them before, yet he knew each of their names and was acutely familiar with their backgrounds and circumstances.

On the left sat the emaciated Nedeljko Čabrinović, a graphic worker from the outskirts of Sarajevo and a product of an abusive home. In the middle was the volatile Trifko Grabež, ironically, the son of a Serbian Orthodox priest. On the right sat nineteen-year-old Gavrilo Princip, a printer and the son of a postman.

The three young men eyed the priest warily and offered no greeting.

Heavy black cloth curtains were nailed to the window frames to prevent light from leaking outside—anything that might alert the authorities that the abandoned house was being used for nefarious purposes. The only armchair in the room was occupied by the oldest man present, Major Vojislav Tankosić. By day, he was an officer in the Serbian army; by night, a leader of the secret Black Hand organisation.

He dropped his cigarette into a chipped cup on the dirty wooden floor beside his chair, eased himself upright, and greeted the priest with a warm smile. "Hello, Father."

Father Belić acknowledged the major, quickly glanced around the room at the other faces—men he knew and trusted—and nodded to each in turn. He pocketed the talisman he carried and unslung the canvas bag from his shoulder. Everyone watched as it hit the floor with a metallic clunk.

Immediately, Danilo Ilić rose from the rickety kitchen chair and moved towards the bag. One eye was partly closed from the irritant smoke drifting from the ever-present cigarette clamped at the corner of his mouth. He unfastened the clasps and began pulling out the contents one by one, arranging them neatly on the floor beside him.

"We expected you earlier. We were worried, Father," the major remarked casually, not looking at him. His attention remained fixed on Danilo and the assortment of goods laid out before him.

"The dutiful work of a priest doesn't end when the sun goes down."

"Was it the bishop?" Tankosić asked, lifting his head. "Was he asking questions again?"

The priest shook his head. "No. Worse… a father brought his son to me and asked that I explain to the boy why he shouldn't use his fists to solve a problem."

Trifko Grabež, one of the young, radicalised Bosnians on the sofa, snickered.

"And?" the major asked, one eyebrow lifting.

All eyes in the room turned to the priest and waited. The irony of his duplicitous role was not lost on anyone.

Father Stevan slipped his hand into the folds of his cassock and produced his tobacco tin. With a flick of his finger, he opened the lid, removed a pre-rolled cigarette, and placed it in his mouth. The major graciously struck a match. Belić lowered his head, drew deeply, then exhaled a stream of smoke towards the ceiling.

"Perhaps if you all attended Mass more frequently," Father Stevan said lightly, "you would already know what I told the boy."

The major smiled and flicked his gaze toward Muhamed Mehmedbašić, who sat on the floor with his knees drawn to his chin.

Catching the look directed at the only Muslim in the room, Belić added with a faint smile, "You too might learn something from a good Christian sermon, Muhamed."

In reply, Muhamed lifted his head and studied the priest with quiet interest.

"Oh?" the priest continued mildly. "And what would you have told the boy?"

Muhamed's eyes sparkled with amusement as they locked onto Belić's. "*Allah* commands justice, doing good, and generosity to kith and kin," he said without hesitation. "He forbids all shameful deeds, injustice, and rebellion. He instructs you that ye may receive admonition."

Father Stevan laughed. "Perhaps I should have the father and the boy come to see you?"

"I've heard your endless sermons as you preached to my brothers here," Muhamed replied with a laugh of his own. "You do quite well without me."

Gavrilo Princip scoffed from the sofa. "And what of us? Will you preach to me as well?" His lip curled. "We are here to do a job, not listen to religious babble from a priest."

The major opened his mouth to reprimand the youth, but the priest placed a restraining hand on his arm. He turned to the nineteen-year-old and studied him with a measure of pity. He knew the three newest recruits were all terminally ill with tuberculosis—bitter, radicalised, and primed. He paused to collect his thoughts. What he was about to say lay at the core of his beliefs, both as a priest and as an activist. "Committing a moral sin to achieve a righteous and just end is acceptable," he said calmly. "Even at the expense of trust." Before the young man could respond, he continued. "Are you here merely to satisfy a thirst for violence, or is there a greater cause worthy of your life?"

Princip took the bait. He rose to his feet, chest thrust out and began to recite well-worn doctrine. "I am a Yugoslav nationalist, committed to the unification of all Yugoslavs. I do not care in what form the state exists—only that it is free from Austria." He glared at the priest as he finished. "And who are you? Are you here to preach righteousness and the gospel—or to do what is necessary for our people and help unify our country?"

Trifko Grabež leaned forward on the sofa in tacit support. Nedeljko Čabrinović stared blankly ahead, as though he hadn't been listening at all.

Danilo paused and looked up—then everyone else followed suit. Gavrilo Princip remained standing, defiant, challenging with youthful insolence.

The room fell silent.

The young man surprised the priest with his audacity. Father Stevan considered his response carefully. Only that morning, he had asked himself the very same question.

He nodded.

"I am foremost a warrior—a soldier—and I proclaim to you and everyone else here that Austria is our first and greatest enemy." The priest slowly swivelled his head, addressing the room, not just Princip. "Just as the Turks once attacked us from the south, so Austria attacks us today from the north. I preach the necessity of fighting Austria and keeping Serbia free from imperial oppression.

I preach the sacred truth of our national position." He turned back to Gavrilo Princip and met his challenging glare. "For the sake of bread and land, for the fundamental necessities of culture and trade. Yes, my brothers, the liberation of the conquered territories and their union with Serbia is necessary—for gentlemen, tradesmen, peasants, and even you, young man." Belić paused to draw on his cigarette before continuing. "And for religious men alike. Those who rule must respect the laws and institutions of our country. And yes, our masters and wealthy owners must be mindful of their duty as well." He took two steps towards Princip and placed a reassuring hand on his shoulder. "Rest easy, my friend. We are all here for the same purpose."

Against the far wall sat Cvetcko Popović. "Well said, Father—spoken like a true man of God." He clapped his hands in appreciation as Princip returned to his seat, scowling. Even Muhamed was smiling; anyone familiar with Father Stevan Belić knew something of his murky past, but his commitment and sacrifice to their cause were beyond question.

The major turned to Danilo, who had the bag unloaded. "Is everything there?"

Danilo nodded, spilling cigarette ash in the process.

"Pass out the weapons as we discussed," ordered the major.

All attention returned to Danilo and the armament laid out before him.

Father Stevan sat on the chair Danilo had vacated. He would not be receiving a weapon; he had completed his role, and his work was finished. Still, he listened attentively as the major and Danilo repeatedly reviewed the plan, leaving no room for misunderstanding or mistake. It wasn't that he intended to involve himself in tomorrow's attack—he had made other, more secretive arrangements and planned to be far away when the Austrians were left licking their wounds at the hands of his Black Hand brothers.

The three newest recruits—Nedeljko Čabrinović, Trifko Grabež, and Gavrilo Princip—had no previous experience with firearms or bombs. In the preceding weeks, under the patient tutelage of Major Vojislav Tankosić, they were instructed in throwing grenades and in operating the Browning FN Model 1910 automatic .380-calibre pistol, which each would be issued. Along with Danilo Ilić and his cell of three additional insurgents, the attacking force would total seven. Each man received a Browning pistol, a hand grenade, some cash, and contact details of local sympathisers who could assist in their escape. In the unlikely event of capture, the major decreed that each man would also carry a vial of potassium cyanide. They were assured that death would be swift and painless.

The heightened tension in the room, so prevalent earlier, gave way to a sombre mood of self-reflection and quiet anxiety as each conspirator considered his part, much like an actor before a final performance.

Deciding it was time to leave, as he still had a long night ahead, Father Stevan Belić rose from his chair, took a single step, and paused. Major Tankosić was discussing the Browning pistol's mechanism with Nedeljko Čabrinović and looked up. Muhamed and Vasco Čubrilović were quietly reviewing their escape route; they fell silent and turned towards the priest. The others, quiet and brooding, shifted their attention to the figure standing alone in the centre of the room.

With all eyes upon him, Father Stevan looked down at the cross he was fidgeting with, compulsively turning it over in his hands as he gathered his thoughts. He raised his head and drew a deep breath. "We must offer forgiveness to those who will be sacrificed, but their sins will be absolved before God—as will ours. The people of this great nation are also God's children, so we act in the name of God." He turned to Muhamed, who listened attentively. "Let us rejoice in the dignity and freedom we bestow on our people, our families— and let God forgive us for our sins."

He opened his mouth to say more, then thought better of it. "Amen," he whispered.

"Amen," a few responded.

"*Allah Akbar*—God is great," Muhamed replied.

Father Belić knew he would probably never see his fellow conspirators again. With a heavy heart, he crossed himself, nodded to the group, and without another word, quietly left the room.

Other historical fiction books
by
Paul W. Feenstra
Published by Mellester Press

Boundary

Moana Rangitira Series
The Breath of God
For Want of a Shilling

Gunpowder Green

Into the Shade

Falls Ende short story eBooks
1. The Oath
2. Courser
3. The King

Falls Ende full length novels.
Falls Ende – Primus (eBooks 1,2 & 3)
Falls Ende – Secundus
Falls Ende – Tertium
Falls Ende – Quartus
Falls Ende – Quintus
Falls Ende – Sextus
Falls Ende – Outlaw

Leonard Hardy's
A Sinister Consequence
A Questionable Virtue

A Gentleman at Heart

www.PaulWFeenstra.net

Facebook.com/AuthorPaulWFeenstra/

Twitter@FeenstrPaul